Virtual World

Kha

By

JL Sims

ISBN-13: 978-0-9905198-2-9
www.fictionalwriter.com
jlsimspublishing@gmail.com

Listen to yourself and in that quietude you might hear the
voice of God.

-*Maya Angelou*

Acknowledgements

I was ten years old when I found my father's body at the foot of his bed—matured—in that moment, he taught me the meaning to life.

To the memory of
Our Fathers

CONTENTS

The Suffering

The eastern horizon exudes a reddened haze, as if bloodied by the millions who lost their lives in the post-nuclear explosions. Leaflets of ash drift lazily through the sky like strips of confetti. Northern winds blow foul gusts of polluted air across the plateau. The contamination intermingles with noxious vapors spewing from countless volcanic fissures scarring the landscape. Earth's diminished atmosphere exposes the world to hellish amounts of solar radiation while the lifeless remnants of an unknown city loiter on the pains ahead, like a ghostly vagabond from times past.

Grey clears his throat and then gives me a gentle nudge. "The nukes will detonate in twenty minutes. If we're not in the tower by then—"

I raise my hand and nod, "I know."

Remi steps forward. "What now?"

He's perspiring profusely and his voice lacks confidence. Remi's odd behavior catches my attention, because Grey is the one who usually loses his nerve under pressure.

I turn away from the devastating sight of radioactive plains and carefully study the enemy garrison to the west. A frontal assault is suicide.

IFA fusion cannons guard the main gate. Losing both of our Jackals and the assault helicopter in the previous battle leaves no way of breaking into the building from aboveground. My initial assault plan is a total failure. We need to find another way inside Tower Yu…

I point to Remi and Hannibal. "Get on the highest ridge and engage the artillery. You'll have to destroy at least one cannon to draw the IFA outside."

Grey's widening eyes exaggerate the bulbous curves of his boyish face. "You're going through the sewers with me?"

I hand him my speargun after resetting its sights. "I won't make it through on my own."

"But our team never split up before, and—"

"You heard the lady!" Hannibal raises a massive pulse launcher onto his shoulder and then trudges off with a Goliath-like gait. Hanni's bodybuilder shape always seem to match his choice of weaponry. "Good luck Commander!"

Remi hands me the nuke's activation key. His stony facial features crease with determination. "Get to that tower and whatever ya do, don't give up. This is da final battle. Everything is riding on this!"

I watch Remi and Hannibal leave as Grey opens the nearest sewer lid and illuminates the gloomy interior with his helmet light. Before he gives the all clear I impatiently push him aside—jump down—and straddle the foul stream of liquid faintly visible along the sewer's floor.

Five-foot long centamides trudge through the

greenish goo directly ahead. Each of the mechanical sentries resembles an armored centipede. One of them detects us when Grey splashes noisily by my side. I blow it apart with a single blast from my shotgun and the mechanical bug screeches when its short metallic legs blow apart.

Several centamides are alerted by the skirmish and reverse course. The scuttling sentries appear to hiss angrily as they release pressurized air from their silver mandibles. Grey stumbles ahead of me as one of them attacks. I yank him away from the centamide's acidic spew and destroy the clanking sentry with a focused blast from my weapon.

"Be careful and get to cover! I can't afford to lose you!"

I push Grey to the opposite side of the sewer and we take positions behind trash as more centamides advance. The lead crawlers spew streams of acid against our barricades. Their hissing mandibles preempt each attack. I emerge from my garbage pile just long enough to destroy the foremost centamides with consecutive shots. Grey impales three more against a dilapidated baby carriage. They explode seconds later, obliterating five stragglers with collateral damage.

I charge a damaged centamide and blast it into oblivion while Grey spikes the remaining pair with a single spear. There isn't a moment to waste so I fire more rounds into the pinned critters and duck below their exploding shell fragments.

Hannibal's roaring pulse launcher echoes above ground and I imagine his snarling war-face boosting

Remi's morale, as it often does mine.

Grey finds an archaic dual engine speedboat inside the main sewer junction. We immediately crank its engines.

"This one's blown!" I kick the crappy contraption.

Grey smiles when his engine roars to life. "We're in luck!"

I jump aboard and replace my shotgun with the IFA assault rifle someone stashed beneath a detached engine casing. Grey assumes the boat's controls as I sit cross-legged and align the rifle's front sight post to my firing eye.

"Full throttle! And stay away from the loading ramps!"

"Gotcha!"

I cock the rifle and release a single shot to ensure the weapon's functionality. Grey forewarns of distant movement when the boat speeds forward. After extending the rifle's scope and identifying automated ceiling drones, I set the weapon's three-round burst mode, steady my aim, and fire.

Rounds leap from the rifle's black barrel and shred the foremost drones. Grey swerves wildly as he avoids their detonating components. I nearly fall out of the boat and pound its strakes out of frustration.

"Keep her steady!"

Grey squeezes the boat's controls to emphasize his commitment. "I'm on it Commander!"

More threats appear. I collapse the scope in favor of the front-sight post and fire at three centamides scaling the walls. Grey sideswipes proximity mines as two crawlers return fire. We barely clear the mines before floating debris causes them to detonate in unison. The blast lifts our boat's aft while dislodging the remaining centamides from their perches. I notice cracks forming along the ceiling after the rear-end slams back into the sewage.

"Go faster," I wave forward excitedly, "the ceiling is buckling!"

Echoes from snapping support columns fills the air. Ominous quaking follows. I glance back and notice entire wall segments crumbling into the wastewater. Just as I begin doubting my decision to bring the rookie, Grey stiffens his grip on the speedboat's controls. His strength grants me the seconds needed to retrieve my utility pouch.

As the tunnel disintegrates behind us, its ceiling peels away in a continuous strip as if ripped from an enormous tape dispenser. Grey tries speeding away from the pursuing collapse but it's futile. The tumbling waterfall of debris gains ground with every second. I pull an EBE capsule from my utility pouch and grab Grey's shoulder.

"Jump the next cargo ramp!"

Grey is bug-eyed. "An electromagnetic bubble capsule? How will—"

"Just jump it!"

Grey aligns with the next ramp when I activate the capsule's emitter. A bluish, semitransparent sphere expands from the EBE's positive node and surrounds the entire vehicle. We'll stay grounded from the field's charge if I can maintain my grip on the capsule.

The ceiling collapses on top of us as we approach the ramp's incline but the sphere's positive force repels the debris. Large stones, pipe-fittings, electrical conduits and even dust slide along the sphere's surface and away from us. Grey is speeding so fast the boat goes airborne. We break through the crumbling ceiling and emerge aboveground as the capsule's charge dissipates. I eject from my seat when the speedboat crashes against the floor and tumble twenty feet before rolling to a stop. The collapsing sewer swallows the boat and a portion of the room's inventory while creating a rubble-filled trench across its mid-line. Grey is already standing by the time I spot him. He races to my side and helps me up as we look around.

"I don't believe we just survived that!"

I shake my head, dazed. "Are you OK?"

"I couldn't be better! We're in the armory!"

An assortment of military weapons fills the room. Grey points to something behind me. I turn, knowing what I'm going to see after gauging his expression.

"Jackals!"

"How many should we use, Commander?"

"We need an entire pack so, program me as the Controller. Upload a virus to the rest."

"Consider it done!"

Grey targets the largest cluster of Jackals and hides behind an armored hovercraft while hacking into their artificial intelligence. I slide behind a stack of crates before more IFA bastards enter the room and prime my electromagnetic bubble capsule's negative node. The first armory door opens before Grey can finish so I lob my capsule into the doorway.

This time, a red sphere expands from the emitter and ensnares an entire squad of guards like dirt on a discarded piece of bubble gum. The sphere fills the entire hallway as it reaches its full girth—mashing the guards against the walls, floor, and ceiling, which buckles outward.

The simultaneous crushing of so many men unnerves me. They fruitlessly fight to escape capture and claw, grab, pull, and push against each other as the sphere molds them into the hallway. Bones snap. Eyes bulge and pop. Bodies burst from compression until a mangled organ soup is all that remains. My skin crawls from witnessing such carnage. Everything finally collapses inward with a loud and sudden BOOM that seals the armory's main entrance with rubble and gore.

I glance towards Grey after gathering a few IFA bubble grenades from a nearby cache. "Hurry! There's a southern entrance! Reinforcements are coming!"

Grey calmly assures me that, "I'll have it done in a few more seconds."

"We don't have a few more seconds! I need those Jackals online, now!"

An automated alarm sounds.

Warning: Breach in armory. All troops in section C must report to level one.

Grey nods, "I'm done! Give the sync command!"

"Greed!"

My voice activates several Jackals. Their seven-foot long canine bodies and angular teeth resemble extinct counterparts from a distant land. The pack stands attentively as I set their protocols.

"Protection mode alpha; echelon five formation; attack mode three; initialize!"

The Jackals move in unison and form a semicircle as I face the group. When I add the 'attack on sight' command, they growl to signify charged weapons.

Grey reaches out with upturned palms. "What about the strays?"

"Program them to prowl while making us exemptions."

"Already done!"

My lead Jackal turns about with raised ears when the southern door finally unlocks. Its sonar targeting system locks onto something in the adjacent lobby. A familiar voice blares from the dark interior after the door slides opens.

"Commander, Di Ehari! Disarm and surrender or you and your men will be killed!"

Does General Gideon really think we came this far to surrender? Grey hacks into one of the Jackal's audio files and synchronizes the program with my voice pattern. I usurp the airwaves through the Jackal's speaker when he gives me a thumbs-up.

"Your president's rule is over, Gideon! Our world has evolved beyond the slavery of self-indulgence! People no longer idolize your kind! Freedom is at hand!"

Gideon rambles maniacally as Grey whispers in my ear, "We've got less than seventeen minutes before nuclear detonation—"

"The slavery of self-indulgence? Haven't you realized by now Commander, that there will always be an Americanized system of rule? There will always be an empire filled with people lining up to subjugate themselves! Why do you call it slavery when one indulges? Are you mad? Haven't you read their books or watched videos from those times? Americans loved conformity, reliance, and institutionalism! The people loved enslavement to trends and popular opinions! They loved conforming to an ideal image of self-worth! They loved serving their most primal desires! America was the perfect empire! It must be reborn!"

"No," I cock my rifle after reloading it. "Yours is a false America run by a corrupt artificial intelligence! Your system of governance will never serve society's interests! Indivism is the only path to independence!"

Gideon laughs. "People don't want individuality! They want dependency! They want someone like me to tell them what to do! These lost souls want someone like me to follow! Hell, most people can't even think for themselves nowadays! I am their conscience!"

A Jackal steps ahead of me when IFA bullets penetrate the doorway. Even though their trajectory poses no danger, the Jackal's defensive programming reassures me. Grey follows my lead and mounts one of the machines. The remaining Jackals gather around us.

Gideon anticipates our maneuver and dispatches a dozen Rollers into the armory. Grey tosses his final black hole grenade as they barrel into the room. It glides through the air like an ancient hockey puck and stops within a few feet of the doorway. When the grenade releases a pool of dark matter across the entrance, six cumbersome Rollers fall into the void and vanish. The remaining orbs stop just short of the undulating hole and unfurl to reveal the men sheltered within. They block the exit with their mechanized suits, form a single-line formation, and then fire at my position. Patrolling Jackals assess the scene and initiate a surprise attack. The howling machines leap into action and smash into the IFA's flanks with such force, that their entire formation fragments into chaos.

"Get ready," I point to the doorway, "we're breaking through on my command!"

"I'm right behind you, Commander!"

I nod, "Jackals one through seven, initiate Carthaginian DE!"

Half of my Jackals join the embattled strays and perform a double-envelopment after the Rollers advance. I hold as a furious battle unfolds. The earsplitting noise of bursting rounds, screeching rockets, and whining lasers fills the armory. I give Remi the signal after setting my only timed bomb atop one of the explosive caches.

"Let's go!"

Our Jackals leap into a sprint and we race into

the empty hallway in a single line formation. The cache blows before we exit and triggers a series of explosions that rock the entire building. Some of the soldiers positioned outside the armory scatter. I spot Gideon as we leave the hallway but he retreats into one of the executive elevators before we can target him. The remaining guards find defensive positions behind metal desks, columns, and anything else that appears solid enough to absorb a round.

"Grey, secure elevator one! Jackals, attack all hostiles firing Class A weaponry!"

My pack charges the IFA soldiers without hesitation. Two of the Jackals fall after running into restrainer nets. Enemy soldiers gun them down when the mechanical beasts prove incapable of escaping the net's electrical bondage. The rest are too elusive for planted traps and pummel the soldier's defenses with a barrage of laser fire.

Grey analyzes the building's structure with his eyelens and immediately yells his discoveries. "Gideon is heading for the top floor and all elevators are locked!"

I find cover inside one of the alcoves and study Grey's uploaded image with my eyelens. "There are multiple stairways leading to the upper floors but the elevators seem to be the only way of reaching the top! Hack into elevator three and open it!"

"I'm on it Commander!"

IFA guards notice Grey crouching by the elevator and fire at him. Only then do I realize that someone has re-hacked most of our Jackals. Before I can relocate, an entire section of wall crumbles from a pulse-launcher round fired from a quarter mile away. The blast crushes numerous guards, and nearly all the re-hacked Jackals. Hannibal exceeds my expectations once again!

"Got it! Elevator three is open!" Grey motions to the parting doors and we duck inside with the last remaining Jackal under my control. "There are only fifteen minutes left before nuclear detonation!"

I hand Grey a scavenged rifle as the elevator rises. "Don't worry, we'll make it."

Gideon's voice booms through our elevator's intercom. "Are you sure, Ehari? Ninety-five floors and a bomb separate you, from me. Have a nice ride!"

"Grey!"

"Already found it!" He assures with a definitive nod, "I neutralized the remote trigger but the bomb has a secondary timer."

"Can you disarm it?"

"No!"

"Time?"

Grey wipes glistening beads of sweat from his brow. "About ninety seconds…"

We use our Jackal to rip open a ceiling panel and climb on top of the elevator. Our mechanical pet severs all lift cables before scaling the shaft with us on its back. The elevator gives way and drops a few floors before its emergency breaks engage. We claw into the forty-ninth floor and dash towards the window of an abandoned office.

Calamitous quakes rumble throughout the

building when the elevator bomb explodes. I feel the entire structure swaying. Lights flicker. Ceiling panels fall. Panic seizes the workers in neighboring rooms. I don't pity their terrified screams. These people worked to suffuse the voices of common citizens. Punishment is at hand.

I place a single rifle round through the office window. Our beast smashes through the cracked glass while using its magnetic claws to grab the tower's outer wall. It carries us skyward as I consult my eyelens.

"The main office is sealed!" I glance back at Grey and try ignoring the extreme heights hovering beyond him. "Find another way inside!"

"I'm disabling all known anti-viral barriers first, and—"

"Just get it done! There isn't much time!"

Swarms of IFA troops are assaulting a derelict warehouse on the ridge below. I have no doubt that Hannibal and Remi are in the middle of that chaos. It's only a matter of time before the opposition overruns them.

"HQ, this is Commander Di Ehari, requesting satellite support!"

General Atkins immediately responds on my crosscom device. "Commander Ehari, what is your strike code?"

"Alpha 45920-164 Omega."

"Code confirmed. Awaiting Helix coordinates."

I use a telescopic laser-pointer to identify the largest cluster of IFA troops. Pressing its trigger changes the green targeting laser to red, thereby activating the orbiting satellite's Helix lens, which focuses the sun's energy to the indicated targets. Seconds later, a golden beam pierces the atmosphere with a lethal dose of solar radiation. Hundreds of IFA troops die when the pillar of light douses them like ants under a magnifying lens. Their smoldering embers form a momentary mist of light when carried away by the wind. The survivors scatter as Gideon's voice reemerges through one of the building's loudspeakers.

"How can you fight for indivism without considering our indivisic rights? Attacking us uproots the very foundation of your beliefs! Indivism permits the advancements of individual agendas! You have no right to contest our dreams of restoring Capitalism!"

"Commander," Grey nudges with his index finger, "I just planted my virus into the IFA security system."

"Good." I check the time on my eyelens and confirm its readings with Grey. "How much time before detonation?"

"Thirteen minutes," Grey answers bleakly—deliberately emphasizing the number's unlucky reputation.

"I know everything about you, Ehari." Gideon chuckles as if harboring secrets about my life that I have yet to discover. "In fact, I know you better than you know yourself! You graduated last in your class and struggled to pass your placement tests. No one wanted to follow your command. Only after the death of all your superiors in the Battle of Trials, were you able to attain the title of Commander. People like you hope a lifetime of failures can be undone with a single success but you'll fail no matter what you do! It's in your DNA to come up short. It's all your kind knows!"

We reach the tower's summit and dismount the Jackal. A circular bay integrated into the roof opens to reveal a Type-3 assault helicopter on a rising platform. Its rotors are spinning and the vehicle appears ready for liftoff. The helo immediately fires its twin eighty-millimeter cannons the moment we enter its cross hairs and the massive rounds nearly shear my head off as we retreat behind a stairway shed. Such power is terrifying. The helo's pilot obliterates a nearby docking terminal with a few playful shots, as if to further demonstrate the cannon's awesome power, and then rises into the air as I shudder with uncertainty.

There's nowhere safe to hide and I freeze–barely able to control my breathing or trembling hands. The helo circles the building. My heart pounds as its echoing rotors thump against the shifting winds. The agile craft seems to be everywhere and swings into view unexpectedly.

"Get down!"

Grey pushes me to the ground as bullets puncture fist-sized holes into the shed—right where I stood, only a second ago.

We roll out of view with our Jackal trailing behind

us, and dash between the tower's utility shacks as the helo circles the roof once again. Its detection system has no problem locating us. I suspect onboard thermal imaging; but whatever the case, we struggle to avoid the helo's pelting rounds. It forces us into a convection canal where we hunker from the gouged chunks of building debris flying around us.

Grey's face glistens with perspiration. He points to a nearby hatch, "Is that what we're looking for?"

I shake my head. His dependency on leadership helps me refocus. "That hatch belongs to the helo but Gideon's control room is directly beneath it! The access door we're looking for is on the northwest corner of the roof!"

"How do we bypass a Type-3 helicopter? It's too mobile to dodge, even with a Jackal!"

I answer Grey's question with another call to headquarters. "HQ, this is Commander Di Ehari, requesting additional satellite support!"

"Commander Ehari, what is your reserve strike code?"

"Alpha 95673-316 Omega!"

"Code confirmed," General Atkins acknowledges once again. "Awaiting Helix coordinates."

"Run for the hatch when I give the command!"

"You want me to be a decoy?" Grey shakes his head, "I'll get obliterated out there!"

"Just do it!"

The Helix satellite is incapable of designating moving objects so I mark the tower's center with my laser pointer and assign the building's perimeter as the target. When solar beams pierce the sky, they randomly strike along the tower's fringe and drive the skittish helicopter pilot away.

"Go! Run!"

Grey dashes across the roof and forces the helo to alter course and attack. He narrowly avoids its bullets as the emboldened pilot slips his craft in-between the columns of solar fire bursting from the sky. Grey stands exposed, and is only halfway across the roof with no chance of outrunning the Type-3, so I set my Jackal to suicide mode after ordering it to climb the nearby radio antenna.

As hoped, the pilot remains focused on Grey and ignores the Jackal. When he makes a final attack run the mechanical beast leaps from the antenna and crashes into the helicopter's side. The helo spins twice before exploding into a fiery ball of twisted metal.

Grey points to the sky, "Watch out for the tail!"

He leaps away from the helo's front end when it smashes into the tower. The rotor breaks free of its tail and I gag from the earsplitting sound of the screeching metal spinning pass me. More helicopter wreckage slips off the tower and falls out of view after lathering the roof with fiery debris. A flaming seat cushion smacks my head in an embarrassing way, but I'm otherwise unharmed. When I call to Grey, he responds from beyond the wall of fire that now separates us.

He waves, "I almost crapped myself!"

"Can you get the access door open?"

Grey marvels at the helo fragments that continue

raining down. "I've already unlocked it and bugged the internal security system! It should be disabled for at least ten minutes!"

"Go to the hanger and find some transport!"

Grey shrugs, "What are you going to do?"

"I'm going to make sure we finish this mission!"

Grey descends into the bay's hatch as I head for the control room. His virus successfully infects all cameras and turrets; they're either non-responsive or behaving erratically. I enter the main corridor as the doors leading to the control room begin opening sequentially.

"Worry not my beautiful queen of destruction, I'll clear the way for you. Let's discuss terms in my office."

Grey's virus must be working if General Gideon wants to negotiate. He's trying to buy time in order to initiate some kind of trap. I lack alternatives and reluctantly proceed through the winding corridor. It widens midway until I emerge—with my rifle raised—inside some kind of garden.

"Amazing, isn't it Commander?" Gideon derives pleasure from my nervousness and chuckles confidently. "This room was constructed to resemble a Roman palace. It's the last of its kind, too. Every stone comes from authentic Italian ruins. A mind like yours isn't capable of conceiving architectural marvels of this sort, is it? Your tribe is responsible for their extinction due to sheer ignorance whereas my people, well… we all know the results of that encounter. You're all primitive, lesser humans, who trail in the path of greatness!"

I scan the room but fail to locate Gideon. "Where are you?" His voice emerges from all corners of the garden as if relayed through a speaker system. It's an unnerving experience. "I thought you were going to face me like a man!"

"Like a man, huh? You can't appreciate the sophistication and civility that were bred into my forefathers!"

"You're delusional! They blew up the entire world! That's civilized barbarism!"

I step into one of the garden's snaking paths and stroll through its vast collection of rare plants. The scenery is a bit mystical, especially after traversing a dead planet. Searching for someone in such an unfamiliar environment is challenging and the mainframe that I'm searching for can be anywhere. The foliage provides an effective layer of camouflage and discerning familiar patterns within its flora gives me a headache. Yet to my surprise, Gideon emerges from hiding and speaks to me from a raised pavilion beyond the garden.

"Why are you here, Commander? What do you hope to accomplish? Unlike that rebellious group of yours, my organization has something called, *a chain of command.* There will always be someone ready to take my place. Killing me gets you nowhere!"

I notice a statue of Zeus standing atop a golden pedestal on the opposite end of the room. A rose garden encloses the statue within a thorny fence. The Greek god holds a massive thunderbolt in his upturned palm. The thunderbolt's tip points toward the garden's center, where a globe of the world rests.

"Why would I come all this way just to kill you? My target is your Commander in Chief. By the way, why do you have a Greek demigod inside of your Roman palace?"

Gideon laughs as I move towards the statue. "You're going to kill my president? Well, good luck with that! You'll never reach him! He's well protected!"

"Is he?" I use my crosscom to play a recording of the president's Chief of Staff.

Recording begins:

"Of course everyone thinks Tower Yu is just a military fort." Chief Drover elaborates, *"But it's actually the guard tower for bunker zero. The bunker lies beneath Tower Yu, so there's no way anyone is going to reach the president. We sealed him up so tight that it'll take a tenth of the world's firepower to dig him out. The IFA is the only nation left with that kind of power and Tower Yu is the only IFA installation in possession of that kind of arsenal..."*

Recording ends:

I can almost hear Gideon gulp and cheerfully add, "Beneath this room is a vast nuclear arsenal."

"Is that what you think?"

"That's what I *know*. This tower serves as the president's personal fortress. One fourth of your arsenal lies within these walls and beneath its foundation. I also know that you're trying to stall me long enough to get your security system to reboot. You shouldn't have trusted your most valuable room to computers. Your guards will need about five minutes to get here now that the elevators are out. That just leaves you, me, and Zeus…"

Gideon immediately goes on the offensive when he realizes my intentions. "Not everything in this room is automated!"

He raises the pavilion's hidden wave cannon by rotating a few levers on a hidden panel. Terror floods my veins as I leap into a sprint in search of cover. Gideon hastily arms the quad-barreled monstrosity and immediately fires into the dense vegetation.

Thousands of rounds level the trees in front of me before sheering a wooden bench and garbage can. I dive into one of the nearby streams and swim beneath the blanket of bullets as they tear apart everything above water. My rifle is lost in the confusion but I manage to descend below the chaos and swim twenty feet downstream before resurfacing beneath a small stone bridge. The wave cannon fire is nearly impossible to avoid and the leveled vegetation to my right is proof. Each of the four barrels showers the room with over three thousand rounds per second. An offensive strategy is out of the question.

"You'll never leave his room alive, Commander!"

Gideon is barely audible over the chattering cannon fire. A few rounds strike water conduits feeding the stream and their enclosed pipes rupture. I allow the surging floodwaters to carry me right to Zeus. I climb the golden pedestal and insert Remi's activation key into the thunderbolt before Gideon spots me. A automated alarm sounds through the garden's speakers.

Warning: Nuclear launch sequence activated. Warheads AKRG-10:1 through Zebt-2:2 initialized.

Gideon stops battering the statue with bullets. "What did you do?"

"I infected those nukes you're hoarding with a unique virus! We never had the weaponry to destroy the International Federation of America, so we used your missiles against you!"

Gideon leaps from his pavilion and dashes to a nearby computer panel in a vain attempt to stop the launch. I leave him to his fruitless task and escape through the main corridor as some of the automated defenses reboot. Two turrets target me as I slip behind the radio antenna. Grey hasn't returned with transportation and IFA reinforcements are arriving.

"Grey! Where are you? I need transport!"

There's no response on my crosscom and three guards emerge from the main corridor with pistols aimed at my hiding spot. I wait until they cross the turret's line of fire before briefly exposing myself. The automatic defense system targets me, but accidentally guns down two of the men as more arrive from the circular bay's catwalk.

I throw my only bubble grenade at the new group of guards and scurry to the furthest corner of the antenna after it detonates. Bubbles form on the heads of those caught within the grenade's blast radius. The victims choke as their crystalline helmets suffocate them with poisonous gas. Some of the men can't endure the torturous toxins and rupture the bubbles with the butts of their guns–bad idea. Their crystal helmets explode when prematurely ruptured, taking the heads they encapsulate with them. The remaining men retaliate with black hole pucks and force me to retreat behind what remains of the maintenance shack.

There's nowhere else to run but I find a single EBE capsule amongst the helo's wreckage and activate the emitter's negative node. After lobbing it at the guards, the red sphere bounces across the roof and ensnares four men before rolling off the building's side. Their screams fade into the wind as a Verticraft ascends the tower.

"You've got to be kidding me!" Just as I resign my life to the armored aircraft, it fires its foremost cannons at the IFA guards advancing on my position. "Grey? It's about time!"

He circles the building and provides suppressive fire as I climb the radio antenna's ladder. The enemy guards are powerless against the Verticraft and retreat as Grey opens the vehicle's rear hatch. I climb inside the hawkish looking vehicle and sprint to its cockpit as Grey steers away from the tower.

"Did you insert the activation key, Commander?"

"Of course! I wouldn't be here otherwise! Is my timer right?"

The launching of warheads partially answers my question. As we hover over the roof, missiles ascend from all four sides of the building and elevate skyward. Each of Tower Yu's odd floors releases its set of eight warheads in sequential order.

Grey taps the instrument panel, "We have less than eight minutes before they return. If we head for the upper atmosphere right now, we might be—"

"We're not leaving without Remi and Hannibal!" Grey immediately alters course while I assume the gunner's chair. "How's our ammo?"

"We're fully stocked. The starboard launcher was damaged in that last assault but it's still functional."

I activate my crosscom. "Remi, can you hear me?"

"Commander? Yeah, I can hear ya, but we're under heavy fire and need support! Bail us out! We're about to get slaughtered!"

"I've got you marked at location 45-17. Can you confirm?"

"Hell yeah," he acknowledges in a panicked voice. "We're right in da middle of a crap storm on da eighth floor of an apartment complex!"

"Can you make it to the roof?"

"Hell no!" Remi briefly shouts something to Hannibal as gunfire fills the background. "We're pinned down! Low ammo! Are ya going to save our asses or not?"

"Air evac, via Verticraft. ETA three minutes."

"Gotcha! We'll try to hold out!"

"Damn…"

"What?" Grey glances towards me with widening eyes. "Why, damn?"

"Whenever Remi says, 'We'll try to hold out,' he really means, 'We're screwed if you don't get here sooner, rather than later.'"

"Then I'll get us there sooner!"

I'm not sure how but Grey slides the Verticraft down wind currents like a sled riding a snow bank. Every time the vehicle seems to lose its lift, he pulls up slightly, levels out, and then resumes his suicidal drop. Small arms fire hits the craft as we near the pickup zone.

"Don't waste time strafing the perimeter!" I point to the building's first floor. "Rollers have the complex surrounded and IFA troops are storming the rooms with Jackals!"

Grey cringes. "What do you want me to do?"

"Open the rear hatch, hover by the eighth floor, and try to keep her steady. I'll man the aft cannons!"

Grey doesn't disappoint. Once we near the building, he keeps the Verticraft nearly motionless. Muzzle flashes ignite the shadowy corners of the eighth floor. When I spot Remi and Hannibal pinned down inside of a bedroom, I direct a hail of cannon fire at the shadowy figures moving throughout the apartment's other rooms.

IFA troops scatter like roaches. The battle intensifies when someone sets their Jackals to suicide mode. Two of the mechanical beasts dash across the apartment and jump through a kitchen window. I destroy them with cannon fire before they smash into our Verticraft and their exploding bodies collapse the apartment's kitchen.

Three more Jackals leap from the roof and tumble by us when Grey veers away from the building. Remi and Hannibal jump aboard after he repositions the craft. Bullets seem to emerge from every floor of the building and I fire the cannons with such ferocity that the barrels redden. Grey elevates quickly but loses one of the engines to gunfire.

"Commander," Grey whines, "I'm not sure if we'll make it..."

I try reigniting the damaged engine as Remi and Hannibal enter the cockpit. They know without asking that we're still in trouble. Both men return to the cargo bay and dump all of its supplies before returning.

Hannibal groans, "You should have left us behind."

He actually appears annoyed that we saved him! Hannibal's willingness to sacrifice his life over mission loyalty or some mistaken sense of martyrdom is disturbing.

"Damn that!" Remi beats his chest excitedly. "I don't know about Hulk over there, but thanks for pulling my ass out of that IFA slaughterhouse! I don't want to miss da fireworks!" The Verticraft lurches when Remi assumes control of the vehicle from Grey. "I saw ya using that dolphin technique I taught ya back in Quazi. Good job, but ya leveled out too fast! Those dives could of been faster." Remi licks his lips, and then steers the Verticraft away from the first of several descending warheads.

Grey cynically notes, "We'll be a part of the fireworks if you can't get above the minimum safe distance."

"I'm a better pilot than ya with one arm! So how much time before da big bang?"

"Just focus on flying the damn Verticraft! We only have five minutes before detonation! Commander, is my count right?"

I read from numbers on the dashboard clock. "Five minutes, fifteen seconds until detonation." I lean back, buckle my seat belt, and light a cigarette. "Find a seat and strap in. If we go down it's going to be hard."

Everyone quiets when the Verticraft's final engine stalls. Remi struggles to maintain our current altitude and just when the vehicle seems ready to die, the engine sputters back to life, and continues carrying us skyward.

Time passes slowly in the final minutes.

I stare out the cockpit's window trying to imagine Earth in its prime. How can we allow the world exist in such a miserable state? Earth birthed us. When the wind mortally howls or the ground rumbles with grief, who are we to turn a blind eye? Humans caused her illness so administering a remedy is the only humane thing to do.

How should one view the end of the world?

My father raised me to believe that only God

can destroy all life and humankind doesn't have the power to obliterate such a "divine" creation. Yet here I am, ascending ashen clouds like a demon, or even worse, a god. Earth now lies doomed and my hand helped trigger its demise. All of human history has culminated to this moment and I feel like the very hand of death that I reviled my entire life. Does this make me a god, or does the credit go to those pale souls who centuries ago, created the instruments of destructions that I wield so valiantly? Perhaps my theology is all wrong; maybe I'm the Antichrist or even worse, the Devil…

Should I have tried to reconstruct the old world? Is it possible past men were destined to annihilate whereas my generation is fated to rebuild? It's not likely. I am no slave to the misgivings of men, nor will I clean up past mistakes—seeking light in the darkness of Hell. I prefer to destroy the world that past injustices created. Why? I reek of God's attitude, that's why! In fact, to despise humankind, is to love the true nature of God. Surely, you've despised something you created. Ah, but you choose not to believe in God? Well then, enjoy your paradise here on Earth. The vacation will be over shortly.

If I could stay at that IFA tower without a premature death, I'd linger until well after the mushroom cloud fades, just to ensure everything is gone. Is this what Hannibal hungers for? Maybe he wishes to unite with that one moment when everything becomes right with the world.

Then, in a sudden flash, Tower Yu's entire

payload detonates…

A brilliant fountain of light rises from below and suffuses the horizon with rolling waves of thunder. The Verticraft's tinted windows can't dim the blinding radiance filling our cockpit. A billowing cloud of fire smacks the aircraft and we thrash about like rag dolls. There's no way to escape the maelstrom. We spin about as fire devours the derelict urban city, plateau, and the mountain range sitting below.

When the nuclear dawn fades, I'm awed by a rising mountain of molten fluid that suddenly bursts from Earth's crust. A terrifying volcanic roar dwarfs all sound barriers. My eardrums rupture and bleed from the deafening intensity. I know only from looking at the Verticraft's console that our nuclear bombardment has awakened all of Earth's super volcanoes. An epic earthquake follows. The planet appears to split in half when a massive canyon of lava erupts from the widening continental fracture racing in our direction.

My stomach curls with fear as I realize we're about to die. The rupture is beyond tremendous. It sets the sky ablaze while vaporizing all clouds. I'm unable to hear the Verticraft's engine and have no way of telling if we're rising or falling. Shock waves grab the vehicle, rattle our seats, and thrash the aircraft from all directions. Crackling flames engulf every portion of the Verticraft as they spiral upward.

We're now beholden to a true demonstration

of power. When lava blasts into the stratosphere, everything inside the cockpit ignites. A flaming vortex rises from the chaos, swallows the vehicle, and pulls it into the fiery hell below. Then, just as I begin to scream, I see… God.

Special Delivery

CHAPTER 1

Ilighten the one-way transparency on my portal and see Remi waving with another one of his goofy expressions. Grey and Hannibal are standing behind him.

I turn away as Remi yells, "We know ya're in there! C'mon E, open da portal! Ya can't hide from us! We're not leaving! We'll camp out all night, just like last time!"

I don't want another spontaneous front yard party, and reluctantly unseal my portal. The oval entrance expands like an eyelid. Remi skips through, bows majestically, and then hands me a purchase slip for cigarettes. My taste buds glow at the thought of a fresh pack. I smoked my last nicotine stick a few hours ago. The peace offering makes up for the unannounced visit, although I'd never admit it.

"Bout time ya opened up! It's raining out there, no thanks to ya!" Remi strolls straight to the kitchen's data chest—opens it—and starts rifling through my consumables.

Grey gawks at my red lingerie. "I hope we're not imposing–"

"Just make sure to put the toilet seat down," I caution figuratively before gesturing admission.

There are no toilets in my condominium, since

they serve no identifiable purpose. Some people still use them as decorative data recyclers but I'd rather insert old info into one of the conduit slots on my wall. Toilets are one of the few things from the physical world that I don't want to emulate. Ancient waste disposal was gross… to say the least.

Grey smiles warmly before finding a seat in the den. He accepts the beer Remi offers only after I nod my approval. Toilets—cigarettes—seats—beers—are pleasure items. Decorative toys, even. We have no physiological need to smoke, sit, drink, or do half the things ancient people did. Regardless… many individuals have a psychological need for these ritualistic behaviors. How can a person retain their humanity without acting human?

Hannibal stands in the portway puffing on a freshly lit cigarette. The photonic fumes aggravate my urge to smoke. I refill my cigarette pouch by using the password on Remi's purchase slip and pluck one of the glassy tubes free when all twenty cigarettes finish downloading. Cycling through the filter's various flavors to find strawberry splash is a bit tedious but it seems like a tasty option. I depress the butt to ignite the tip, take a deep drag while staring at those droplets of rain that Remi was in such a hurry to flee from, and exhale.

"Aren't you guys going to the Palladium?"

Hannibal releases a long, steady stream of cloudy photons before answering.

"We went."

"So," I wonder in-between puffs, "what happened?

You couldn't have been there for more than an hour."

"We weren't."

My exhaled smoke transforms into a bushel of strawberries that ripen on smoky stems. They dissipate into a pink mist when mixed with Hannibal's turkeys. How can anyone enjoy turkey-flavored cigarettes? Disgusting!

"So what happened this time?"

"Do you really have to ask? Remi is what happened. He started a fight with a couple of eggheads so Boc kicked us out."

"What did you expect? Remi is Mandible 9's official hothead. I swear though… this has to be the one-hundredth time! And you wonder why I don't go to the Palladium with you guys. How many did you fight?"

Hannibal shrugs after taking another long drag. "He fought three of them on his own. Remi must be taking superman pills or something. All I had to do was sit back and enjoy. It felt good just watching a fight for once."

"What did Grey do?"

"Our newbie?" Hannibal almost laughs when his eyes glaze from the memory. "The bastard was raising all kinds of hell but nobody was paying attention! Remi is too rowdy to have the spotlight taken away from him."

Remi jumps up from his chair. "That's because I'm da spotlight guru!" He lightens the transparency on one of my walls until the backyard becomes visible, and then flexes for an invisible audience—his spiky blonde hair dances about like blades of grass. I try ignoring Remi's senseless actions but his absurd posing stirs giggles. Remi settles down only when he feels I've been properly entertained.

Hannibal observes the peaceful scenery I designed years ago. Infinitely variable clouds change according to prewar environmental conditions. A sprawling mountain range stands beneath them. Every weather pattern is unique and no two days are ever the same. My clouds have thickened and turned gray while random streaks of lightning brighten the darkening sky.

Countless people have created similar programs but with mixed results. Some clouds lack enough variance while others create abnormal atmospheric conditions that alter the laws of gravity in unrealistic ways. The public considers my program to be the "realist" version. Yet in reality, how can anyone truly determine what's real from within our virtual world? Nobody knows what a real white cloud looks like anymore. I mean, not *really*. Our perception of clouds derives from old video recordings, ancient meteorological data, and survey drones. How real are those?

"There was another terrorist attack," Hannibal mumbles, "inside the Sphinx hotel."

"I know."

My cigarette finally depletes. Instead of using a wall slot, I place the butt into a palmetto-shaped ashtray sitting on my banister; a birthday present from an old neighbor. It recycles the unused bits of data somewhat like an ancient garbage disposal.

"I saw the aftermath on PSN. Some of the causalities were kids."

Hannibal shakes his head. "Thirty kids."

My vision frays into static when a few ionic sparks escape their ocular confines and run down my cheeks like escaping convicts. Children soften my heart in unexpected ways. Damn kids…

Thirty of them died!

Just one would have been too much, but thirty? What's the virtual world coming to? Hannibal has no idea that I spent the past hour crying over this exact issue. Then again, maybe he assumes as much. My team knows me well enough to predict my behavior with a fair amount of accuracy.

Grey asks, "Hey E, can I use your lift for a store trip? Remi needs some special barbecue sauce that we can't download online. He wants to grill some wings."

"Yeah, *my wings*," I chide without facing him. "The lift number is 5543-4321-8763."

"Thanks…"

Grey seems hesitant to leave. He senses my distress but chooses not to approach with Hannibal hovering about and eventually heads off to the download store.

Remi bounces in his seat. "Hey, we're on da news again!"

I use Hannibal's sleeve to balance the teary charge from my sparking eyes before returning inside and plopping on my lounge chair. Mandy Alyssum reports breaking news on the den's wallscreen.

"It's been nearly a decade since *The Suffering* was introduced to the gaming world. The game has a reputation for its remarkably unique and seemingly impassable level designs. Gamers are accustomed to playing simply for the pleasure of dying in uniquely gruesome ways. Although some came close to defeating *The Suffering*, none proved successful. A few of the most notable teams include Psychotic 357, commanded by actor Jean Mayweather. Turbulent Hammer, commanded by columnist Po Hudani and the infamous Cocaine Jailbirds, commanded by Newark Chief of Police Antonio Victor.

That changed yesterday when a relatively unknown team conquered level thirty in one of the greatest performances ever witnessed. Led by Di Ehari, Mandible 9 not only beat the game, but accomplished this remarkable feat together, with all members surviving to the very end."

"Damn!" Remi laughs until his face brightens. "She's using one of ya high school graduation photos!"

"And the ugly one," Hannibal garishly adds.

"The ugly one?" I throw one of my slippers at Hannibal. "I like that picture!"

"Sorry, but you look like a drunk chipmunk in that photo!"

"Di Ehari," the reporter continues in a rehearsed tone, "is best known for her Clouds of Life simulator.

The program's stunning rendition of infinitely variable cloud formations has gained praise from artists, level designers, and leading pioneers from the scientific community. The original members of Mandible 9 include Stephen Remi and Otum Hannibal. Yung Grey, the newest addition to the group, is also one of the lead programmers behind the geological earthquake simulator, Quaker. All members are in their early to mid twenties."

Hannibal leans forward when clips of our in-game performances flash into view. His brawny frame nearly tips over my loveseat.

"Do you think my muscles look bigger on-screen?"

It's a question worth ignoring.

Remi revels in some of his past heroics. "That's when I destroyed da mechanical Centaur boss in level eighteen! Damn that was a fun mission!"

"Mandible 9 isn't without its problems, however." Miss Alyssum elaborates with a raised brow, "The team struggled to remain in the Worldwide Contenders Board of Competition since their induction into the gaming league. While on the brink of failure, former member Johanna H. Scarlet abandoned Mandible 9 in favor of the Bloody Membranes—a popular team that currently holds top honors in the *Cyclone* series action drama. And earlier today, all male members of Mandible 9 were seen fighting at the Palladium in Upper Westchester."

Remi stands up and poses by the wall, again. He looks and dresses like an eighties rock star. "Damn, she's airing that already? Alyssum is making me look like an animal!"

Hannibal fondles another cigarette without actually lighting it. "You *are* an animal," he casually instigates.

The reporter uses select images to highlight scenes from various games. "Titles such as *Heaven's Gate, Cyclone,* and *The Great American Adventure,* have become the premier form of entertainment for seven out of ten people. Virtual games are now the vanguard of media entertainment. Players who assume pivotal roles in the most popular love, drama, mystery, horror, comedy, and action stories have become worldwide celebrities. Nevertheless, with the completion of *The Suffering* comes an inevitable question; have we gone too far? It's been nearly two thousand years since the virtual world's creation. As the virtual world exists in tandem with its physical counterpart, should we reenact the very war that led humanity into near extinction? Here to answer that question is Dr. Hugel Grant from the Institute of Virtual Science and Technology. Hello doctor."

"Thank you for having me," the portly doctor nods.

"You've been a critic of *The Suffering* ever since its release ten years ago. How do you feel about talks of a sequel?"

"It's a bad idea, obviously. Stephen Remi is the perfect example of why the past needs to stay buried in the physical world. Mr. Remi instigated a fight in a respectable Upper Westchester club shortly after leaving *The Suffering's* apocalyptic environment. His behavior shows symptoms of virtual induced dementia. VID escalates the longer a participant remains exposed to these types of… games."

"That's bull," Hannibal contests, stroking his cigarette with a bent forefinger. "Remi always acts like a demented animal."

"Yeah I—" Remi glances towards Hannibal and scowls, "Hey, screw off Elephant Man!"

"The issue is one of morality," the doctor remarks smugly. "Our virtual world was created to simulate the best aspects of the physical world—not follow its most heinous examples of human behavior. With the introduction of virtual entertainment, people are finding it difficult to separate our reality from those found in these pointless games. We need to do the responsible thing by putting restrictions on what type of content can be rendered."

Mandy Alyssum asks rhetorically, "If we forget our past, aren't we doomed to repeat it? Some argue that restrictions of any kind are a violation of our indivisic rights. I'd like our viewers to watch a clip from yesterday's interview with Miss Di Ehari, Commander of Mandible 9."

After a brief pause, the newsroom containing Mandy Alyssum and Dr. Hugel Grant overlaps with prerecorded footage of my team. Everyone is sitting on a couch with Alyssum facing us from her own chair.

"Even in the physical world, athletics and video games were predominately conquered by males. Most games feature male protagonists of a single race. Di, you've managed to dominate a game within a field saturated by men. Do you see yourself as a pioneer?"

"I couldn't have beaten *The Suffering* without my team. Nothing about that game is singular. Mandible 9 was successful because of our collective effort."

"But you're the team leader, correct?"

"Well… yes."

"As Mandible 9's leader, how do you feel about the criticism surrounding the game? Its release and subsequent completion triggered worldwide protests. Some people even claim to be horrified by *The Suffering's* content."

I look directly into the camera and say sternly, "If you don't like the game, then don't play it!" Alyssum smirks as I return my attention to her adding, "Our world is divided into Realms for a reason. If you dislike certain people and want to live exclusively around your chosen kind, there's a Realm for you. If you want to exist in the company of only one sex, there's a Realm for you. There's a Realm for every imaginable preference. There's even a Realm for those who choose to live within their own custom environments and yet another for non-virtual gamers. I prefer the Free Realm."

"Why is that? The Free Realm is violent, disruptive, and the most unstable of all Realms."

I nod agreeably. "This Realm is the closest facsimile of Earth. Our existence owes itself to many races and both genders from all over the planet. A collaborative effort from individuals with opposing views and theories created the virtual world. The Free Realm is meant to mirror their reality."

"And what reality might that be?"

"It's one where people must contend with the differences of others."

"But many of *The Suffering*'s critics are gamers, Di. What about them?"

"Again, they don't have to play the game."

"That's an interesting statement, mainly because you said in a previous interview on the Glass Network, that you have no plans on replaying *The Suffering*. Would you care to explain your reasons for abandoning a game that's given you intervirtual fame?"

"I never played the game with intentions on becoming famous."

The reporter leans forward. "What were your intentions, then?"

I glance towards my team and continue with their encouragement. "I first learned of the Rupture on my ninth birthday—and was horrified to learn that all of humankind now exists within the Nexus—and that Earth is completely dead. The planet teemed with life once but now, we're all that's left. This... photonic world instantly became a prison to me—especially after studying all the old holobooks, videos, and texts from the past—I wanted to feel connected to the physical reality that exists outside of the Nexus and maybe... understand what brought us here.

That's why I played *The Suffering.*"

Alyssum nods. "Even though we live inside the Nexus, we still exist within the physical world. In fact, many believe our new form of existence marks the height of human evolution. Consumption for example, primarily serves as a tool for downloading new updates and viral patches. All we need are the raw materials that our remote laborbots harvest to maintain themselves and the Nexus."

"True," I nod, "nevertheless, we're doomed if something happens to the laborbots. Moreover, even if we live for a million years, virtual humans can only exist as we are now. Real humans evolved, whereas our evolution has peaked."

"We evolve all the time. Sequential updates, addons—"

"No," I politely interrupt, "I mean as a virtual person, our evolution is strictly based on our perception of what evolution should be, within a virtual state. Not only are we lacking nature's guidance, humans are now dictating the pace at which we develop. I don't see how this can end well. Bearing the burden of self-development is perverse and the opposite of evolution."

Alyssum lowers her holopad. "What do you consider it, then?"

"Corruption."

My interviewer leans back, folds her hands, and then places them gently on her lap. "We exist because of, and as forms of technology. This technology continues to advance because of us. Isn't it fair to say that because we're dictating the pace and direction of our evolution, we now have the power to supersede extinction?"

"That notion is what *The Suffering* is about," I respond carefully, "humans dictating the pace of their evolution with hopes of superseding extinction. Is it truly possible to dictate such a path, regardless of the means? Our evolution and our demise remain in the hands of nature. Even though we exist inside the virtual world's Nexus, the Nexus exists within a very volatile physical world. Who knows what the next calamity might be. We remain trapped on the very planet that drove us into a photonic environment. And I'm willing to bet ancient humans would have preferred life in the physical world as opposed to this place."

"But you still haven't answered *why* you've decided to stop playing *The Suffering*. What happened to you at the end of the game? Why did you scream in the final moments?"

I look disconcerted on-screen. It's obvious I'm struggling with something much deeper than the philosophy of a game.

"I can't say."

"Can't say," Mandy Alyssum prods, "or won't say?"

The reporter relents when I remain quiet. "Now that you've decided to move on to other games, will your team seek a new commander and continue playing *The Suffering*?"

"No!" Hannibal, Remi, and Grey cry in unison from the sofa.

She turns towards Hannibal. "Why is that?"

"Ehari is more than our commander; she's our friend. True friends never abandon one another."

"Funny you mentioned that. During a previous interview with Johanna H. Scarlet, she said playing under Di's command requires infinite patience. Care to elaborate?"

Remi leans ahead of Hannibal and Grey to add his two cents. "Scarlet was always jealous of E, plain and simple! E is a thoughtful tactician. It's like comparing a checkers player to a chess master!"

Alyssum asks Grey, "How do you feel about taking Miss Scarlet's place? She proved her resourcefulness by skillfully hacking *The Suffering*'s programming, and alerting Gideon's in-game AI of your presence. Her interference nearly cost you the victory."

Grey smiles with enough warmth to melt a glacier. "Everything she hacks, I hack better. Besides, I'm on a winning team. Where's she?"

Once the video returns to its original set, Alyssum asks Dr. Grant, "Will you admit *The Suffering* may have a valid purpose? Perhaps even a necessary one?"

The doctor shakes his head, no. "Nothing is wrong with most virtual games. *The Suffering* however, seeks to exploit and popularize humanity's greatest tragedy. Nothing good can come from it. Perhaps this is the reason why Miss Di Ehari has chosen to abandon that despicable game?"

Remi throws a credit slip at the wallscreen." That grump needs some ass!"

I lift my hands in disgust. "Can you form one sentence without an obscenity? You're making my ears bleed!"

"That's how we got into that fight at the Palladium," says the rookie.

When I turn around, Grey raises a few bottles of specially programmed barbecue sauce for all to see. I notice glowing lipstick on his forehead and wonder about the innocent soul he managed to coax into leaving it there. His boyish smile and puppy dog eyes never fail him.

"What am I doing with these?"

Remi jogs across the room and pushes Grey into the kitchen. "Ya're going help me make some of da best DAMN wings ya ever had!"

I cringe, grab my remaining slipper, and launch it across the room—striking Remi between his shoulder blades. He playfully stumbles and falls. As I get ready to join them in the kitchen my chiming portal bell snags everyone's attention.

Hannibal motions me away. "Don't worry E, I'll get it."

Carol waves when he unseals the portal. "Hi E! Congratulations on your victory! That was one heck of a final battle!"

I wave to my neighbor. "Thanks! I didn't know you played virtual games."

"I enjoy watching more than playing. Some of

those games are better than movies." Carol points towards her home. "The servers delivered something big to my condo but it has your name on it. I think there was a delivery glitch."

"Beastly! I'll be right over!"

I hop pass Remi and Grey as they shadowbox in the kitchen and slip into my bedroom—making sure to lock the portal before searching my walk-in closet's catalog display for something to wear. Sure, my escapade will only take a minute or two, but a girl still has to look good, right?

Style is always important to me. For instance, an old looking pair of sweatpants requires an equally old looking shirt. Keep in mind that neither should appear tattered. That was last week's style. Color is always vital, as it defines my guiding emotion for the day. Everything has to match, of course, but not obsessively so. Get me started on accessories and I can be here all day! My closet has over thirty-three thousand articles of clothing data. There are so many combinations that I always spend more time getting dressed than necessary. Then, seemingly out of nowhere, I hear a loud and sudden BOOM!

My entire life flashes before my eyes as I'm lifted into the air—floating, as though in water. The sensation is fractional. When the moment passes, an invisible force throws me against the closet door and knocks a few breath programs out of my lungs. My head throbs, both shoulders ache, and my vision blurs with static. Nothing outside of the gaming world has ever dazed me with such force!

Then I notice blue flames rising from where my windowed wall once stood. Blue photonic fire is indicative of data recycling. The process of reclaiming damaged or outdated information is usually restricted to recycling centers. I have no idea where these flames are coming from but they'll definitely kill me if I don't get out of the bedroom.

I try standing and scream when my legs refuse to move. My voice sounds muted—either from deafness, or breathlessness. Tears spark against my checks as I try climbing over some broken furniture blocking the closet. Aqua blue flames reach out like the hands of a demon and fondle my overturned bed with fiery fingertips. A pink hue lathers the meshing of items lost in the fire. Once the textures destabilize, their inner framework scrambles until the resulting error causes viral scanners to erase the object from my room—or in layman's terms, 'death by deletion'. I'm lost in a moment of shock when Remi and Grey hack through my bedroom portal.

Remi is the first to enter. He leaps over my burning bed and scoops me into his arms while Grey uses a nightstand to help push smoldering objects out of our way. Remi follows Grey through the kitchen and when I try speaking, only a scrambled set of syllables escapes my lips. They exit through the front portal, run to the first available projection step, and then use it to propel down the street. Remi gently lays me on someone's fur lawn. I look back and nearly faint after realizing Carol's house is gone. Blue flames engulf my condominium along with two other homes. People begin filling the jumpwalks as if they're ancient sidewalks. Some project about and try helping those caught in the blast. Others stand mesmerized on their lawns and porches. It's complete chaos.

I barely moan, "Hanni…"

Remi looks around and cringes. "I think Hannibal went to Carol's place right before da explosion!" He reaches out and grabs Grey's collar. "Stay with E! I'm going to look for him!"

Grey takes my hand. "Don't worry I'm not going anywhere!"

Remi uses one of the jumpwalk's projection steps to propel into the growing crowd in front of my condo. Grey tries comforting me when I utter a few intelligible words.

"Shhh… don't talk. Lie back. You need to regenerate."

"Carol… Hanni…" I feel my energy fading as Grey's trembling arms embrace me and I wonder if I'm dying. What little strength my body retains evaporates when I try moving. My pulse slows when an eddy of darkness swallows my consciousness. Everything blackens as I listen to my rhythmic heartpulse getting weaker… and weaker… before melting into silence.

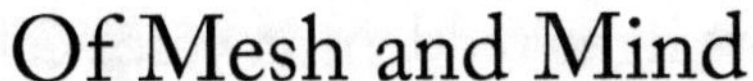

Of Mesh and Mind

CHAPTER 2

Iawaken on a strange pod-shaped operating table shivering from electric chills. Millions of splintering lights—rising from its rubbery mattress—pierce my body and dissolve into a green mist a few inches above me. A ball of hovering blue light pours magnetic rays into my skull. I can feel its luminescent beams sifting through my synapses. The simple act of thinking interrupts the ball's progress and when its light reddens, a voice calls out.

"Hello Miss Ehari. You are in the Tia Muhammad Medical Facility. The asonograph is nearly finished analyzing your synaptic pathways. Please remain quiet."

I instinctively disobey. "Where are my friends?"

"They are up here in the control room, and will rejoin you in the reception area when the graphing process completes."

I look up and see Remi and Grey waving through a particle window, but the rest of my body fails to respond.

"Why can't I move?"

"You have been suppressed with a photonic anesthetic. Your bodily functions will be restored shortly."

I survived the explosion! Beastly… but what

about Hannibal? What happened to my condo? Where's Carol? Why did everything blow up? I clench my teeth at the possibilities.

When the red glow hovering above my face fades, the splinters of light drawn from the mattress reverse course and retreat into the bedding. Gravity, sensation, and control, return to my body. I sit up and look around once the energy surging through my vascular threads completes its saturation process.

It's an average hospital room. Gray decor—smooth tile flooring—a single transparent wall belonging to the control room—nothing special. The only portal opens as if activated by my awareness of its existence. A slender woman with green eyes enters. The doctor's fiery red hair overshadows her pale skin and white lab coat. I'm unsure if the explosion of color is due to my refreshed consciousness, or her curly follicles' natural vibrancy.

"Good morning, Miss Ehari. I am Dr. Panels. Welcome back. How are you feeling?"

"Where's Hannibal?"

My question seems to distract Dr. Panels from her script. Still, she recovers her composure quickly. "Mr. Hannibal is undergoing synaptic surgery in the adjacent room. I can escort you now that we are done repairing your injuries."

I cringe. "How badly was I damaged?"

"You had a minor reverb concussion. There is nothing to worry about. All of your photonic synapses are functioning correctly."

"Thanks. Can you tell me about my neighbor, Higgins Carol?"

The doctor's reassuring smile quickly fades and her new expression speaks megabytes. Nevertheless, I wait patiently for verbal confirmation of my neighbor's demise.

"I am sorry but… Miss Carol did not survive the explosion."

My heartpulse nearly stops, again. I maintain insulated eyes even though static builds within my sockets. I never cry in the presence of strangers, if I can help it. Still, my trembling lips are softening the emotional barrier I'm trying to sustain.

"Your friends brought some clothes for you. When you are ready…" The doctor points to a few purchase slips on a nearby table. I know before acquiring anything with the downloader, that I won't like any of the selections.

It sucks to be right sometimes.

The shirt is too small, the pants are too baggy, and of course, everything is mismatched. At least the velvet sneakers are snug. I adjust the color tag on every article. The shirt is now pink with black pants and matching sneakers but their cheap standards have no auto fit options, which forces me to accept the given sizes. I follow Dr. Panels out of the room and find Grey waiting near the control area with Remi. They immediately blanket me with hugs.

Grey greets me with a boyish smile. "Glad to

have you back."

"There's my Chipmunk!" Remi gives my stomach a few playful jabs. "I knew ya'd make it! Ya're da Iron Maiden!"

Those swelling tears that I effectively hid from Dr. Panels are generating sparks. I bury my head in Remi's chest while Grey gives my back an affectionate rub. I normally shun emotional displays of this sort.

Dr. Panels asks, "How are you feeling?"

"Strong," I answer weakly. "Thank you."

"Even though you appear fully regenerated, I suggest undergoing a maintenance exam with Dr. Harish. A room has been reserved in case you decide to stay. Mr. Hannibal requires my attention now."

"Of course." I wonder nervously, "How is he?"

"Mr. Hannibal is in critical condition. We performed every possible procedure in an effort to stabilize him. We are waiting to see if he is strong enough to survive the graphing process. The blast damaged a portion of his synaptic network. Even if Mr. Hannibal survives, he may never be the same."

I pull away from the hug-fest but tolerate arms around my shoulders and waist.

"I understand. Where is he?"

"I can take you to him. Please, follow me."

Dr. Panels has a brief discussion with a nurse from across the hall before leading us to the same control room where Remi and Grey anxiously awaited news of my recovery. When she unseals the portal, I pull away from my friends and project up the angled jumpwalk to the next level.

The atmosphere is too dark, especially for a control room. Aside from a dimly lit ceiling, an array of instrument panels provides the only means of illumination. Glittering antiviral particles float about as they electrically sterilize the room. Stacks of popular magazines sit atop end tables. An open art journal rests on an empty seat with video articles about digital painting playing on mute. A semitransparent wall encases an aerial view of the uncomfortable operating table that helped save my life. The dimming glass obscures the room's new patient—like a two-way interrogation room from an ancient detective movie. When I approach the opposite wall and see Hannibal resting quietly on the table below, a few more tears spark from my eyes.

Needling light from the asonograph focuses on the hole in his skull's meshing. The floating arm controlling its synaptic bulb moves incredibly fast as it repairs the damage to Hannibal's neural network.

I cuff my mouth, "What happened?"

"Terrorists," Remi answers without pause.

"Terrorists? Are you kidding me?"

He shakes his head slowly. "It's true. The Calling is responsible. They actually tried to delete us."

My hands curl into fists. "The Calling? Are you talking about that radical Catholic group? Why would they want us dead?"

"I don't know. It has something to do with preserving the moral fiber of human society. They think we're Satanists for acting out those roles in *The Suffering*."

My eyes widen with disbelief. "A quarter billion people play that game!"

"Yeah, but we're the only ones who beat it," Grey notes regretfully, "…that's why they want us dead—as an example to the rest. The Calling hid an explosive virus inside a large message container and then vmailed it to your condo. Their bomb would have killed us had the address servers aligned the virus to the right house. Apparently, there was some kind of delivery glitch."

"But you're Catholic!"

Remi points to Grey, "He's not a Bible thumper no more."

Grey grabs the art magazine and stares at a video article. I study him, wondering what's going through his mind. "So you left the church?"

"Yeah, because they kicked me out." I watch Grey scowl with frustration and even hear a few mumbling curse words seep through his parted lips. "Maybe it's for the best, since the authorities have no clue about who's responsible. How can I feel comfortable going to mass after this? I could be sitting next to the same terrorist that tried to kill me and not even know."

"Wait… you were almost killed by Catholic terrorists, and instead of giving their support, the official church excommunicates you?"

I sit down and bury my head in both palms. It seems unreal that any of us would be the target of a terrorist group just because we played a game.

I scream, "That's what this is about? Some fanatical creeps deemed us unworthy to exist! And it was all because they disapprove of our choice of personal entertainment?"

I stand up and knock the nearest end table over with a raging kick. "Ouch! My toes!"

"Calm down," Grey quietly advises.

"No!" I scream so hard my throat rattles. "Carol is gone! We nearly died in my home! Hannibal is lying on his deathbed and the bastards responsible are still free? This is bull!"

I feel like kicking over another end table but my toes still hurt from the first outburst. Dr. Harish will probably lecture me about it during the physical. Remi places a hand on my shoulder but this time, I shrug it away. When "physical" contact fails to calm my agitation Remi tries sedating me with information.

"Two agents from da Virtual Bureau of Investigation are waiting for ya in da atrium. They probably have more info."

A distraction is exactly what's needed right now. I take the lead and motion for Remi and

Grey to join me.

"Let's go."

Remi points to me, "They only want to speak to ya."

"Just me? Why?"

He waves his hands about like a thief caught stealing a precious artifact. "Don't know, but I saw other big wigs with them."

"Who?"

"They looked like scientists."

"VBI agents with scientists?"

"Yah, I know." Remi's brows wrinkle. "Makes no sense."

I ask Grey, "How do you know The Calling is responsible for the bombing?"

"Everybody knows. That self-proclaimed Pope of the Underground announced it over the Virtualnet. Mandy Alyssum did a special on it. Apparently, they launched a wave of viruses into the Protestant's, Baptist's, Hindu, Buddhist's, and Muslim Realms before bombing your condo."

"I forgot about my condominium. What happened to it?"

Grey shakes his head. "There's nothing left aside from defragmented rubble."

"Damn those bastards! My latest cloud simulator updates were in there! Three months of work… gone!"

I kick over another end table—this time with

my good foot—and successfully keep my toes injury free. Just as the table lands on its side, Dr. Panels opens the portal and enters the room with a husky looking man and a stone-faced woman. The fitted suits, meticulously groomed hair, and specialized neural links reek of VBI protocol.

The husky man looks directly at me. "Are you Di Ehari?"

I cross my arms. "And you are?"

"I am Agent Grills. And this," he says motioning to his partner, "is Agent Dennington from the Virtual Bureau of Investigation. We would like to speak to you about yesterday's attack."

My eyebrows curl with intrigue. "Do you know who's responsible?"

"Please, follow us Miss Ehari. We can discuss this matter in greater detail at our office."

"What about Remi and Grey?"

"They'll have to stay behind."

"Why?"

"Everything will be explained if you follow us." Agent Grills steps aside and gestures towards the portal as if it's a prize in a game show.

I turn towards Dr. Panels. "What about my exam?"

"The exam can wait. I will keep a room reserved for you."

The doctor assures her promise by immediately setting the conditions with her holopad. I'm hesitant. Normally, my crew goes everywhere with me, but things are different this time. Somebody needs to stay with Hannibal while I get answers.

Remi snatches Grey's vr-com and hands it to me. "No worries. We'll keep an eye on Mr. Muscles. I'll call if anything happens."

Grey doesn't protest but I give his vr-com back and demand that Remi hand over his instead.

"But why take mine?"

"Basically, your mother is the only person who calls you with it. I'll let her know you're fine if I hear from her."

"But, but what if—"

"Besides, I know you're the one who bought this crappy shirt for me."

Remi grins mischievously. "How did ya know?"

"It's ten sizes too small! I look like a sleazy jumpway hooker!"

"Sorry…"

"Sure. You're unbelievable… Hannibal is on his deathbed and you're pulling crap like this?"

Embarrassed, Remi's face brightens from the surge of light running through his vascular links. There's nothing more to say. I leave with the agents after glancing down at Hannibal one last time.

Emergence

CHAPTER 3

I follow both agents to a jumpwalk and use its projection steps to propel to the closest lift. Each step thrusts our group fifty-cubes—or virtual feet—forward. Entire hospital sections fly by like slides in a PowerPoint demonstration. We pass Pharmacology, Radeonology, Oncology, Pediatrics, and the Holostetics departments before reaching a transit hub.

Our chosen lift is from the Glair series. I prefer this model because it resembles those antique elevators from the twenty-first century. Unlike other versions, G lifts are spacious enough for about twenty people. They also reanimate environments while in transit. I enjoy watching my destination forming around me before I get there. We step aboard, seal the access portal, and wait for Agent Dennington to activate the terminal.

"Set our transit to the Virtual Bureau of Investigation; office 67B865UI453HGHY4."

Automated Voice: Office confirmed. This destination requires security clearance from authorized personnel, only. Please enter code now.

Agent Dennington enters her code when prompted.

Automated Voice: Code confirmed. To initiate transfer, please verify authenticity with a valid nail print.

The security system quickly confirms Dennington's print and allows the lift to begin imaging our new locale. It only takes a few seconds for everything outside the lift's glassy walls to fade into absolute darkness. Seconds later, rectangular bits of our new environment appear to stick against the lift's outer surface. Once all of the pieces form a complete picture of Agent Dennington's office, the image expands into a three dimensional space.

I follow Agent Grills through Dennington's office and sit in the leathery chair he offers me. His stone-faced partner idles by Grills' side as he slaps an image sheet onto her desk. Agent Grills slides his fingers across the thin sheet and turns the holographic pages until he finds what he's looking for.

"Before we begin, I need to ask you about something that may be unrelated to the current case."

"Like what?"

"Something… personal."

"Why ask?"

"It may be important."

My eyebrows curl. "Go ahead."

"I did not realize until yesterday that people still exist with Texitus disease. Aside from you, the only other known carrier is Otum Hannibal. The odds are remarkable that you are friends. But it is equally odd that your condition was not eradicated after the Rupture."

"Sorry to disappoint you," I reply dryly.

Agent Grills looks up, leans back in Dennington's chair, and then waves me down. "My inquiry is not meant to be offensive. Our superiors think your condition is inconsequential but I believe your disease is a vital component of both recent and future events."

"In what way, exactly?"

"After defeating *The Suffering*, you have been profiled by certain religious organizations as either saintly or demonic. Beliefs like these usually stir violent outcomes."

"You think radical Catholics were targeting me because I have a texture disease?"

"They are, targeting you. Even though The Calling failed their assassination attempt, evidence suggests they will try again."

I can barely conceal my bulging B cups with folded arms. It's hard looking serious when my animated butterfly tattoo is flapping around my exposed belly button.

"How can my condition have anything to do with this?"

Grills fixates on his holopad as Dennington responds to my discomfort. She unseals her locker, downloads an outfit from a list displayed on the interior screen, and then offers it to me for fifty credits. I graciously accept the white blouse and slacks even though I'm sure they're her least favorite articles. Although a bit too formal for my liking, the clothes are leagues better than what I'm currently wearing.

I slide the clothing tag across Remi's vr-com and allow the embedded creditor program to deduct the appropriate funds from his account. Once the transaction completes and the items fully download to the device, I save the purchase slip to Remi's vr-com, activate its tag, and allow the outfit to autofit onto my body.

My new slacks fit perfectly. It takes only a moment to modify the color. Black compliments my overall mood, so I adjust the color of the slacks accordingly but leave the blouse white. The collar relaxes after deleting a few buttons and I retract the sleeves by tapping their cuffs.

Agent Grills raises a V-ray of my body's genome that he retrieved from Dr. Panels. "The assassins believe you have ancestral ties to the physical world. What I find interesting, is that Dr. Panels believes your texture contains a unique sequence that may provide one of the keys for returning to Earth as flesh and blood humans."

"That's ridiculous."

"Actually, it might be scientific truth." Grills points to the V-ray and then slides his finger along a key segment. "This sequence is unique. No other human has it, not even Hannibal. Mutative origins were ruled out. In fact, the sequence appears to be a natural element of human ancestry."

I stand up and pace about the room. The extra sequence could be good or bad. It obviously has something to do with Texitus disease.

"How can The Calling know this? I didn't even know this!"

Grills examines the V-ray closely, as if noticing something new. "We think Johanna H. Scarlet informed them."

I tense at the mention of Scarlet's name. She's a master hacker who's capable of discovering just about anything—would she have me killed over an anomalous sequence? Is my ex-best friend truly capable of murder?

"Why exactly, does The Calling want to delete me? Is it because of the game or the disease?"

"These fanatics view physicality as the cause of all suffering. Assassinating you will extinguish any hope of returning to that state of reality. They believe the game and your unique sequence are intertwined."

"What can be done to stop them?"

Agent Grills sets the V-ray aside before placing both hands palms down on the desk. This man's every action seems purposeful—as if he's an actor in a play.

"What is your religious affiliation, Miss Ehari? No record of this information has ever been documented."

"Why ask? Is it because you're Catholic, or because it's pertinent to the case?" Agent Grills appears baffled by my intuition so I point to the closed closet. "I noticed a rosary's imprint hanging on the hook inside Dennington's closet before the room fully materialized. Glair model lifts are buggy that way."

"And?"

"And, that rosary has blocked insignia on it, which is for men. Does it belong to you?"

Dennington leans forward while eyeballing me and whispers something in Grills' ear. He glances towards the closet and speaks without looking in my direction.

"I am asking you because the information could be pertinent to the bombing."

"Really? So you expect me to believe that a Catholic background doesn't influence your opinion towards me?"

"The influence is positive."

"And what about Agent Dennington?"

"She is here to help you, too."

Dennington's stony face softens. She has obvious reservations about exposing their relationship. Grills continues after an awkward silence.

"Disregard my last question. Now… we have been tracking Oliver Milke's terrorist group for twenty-eight years. This so called, 'Pope of the Underground', has remained hidden within the virtual world's infrastructure the entire time. We found evidence at your condominium that is helping to track Milkes and others within The Calling who might be responsible for the attack."

"What kind of evidence?"

"You were working on an update to your cloud simulator prior to the explosion, correct?"

"Well… yes. How do you know that?"

"Portions of your holopad were discovered intact. We analyzed the photonic drive and extracted some of its data. I am sure you are aware that programs emitting a constant tracking field, or that monitor the environmental conditions outside of your home, are illegal."

"Yeah, so? I need that program for my work. Are you going to arrest me?"

"Its usefulness in this case will absolve you of all criminal charges. Now, seasonal program 67-435345 was the one you used, correct?"

"Yes," I acknowledge with an affirmative nod, "it helps to assess how clouds should be implemented into the environment."

"That program has a field radius of one hundred and ninety-cubes. Some of the projected calculations include wind speed, gravity, and temperature. While seasonal program 67-435345 normally serves as a meteorological thermostatic simulator, we modified its codes to track abnormal patterns within the environment; particularly the presence of foreign properties."

I thank Dennington for the clothes before sitting down. Her polite head tip is the only gesture of emotion she's willing to complement her generosity with.

"How can a seasonal program be of any use in your investigation?"

"In an automated effort to erase processed environmental data, seasonal program 67-435345 normally removes the presence of anything which replicates speed, gravity or temperature from its standard calculations. Instead of deleting this information, the program stores the data inside of a temporary cache. We added these missing anomalies to the environmental conditions surrounding your condominium prior to the explosion."

"Wait… so you're using my seasonal program to reanimate the terrorists?"

"Yes. Factors such as gravity and temperature are similar to footprints. After combining these absent deductions with the program's environmental data used for your cloud simulator, we determined the height, energy rate, and gait of the four people involved. Your fog reference data was the key to solving the mystery. We overlapped these anomalies with the updated version of your simulator, and used the fog as a kind of… mold, that formed three-dimensional shapes of all four individuals involved."

I chew my bottom lip while considering the idea's cleverness. Who, other than the VBI, would have thought of such a thing?

"Unfortunately," Grills elaborates, "there are limitations. For instance, we failed to determine the exact appearance of these individuals because their body molds have no features. Texture shades, hair and eye colors, for instance, are also unknown."

"But that shouldn't be hard to discern. A graphic artist can color in those details, right?"

"Identification is proving difficult. Each of these individuals wore masks, and even with an accurate profile, finding people who recognize these terrorists may prove difficult.

"We also believe that when your seasonal program caused the delivery glitch, all four suspects arrived through a scrambled network and attempted to realign the bomb with your condominium."

I'm impressed by the bureau's resourcefulness. "My friends need to hear this!"

Agent Grills raises a finger before I can stand. "The agency prefers secrecy in this matter."

"Why? Everyone has to know about this!"

"Every member of The Calling has spent decades evading capture. These clues are our first breaks in the case. If the terrorists learn of their exposure we may lose the advantage of surprise."

I consider the common sense behind Grills' reasoning. "Damn, you're right… can I see the molds?"

"Certainly."

Agent Grills plays a recording of the perpetrators using the room's spectral holograph. A spiral bulb centered on Dennington's ceiling, releases a

Christmas tree of light against the floor. The VBI's three-dimensional fog molds become visible inside the cone of light. I circle the group a few times and pause when one of the figures stands out. There's something familiar about its unusually thin arms and the style of clothing. My eyes swell with recognition after a few moments.

"That's Scarlet!"

Agent Grills looks shocked. He stands up and hastily walks towards me with that ugly transparent holopad cupped underneath his shoulder.

"You think this mold belongs to your former teammate?"

"I'm positive that's her!"

"How can you be sure?"

"At first glance," I begin gesturing to the torso, "she looks like a man but that's only because Scarlet's wearing a flame resistant vest. She designed that one herself and used it in a game we often played. Her crest is right here," I point to the indented logo on the back of Scarlet's vest.

Agent Grills uses his holopad as a window viewer, and adds Scarlet's body textures to the mold. It's a perfect match. Dennington repeats the process by adding textures and facial data to the remaining molds.

"The Bloody Membranes," she gasps, lowering her holopad. "We need to assemble the anti-terrorist task force!" Dennington rushes out of the room as I study the other figures.

"Dennington appreciates your help," Grills acknowledges on her behalf.

"Of course, but where's the bomb mold?"

"The bomb mold is being analyzed at our forensic facility. You should also be aware, that when Mr. Hannibal went outside, the perpetrators detonated the bomb prematurely. Evidence suggests he tried stopping them. His interference may have saved your life."

"Well, that sounds like Hannibal."

"The main reason you are here, however, involves something of greater importance."

"You mean aside from the bombing? What's greater than that?"

Agent Grills returns to Dennington's desk and gathers another holopad from a safety deposit cache. "One of our cameras in the physical world discovered something… compelling, and words cannot convey the magnitude of this discovery." The emblem on Agent Grills' identification tag reveals that this man is not a VBI agent like Dennington, but a high level VIA agent.

"So, you actually work for the Virtual Intelligence Agency, and *not* the VBI?"

"Yes."

Agent Grills moves from the desk slowly, as if afraid to do so. He activates the wallscreen to my right with his personal neural lens. At the prompt, Grills inputs the proper password via neural signature. An image of Pyramid Valley appears on the wall. I instantly recognize the place. One quarter of our active laborbots are mining minerals from there. Everybody has operated one of the bots at some point in their life. The agent chooses an immersive viewing option and the wallscreen projects three-dimensional variants against the floor, ceiling, and walls. A virtual duplicate of the Pyramid Valley mining compound quickly surrounds us. Grills switches to one of the compound's most desolate areas and allows the footage to play. I impatiently look about until something walks across the windswept plateau directly in front of me.

"Oh my God…" I'm startled, and step back even though it's just a hologram. "What's that?"

"You are looking at some kind of bipedal creature." Grills pauses the footage of the strange reptilian holograph so that I can have a better look. Although radioactive dust shrouds most of the creature's features, there's no doubt that it's some kind of sentient being. I slowly circle the holograph and stare at it for nearly five minutes without speaking.

"What could possibly survive in such a hostile environment? Earth is a desolate landfill!"

"The most prominent minds from the Institute of Virtual Science and Technology are scrambling to discover that answer. The perimeter camera that captured this footage is located thirty miles south of Pyramid Valley. It monitors atmospheric conditions preempting a volcanic fissure. This seems to be the creature's point of origin."

"Do scientists think it's a human descendant?"

"It is a bipedal creature with unusually long arms and an oblong head. They have yet to reach any concrete conclusions but its stride is indicative of a humanoid pelvis." Grills uses his neural lens to switch the hologram's perspective to an animated rendering of the creature's body. He points to its torso adding, "The shoulders have depression mechanisms that allow both arms to digress into the body."

"What does that mean?"

"Its body seems engineered for survival within a variety of pressurized conditions. We know nothing aside from that."

I'm awestruck. The brownish red humanoid thing looks like some kind of walking, semi-electroluminescent alien from a sci-fi movie. Its face, oddly, appears neither human nor animal. All of its sensory organs—from my uncultured hypothesis—seem to be inside the creature's body.

"So, what do I have to do with this?"

"The Species Project began after this discovery. Its goal involves reintegrating humans into the physical world. *The Suffering* was created by the Institute of Virtual Science and Technology as a tool for testing secondary candidates."

"Secondary? So there's already a team deployed?"

"A team *was* deployed."

"What happened?"

"That information cannot be disclosed to you

at this time. Needless to say, a mission failure occurred."

Agent Grills methodically switches the room's perspective to its original state before using the spiral ceiling bulb to display the holograph of a woman with purple hair. The odd seams along her appendages allude to a manufactured origin. He exaggerates its appearance by adding a rotation feature to the hologram.

"This unit is called MAJOR. The acronymic code-name is manned, anatomical, junket, operating within reality. You are looking at the most advanced cybernetic body ever created. MAJOR resembles a real person, yet functions similarly to remote laborbots."

"Why did they give MAJOR an anatomical designation? Doesn't it function like a bot?"

"This unit is a cybernetic prostheticalanatomy. MAJOR can be placed in various autonomous modes during emergencies and is capable of reactivating the Nexus with assistance from an advanced artificial intelligence."

"Why make a CP that looks like a female? Wouldn't a model similar to the 7600 bot series be better? Bots with spider bodies have always proven the most reliable."

Grills dismisses the notion with a jerky shake of his head. "The complexity of certain tasks requires the flexibility of a human form."

"And the purple hair?"

"Instead of relying solely on external light sources, the purple follicles in MAJOR's hair contain properties that can illuminate the darkest night for up to one hundred physical feet. The color is a natural by-product of the chemicals used to achieve this effect. Engineers behind the CP's creation considered many factors at great length, including species and gender. Extensive research indicates that a female humanoid is more likely to elicit a docile response during first contact with intelligent life, than a male humanoid."

"Is there a male version?"

"There was. Unfortunately, its design proved unstable.

"Why do MAJOR's eyes look unusually ovular?"

"Winds within the Wasteland can be harsh." Agent Grills points to the CP's face. "Slanted eyes can help traverse certain environments. It is probably an unneeded feature, because the CP requires an advanced environmental suit."

"So, this is the reason for a VBI, VIA, and IVST joint venture? This is a bit overwhelming!"

"I completely understand," Agent Grills agrees while moving closer to the cybernetic prostheticalanatomy. "But it is imperative we cover the basics quickly."

"The basics of what?"

"Decades of work went into creating this particular model. We need to make sure you are capable of operating it."

"Is this why I'm really here? You want me to operate MAJOR and then look for that… that… thing in the Wasteland?"

"Correct. Be aware however, that operating MAJOR extends beyond simply controlling the CP. Integrating your mind into the machine is a requirement. We need to make sure that you are psychologically prepared for such an endeavor."

I grip the curves of my hips. "What do you mean by that?"

"I know what happened to your brother, Miss Ehari."

My vascular threads prickle with electric angst. I'm not exactly sure if Agent Grills has real information about my brother's demise, or if he's about to regurgitate recycled hearsay.

"Gardeners beat around the bush. I thought you were a VIA agent—"

"Your brother downloaded his neural network into a laborbot four years ago during a routine assignment and disappeared while working in Pyramid Valley. Most people think he wandered too far from the compound and was lost in the nuclear storm sweeping across the area at that time. Nobody knows for sure what happened. His death resulted in new safety measures for all citizens operating laborbots."

"Is that it?"

"Should there be more?" When I clench my fists, Agent Grills leans back and speaks with a softer tone. "Sometimes there are no answers. I know you wish for closure. In truth, his disappearance is a mystery even to us. Numerous scouting parties failed to find any trace of him. It grieves me to say this, but class C nuclear storms create some of the most violent winds known to man. It may be possible those winds carried your brother to the other side of the planet, or dropped him four miles outside of the compound. We may never know the truth."

"What about Mandible 9?"

"As you may have surmised, *The Suffering* tests multiple aspects of the teams that play it. Roughly, two hundred and fifty million active participants became our potential candidates. The game's creation helped determine who should lead the mission and the expertise required for its success. Although it is not mandatory, we actually prefer your team's involvement. They have already proven themselves capable under extreme pressure and survived circumstances that mimic the environmental conditions you might face in the physical world. I will brief them when the time arises. If they are willing to accept the terms of this assignment and complete additional training, they will be asked to participate."

"You shouldn't waste your time. They follow my lead."

"No disrespect Miss Ehari but I have protocols to follow. Each member of this expeditionary team must be set aside for an individual assessment."

"It's my team, Agent Grills."

"This is my assignment, Miss Ehari. If you decide to join this project and traverse the Wasteland, I want you to know that our entire team will be monitoring your every move. You have no authorization to run your own personal search mission for your brother's remains. There cannot be any doubt about your assignment. Species-5478, or evidence of its existence, is your only mission."

I stare at Grills for a moment and then cross my arms. "My team is not just a collection of friends that I play games with. Hannibal and Remi have been with me since my parent's death and helped me when my brother disappeared. We argue, laugh, cry, and care for each other as a family. Even Grey was there when I nearly died in my own home. If you expect me to ignore the sacrifice my brother made while excavating the Wastes during a government mandated labor assignment, then I dictate my team's involvement. Not you."

Agent Grills studies me before standing. "Is it safe to assume that you have decided to partake in this project?"

"Your assumptions are correct." I smile with a bit too much enthusiasm. Who in their right mind would refuse an opportunity like this?

"Instruct your team of the mission parameters and prepare them for a lecture at 0800 hours tomorrow."

"Of course." The agent takes my hand when I reach out, and shakes it firmly. "So The Calling was right after all."

"What do you mean?"

"If I'm able to assimilate into the physical world with MAJOR, then their concerns about me are somewhat true."

Before Agent Grills can respond, photon fire blares from beyond the room's portal, and I shriek from the unexpected fright. The lights dim when Grills generates a handcannon from a government mod programmed into his cuff. He jumps in front of me as the portal opens to reveal the silhouette of an armed woman who now blocks the exit. She raises a weapon as Agent Grills targets her; someone is going to die.

The Audacity of Death

CHAPTER 4

"Wait," Dennington pleads with her arms raised, "hold your fire!" Agent Grills allows Dennington to pass through the entrance. She seals the portal and then addresses me directly. "The Calling is here! They came for you!"

A risky bombing at my condo is one thing… but assassination at a VBI office? The audacity is mind numbing!

Grills checks his neural link for a secure government line and finds nothing. "How did they break into the central hub? It has thirteen different anti-intrusion fences!"

Dennington waves her hands about like a frenetic mental patient. "We never linked to the government network! The terrorists intercepted our connection at the medical facility! They redirected us to an obsolete depository for historical data! When I stepped through the portal, a contamination scanner almost deleted me! I struggled to get back inside this room!"

I panic after realizing we're nowhere near the VBI headquarters or civilization. "You mean we're about to get purged! We're floating around like bait in a shark's tank! We have to re-link with a secure network!"

"Calm down," Grills advises. "We—"

"No!" I retaliate with such distress that my voice sounds foreign. "We have to get out of here! The scanners will find us if we stay! Do something!"

Agent Dennington responds by placing a firewall on the portal. Grills offers me an antiviral vest. I waste no time donning the protective gear.

"Let us handle this," Grills insists. He tries messaging headquarters once more but doesn't receive a response. My trembling hands draw false assurances. "Stay calm Miss Ehari, we will protect you."

His promise does nothing to reassure me. In fact, my concerns intensify when I feel a surge of positive vionic energy flooding the room. Agent Grills raises his weapons when the portal's firewall bubbles inward like chewing gum.

"Stand down or I will use deadly force!"

"We've come for Di Ehari," a raspy voice announces from beyond the portal.

"I am Agent Paul Grills with the VIA! Stand down or you will be met with deadly force!"

A second voice warns, "We answer to a higher authority! We'll never surrender! Submit the profligate to us or suffer damnation!"

Dennington knocks her desk over and pulls me behind it. "We must be linking to a terrorist network! Stay down and do not move!"

I follow her orders without question. Both agents

use furniture to create a rudimentary obstacle course before joining me behind the desk. Agent Dennington activates a security program as Grills targets the portal.

Grills tells Dennington, "Hold your fire until I give the signal," and then points to the portal with a steady arm.

"OK," Dennington acknowledges, mimicking his actions.

I scream when the portal suddenly bursts open. Five armed assailants rush into the room firing photon flares from barrels fused into their knuckles. Both agents duck behind the desk as shimmering red rounds fly across the room and attach burn programs to the wall. When the assassins charge our barricade, ion nets snap up from the floor like mousetrap hammers and ensnare the would-be assassins. All five men are smashed into the ground and reduced to piles of non-programmable meshing. An appalling amount of gore coats the floor with an electrostatic paste that appears eerily organic.

Grills shouts, "Fire!"

Dennington swiftly crests the barricade and shoots through the portal with her handcannon. She catches another assailant just as he enters the room and the carnage is unlike anything I've ever seen! Dennington's rounds rip into the assassin's face and jackhammer through his brain's neural link. Red streams of data squirt from the opened vascular threads. The victim slumps to his death as I turn and vomit two recent downloads all over the floor. A beaming multicolored light catches my attention when it pierces a portion of the ceiling.

I lean into Dennington yelling, "Contamination scanner!"

Agent Grills tosses an explosive program through the portal when he notices the shimmering beam eating the building's architecture—devouring everything within its path. His explosive detonates with enough force to sever our link with the terrorist network—dropping the room into a virtual free fall as a final crazed Calling member slips through the opening and leaps over our barricade.

Grills and Dennington fire but miss their target. The assassin seizes the opportunity and stabs me with a photonic blade but luckily, my antiviral vest blocks his initial thrust. Dennington kicks the assassin in the ribs when he raises the blade for a second attempt. He tumbles sideways allowing Grills a clean shot that opens his chest. The assassin yelps twice before dying with gaping eyes focused solely on me.

The room lands in a historical recycling pool and aligns with a bit collector. As we ride along the collector's rail, the room merges with other data and joins an incomplete stack of blocks that have yet to form a fully recyclable cube. The room's anterior wall disintegrates as the contamination scanner continues reprocessing its architecture.

"The scanner is coming," I warn, pushing pass both agents, "it's time to get out of here!"

We leap through Dennington's portal and

into an outdated rendition of the Sistine Chapel. The chapel's portal leads to a glitched suburban kitchen with flickering walls. After entering and exiting a blur of portals our group ends up in an unformatted Malaysian banquet hall. The pursuing contamination scanner hums with the ominous sentience of a psychopath. Deletion at the hands of its deionizers petrifies the photonic plasma flowing throughout my vascular threads. Even worse, many of the upcoming portals lead to solid or corrupt blocks of impassable data, requiring backtracking. These dead end rooms increase in number as we near the recycling pool's prompt station. The actual station has an interface mandating activation in order to leave the area but neither Grills nor Dennington can do this without government support. Plus, The Calling has blocked their neural signatures with some kind of dampening field. Thank God for criminals like me... because I'm able to reach Remi with my illegally modified neural link.

Ehari: Remi, can you hear me?

Remi: E, where are ya? We just—

Ehari: Shut up! I need help! I'm trapped inside a historical recycling pool's purging tank! I need the command line for this prompt station!

Remi: What da... give me a minute...

Ehari: A minute! Are you crazy? I don't have a minute! A data scanner is purging everything behind me!

Remi: Crap! Ok, so... first, ya need to break

across da bridge to use a command line like that!

Ehari: What? How?

Remi: Find da divide!

Ehari: The divide? That can be anywhere!

Remi: Just find it!

I blurt out, "We have to find the divide!"

Agent Grills motions to the next portal. "Follow me!"

The agent's discovery of a sequential trend allows us to bypass all sealed data blocks. We need every second too, and barely exit the block in time. A wide gorge of light awaits us on the distant end. It bisects our path to the prompt station.

Ehari: We made it to the divide! I can see the bridge! How do we cross it?

Remi: Ya have to evoke da station command!

Ehari: How do I do that?

Remi: Do ya know what era ya're in?

Analyzing the clues to our whereabouts is difficult. Innumerable forms of data are raining down from the above reference filters. Everything from clothing, buildings, gadgets, and strange miscellaneous items are falling into the recycling pool. All of the objects relate to a single age that eludes me. Dennington responds to my confusion.

"What are you searching for?"

"Anything that might tell me what era this pool is intended for!"

"Try fifteenth century AD."

Remi: Who is that? She sounds sexy...

Ehari: Remi! I swear—

Remi: I got it, I got it! Transmitting da command to ya now!

I use the phrase, 'Illusionary Colonial Renaissance' to unlock administrative access to the bridge. A glassy tube materializes seconds later. We cross the divide as the pursuing contamination scanner envelopes the data cube's last remaining blocks of obsolete information. A brilliant rainbow colored burst sprouts from the depleted hub as we race across the bridge and enter the awaiting station. The evaporated light rains down as every remaining bit of data absorbed from the blocks, condenses into a reformatted plate of free space.

Once we're safely inside the command station, Grills initiates new protocols that force the purging process to freeze. All operations go into standby and an emergency access corridor opens below the building's projection steps.

Agent Grills takes my hand. "Follow me, Miss Ehari."

I happily oblige and, stoic as usual, the agent leads us into the awaiting corridor and back to the safety of a filtered maintenance network. Both agents reestablish contact with their perspective parties. I'm still too afraid and hesitant to do anything. My brain feels overloaded from all of the excitement.

Remi: E! Where are ya? Are ya ok?

Ehari: I'm fine, I thi—

Remi: There was an attack here at da facility! Da Calling was looking for ya!

That did it. I can only take so much stress… and feel faint from exertion. My brain's neural network shorts and I temporarily lose control of my legs. Of course, Agent Grills is there to catch me…

Ehari: We need assistance!

Remi: No worries little Chipmunk, da VIA is monitoring our link. They should be opening a portal at yar destination any second now.

I see the exit before Remi finishes his sentence. A team of specially armed VIA agents spills through the portal on our end of the corridor and race by without giving us a second glance. Grills leaves me with Dennington before departing with the anti-terrorist search team. Dennington guides me through a maintenance exit filled with counterintelligence personnel.

I hear someone mumble, "They might kill her the next time," as we pass by, and I break into tears.

A Tale of Two Worlds

Chapter 5

Three days have passed since The Calling's latest attack but it feels like the attempt happened yesterday. I barely had a thought to myself for sixty-three hours. Investigators are pouring over every detail of the assassination attempt from the perspectives of both agents and then my own. For now, the VIA is treating the failed attack at the Tia Muhammad Medical Facility as a separate event. By interrogating my friends individually, the Virtual Intelligence Agency thinks it will be easier to discover any secrets Mandible 9 may be hoarding. Of course, we have nothing to hide and willingly submit our memory fragments of the attacks to the proper authorities. I feel like a twenty-first century crime suspect giving up a DNA sample when medical and forensic specialists download the entire sequence of events from our neural networks and analyze every detail. Surrendering these memories will validate our steadfast proclamations of innocence. That means we know—even before the authorities—that the real culprits remain at large.

Agent Grills relocates my team to a safe house. I have no idea where we are and suspect we're off the government network. That would normally make me nervous but considering recent events; the anonymity is actually comforting, especially since I have administrative access to this facility and no sense of confinement.

"You can leave whenever you like but any return trips are subject to our approval," says Agent Dennington, as though reading my mind via neural link.

"I understand."

I've been so absorbed by my own thoughts that I didn't notice her standing behind me. Giving up the portal's access key is mostly symbolic. Everyone knows that I'll probably stay in this facility until someone captures the perpetrators. Leaving is too risky. Not only do I lack the skills to evade assassins, there's nowhere else to go.

Dennington decides to sit next to me. Maybe she thinks with all that's happened, proximity will get me to open up to her. People often misjudge me in such ways.

"To operate under our protection program, your port of origin must remain confidential at all times. We need to limit the risk of leaking your whereabouts to the public. Do you agree to these terms?"

A verbal signature is all that's required to sign the terms and conditions form on Dennington's holopad.

After careful consideration, "I agree to the terms."

My confirmation also grants unfettered access to the new VIA facility, which Dennington specially formatted for my team.

When my friends and the agency's staff enter the building, our new abode automatically implements anti-intrusion software. I have no idea what some of these advanced safety measures actually do. Top-level security of this sort is a bit worrisome. Dr. Panels and a handpicked team of specialists have already been looking over Hannibal's care in the medical department. All new arrivals settle into their rooms but I decide to view news reports on a wallscreen in one of the lounges.

One thing is for sure; I have never, in my entire life, smoked this many consecutive cigarettes!

The Virtualnet is flooded with events pertaining to the terrorists. Most of the channels I tap into exhibit some rendition of the bombing at my condo, the Tia Muhammad Medical Facility attack, or footage of me passed out in Grey's arms. Although officials from the Virtual Bureau of Investigation are making most of the public statements so far, the president's State of the Union speech will virtualize the event to every Realm this evening.

To sum it up; somebody found a way to modify blue fire. I'm betting on Scarlet. It's common knowledge that photon-based weaponry destroys the bonds binding our meshing, yet the reformatted blue fire engineered by these terrorists incinerates virtually everything else. Carol wasn't the only thing to die because of the bombing. Two thousand years of relative peace have ended. People are panicking because there's now a way to destroy the virtual world from the inside out. This is the very thing the original programmers went out of their way to prevent.

I've been quietly watching various newscasts all day, or night… whatever. I don't even know what cycle it should be. Discerning the passage of time is hard with all that's happening. Hours are leapfrogging from one report to the next; all while humanity regresses to a barbaric time when humans had the power to annihilate the world in which they lived. People will surely die as the revelation of modified blue fire permeates the masses. In fact, Realms to alternate realities are beginning to open after centuries of isolation. Some societies have evolved into such abstract entities they've literally become alien to others. Eight media outlets have already reported new conflicts between some of these Realms and the rising violence is the latest intellectual commodity bartered by newscasters.

I barely notice Agent Dennington leave or Dr. Panels when she enters the room. "What happened to your toe," she asks halfheartedly, as if indicting by tone, the gravity of greater issues and the minuscule importance of my injury.

"I kicked over an end table."

Instead of admonishing me right away—as medical professionals seem obligated to do—Dr. Panels assesses the damage with some kind of portable diagnostic tool.

"Your texture remains in good condition and all of your vascular threads seem to be operating efficiently. I found minor fracturing along some of your texture links, but they should finish reformatting within a few hours."

"What about Hannibal?"

"He is stronger than I expected. His brainwaves have undergone a remarkable transformation after the Tia Muhammad Medical Facility attack. There was a thirteen percent spike in Mr. Hannibal's healing rate. The rest of his meshing is now regenerating at an increased ratio. He should be leaving the asonograph shortly. My tests indicate minimal damage to his brain. In fact, I did not think a recovery of this magnitude was possible."

The news generates relief algorithms in my vascular threads. I relish hearing something good despite everything that happened.

"When can I see him?"

"You can wait for Mr. Hannibal in the control room after I finish inspecting your neural network." The doctor adds teasingly, "Just try not to assault anymore end tables, please."

"I'll try… so what are Hannibal's most serious injuries?"

"Mr. Hannibal suffered slight decay to the second channel of his ninth parallel, along with minor neurotic corrosion within the persobial region of his brain."

"What's that area responsible for?"

"The persobial region deals primarily with personality. Although highly researched, it remains one of the most misunderstood sections of the synaptic network. When scientists transferred the first neural signatures into the Nexus, their long-term knowledge of how brainwaves operate within a virtual environment remained largely enigmatic."

"So personality disorders became the biggest hurdle?"

"Yes. Neural imaging gave prewar scientists the ability to separate a synaptic fingerprint from an individual's brain, and place it elsewhere."

"Like in a freaking cold drive…"

"Early pioneers did not realize those drives were too small," Dr. Panels admits.

"Hell drives," I add meanly.

"Yes. Those were bad times. Now fast-forward two thousand years. Even with our technological advances, science has only scratched the surface of synopticology. Although we made great strides elsewhere, we have yet to map all of the brain's functions—particularly those of the persobial region."

"What are you saying?"

"Mr. Hannibal is stable. Unfortunately, he may not be the same man you knew before the assault."

"Is Hannibal capable of joining the mission?"

"The VIA is not planning on disqualifying him. That decision falls on your shoulders. You are the one that knows him best. Mr. Hannibal's synaptic pathways seem entirely repaired but there are aspects to a person's personality that cannot be measured with equipment. Memories, talents, educational level, etc., all remain intact, but there may be a difference in his behavior. You are the main person capable of assessing whether or not he acquired a personality disorder that will hinder his participation from the Species Project."

That's very hard to swallow. What if the man I knew is gone? Can I accept a new Hannibal? Would he accept me? This problem has the potential of ruining my team's cohesion.

"So… he's undergone some form of mental trauma?"

"Well, in a manner of speaking, yes. Humans in the prewar era were susceptible to a variety of neurological conditions which altered personality."

"Like post-traumatic stress disorder?"

"What do you mean?"

"Some of the artificially intelligent soldiers in *The Suffering* went crazy from prolonged exposure to war. It seems odd, because you'd think a person would adapt to such environments or situations over time."

Dr. Panels casually slips her medical holopad underneath her elbow as she ponders my explanation. "I wish it were that simple. Human brains are susceptible to a wide array of syndromes. The transference of biological-based brainwaves into the Nexus provides an example of how adaptive human neurology can be. Yet, the synaptic network proves incapable of handling extreme loads regardless of the medium. In the physical world, survivors of tragedies sometimes required years of rehabilitation when recovering from the horrors of a single near death experience. We are virtually the same even though scientists replaced our physical brains with photonic variants capable of accelerating trauma."

"Holographic meshing helps."

"Absolutely. The genetic norms for sentient life forms the baseline for behaviors in all creatures. In short, physical limitations engender mental limitations. This is why a dog cannot think like a human. A canine's very design encourages barking, instead of speaking. People once thought, that the neurological makeup of the human mind dictated a person's sexual proclivities. However, during the early years of synopticology, prenatal neural transfers of "girl" minds into "male" meshes resulted in male offspring. Transferring prenatal "male" minds into "female" meshes resulted in female offspring. Individuals have a natural inclination to base gender on the body they incorporate."

"Why are there homosexual people, then?"

Dr. Panels smiles. "There is an inherent ten percent variation in all controls groups, where any number of abnormal behaviors may occur."

"Are you calling gay men and women abnormal?"

"Scientifically speaking, choosing a non-reproductive lifestyle is abnormal. It is no more abnormal though, than being among the ten percent who commit other unconventional actions endemic to gender; meaning, it's a perfectly natural derivation from the norm."

I shrug, "So which is the motivator?"

Dr. Panels raises her holopad and sifts through pictures of prewar human anatomies. She transmits images that illustrate her main points to the wallscreen before us.

"Reverse gene dating proves that environments can motivate any species into adapting new evolutionary traits. Once a sentient species molds into existence, cognition is directly relative to the form of that species. The environment is central to evolution and plays a guiding role at every stage of a species' development. This is why prewar people, for instance, would gain nose and ear hairs over time, or why birds had wings, or why fish had fins and streamline forms, and so forth. Those mechanisms were compensators for environmental anomalies.

Adaptive mechanisms will not evolve in sterile environments because there would be no use for them. A notable example includes prewar humans venturing into outer space. They lost bone density while floating in weightlessness. Their bodies adapted to the absence of gravity and began to evolve into something different after only a few months. The very reason human beings came into existence is due to environmental factors such as animal interaction, temperature, nutritional availability, gravity, or even day and night cycles."

I furl a brow, "What about us?" If we've gone from bone and sinew, to mesh and texture, how will our evolution be affected?"

"That question is hard to answer. What I can say,

is that the virtual world we created is molding us."

"But," I point out, "we mold the virtual and physical worlds by interacting with them."

"Maybe…" Panels nods, "but if we are molding these worlds, what are we creating?"

"I'm not sure…"

Dr. Panels smiles. "Neither am I. Nevertheless, regardless of our sentient virtual state, humans remain susceptible to the physical world. Some might argue physicality is the primary force molding humanity into virtual facsimiles of our former selves."

"You were saying something interesting about mental limitations…"

"When prewar humans found themselves in abnormal situations, such events generated additional neural pathways within their brains, which aligned with older and more stable pathways in order to balance any ill effects from the new experience. This is why psychiatric therapy was so effective. Guided construction of healthy neural pathways had the ability to heal psychologically damaged sections of the neural network with positively reinforced pathways. Sometimes, however, these routes overlapped."

"They'd go crazy."

"Correct. Wet brains were more susceptible to violent tendencies and psychotic disorders than our virtual counterparts.

"Nevertheless, extreme mental illness would only occur if an alternate neural route failed to develop properly. In those cases, some people regressed from the bad memories or blocked them from their consciousness by establishing neural road blocks.

"Controlling pain is one of the most important equations in our mentally stable environment. By deactivating pain receptors that exceed three thousand peps, we have effectively eradicated many neurologically related conditions."

I accompany Dr. Panels to the wallscreen even though I prefer to remain seated. "That's true, but we're more susceptible to the effects of pain now. When people were made of flesh and bone they could survive a dismembered limb."

"Only if their blood loss and rate of infection were nominal," Panels clarifies, "otherwise, yes."

"Right… but if a person's pain receptors get damaged like that in a virtual accident, they die. A severed limb may as well mean decapitation."

She frowns. "That doesn't happen often. Only two out of every one hundred thousand accidents produces those results."

"I think mind numbing pain is a vital part of the human experience. It forces people to respect life."

The doctor concurs after considering my analysis. "I agree. Either way, life in the virtual or physical worlds will never be perfect. Existence pays its toll through suffering."

Dr. Panels finishes the exam in silence and uses

her medical holopad to input a prognosis of my condition.

"All right Miss Ehari, it looks like we are done here. If you have any questions feel free to contact me."

The doctor extends her card and I gratefully record the encoded information with my neural lens. A single flash—and we're finished.

"Thank you, Dr. Panels."

"Please, call me Rina, if you like. Do you remember where the control room is located?"

"Down the hall, pass the lounge, turn right by the lift, go just beyond the waiting room, take the second left, and then go to the fourth door on the right."

Panels steps back, befuddled. "A simple yes would have sufficed!"

"Sorry," I shrug brutishly, "that's a neurotic gaming habit."

I return to the control room and find Remi plugged into a regenerator socket. He *almost* looks like a sleeping baby curled up in the room's corner. A big, loudmouth baby, that is. Grey is using his neural link to send mental messages to a few girls. I want to ask more questions about Hannibal's condition but decide not to bother either of them just yet. After sliding into one of the lounge chairs, Grey mutes his thoughts and then hands me something.

"That agent from the VIA said you'd need this."

"A Trinity optic lens? When did he give you this?"

"About twenty minutes ago. He couldn't wait for you to finish your physical and said something about official business."

My neural signature activates the device when I retrieve it from Grey. A message icon blinks on the oval screen.

"It's the new model," I gloat.

Grey is too busy messaging his plaything to respond. I wonder… is he chatting with the same girl who smeared his forehead during that barbecue sauce run? His boxing gestures suggest their discussion is about Remi's fight at the Palladium, of all things.

The oval lens resembles one of those ancient Egyptian eye symbols from a forgotten god. After tethering the add-on node to my neural link, a holographic screen pops up in front of me. My fingertips appear to touch a semitransparent panel when I reach out. Special input programs allow for hand gestured inputting. Using aerial signs for quick commands is easy. There's even a hands-free option that allows the optic lens to hover while using it. I play with the floating texts before activating the message icon and a holo recording of Agent Grills materializes.

"Hello Miss Ehari. I took the liberty of acquiring this Trinity optic lens for you. The line is secure and you can use the device for personal business, if desired. Be aware that in light of the recent terrorist attacks and the secretive nature of the Species Project, all of your communications will be monitored until this mission is either complete, or the president

de-classifies the project. If you have a problem with any of the requirements, you can back out before tomorrow's briefing. Our department will remove all memory segments from your neural network, which contain information pertaining to this project, at that time. However, once you begin the assimilation training for MAJOR, consider yourself an official employee of the government.

"The bureau has enclosed a list of documents, laws, protocols, regulations, penalties, contact information, and expectations of our department and the agency. Study each section carefully and when you review them with your team, make sure that any discussions concerning the project occur at the locales indicated by the optic lens, and nowhere else."

When the message ends, an automated voice asks if I want to replay the recording or view the enclosed documents. I choose to view the documents and discover a forty-nine page project handbook. By the time I finish reading it, Remi awakens, Grey disconnects from his neural link, and Dr. Panels returns and begins monitoring Hannibal's condition.

Remi nudges my shoulder. "Are ya finally going to tell us what's going on?"

I deactivate the optic lens and the device switches to an encryption mode that can only be unlocked with my active synaptic signature. Is it a Trojan Horse? I slide the optic lens into one of my memory pockets and wonder how long it'll take Grey to hack it. Remi relentlessly digs for more information even though I dismiss his initial inquiry. I need some time to process the material and ascertain my team's role in this new project.

"Come on already, we know something's up! Ya've been quiet ever since ya got back from da VBI headquarters. Ya're never this quiet! Ya're always like, 'Blah blah blah this, and blah blah blah that—"

"We'll discuss it later."

Remi stands in front me defiantly. "Damn that! Just tell us what's up!"

"Later!" I toss Remi's retro, smartphone-looking vr-com back to him, and wave Grey away when he asks to see my Trinity optic lens. "You just had the lens. Why do you want to see it again?"

"I just want to check out the case design…"

"No! I swear you're turning into Remi!"

"I hope not… trees get more sex than he does."

Remi throws a digital magazine. "Screw off geek!"

I step in-between them. "Stop! Can we please not defile every place we go! Have some respect for Hannibal!"

"Mr. Hannibal is waking," Dr. Panels intercedes while tapping furiously on her instrument panel, "I think you should come."

Waking Giant

CHAPTER 6

I sprint to Dr. Panel's side—pressing in as she inputs her final command into the control room's main console. The doctor tries consoling Hannibal.

"You are safe now. Try staying still, and remain quiet. The asonograph is repairing your synaptic link. All of your friends are here in the control room. They will join you in the reception area when the graphing process completes."

Hannibal sits up and forcefully pushes the mechanical arm controlling the synaptic bulb. He's normally compliant but now appears extremely agitated.

"Where are they? Ehari! Where are you?"

"Please, try to relax. Your photonic anesthetic has worn off. You need to lie down bef—"

Hannibal stands up and looks around. "Who are you?"

"I am Dr. Panels. You have t—"

"Let me out of here!" Hannibal pushes the entire operating table over. Dr. Panels quickly steps aside so that I can use the console's orbed spectral-phone.

"It's all right Hanni! We're in the control room!"

Hannibal pauses and looks up. "E, is that you?"

"Yes! But please, calm down! You're in a rehabilitation center at a VIA safe house."

Hannibal complies when he spots me and lowers the asonograph before throwing it into one of the walls. Dr. Panels deactivates the spectral-phone when I questionably glance at her.

"Why does he look so dazed?"

"Mr. Hannibal moved the synaptic bulb too early. He needs to lie back down in order for the process to finish."

"I have to get down there first."

Everyone follows Panels out of the control room and waits for her to unseal the operating chamber. When Hannibal emerges, he gives me a smothering bear hug before squeezing Remi and Grey's shoulders in a manly manner.

He looks straight into my eyes and says, "There was an explosion."

I chew my bottom lip. "I'll explain everything. But first, how are you feeling?"

"Dizzy, and my head hurts."

"You need to lie down for a few more minutes. The asonograph has to finish repairing your synapses."

Hannibal rubs his chest with light strokes. "My data was spilling everywhere." He whispers, "I thought… I was deleted."

"Please don't freak out when I say this but… most of that data belonged to Carol."

"Carol? Is she…"

"Yes." I wrap my arms around Hannibal, hoping

to quell the pain.

"What happened?"

"Terrorists. The Calling is responsible."

That's enough to get Hannibal moving but it only stimulates his curiosity. He follows me to the control room where I explain The Calling's involvement and the damage to his synaptic brain. Hannibal takes Carol's death hard. They became close over the past year and seemed destined for romance. He doesn't cry but there's noticeable heartbreak in his eyes. It takes time, but I eventually convince him to finish the asonographic procedure before leaving the medical area.

We spend the rest of the afternoon bonding at Hannibal's new place. He shuns the city environments—that the rest of us prefer—and institutes the same cliff settings used at his original home. The beautiful view overlooks a place called Pine Forest; the last of its kind before the war. Even though it stirs ominous sensations associated with prewar life the environment is much better than the VIA's stuffy default rooms.

Everyone gathers at the patio table as Grey brings two plates filled with succulent portions of chicken and seasoned fries; courtesy of Remi's scavenger exploits. Even though we're not capable of starving in the traditional sense, our taste buds salivate at the smell of delicious herbs and spices. Consuming food and drink has become a social tradition for people like us, and a good way to download the most recent updates. Hannibal normally gives a prayer of thanks but passes that duty to me this time. Is this another personality change? Not to mention the role of prayer guide doesn't suit me.

"Dear… Lord… we pray for forgiveness, and ummm… thank you, for providing in times of plenty, and in times of need. We ask that you allow a place for us in the sanctums of Heaven. We ask that you absolve those who would seek to do us harm and to give us the strength to forgive their transgressions. Thank you for returning Hannibal to us. Thank you for keeping us safe. Please, bless this food as we beg forgiveness for our sins. Amen."

Remi blurts out, "Hell yah! Damn these wings smell good!"

I sigh as he grabs the biggest wing on the plate and stuffs his foul mouth with it. Why bother scolding him? Grey joins Remi's feast as I nibble on seasoned fries. Hannibal examines all of us then asks the million-dollar question.

"Grey said you were visited by government agents. What did they want?"

Where should I begin? My team never went on any "real" missions before. Well, maybe Hannibal. He was a prizefighter but the rest of us are amateurs to actual conflict. Wait, I take that back. Remi is *not* a stranger to conflict and even Grey worked for the Blue Fire Department. Damn… I guess my insecurities come from being the only person without any real life conflict experience! Sure, games like *The Suffering* feel real, but no matter how intense the action gets, there's no actual threat of death. In fact, the condo bombing marks only the second time that I actually faced true deletion.

"Some women curbed their eating in the physical world because they didn't want to gain weight."

I slowly twiddle a fry between my thumb and forefinger. The newest progression downloads are coded inside and I'd slowly lose functionality without them. I find oral downloads more convenient than tanning updates into my body. Still, I'm not really in the mood to eat.

"Now that we directly control our body sizes through programming, most women don't bother eating because we're not hungry."

Grey looks like a child with barbecue sauce dripping from his chin. "What's your point," he asks in-between mouthfuls.

I push my fries in his direction. "Most women are never full."

"I don't get it." Grey plucks one of the fries from my plate and chomps it before finishing his thought. "What does this have to do with the Virtual Bureau of Investigation or the Virtual Intelligence Agency?"

"Ehari isn't talking about government agencies," Hannibal suddenly replies. He faces me and adds, "You're talking about yourself. You've never been satisfied. Beating *The Suffering* or creating the world's best cloud simulation doesn't gratify you. None of it fulfills. Am I right?"

My smile approves Hannibal's astute deduction. He still understands me. It's comforting to know that at least this part of him remains. I activate a cigarette after changing its flavor-strip and take a drag. The tropical breeze scented fumes fill the room with an earthly aroma when I exhale. This time, the fumes form into various fish that swim about before dissolving into streams of smoke.

"Agent Grills briefed me about a top secret project run by the Institute of Virtual Science and Technology, and the Virtual Intelligence Agency. I accepted a proposal on everyone's behalf to aid them. Your official acceptance of the enlistment terms is required by day's end. Participation in this project will be historic."

"Historic?" Hannibal sits up. "That's a big word. Does it mean we're going after the terrorists?"

"No. Our goal is much bigger. We're going on an expedition into the Wasteland."

Remi spits out a chicken bone. "Da Wasteland? Why go into that deathtrap? I'm not interested in a mining contract!"

"This isn't a labor assignment. We have orders to identify and confirm the existence of a new species." I remotely connect my neural link to the nearest wallscreen and relay its contents for all to see. "This footage was taken from a camera monitoring Pyramid Valley's perimeter."

It takes a few seconds for my team's puzzled expressions to morph into astonishment.

Remi cries out, "Something actually lives out there? Holy crap! Holy freakin crap! That thing could be our ticket outta da virtual world!"

Grey drops a wing without even realizing it. "Maybe we can use its genes to recreate humans!"

For once, Remi agrees with him. "Yah! Can't see it clearly but… it looks humanoid! Well… kinda humanoid…"

Grey leans forward. "Is it a descendant of humans?"

"Nah lamebrain," Remi finger wags, "it's some kind of evolved lizard, ain't it, E?"

"Unknown."

"Come on! What in da Hell is it?"

"As I've already said, we have orders to identify and confirm the existence of that creature."

"But its existence is already confirmed!" Grey wisely notes. "The recording—"

"Calm down, we're being monitored by the VIA."

"What?" Remi looks around as if expecting to find someone hiding behind one of Hannibal's sofas. "We're being monitored?"

Remi immediately tries assuming a greater level of professionalism when I explain the conditions of our enlistment. I supplement my oration by vmailing copies of the employee handbook to everyone's neural links. They scan the holographic handbook while intently listening to my explanation of the bureau's protocols.

"Read everything thoroughly. The agency will delete those files remotely when you finish. If at any time you wish to review the material speak to me and I'll provide a temporary copy."

Hannibal deactivates his neural link and then asks, "Who are we working for and when do we start training?"

"It's a joint venture between the IVST and the VIA. The Institute of Virtual Science and Technology created the Species Project. However, we'll officially be employees of the Virtual Intelligence Agency. They're overlooking the project and expedition.

As for your second question; training has already begun. *The Suffering* is an IVST testing simulation for new recruits. We meet the project heads for a full briefing tomorrow morning at 0800 hours. Agent Grills vmailed the mission parameters to me and I'll explain more when you accept the VIA's terms and conditions. Integration training begins after Carol's funeral."

"I've already accepted!" Remi proudly announces while butt dancing in his seat.

"So have I," Grey proclaims with moderate enthusiasm.

Hannibal examines me closely, as if trying to deduce whether I'm suffering from a mental lapse. "Are you sure this is a good idea? I mean… working for the IVST in any capacity seems wrong, considering your brother's disappearance."

"I've made my decision. Now make yours."

All right E, if you say so. Hannibal takes his time reading the VIA's terms. When he finally commits, everyone displays gestures of relief as he orally signs the agreement with care. So far, Hannibal seems mostly himself. I feel bad analyzing him like this. He, in turn, expresses afterthoughts. This is classic Hannibal.

"So *The Suffering* is a government funded program, huh? I always felt like something was off about it. It just felt too real. Some of the tactics those soldiers used are beyond the scope of civilian programming."

I get everyone's attention with a firm fist pound against the tabletop. "Focus on the Wasteland! Be prepared to contend with physical danger! Earth is one of the most toxic and volatile planets in the solar system. Everything out there is chemical-based. That means, you have to exchange the laws of virtuality for a state of substance. You have to master your new bodies' limitations. Pressure, gravity, and weather, are only a few of the obstacles we may encounter. Learn how to deal with these conditions or die by them. Can you truly handle survival in another atmosphere? There are no continue options in the physical world. If you die out there, game over."

Grey is the first to speak up. "I understand the risks. Many people have died out there. We'll be careful."

Hannibal makes another inquiry after a moment of silence. "I take it we're not using imprinted mechs?"

"We're utilizing experimental technology on this expedition. Cybernetic prostheticalanatomy is the IVST's scientific designation for these machines"

Remi leans back, as if shoved by the word's enormity. "What in da Hell are those?"

"They're advanced cybernetic units that mimic the human form. Of the two models, my Type XX requires full assimilation, whereas your Type XY variant will function much like the laborbots we're accustomed to operating for mining purposes. Most of the people that I consulted with call them CPs."

Remi rests his chin in both palms. "What do ya mean by, assimilate?"

"I'll have to fully integrate with the machine. My Type XX CP, is the lifelike model, and contains more sensory advancements than the support counterparts you'll be controlling. It not only replicates the human form but also possesses enhanced acrobatic, cognitive, and technological capabilities. Your Type XY CPs have enhanced strength, surveying, combat, endurance and analytical capabilities. Type XY versions also consist of atomically fused titanium imbued armor that can withstand conditions far exceeding my model's limitations.

My XX CP however, will allow me to experience life with all of the senses that our ancestors possessed. This is why I must literally become "one" with the machine. If the assimilation proves successful, Type XX models will be mainstreamed within twenty-two years."

Grey studies me with wrinkled brows. "Is it really

possible to imprint the physical world this way?"

"Yes. Anything is possible." When my answer fails to satisfy him, I offer an example. "We do it all the time with laborbots."

Grey smirks. "We're photonic entities, existing in a two-dimensional reality, experiencing a three-dimensional rendition of the physical world. The bots used for labor on Earth modify footage of the Wasteland so that we can interpret the image. People maintain their photonic states while using laborbots and control them like ancient astronauts piloting spacecraft. But if an XX cybernetic prostheticalanatomy can do what these engineers claim, you'll *become* the machine. That's like ancient humans going from three-dimensions, to a fourth. In order for that to happen, you must transition from our photonic plane, and into the CP's physical state. How can they be sure your mind retains the ability to perceive a three-dimensional realm? Has there been animal testing?"

I hate it when Grey does this. He knows the answer yet insists that I state the obvious—perhaps demonstrating to the VIA, his mental acuity.

"You already know the law forbids any form of animal testing unless it's permitted on humans. So yes, this means the engineers who created the Type XX have no idea if it'll function as intended. The CP's advancements make test runs impossible. However, if the integration process proves successful, I'll be the first human to reenter three-dimensional space since the Rupture."

Everyone quiets. This is the stuff of science fiction. We all grew up watching the cartoons and movies of explorers reentering the physical world. It's been a fantasy endorsed by the young and old alike. I once believed returning to Earth was a daydreamer's fairy tale or a conceptual argument for theoretical physicists. It just seemed so unlikely but then I saw footage of a cybernetic prostheticalanatomy… and became a believer.

Grey furthers his inquisition. "So this tech can't be tested?"

"Well, not exactly. A male prototype was released three-years ago but there was some kind of system failure during a diagnostic check. Apparently, the body never launched as intended, and shut down."

"So instead of viewing a three-dimensional plane, you might enter that CP and see a distorted world, static, darkness, or maybe nothing at all. Maybe it'll kill you."

Grey's incessant need to reassess the situation is irksome, but also part of the reason why I brought him into the fold. I interlock my fingers, tap both thumbs, and consider the possibilities.

"All of those scenarios are possible. The engineers aren't sure if our prolonged existence within the Nexus altered our ability to perceive Earth in its true form. Changing from a biological state into photonic entities may be irreversible. But consider the possible benefits. Successfully dual channeling the human mind from opposing states will mark the next leap in our evolution."

Hannibal rubs his chin. His eyes appear glazed. "I wonder what the physical world really looks like."

"It should mimic this reality exactly. Even though we exist within the Nexus' two-dimensional plane, our minds perceive a three-dimensional environment. The entire basis of our virtual world extends from the physics and spatial properties of its physical counterpart. Reintegration should be seamless."

"Yeah, should be…" Grey says, "but not all Realms are the same here. And are we truly experiencing three dimensions in the Nexus? Sure, this room looks and feels as if it has three-dimensional depth, but we still exist within the Nexus, in a two-dimensional plane. Three-dimensional rendering isn't the same as three dimensions in the physical world."

"Your concerns are valid but there's nothing I can do about them. I'm aware of the risks but consider the gains. Yes, I may become mentally handicapped, have my mind erased completely, or die during the assimilation process. Similar things can happen here in this world. Nobody lives forever. Nevertheless, our ancestors covered all the bases when creating a simulation of physical reality. They didn't commit themselves to the Nexus until they felt the environment was adequate. Their focus was always on perception. If they believed the virtual world is an identical simulation of the physical one, then I concur by default."

Hannibal stands and looks through the windowed wall exposing Pine Valley. It's hard discerning what's on his mind. Hannibal was always a difficult man to read, though.

"What about our souls?"

Hannibal's question catches me off guard. Grey speaks before I can think of anything to say.

"What do you mean by, souls? There's no such thing!"

Hannibal crosses his arms before facing me. Losing Carol seems to have seeded his mind with spiritual anxiety, because the question of souls is indicative of entrenched mourning.

"Haven't any of you wondered if we're real people? How can any of us be sure that we even exist?"

"Someone once said," Grey quotes, "I think, therefore I am."

Hannibal eyes Grey with disbelief. "So a rock doesn't exist, because it doesn't think?"

"A rock isn't aware Hanni, and without something acknowledging it, fails to exist."

Hannibal's eyes narrow into a hawkish glare. "Well, if a rock fails to exist without something acknowledging it, than how can any person exist in the absence of a rock? Without something to acknowledge, a person is nothing."

"Yah," Remi chimes in, "what he said!"

Grey's confidence wavers only slightly. "Existence is based on knowing, not being."

"You're assuming to know what it means to exist. Knowing of existence, doesn't equal understanding."

Grey smiles humorlessly. "I understand existence better than a rock."

"You don't really *know* that." Hannibal takes a few steps towards Grey and hunkers over him. If Grey could sweat like an ancient human, his forehead would probably sprout beads of perspiration. Instead, it begins to sparkle slightly. "How can you understand existence without knowing how we came into being or what happens when we die? True understanding involves knowing what happens before and after life. Existence isn't just about this moment because if we truly exist, then we must have always been around. Otherwise, we never were, and are no more alive than a rock."

"You're starting not to make sense. I suppose, that's why you believe in souls. Do you think we have some imperishable part of ourselves, like gods?"

"Isn't that what you believed as a Catholic? If God exists, that "image" we're made of in the Almighty's likeness would be the infinite part of ourselves that changes states because it cannot be destroyed."

Grey stands up and sits on the edge of the table. He fails to imbue any significant amount of imposition. "I'm no longer Catholic and don't believe any of that crap anymore. Besides… knowing of God or of souls, doesn't equal understanding."

"If we have souls," says Hannibal pivoting, "then that would explain why we understand our existence, and that of God's. But what if we're just leftover characters in an abandoned simulator? How do we know physical humans created us? What if the virtual world is our true reality?"

Grey pushes the issue. "That's like asking what

came first, the chicken or the egg?"

Hannibal pushes back. "No, it's like asking what comes last, the egg or the chicken?"

"That's enough!" I stand up so fast, my chair falls. "Try looking beyond yourselves for once. The true purpose of this mission goes beyond the value of our individual lives or confirming the existence of species-5478. Our existence as a species relies on the success of this project. Modified blue fire is the only reality that matters now. The clock is ticking and runs out when somebody finds a way to use it as a weapon of mass destruction. Our Nexus is now susceptible to annihilation from the inside. Extinction is not only a possibility, but also a likely probability. This project might be the only way of saving humanity. Success could mean reintegration into the physical world on a broad scale. That alone, is enough to commit our lives."

Remi grins. "So two thousand years ago, people left da physical world to avoid killing themselves. And now, we have to leave da virtual world for da same reason."

Where the Dead Lay

CHAPTER 7

Knowledge acquired from *The Suffering* now proves invaluable when learning about various gadgets and terminology used in the IVST's testing labs. I keep abreast of all protocols and emergency procedures, even if it means the scientists and engineers have to delay the project in order to address my concerns. Postponements aside—my team is ready to enter the physical world after only three months of practical training.

Many within the scientific field consider the original process of transferring brainwaves from a biological human into the Nexus, rudimentary; especially by today's standards. The human body served as the primary conductor in the initial transfer, and was destroyed in the process. People sealed themselves inside an insulated container that looked like a coffin and hooked into an enclosed respiratory hose. They filled the coffin with a conductive liquid that held elements such as—carbon—calcium—phosphorus—sodium—magnesium—and other properties similar to the human body. By applying the appropriate charge through a magnetic coil, the subject underwent a form of neural shock as his or her synaptic network transferred through the liquid and into a conduit known as 'the spinal tap'. This device decoded the synaptic pattern into a code, which it proceeded to upload into the Nexus.

Things are much different now.

The incubation tub that we nicknamed 'the womb' exists in the physical world's IVST facility. It nurtures my new cybernetic prostheticalanatomy within an egg-shaped cocoon made of insulated glass. My mind will enter the CP through a multi-threaded fiber-optic umbilical cord. This is how the engineers will transfer my synaptic network if all goes well. They say the process will take seventy-two hours but how my mind chooses to interpret the passage of time remains a mystery. I can only hope the transfer will at least feel expedient.

Working for the Virtual Intelligence Agency is more intense than I expected. The prerequisites for operating a cybernetic prostheticalanatomy far exceed that of controlling a laborbot—due to the complete neural assimilation requirement—and unlike the excavation or construction bots used on the mining compound, the synaptic transfer required for operating the CP's prosthetics leaves no method of remotely recovering my brainwaves if I irreparably damage the body. Returning to the IVST research facility is the only way of reentering the virtual world. Isolation from humanity is a terrifying prospect but complete assimilation with a cybernetic prostheticalanatomy is the closest I'll ever come to having a human body.

"Onboard virtual sync is complete," says Mother

Nature, my official VIA station officer. "Synaptic framing in progress. Good luck everyone."

I focus on linking with my cybernetic body while the rest of Mandible 9 commits to something similar inside their own decompression chambers in the neighboring room. We're required to lie down on particle beds fused inside light chambers. Concave indentations on both sides of the bed allow access to input panels. After entering my final confirmation code, Mother Nature finishes her countdown from behind a tinted containment wall.

"Three, two, one… code validates. MAJOR is stable and awaiting synaptic fusion. All communication relays are online. Initiating Genesis self-diagnostic sequence program 1.11.21.3."

The first MAJOR went corrupt during its initial self-diagnostic run. All those geeks in the virtual labs have been dreading this moment and anxiously await the results from my CP's startup. Clusters of rotating nozzles lining my chamber's ceiling are now descending as they gradually release a photonic mist. The bubbling particles of light synchronize with the inner vascular threads beneath my texture's subcutaneous layer. This particular procedure should preserve my genetic meshing inside the chamber for its return trip.

The particles accumulate into a thin sheen across my body, giving it a golden aura that dampens all light from the room's monitors. I become extremely agitated from the prickly sensation. Mother Nature immediately responds by decreasing my rate of compression and the lights dim as she speaks.

"Try to relax," Mother nervously advises through a spectral-phone. "Separating your mind from its mesh is a precise science. You have to place yourself into a meditative state in order for the process to work. We need your synaptic pulse to beat within a normal range."

I practiced meditating a thousand times but it's hard placing my mind into a state of dormancy—especially now. A million thoughts are zigzagging across my synaptic network. I admit though… experiencing the effects of compression actually calms me. I relax as the photonic mist absorbs the outer layers of my body, which evaporate into the upper half of the meshing chamber, where the textures stick to the mirrored underside. My pulse decreases when the chamber compresses the vascular threads in my skeletal meshing. Grey's distant moans grow louder—reminding of my team's similar ordeal.

Although the first test subject passed this part of the integration process, he failed to establish a neural link with his cybernetic prostheticalanatomy. System failure occurred soon after and the cause remains a mystery. Most scientists believe the subject's irate temperament caused the malfunction; hence my required meditative state. Yet, my mind does more than relax, it loses cognitive density. My entire synaptic network relaxes its bonds when the mental tethers binding the various sections weaken. I lose all sense of time as my thoughts dilute into near nothingness. The dream, sub, auto, primal, and emotional states of consciousness slowly dissolve into a palette of viewpoints.

Is it finally time to converge with my cybernetic prostheticalanatomy?

This new urge… no, this new outlook… this narcotic perspective courses through every portion of my being and feeds on the marrow of my soul until I pull away from all that keeps me alive.

The time has indeed come…

Dr. Panels rejected all of the VIA's warnings and downloaded her own modified cyanide program into my meshing—an act unknown even to the IVST scientists monitoring my condition. Rina explained to me weeks ago that there's no way of transferring a person's synaptic network without removing it entirely from the individual's meshing. She believes the only way to do this, is through death. Transference of the "reawakened" consciousness mimics the ancient act of resuscitation. Rina theorizes that the original subject failed to transfer into the awaiting CP because he was conscious throughout the ordeal. Complete deactivation of the entire synaptic network is the only way of moving it to a new location. Otherwise, key portions will remain in their original locale. Many in the scientific community refuse to accept her theorem. My instincts tell me that Rina is right but I remain tense, because there's plenty of time for the techs to find her poison and prematurely revive me. If they catch us, or if she's wrong, Dr. Panels will lose her medical license and face prosecution for attempted or actual homicide. Of course, I'll face expulsion from the program if I'm not deleted.

I recognize the sacrifice required even if the VIA refuses to acknowledge the truth. That leaves Rina and Mandible 9 with only one chance at success. My doctor has prior notes, observations, and records from the first physician expelled from the program. A lot of the evidence she presented goes over my head so I have only my belief in Rina's expertise, anxieties, and many questions.

Oh and I question everything!

Is Rina simply another assassin trying to kill me? Will my entire mind transfer into MAJOR? If so, will there be room for growth? Will I lose a part of myself if my mind doesn't fit inside the CP? If the process works, will I have to die again, in order to re-enter the Nexus? What if my mind freezes inside the CP and I'm unable to operate it? Will I become a cybernetic paraplegic if that happens? Where does the machine end and I begin?

My thoughts wander into abstraction as the process intensifies…

What fraction of the mind is present in consciousness? Is that fraction a sum of the whole? Does virtual schizophrenia cause divided mind syndrome? Is communication the only way to combine minds? Is killing someone the only way to subtract a mind? Is giving birth the only way to add a mind? What fraction of consciousness remains after death? Is that fraction a sum of the whole?

I can feel the cyanide now—my thoughts are becoming increasingly erratic as the poison devours my life—it's soooo cold—yet, the seeping cyanide coursing through my vascular threads is not the origin of this freezing sensation. The sense of death encroaching upon my body is the actual cause. It feels like a cold sponge absorbing the life directly from me. But death isn't just absorbing life from me... it's absorbing my soul!

Such emptiness is terrifying! The void of lifelessness frightens me! I want to live now! I want nothing more than to live! Why did I risk my life so foolishly? I try fighting it but the poison is so strong that I can barely think of anything else!

Then, without warning, I di—

A Ghost in the Shell

CHAPTER 8

I am a soul without form, lost within a void. Darkness rests upon the deep. And the spirit…

God?

God!

God does exists…

Yet, not as I thought. Not as a being. Not as an entity. God knows everything because God is everything… God is the source. God is the embodiment of existence.

The ancients knew this Secret. To die, one must first have Life; Is there any other way to achieve That? We pretend as though we enjoy life, but we Don't—nobody wants to simply Exist.

We seek immortality.

The Source Code.

I found it, and draw from this well of infinite life—like everything else—including the source, which draws upon itself. We consume each other. We become each other. This is where I am reborn. Distilled within the source, my life spawns from this unbridled expulsion of infinite life. The source inverts our universe. The source encompasses everything; enslaving my previous existence with its entrapping thralls. When the source sways, flickers, or shudders, so does the void in which I exist. What does this mean? Extinction? Rebirth? Reincarnation? And the source links to the void like bonding atoms creating a new element. I can see everything because the source pulls from every direction expanding my view until…

:ATEN:

0 (-0)

[CEREBRAL AUGMENTATION]

[MODE]

[PROCESSING]

CHANNEL 1	CHANNEL 2	CHANNEL 3	CHANNEL 4
NEURAL PROCESSOR INTELAMD	COGNITIVE MEMORY SOLID STATE 0009	POWER SOURCE SUB-FRACTAL	SYNAPTIC NETWORK DI EHARI
XX-25 PROCESSOR CPU ID: PE 2:1 PATCH ID: JE 6	MOTOKO K 1995 PARALLEL AGGREGATE VER. 2	IVST BIOS V2.00 PNC	GHOSTING MASAMUNE
CENTILLION CORE 6.0 22 141 29(27) x 7	MEMORY TESTING 7978890 BB = OK	ENERGY COUPLING STABLE	CEREBRAL INTERFACE ENCODING NEURAL IMPRINT

Thump-thump, thump-thump…
Thump-thump, thump-thump…

Thump-thump, thump-thump…
Thump-thump, thump-thump…

Thump-thump, thump-thump…
Thump-thump, thump-thump…

My consciousness is adrift. I can vaguely perceive the amniotic fluid my body floats within. The systematic thump-thump of my heartbeat initiates the rhythm by which my instincts activate. Every thought forms around the beating.

Thump-thump, thump-thump…

The beating sets the initial pace of my cognition.

Thump-thump, thump-thump…

One two, A–B, z^2… the beats have a perfectly placed pause that intentionally identifies the set. These thumps commence the cognitive response of duality. Male and female—good and evil—this and that—night and day—awake and asleep—happy and sad—life and death. Like a ship breaking its moor, my thoughts are unhinged from the docks of virtuality and rocked by the turbulent state of the physical world.

My neural network overloads with synaptic impulses and tries adapting to the anomalous configuration of cybernetics. I squint at the twisted images floating before me and feel—what I believe to be—nauseated. Odd sensations flutter throughout my cybernetic body. My prosthetic lungs aspirate amniotic fluid and shudder violently. Breathing is torturous. Writhing in pain, I pull the thermostatic umbilical cord free and bash the incubation tub's glass lining with my fists. Instead of feeling liberated by this new existence, I struggle against the stifling warped reality of physicality.

"PleesowihffCAlmoodoown!!!OoEHaRRriik ldi!"

A familiar voice calls from somewhere nearby. Yet, even understanding familiarity is a laborious endeavor. In fact, understanding language, or interpreting sounds are arduous tasks. How do I reassemble my shattered mind?

I never experienced such mental upheaval! The chaos is driving me insane! It tears at the fringes of my mind! I'm losing my hold on reality but… wait… now I feel something… that is… a part of… me?

Fingers?

Toes?

Yes! My fingers and toes, fingers and toes… all

reacting erratically to my impulsive thoughts. They become the new anchors for my mind.

Fingers, toes…

Fingers, toes…

Their purpose becomes clear. I use my clenched fist to bash the womb's inner lining and fracture it. Voices call out, ordering me to stop. Nothing is going to stop me! I feel confined and suffocated so I strike out with another solid punch. My fist shatters the pink glass. Amniotic fluid floods the convection drains beneath the incubation tub as I fall into the womb's concave support frame. My body ripples with shuddering spasms as I vomit but there's something far worst surrounding me now… gravity? The unfamiliar and smothering sensation encroaches on every inch of my body, compelling me to escape.

I climb out of the support frame, drop to the floor, and crawl away from the womb like a slave breaking the bonds of captivity. Still gasping for air, my thoughts gradually saturate with memories of the virtual world.

After collapsing to the floor, my watering eyes focus on the physical world's brilliance. Some of the laborbots used to construct this facility and my new body stand poised along the walls in standby mode. Most of them have odd appearances. Some resemble mechanical skeletons. Others look like robotic spiders. All are offline, due to fears of electromagnetic interference disrupting my integration.

The detailed replica of a sycamore tree is the next thing to capture my attention. It towers in the room's center, guarded by a small circle of artificial grass. Each blade stands out with incredible vividness. The sycamore's feathery leaves swaying in the air conditioner's breeze mesmerize me. Their sharply defined textures and colors exceed the Nexus in every way. When I reach out and touch the tree's plastic bark, odd sensations tingle through my cybernetic nerves as this unfamiliar dimension of time and space continues unraveling. I withdraw from the unpleasant roughness and begin hyperventilating. Mother Nature's voice reemerges in my crosscom.

"You made it through the hard part, Di! Now please, try to relax… your neural network is adjusting to the CP's cybernetics. Take deep breaths and try to remain still."

I follow mother's advice and close my eyes. Physical life is a surreal conglomerate of heightened perceptions. The vibrancy of sight—the acuity of sound—the sensitivity of touch—the zest of taste—the fragrance of scent—all of these enhanced sensations are barely containable. I feel like this new body is an entity unto itself and my mind is a foreign invader attempting to conquer hostile territory. After a number of deep breaths, my prosthetic heart finally begins slowing. Mother Nature is joyous. Her voice fills the room's intercom with rapture as my mind and body merges.

"Remember, MAJOR's autonomous systems

must activate during startup. Once the error control routines finish, you can deactivate individual components, senses, and abilities, as needed. The CP's system requires all sensory functions to remain active until they synchronize."

Exploring my shapely new CP is an experience unlike any other. Sliding fingers over its moistened skin reveals a remarkably soft texture. Although, in reality, I'm not actually sure what true softness should feel like. Nevertheless… this seems right. The artificial organ is smooth and slightly elastic. It's remarkably sensitive to the environment, but not excessively so. According to the IVST engineers, this special membrane is tough like metal but fashioned to mimic the epidermal and subcutaneous layers of the human skin. They did a remarkable job as far as I can tell.

Staring at my visage in the floor's shiny surface evokes a myriad of emotions. The CP replaced my virtual texture's natural mahogany tone with a pasty pale color. Its eyes, nose, and facial features are so different from my natural appearance that I hardly believe this new reflection belongs to me. The purple hair offsets my sensibilities and even its voice contains a higher pitch. Strangely, although this CP is not my actual body, a strong sense of ownership overwhelms me. I suddenly become acutely aware of my nakedness and search for something to wear.

Magnifying portions of the environment with pinpoint accuracy occurs willfully. The bright gray paneling and hexagonal rivets used to seal the birthing chamber take on new dimensions when zooming on them. Raising and lowering both arms is second nature and function similarly to that of my natural photonic limbs. Slight aches and pains in certain body parts indicate potential weak points. I fight gravity's restrictive hold while trudging across the birthing chamber and head towards the robe hanging next to an open shower.

Mother's voice quivers with enthusiasm. "You are the first person to fully integrate with a Type XX cybernetic prostheticalanatomy! How do you feel?"

I use a deep breath to expel lingering amniotic fluid from my lungs, then relax after a few coughs. "This is unbelievable," I croak happily. "This prostheticalanatomy makes me feel… attuned to the environment! My virtual body never harnessed such sensations. I can barely absorb this level of perception."

"How is your sense of balance and weight?"

"My balance is stable but moving is hard. Why do I feel so weak?"

"That is gravity. As you know, gravity exists in the virtual world only by design. We experience the effects of gravity but not the sensation. As in the physical world, virtual objects tend to fall at a constant rate. However, in a virtual atmosphere, their weight is imperceptible. You are now experiencing the true physiological effects of gravity."

I try shrugging the sensation away but there is no ridding myself of this nagging *gravity*… "It feels oppressive! Gravity makes every motion uncomfortable! Moving shouldn't be so laborious!"

"You should grow accustomed to it. Gravity was a customary part of human life."

"I know, but it feels extremely awkward. Trying to explain this sensation is difficult. Moving takes so much effort. Gravity feels like an invisible atmosphere of pressure."

My physical body conforms to its natural gait by the time I reach the shower. Unlike my photonic counterpart, this body requires a different stride due to its longer legs. I reach for the robe but Mother Nature quickly intercedes.

"You need to shower first," she warns in a harsh tone, "the amniotic fluid contains chemicals that will harden if you fail to wash them off. Your sensory perception will be affected by the resulting crust."

I approach the silver nozzle cautiously—unsure of gravity's true effect on water. Will the spray push me to the ground? Will it hurt to shower? There's an entire laboratory filled with women and men watching my every move through wall cameras. That alone makes the experience very… awkward.

"This is so cliché."

"What do you mean?" Mother Nature's voice sounds genuinely confused, which is shameful.

"You know what I mean! Do I have to shower

with so many people watching? I feel exposed. This is like a scene in one of those twenty-first century movies."

"You don't need to be worried, Di. Every person inside this room spent decades creating that cybernetic prostheticalanatomy. You have no reason to feel ashamed. They know that body better than you do."

"I guess, but that doesn't make it any better. That's actually more disturbing for some reason…"

"Trust me," she suggests with a jolt of authority, "we need to monitor your motor skills and assess the functionality of your movements. Engineers are taking important calculations even as we speak. For instance, taking a shower will give us invaluable data along a wide array of variables, including—"

"Fine!" I can almost picture my frustration pushing Mother Nature's scrawny butt away from her station. "Let's not drag this out any longer than necessary."

I activate the shower's preset button and let the steamy spray to wash over my prostheticalanatomy. The sensation of soapy fluid instantly soothes with a beastly amount of comfort. Water feels remarkably similar to H_2O in the virtual world. Yet, the manner in which gravity pulls the various streams down my body is an unexpected pleasure. The CP's skin flushes with new sensations… thwarting my original wash-and-go plans. I've come to understand how a simple shower can counter the nuisances of getting dirty and the ill effects of gravity. What else is the virtual world lacking?

I take much longer than necessary—nearly becoming oblivious to the onlookers when they grow suspiciously quiet. When finished, I bypass the robe, towel off, and don the skintight environmental suit I find in a hermetic chest. It would be nice to know why the suit has to be so tight but there's probably some lengthy scientific explanation, so why bother asking?

"We are receiving excellent feedback, Di. General and fine motor skills are working better than expected. Now assess your vision."

"Well, everything appears extremely vivid but not like resolutions in the virtual world. This environment has a rich organic look."

"Can you see the chart in front of you?"

"Yes." I acknowledge, pointing to it with my index finger.

"Can you read the letters?"

I lick my lips, just to feel the salivating effect of my saliva. "Do you want me to read the words encoded inside the ink, or the surface lettering?"

A few excited engineers laugh at my progress. Mother Nature continues after listening to suggestions from one of her advisors.

"Try reading the coded words."

"No problem. God, indivism, greed, war, death, individualism, peace, slavery, freedom,

Satan."

"You will find a set of colors on the board to your left. Can you identify them in descending order?"

"Sure. Violet, blue, green, yellow, orange and red."

"Analyze your sense of touch. You will find an assortment of objects on the table to your right. Pick them up and explain how they feel. Count each step you take and report the number."

I check my balance before approaching the glass table. Each toe wiggles independently as desired. Both legs move without hesitation, with only a slight stiffness in one ankle.

"Thirty-four." After reciting my steps, I pick up the steel wrench and plastic ball from the glass table, but drop the wrench almost immediately. "I think my left arm is broken! The wrench felt a lot heavier than the ball!"

"It is supposed to. Did you pay attention in class?"

"Wait… so this is what gravity feels like when holding items with different weights?" I purposely drop the ball and watch it bounce towards the tree. "Why does the wrench hit the ground faster than the ball? I thought everything in the physical world falls at the same rate of descent."

"In a vacuum free from the restrictions of air molecules, both of those objects will fall at the same rate."

I crouch and rub the tool with my fingers. "The wrench feels exactly like objects in the virtual world. The original programmers mimicked textures well, except for the soothing sensation of water. They completely dropped the ball on that one. There's no way to explain how good that shower felt!"

"Noted. Now Di, do you see the punching bag to your left?"

"Yes." I observe the assorted training equipment strategically placed throughout an open gymnasium.

"How far away is the bag?"

The sensors inside my pupils calculate an accurate measurement of the bag's weight, mass, composition and distance.

[SCANNER]
|TARGET LOCKED|

|37.8 FT 4.5 IN|

"Thirty-seven cubes… I mean, thirty-seven and one eighth feet, four and a half inches." I assess the distance of other objects in the room while awaiting a reply.

"Fantastic, Di! Now approach the punching bag and try striking it with a closed fist."

I jog to the bag and give it a swift kick before pummeling the cylindrical stuffing with a combination of punches. Mother Nature watches breathlessly as I turn towards the obstacle course, scale the seventeen foot barricade, swing across the awaiting rope, and then slide upside down the firefighter's pole on the opposite end of the course. I land on my hands and gracefully circus walk across the floor before flipping to my feet.

Someone says, "Amazing," to Mother Nature, and his voice is loud enough to hear through the room's intercom. An arsenal of weapons awaits my sweaty palms in a glass cabinet hanging on the nearby wall.

[SCANNER]
|ANALYSIS|

|STANDARD MILITARY DUAL INTEGRATED|
|WEAPONRY|

[WEAPON 1]
|753 CAL FUSION-BARRELED MAGNETRON|
|PISTOL / SONIC DISRUPTER|

[WEAPON 2]
|50.56 MM M16 A922 PULSE RIFLE /|
|ORBITAL GRENADE LAUNCHER|

[WEAPON 3]
|78 GAUGE GATLING BARRELED|
|SHOTGUN / GRAVITY MINE DROPPER|

Mother Nature suddenly deactivates all of the room's lights when I grab the magnetron pistol. My hair instantly adjusts by shedding a luminescent glow. The purple-white light not only illuminates the darkness but also highlights trace particles that are invisible with normal vision. Without warning, target dummies pop up inside the firing range.

I land precise headshots on all three dummies while acrobatically avoiding a volley of paintballs discharged in my direction. On impact, the spiky rounds cause the heads of each dummy to melt like hot butter.

"Very impressive!" Mother exclaims.

She joins the clapping crowd of officials, engineers, doctors, and scientists in the background. I wonder if the president is present. They have yet to realize how my physical elation far exceeds their primitive virtual exuberance.

"I feel like a superhero in this body!"

"Remember Di, you are only human."

"Well, a replica of one, at least."

"Those archaic weapons are probably going to be useless on this assignment. If you find species-5478, it is likely to be a non-hostile organism. The creature's appearance alludes to docility. In fact, most of your duties will probably involve surveying. The compression packs hanging on the wall have all of the tools you utilized during simulator training. Take one. Proper planning is the best measure for preventing poor performance."

I retrieve one of the metallic backpacks and check its contents as Mother Nature coaches through the intercom.

"The rest of your team successfully transferred into their CPs and will be waiting for you in the preemptive chamber. Their cybernetic prostheticalanatomies are much sturdier than your Type XX and can handle a wider array of environmental conditions. Use them to your advantage."

"Understood." I fondle one of the compression packs as Mother continues.

"We may not be able to maintain constant external communication due to the chemical and electromagnetic imbalances in Earth's atmosphere. You might be on your own after exiting the facility. If you encounter problems that keep you from returning, activate your cybernetic prostheticalanatomy's internal beacon and wait for emergency bot evacuation. Follow our designated route. Deviate *only* if there is a good reason."

"Got it."

"Alright Di, we need to finish the operations and communications checks before I can clear you for departure. You also need to undergo a level twelve medical exam and test MAJOR'S sleep function."

"I'm ready, Mom. What's first?"

"The most important facet of ancient human interaction involved how information was downloaded through the senses. They did not have neural links to sort information."

Mother Nature is right. I feel raw and exposed. My new body registers everything around me without any kind of filtering.

"That's why torture was so effective, right?"

"Correct. All pre-Nexus humans absorbed information like sponges. If a person harbored data another wanted, forcing the victim to download unwanted pain was an effective way of hacking into their mind. That is also why video and audio media was such an efficient means of mental programming. A victim could not reject what they saw or heard after an aggregator already inserted the information into their mind. This type of mind hacking was not even perceived as a mental violation until after the nineteenth century."

I shrug, "So pain was the most invasive means of forced programming?"

"Not necessarily. Backdoor hacking often worked better. If information was downloaded into a person's mind without their knowing, programmers could alter the individual's thoughts with greater efficiency."

"Right. I remember this lesson from one of the training courses. Traditional humans didn't have antiviral neural links. Malicious, Trojan-like content was conveyed through media, books, music, and other forms of data."

"Correct. Early programmers discovered that one of the most decisive means of altering a person's behavior is through dialogue scripting. The simple act of speaking became a tool for downloading whatever information they wanted, into the recipient's mind, and usually without their consent. Most people did not realize at the time, that unauthorized conversations are an invasion of mental privacy."

"It's the most controversial part of the Free Realm," I add. "But at least we have the ability to delete unwanted content from our minds."

"Ancient humans had no delete option. For instance, by telling someone not to think about a blue cow, the programmed individual had no choice but to think about a blue cow. Interrupting someone during a conversation was another way of forcefully integrating a mental script. However, there were less intrusive means of accomplishing the same goal. Directors of twenty-first century shows and movies would often portray the same race of people together at jobs, in relationships, or at other gatherings. By doing so, they covertly inserted Trojan thoughts into people's minds rejecting interracial relations."

I agree with her rationale. "That's also why people didn't recognize greed as a mental illness, or how the Capitalist system survived for so long. It's amazing how ancient humans were fooled into thinking it's OK for a few people to have all of the world's wealth while the rest suffered in poverty."

"It was more complicated than that."

"Was it? If there are ten people in a room, and most are starving and in need of medical care, is it right for one person to hoard all of the food and medicine while the others suffer? What was the point of being a billionaire? People didn't even use their wealth to devise great projects; like building a base on the moon or constructing an underwater town. They simply hoarded riches for the sake of keeping them from others. What was the point of sitting on mountains of wealth and watching others suffer? Did it make rich people feel better about themselves, before they died like the rest of the population?"

"It is easier to control people with fantasies of wealth than with chains and whips. Rich people weren't the problem, in-so-much as those who aspired to be like them. Greed was one of the worst mind Trojans ever created. It worked, because the few in power controlled media consumed by the masses. They made the idea of overindulgence not only seem normal, but they also supported the often heinous methods by which the acquisition of wealth came at other people's expense. This of course, only benefited the minority in power.

This is also how the act of talking became the premier form of communication. It was the most invasive, pervasive, insidious, powerful, and the most direct violation of the human mind. Unlike the Free Realm, people didn't have the option of choosing what information they wanted to download. Individuals simply spoke to one another without even asking permission about the content they were going to divulge. Mental raping ran rampant in those times."

I nod, wondering how people could live so willingly as slaves of a status quo. "I can't imagine living without the Free Realm's discussion filters.

Banning certain conversational topics seems so natural. Mentally raping a person by talking to them about forbidden content should have always been a major crime."

"Di, I am only bringing this up as a reminder of why the physical world is so dangerous. Physicality is a world of senses. They will impose themselves on you. Respect them, and your senses will serve you well."

Mother Nature's final departure requirements take nearly three additional days and exhaust my remaining patience. She analyzes and tests every aspect of my CP before giving me the clearance to leave the facility. An electric lock seals the chamber's bay door and requires a series of command codes in order to open. I have no idea why this is necessary. Do they actually think someone is going to break into this place? Well… there's the slight possibility that species-5478 could try to enter, so I suppose safety measures validate the security. Still, I certainly don't enjoy waiting for the numerous locks to disengage and when the circular hatch finally opens, I find my team waiting for me inside an enclosed dome beyond a secondary hatch forty feet away.

They look like iron men in their grayish cybernetic bodies and there's no way of telling them apart aside from a series of small numbers etched into their collars. Each unit stands nine feet tall. Engineers housed all vital components within their cybernetic bodies. A concave radar unit congruently oscillates along the curves of their backs. Red armor similar to that of Roman Praetorians protects their bulky inner limbs—the only colorful feature aside from blue seams. The Type XY's feet resembles the hooves of classic anime mech suits, with normal looking hands the size of my chest. They also have human-shaped eyes, ears, and mouths, but lack any kind of nose or similar protrusion in that area of the face.

My team cheers when I step forward and welcomes me into the physical world as if it's their lifelong home. There's no use gossiping about our emergence. I set the operational tone by immediately getting to business.

"Is everybody online?"

"Affirmative!" They acknowledge in a stern collective.

"We'll have to do something about your identities." I remove a black laser marker from my compression pack and point to the first CP. "Who are you?"

"It's me, Grey."

"No he's not!" The second CP steps forward. "I'm Grey!"

Remi laughs and then quickly apologizes as I face Grey. Instead of labeling him by name, I draw a Trinity optic lens on his chest, and some spectacles around his eyes.

"Glasses? Hell yeah!" Remi claps, "That's perfect!"

"Sync your CP's audio projectors to your vocal patterns. I shouldn't have to look at you to figure out who's talking."

I resist the temptation to draw an ass on Remi's cybernetic face, because that will only incite him into a cursing frenzy for the next several hours. Instead, I mark his chin with an exclamation sign, and then emulate his trademark goatee and spiky hair. After drawing large pecks and a six-pack onto Hannibal's torso, I immediately give my first order.

"Species-5478 was last seen near the Mississippi volcanic river, east of our current location. My CP is the only one capable of advanced scientific fieldwork so stay behind me after we enter the Wasteland. I do not want your elephant feet trampling clues that might lead to 5478. March in a single file formation. Keep your scanners on and don't mentally or physically wander."

Hannibal salutes. "Affirmative Commander!"

"Nah Hanni… Commander won't do anymore. Ehari deserves a promotion!" Remi decrees with a two-handed salute, "Her new title is Major!"

Grey gives me a thumb up. "Yeah that's perfect! Fits her like a glove!"

"Technically," Hannibal protests, "a Commander is higher ranked than a Major. And they're in different fields, too."

Remi stomps his massive hoof. "That don't sound right. Besides, she's not commanding ships in *Da Suffering* anymore."

"Technically, it's still a demotion."

"Technically? It's a damn nickname! We ain't even in da military! There's nothing technical about a nickname!"

"Enough chatter!" I step in-between Remi and Hannibal. "Focus on the mission!"

Remi glares at Hannibal and says, "Affirmative, Major!"

We negotiate three pressure-sealed corridors before reaching the final chamber. I double-check my environmental suit before activating its long-range sensors and verbalizing the commands necessary to open the final ten-foot titanium door. Everyone quiets when the locks slowly unlatch and auburn rays pierce the chamber's white interior; as if the blades of light were slicing the door open. At last, I make history as the first humanoid to step onto Earth in over two thousand years. A fiery gust of wind—blowing flames through the doorway—heralds the historic moment.

I stare into the daylight. "Every step we take quarters our march through history."

Sunrise Falling

CHAPTER 9

The underground cavern preserving what's left of our entire civilization is located in a valley sheltered from the sun's punishing radioactive rays and Earth's magnetic showers. We spend hours hiking through tunnels and gullets in order to reach one of the most hazardous plains in the solar system.

Simply stepping into the Wasteland is enough to demoralize everyone. Not even the momentous task of finding species-5478 can erase the hopelessness of a dying world—especially one that mirrors the angst of humankind.

Earth's pollutants and strange gravitational shifts create unpredictable phenomena. The air writhes with toxic brumes stacked atop one another like planks of wood. Heavier contaminants scour the planet's surface, scrubbing away remnants of life, while lighter toxins magnify the sun's ultraviolet rays. Scorching winds blister anything left within these scathing layers of multicolored smog.

Blue skies filled with billowing white clouds are distant memories relived only through my simulator. In physical reality, the reddish brown air contains glittering particles that distort and magnify the sun until it appears to jiggle within Earth's swirling stew of atmospheric gases. A strange distortion effect changes the incoming solar rays into an anamorphic palette of colors that alters the sky's hue every few minutes.

Sluggish clouds crawl across the firmament and smear the air with descending rivulets of chemical soot. The resulting showers are capable of burying anything beneath tons of ash within seconds. Gravity-based clouds pose the greatest threat. Although customary in the "winter" season, I air on the side of caution, and make certain my team maintains a wary eye for their presence. Perimeter cameras record many of these radiant blue clouds lifting enormous objects miles into Earth's atmosphere only to drop them into the distant horizon.

A flaming tornado twirls lazily across the otherwise desolate landscape and a mountainous wall of fire trails the funneling inferno for thousands of miles to the east. It eventually vanishes inside the horizon's murk but the flaming wall remains. There's little to burn other than rocks or sediments, but the misty gas bubbles spewing from volcanic vents provide the perfect catalyst for prolonged fires—especially when vacuumed inside fiery tornadoes.

The landscape stirs flashbacks of *The Suffering*. In the final moments of the last mission, super volcanic eruptions shattered Earth's crust as tectonic explosions blew immense continental fragments into outer space. That blast was probably the most historically accurate event of the game. Nobody realized the planet's inner core was really a ticking time bomb. Had people realized as much, they would have probably left the planet long ago instead of fighting over future of rubble.

Vibrations from the rupture sent Earth into a wobbling orbit for centuries afterward. Although its rotational axis stabilized after the first millennium, the planet's yearly trek around the sun remains abnormally elliptic. Summers are now extremely hot, followed by unusually frigid winters. The area formally known as North America sustained the worst damage. Any land that failed to crumble apart now floats across the planet's swelling lava seas.

It's hard to believe humanity destroyed a planet teeming with life in favor of a desolate one. The retro videos featuring green plains, crystalline waterfalls, and blue skies must be a lie. Perhaps those videos are the fantasies of hopeful minds wishing to leave this insidious world in favor of something beautifully organic. Hope of this kind is delusional when you live in Hell.

Although a nonessential function of my virtual body, I now feel the urge to take a deep breath and sigh. Instead, I look around and wonder why our species longs for the remnants of their former selves.

Why for instance, create a humanoid body that sighs? Those hacks from the virtual world could have designed some kind of flying, spidery machine for me to control. Traversing the Wasteland in this "human" body is going to be a hassle. It even requires an environmental suit! This is why I hate leaving the virtual world for laborbot duty. Reality in the physical world is depressingly harsh.

Hannibal calmly announces, "The VIA is officially off-line. Atmospheric interference is the cause." I find his focus impressive, considering the distractions. He checks a few more readings before asking, "Should we continue recording the entire journey?"

I wave my team onward after finding a negotiable path. "Keep your primary cameras on their sustained recording modes. Our entire expedition needs to be documented for historical posterity."

"Affirmative, Major."

I use my CP's eyelens to plot a path into the Wasteland and set fourteen separate waypoints to help mark our progress. "We're going to follow the last known route of species-5478. Be on the lookout for anomalies and stay together. I'm keeping point."

Individual regions of weather no longer exist; everything now occurs globally, like on other dead planets.

Winter is usually the most unstable season. Acidic ash, sulfuric pellets, frozen gas petals, and radioactive waste often rain slowly up from the ground and fill the sky with summer's next batch of toxic cloud cover.

Spring consists of silent days that are void of the slightest gust. Although lava fissures are abundant during this time, the frequency of earthquakes decreases and radioactive showers lessen.

Summer consists of flaming clouds that eventually spill their contents upon the earth in showering tempests of hellfire. Solar tornadoes are the worst by-products of these storms. They first appear as circular gaps of gas that spawn in the upper atmosphere. The oval windows grant a momentary glimpse into the universe before funneling the sun's radioactive heat into towering hourglass shaped infernos.

Earth's magnetic field is in a state of flux during the fall. Gravity frequently increases to alarming rates during the first couple of months, before sporadically decreasing to near non-existent levels without warning. Anything caught on the surface risks a lethal crushing under its own weight, or propulsion into orbit along a magnetic stream of radiant purple waves.

When humanity's incessant nuclear bombing agitated Earth's core, the ensuing explosion cracked our planet's equator as both hemispheres spun apart like a bottle cap. It seemed that nature or perhaps even God, decided to pause our bickering with a true demonstration of power. In fact, humanity's brutal rise to global domination was born within nature's temporary cessation of arms.

If we're the products of a docile and hospitable planet created for us by a benevolent God, then what is species-5478? What kind of being arises from the bedlam of God's destruction?

Few people believe in God anymore. My era incorporates people who use the advent of technology to justify godless proclamations of wisdom. Yet, these very people glorify themselves as gods, because of the technology they wield. Does that mean they don't believe in themselves? Does technology or the ability to create tech, have anything to do with God?

My mother would often say, "There is no God, because there's no proof of God's existence."

My father would always contend, "There is a God. Our existence is proof."

From what I know of history, humans became the epicenter of turmoil on Earth because we're the most intelligent species on the planet. We did unimaginable acts of terror to ourselves and other forms of life—all while destroying Earth. If we cannot temper ourselves from chaos, why expect benevolence from a higher form of life? It seems that God only needs to be more intelligent than humans are, in order to function as our creator. There's no requirement for an omnipotent God. Yet, if God is omnipotent or at the very least, the universe's creator… perhaps, this is the reason why the cosmos and humankind exist in such hostility. We'd be a microcosmic reflection of God's image.

Grey says, "Major, I'm reading one hundred

and seventy mile an hour winds. Temperature is at four hundred Fahrenheit. It's extremely calm out here."

"You call that calm? Give me a seismograph reading."

He probes the area with his scanners until something registers. Grey eventually steps to my side and points west with his rhombohedral forefinger.

"A category twenty-four earthquake will emerge from a chasm just beyond those mountaintops. Estimated time of arrival is one hour—with a forty second duration."

"Effects?"

Grey debates his calculations before answering. "Trivial, if we're not standing by any volcanic springs."

"We're going to locate the camera that filmed species-5478 and continue from there. Stay close."

I scan the landscape and fail to see anything beyond the dark red haze lingering above the western plateau. After testing multiple eyelens settings, the optical wave function proves to be an effective filter. My team focuses on searching the area for hazards with this new criterion.

The notion of walking *everywhere* disturbs me and my team's obnoxious elephant stomping isn't making the hike any better. The virtual world's various modes of instant travel are more than a comfort—they're a way of life. After hiking silently for two whole hours, I feel a distinct need to pass the time.

"How tall is species-5478?"

The spontaneous question draws enthusiastic grunts from my men. They too, seem happy to have a distraction from the harsh surroundings. Grey, Hannibal, and Remi hastily sort through their neural data for an answer. Like most things, answering my question becomes a sudden challenge that demands a winner and in this case, Grey is the victor.

"Species-5478 is exactly 8 feet and 3 inches high. Why do you ask?"

Hannibal and Remi curse when I acknowledge Grey's speed and accuracy. "Something that tall must have a food source. What does it eat?"

Hannibal's knowledge of prewar biology supersedes our own. He enthusiastically says, "Ancient plants utilized photosynthesis to convert the sun's energy into food. Of course, they also required good soil and water. Maybe 5478 extracts energy from the sun in a similar way?"

I shake my head. "That doesn't seem likely. I compared 5478's body to other prewar life forms and found a startling similarity to mammals. In particular, those things called lemurs. Have you seen a holo of one?"

"Lemurs? Yes, they were bipedal mammals similar to monkeys."

Grey steps ahead of Hannibal. "I studied the

biological and chemical makeup of prewar life, too."

"Well, what did you learn?"

"There were numerous life forms that thrived in some of the harshest environments on Earth. I think they were called—"

"Extremophiles," interrupts Hannibal, who then steps ahead of Grey. "Many creatures fell into that category."

"How harsh are we talking?"

"Extremophiles thrived in conditions generally thought to be unsuitable for maintaining life; like extreme pressure or heat. Usually, a kind of self-regulatory system aided their existence. I read about tiny crustaceans that could generate anti-freezing compounds that allowed them to withstand sub-zero temperatures. There were interesting varieties, too. Some used concentrated sugars, amino acids, salts—"

"So basically, you think 5478 is feasting on extremophiles?

"It's possible. In fact, species-5478 can probably classify as an extremophile."

It's great when my boys do their homework. I give Hannibal an affectionate butt slap. "The geographical layout of this sector appears different from the IVST maps. How stable is this area?"

Grey laughs. "There's nothing stable about Earth or its atmospheric conditions. Expect all kinds of unpredictable changes. You know... there was a time when the word 'season', actually meant something. People could forecast events based solely on routine atmospheric conditions. That's impossible nowadays."

"Yeah, I made the virtual world's most popular cloud simulator, remember?"

Grey appears absorbed in his own thoughts. "Of course," he continues nearly oblivious to my words, "but the world you based that simulator on will never exist again. It has no purpose."

I turn toward Grey and look directly into his red eyes. "There's always a purpose in remembering how things were."

"Damn," Remi pokes Hannibal in the stomach, "butthead got her started."

"The issue is one of cause and effect," I state loudly. "Properties from the past created this environment, just like this environment will affect the future climate."

Grey huffs like an out of breath track runner. "I disagree, of course. Some things have no purpose. They have no cause or effect. They're just random. Like the creation of our planet."

"That's absurd. There's no such thing as senseless randomness, especially in regards to our planet. Earth's very construction is too precise to be an advent of chance. All phenomena have a purpose. Even randomness is a form of order we have yet to calculate. And the complexity of our planet is proof of an intelligent designer."

Grey doesn't bother hiding his snide. "Let's agree to disagree."

"Let us," I suggest a bit too spitefully. "This world is not a creation of randomness. Earth exists in a state of precision, especially the old Earth. Solar and lunar eclipses—a self-sustaining ecosystem—perfect weather patterns—sustainable gravity—Earth was even the right size and distance from the sun to support life. Our planet was like a cog spinning in the machinery of the universe. There are too many moving parts for all of them to occur randomly and they certainly did not come together by chance."

"You don't know what you're talking about. The extreme size of the universe allows for random events like the creation of our planet, to appear purposeful."

"Randomness is an illusion. If I flip a coin at random heights and with random force, there's absolutely no chance that it will land on the same side indefinitely. That would be true randomness. Your version of randomness is actually proportional balance, in which every option must arise in equal proportion. That's a definitive certainty, not a random occurrence. In a truly randomized universe, there's a chance that a coin will never fall on the same side twice. Such events never happen in our reality even though we claim they're possible. The distribution of a coins' chances to land on either side is one hundred percent, because both options will present themselves equally within our medium of time of space. All options within our reality, no matter the quantity, must be realized equally in order to exist. The reason people gamble, is because they know randomness is a figment of the imagination. People gamble with the odds, not randomness."

"Odds *define* randomness. But even if you're right, which you're absolutely not, mankind has proved smarter than all other life, because we continue to beat the odds and survive our own misdeeds."

"Humankind has accomplished no such feat," I argue. "We only proved that when a species becomes too smart for its own good, the problem of excessive intelligence will solve itself. There's no need for something higher on the food chain. We're the problem and the solution."

"That's not true. We continue to exist, don't we?"

"Yes, but as what, exactly? We claim the banner of humanity. We call ourselves people but we're not truly human anymore. We live half-lives in a substitute and flawed world. Part of the reason we're out here is because we're trying to escape the impending destruction of the Nexus. Humanity spends its existence running from itself."

"You're somewhat right." Grey elaborates, raising his voice a few decibels. "We're more than human. We've evolved."

"You think we evolved because we hid inside the Nexus?"

"I think we evolved, because we came out of it."

Hannibal grunts, while Remi shakes his head. OK... Grey *could* be right, and often tends to be. I put him on the team for that very reason.

"All right, let's hear more, wise one."

"Life on this planet while pleasant to look at, ultimately served its purpose by providing us with the keys to the virtual kingdom. The organic world was fragile and never meant to last. Had we not stirred the Earth into exploding, it probably would have done so on its own. A worldwide earthquake, meteor, epidemic, or some other calamity would have eventually erased all life on the planet. We preemptively interrupted this natural cycle of life and death. In fact, now that you're operating that cybernetic prostheticalanatomy, you can experience an enhanced version of what it felt like to be human. How isn't that evolution?"

"We have no idea what it really felt like to be human. There's nothing to compare this body with, other than virtual existence. Besides... true evolution is not just about physically improving oneself." I stop, turn to Grey, and point to the desolate landscape. "We're not lone entities separate from the environment. We are a part of the environment! All of our scientific efforts focus on recapturing our humanity. My cybernetic prostheticalanatomy is nothing more than an elaborate attempt at restoring our former selves. Searching for species-5478 is an extension of that goal."

Remi interrupts us while pointing east. "Blah blah blah… sorry to interrupt ya *fascinating* discussion, but do ya see that? My sensors say it's a class nine gravity boulder. What should we do?"

I examine the spherical distortion rolling across the plains. The tumbling abnormality measures six feet in diameter and refracts light within its spherical core.

"Hold your positions." I climb a small knoll and magnify the boulder with my eyelens before messaging Remi. "Do you see anything else?"

"Nah."

I chew my bottom lip. Some habits are hard to break, regardless of the body I'm in. "Assessment?"

"That one only weighs seven hundred and ninety-five pounds. Boulders that size are usually limited to plateaus but they tend to move in groups. We should be careful. There might be more. Da camera we're looking for should be on a hill just beyond that upcoming ridge. Climbing it will place us above da danger zone."

This particular area is a microcosmic piece of the global environment. At least that's what the IVST scientists say. Ever since humanity entered the virtual world, creating aircraft capable of traversing the ever-changing atmospheric conditions has been a struggle. Although our scientific community utilizes tools like my cloud simulator, old aircraft footage, and military records, they're not quite able to design an aircraft capable of negotiating Earth's environmental irregularities. With much of the skies off limits, mapping shifting global conditions is next to impossible. Fortunately, by the time I lead my team up the next hill, I make a small discovery.

"The air is much clearer at this altitude. I can see nearly twice as far now."

Grey scans the area. "This camera isn't equipped with ultraviolet filtering, which makes capturing footage at this altitude much clearer. All cameras within this elevation should be upgraded accordingly."

Remi documents Grey's findings and helps scan the area for more irregularities.

I motion to Hannibal. "You're with me. We're going to investigate the exact spot where the perimeter camera spotted species-5478."

"Affirmative, Commander." Hannibal glances towards Remi before trudging off.

I feel like a kid when jumping down the rocky hillside in my agile body. As MAJOR's internal sensors monitor Earth's gravity, they adjust my weight to cushion each fall. Even though descents are intense, the actual landings are gentle.

[SCANNER]
|ANALYSIS|

|SUBTERRANEAN BODY DETECTED- OVERLAY|
|SEQUENCE IN-PROGRESS|

"I found something!"

Hannibal's heavy Type XY is the complete opposite of my five and half foot Type XX. He slowly trudges down the hill's incline and leaves deep depressions in his wake. Once Hannibal reaches the bottom, he immediately focuses on the scorched earth.

"What did you find?"

"There's a tunnel beneath us!" I motion with crossed fingers, "And it bisects species-5478's last known path!"

"That's odd. Are you sure it's not another lava vein?"

"I'm not sure of anything but after studying the footage, I can tell by looking at these land markers that the creature altered course in this spot. That's not a coincidence."

Hannibal assesses the area with his own instruments. "I can't find any tunnels."

"Try using sonar. The vibrations from your sensors should bounce off the interior walls."

"All right." After a few seconds, Hannibal gives me a nod. "OK, got it. The tunnel appears to be two hundred feet below ground. You're right about the video, too. 5478 stepped into the camera's view from a southeastern direction, and then altered course right where the underground passage intersects its path aboveground. It followed the cave from here and headed north. Why would species-5478 do that?"

"Maybe it found the tunnel and wants to

explore it. Or maybe it lives inside a nearby cave. I'm wondering how 5478 was able to detect an underground passageway. We had to use wave vision to find it." I pause long enough to give Hannibal time to document our findings.

He looks about with growing intrigue. "How *did* it know about the passageway? There aren't any land markers for identifying underground cavities. What should we do?"

"I'm not sure. We can follow the tunnel north or travel east, toward 5478's point of origin. Protocol suggests following the last known course of any target but this expedition is not routine."

Hannibal looks in both directions. "So which way should we go?"

"My scanner is highlighting hundreds of unexplored cavities to the north. Most appear to have entrances situated inside a nearby canyon. Maybe 5478 lives underground like the rest of us. If so, those caves will make an ideal home. Gather the team. We're heading north."

Suffering is 9/10 of the Law

CHAPTER 10

Operating individually is the natural instinct of any Nexusborn person. We tend to admire how powerful one person can become without the aid of others. Independence is power within virtuality but with physicality, there's strength in numbers.

I feel a strong urge to keep everyone together. Memories of prewar movies—some of which are cheesy—influence my thinking. Yes, I admit an obsession with the classics… but hear me out! Many prewar productions are better than our current soap operas, which seem to be clones of the same cast and plot. It's hard putting a finger on why creativity has taken a nosedive lately but there's little substantive material to watch nowadays. This is why I enjoy prewar movies and virtual gaming. In these productions, people who separate from the group die because of the general philosophy behind strength in numbers. Something always happens to those who stray. Even stragglers in the animal kingdom became the primary targets of predators.

Remi passively indicates his interest in taking point by saying, "Da canyon we're looking for is just beyond that ridge."

"Hang back. I'm going to scout ahead. If there's something in that canyon I want to get the drop on it."

Grey wastes no time voicing his displeasure. "Those quakes were due over ten minutes ago. Maybe you should wait before heading out to investigate."

"Quake energy can be diverted elsewhere or fail to occur entirely. Keep your crosscoms open. If anything happens, stay here and wait for my orders."

"Affirmative," my men grudgingly acknowledge.

I go against instinct and leave my team standing by a meteoric crater. Dark fumes rising from volcanic vents cover the ground with a thick haze. The malignant smog is impenetrable with visual filters and requires the use of sensors in order to monitor ground conditions. I eventually reach a rocky protrusion where the miasmic waterfall of chemical soot wafts over the canyon's edge and falls into the awaiting gorge.

"The smog is drifting down the canyon's side and masking most of the cave entrances. There's a river of lava flowing along the bottom of the canyon. It looks as though the planet is cracking open in this area."

Remi's crosscom signal weakens slightly. "How many cave entrances do ya see?"

"There appears to be eighty-two on this side of the canyon. It's easy to see why they eluded the exploratory mechs. This river is emitting abnormally high levels of heat. The temperatures are distorting my visual filters. Laser sensors are the onl—"

[SCANNER]
|WARNING|

|SEISMIC DISTURBANCE DETECTED|
|ANALYZING GRAPHICAL INTERFACE|

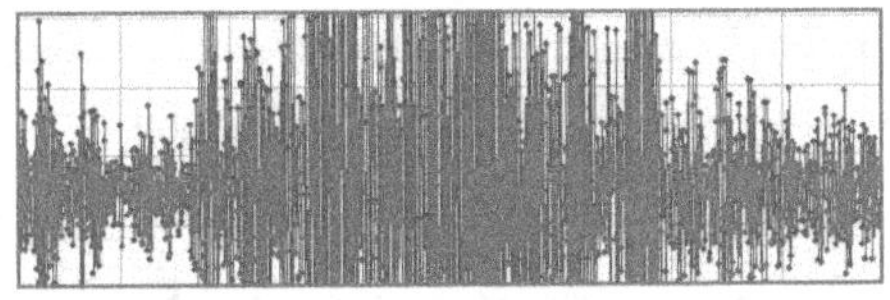

|GRAVITY / WEIGHT REALIGNMENT IN-PROGRESS|

Tremors throw me to the ground. "Damn, the earthquake!" I crawl away from the canyon's ledge after failing to stand. Getting a grasp on the nuances of balance is next to impossible. Instead of regressing, the tremors gradually escalate until large fissures form in the surrounding earth.

"E, get out of there!" Hannibal warns, "The ground is crumbling apart!"

Too late…

A gigantic slab of earth breaks away from the ledge and carries me towards the awaiting lava miles below. I activate the spiked cable linked to my compression pack and aim the pointed end at the canyon's inner wall. One strong ejection is enough to propel the cable into a fixed position. The CP's gravity sensors readjust my weight as the slab continues falling without me. I practically float to the wall and dangle there as though hung in a noose.

[SCANNER]

|WARNING|

|FREE-FALLING OBJECTS DETECTED|

Remi's voice blares through my crosscom, "Damn it! E disappeared inside da canyon! I can't find her with any of these sorry ass sensors!"

The earthquake shakes the cable so forcefully that it might dislodge at any moment. I grab my rifle and shoot some of the debris but my rounds are ineffective against such large targets. Enormous boulders whiz by as I struggle to gain momentum. The earthquake has complete control over the cable's movements. It swings me back and forth like a pendulum until I fire at the canyon's wall. The force pushes me away from an avalanche of debris but a few stones strike the cable and pull me forward prematurely. I swing between falling slabs and land inside one of the tunnel entrances. The earthquake continues its fierce convulsions as the cable retracts into my compression pack, and I press my body against the tunnel's concave wall in time to escape falling stalactites loosened by the tremors. The moment feels eternal and the quake... everlasting, but it eventually subsides and my body's involuntary spasms digress after listening to the churning volcanic fluid running along the canyon's base.

I cautiously lean out of the tunnel entrance and observe the final bits of loosened sediments falling into the orange river. That could have been me—burning alive in a toxic stew of lava and God knows what else! A shudder passes over me when I consider my absurd luck and the possibility of aftershocks. Never have I known such intense sensations. My stomach feels empty, yet unbelievably swollen. What's the purpose for all of these strange physical after-feelings? I return to the safety of the tunnel's interior and slouch against one of its walls.

"E…" says Remi.

Hannibal calls out next. "Are you there?"

Grey wonders, "Is she dead? Is anybody getting a reading?"

Remi defiantly yells, "She's got to be down there somewhere!"

"I'm alive. Give me a second."

Sighs of relief flood my crosscom. They actually sound more relieved than I feel. How is that even possible?

Remi asks, "Where in da Hell are ya?" I even hear him whisper to the others, "I told ya she'd make it…"

"I'm inside one of the tunnels. If you learn how to use your scanners, you wouldn't have to ask so many damn questions!" Of course, my anger stems from almost getting myself killed and not from superfluous questions. I pause long enough to temper my emotions. "Sorry. I just…

I should've been smarter. Grey, give me your read on aftershocks."

"Ahh, sure. I'll need a few seconds."

I use those few seconds to steady my nerves. Dismissing Grey's advice was foolish. On top of that, my pre-planned insertion is ruined! I'm off course and carefully consider my next move.

"There's about thirty minutes before the next of three possible aftershocks. All are minimal yield. Should we try reaching you?"

"No, hold your positions."

My gut sickens from the memory of falling into the canyon. I reel from visions of my burning, mangled body, and vomit battery fluid into my environmental suit's vacuum hose. The hose sends this irreclaimable liquid to my compression pack's waste disposal unit, which reports a twelve percent energy drop to my CP. I refocus on my surroundings after resetting the mission timer.

The tunnel is everything I expect. It has a gloomy interior, uneven pathway, and no signs of life. Although air flows towards the exit, my sensors reveal an absence of expected volcanic particles and gases.

"Hey guys, what would explain the complete absence of sulfur and tephra inside this tunnel? The air blowing out of here lacks traces of either."

Remi, oddly, is the only one with a clue. "That tunnel might stem from another source. Exploring that bastard is da only way to know for sure."

"How far did I fall?"

"Ya fell about a mile into da canyon. We have ya marked on our scanners but with all da interference, getting a fix on that tunnel system is a headache. It might be too far down."

"My sensors can chart the tunnel. Wait for me to link my array to your scanners. You should be able to create a three dimensional map of my position."

I make the required adjustments before exploring any deeper. Shadows paint every curvature of this dismal tunnel. I decide to use MAJOR's luminescent hair to light the path instead of relying solely on sensory vision. My CP's purple follicles stand on end inside the environmental suit's glassy helmet and illuminate the distant crevices of the tunnel. A steep incline becomes visible and considering what I just survived, scaling it will be child's play. Hannibal messages me as I start my ascent.

"How are you doing down there?"

I wave my hands in an overly annoyed manner, since gesticulations are only visible to me. "Things are *great*."

"I know this probably isn't the right time but… can I ask a personal question?"

"What?"

"I want to ask about *The Suffering*."

"What do you want to know?"

Hannibal clears the static from his vocal emitter. "You saw something at the end of the game when the super volcanoes exploded. It was something that wasn't a part of the game—right? What was it? What did you see?"

I freeze along the incline. My vision transcended all forms of reality. The sight of God imprinted my memory with such potency that I could live a thousand lifetimes without forgetting it. Why I witnessed such a thing is beyond me. I'm positive it wasn't a hallucination but I have no way of explaining or even describing what I saw—even with my vast vocabulary. In fact, I have yet to fully process the experience and continue climbing after considering the answer.

"This isn't the time, Hannibal. Find me an exit or at the very least, a suitable relay area. The static interference is annoying."

I listen to the pause following Hannibal's static filled crosscom. I'm concerned about his line of questioning even though it's well within his nature to ask such questions.

"Affirmative, Commander."

I'm assuming Hannibal is going to bring this up again. Maybe his timing will be better on the next occasion. Either way, Hannibal's mental state no longer matters by the time I reach the summit.

"Guys, I found something!"

Remi's enthusiasm bursts through my crosscom. "What? Come on E, what in da Hell is it? Tell me! Come on!"

"I think I found a stop sign."

"Stop jerkin us around! Is that supposed to be a joke?"

"Seriously, I think I found a stop sign!" I touch the metallic octagon and smile. "I'm rubbing the surface right now. All but the most trace elements of red paint have faded but I can still see the word 'stop' on front of the sign."

"Are ya sure? What's da sign made of?"

"It looks like the base element is aluminum. I see two mounting holes fixed into a u-channeled steel signpost. Is this the real thing?"

Grey jumps on the frequency and says, "Flash it!"

I circle the signpost and record light-based footage with my eyelens. Grey quickly checks the specifications.

"It matches the prewar DOT and MUTCD regulations. That has to be the real thing! How could a stop sign exist in such good condition after two thousand years? I detect almost no signs of rust..."

"There's something odd about the atmosphere in this tunnel. I need to go deeper—"

"Wait," says Hannibal, "you should excavate that site first!"

"I'm not an archaeologist!"

"Come on E, you need to slow down!"

"No, I need to see what's ahead! We're looking for species-5478, not human artifacts!"

The cave expands as if remnants of a road linger ahead. I leap across rocks until the cave's hollowed interior reveals something puzzling.

The Scuff Marks of History

CHAPTER 11

"Whoa… guys, you've got to see this!"

"What?" Remi wonders excitedly, "What in da Hell do you see? What's with da suspense, Chipmunk? For da love of God tell us!"

I send a live feed of the glowing blue curtain hanging in front of me. The transparent film seals the cave from top to bottom and emits some kind of the electromagnetic aura that stimulates my synthetic senses.

I hold up an open hand and observe blue light diffusing through my environmental suit and my CP's fleshy cybernetics. The glow has unique properties. Instead of highlighting my skin from the outside in, the blue film appears to spawn light from within my body—as if it's is some kind of X-ray machine. I throw caution to the wind and reach out with my left hand. The action generates a universal gasp from my team as they watch. I press my gloved palm against this strange substance and it slips through effortlessly.

Remi asks, "How could ya just… touch it like that? Ya got more balls than a pool table!"

Instead of rebuking me Grey asks, "What does

it feel like?"

"It's tingly, unobtrusive, and soft as water but charged like an electrical current. I think this film could be a part of something mechanical. It's extending my sensor's range somehow. My scanning ability has increased a hundredfold and I'm detecting a large cavern directly ahead."

"You need backup," Hannibal advises. "I think one of us should accompany you. We found an alternative route into that tunnel system."

"Agreed. Get down here, ASAP."

"I'll be there before you know it."

Anxiousness riddles Grey's voice. "Hey Major, maybe I should come too. I can help analyze your findings."

Grey's cognitive prowess is a great asset but I'm not sure what's down here and feel more comfortable with Hannibal's combative expertise.

"Negative. I want you to stay aboveground with Remi and monitor our progress. This area looks unstable and those incoming aftershocks might cause a cave-in."

I return to a point near the tunnel's entrance and wait as Hannibal uses a laser to drill through the stone barring his channel from my own. We immediately head back to the blue film once he's through. Excitement fills me but Hannibal seems unusually calm. Once we reach the translucent barrier, he takes his time analyzing the area but learns nothing about the film's properties. It consists of unknown elements that further enhance the curtain's mysterious origins.

I point to the film. "We should cross over."

Hannibal turns his entire metallic body towards me. "Consider this carefully. We have no idea what that film consists of, where it comes from, or what effect it might have on our CPs."

"It didn't do anything bad to my hand."

"You don't know that. The film could have some long term effect similar to radiation poisoning."

"Stay behind if you like but I need to know what's further ahead. Half our team is aboveground. If anything happens, they have orders to go back to the preemptive chamber and return with help. We have an obligation to investigate any clues that might lead to species-5478."

I step pass Hannibal and reach out with both hands. Blue light lathers my palms with energy. When I step through the film, my body feels an invigorating burst of power and I waver slightly as though awakening from a deep sleep.

Hannibal reaches out. "Are you alright?"

"That's strange…"

"What?"

"I think the film fully charged my battery."

"Do you detect any other changes?"

"Yes. That earthquake seems to have moved the film's border. It originally extended beyond the stop sign. Air on this side of the film has so many unfamiliar particles that my sensors are having difficulty sifting through them."

Hannibal grudgingly steps through the film and follows me into the cave's depths. Unlike my Type XX, his cybernetic prostheticalanatomy appears completely unaffected by the film.

We quickly discover a large chunk of concrete. It doesn't appear to originate from an actual street but *is* indicative of the sidewalks that usually bisect ancient avenues. The data I'm transferring aboveground seems to excite Grey the most.

"That place is amazing! All kinds of unknown and synthetic elements are down there! I can barely process it all—a heavy saturation of oxygen—various composites—prewar particles—what did you find? Is that some kind of a lair?"

"Do you see anything that can help me locate species-5478?"

"I'm not sure but I'll keep you posted."

Grey sifts through data while I venture deeper with Hannibal. There's no doubt that we're on to something—but what, exactly? My tenuous pace evolves into a nervous trot. I spent so much time familiarizing myself with my team's cybernetic bodies that I forget most of my first contact protocols.

What should I do if we actually encounter species-5478?

There are countless scenarios. For instance, what's the best method for determining a species' intelligence? How do I verify or even interpret its violent or peaceable tendencies? What forms of communication should I employ? Should I try speaking to it? What if my vocal vibrations harm species-5478? Would sign language be the best option? Hand movements might be threatening so what about projecting mathematical equations? Maybe giving it a gift would be the right answer.

Who can say?

Now, how would most people react if an exotic creature tried communicating with them? The outcome would probably depend on whom the creature chose to contact and the circumstances therein. Knowing the average human, there would probably be a vast number of reactions. Paranoia, fear, intrigue, and violence would be only a few of the possibilities. A person might act fearful when alone, but may act bold within a larger group. Is that what I should expect from species-5478? Could 5478 have similar personality traits to that of humans? Does it even have a personality? What kinds of groups does it form? How do they relate to one another?

Then there's my reaction to species-5478…

Would my nerves hold up? Could I avoid misinterpreting its actions? What if it ignores my presence or happens to be smarter than I am? What happens then? What role would I play in the presence of superior life? Do I act as a subordinate dog might, and assume the trusting and obedient role? Do I seek less peaceable conditions for coexistence? Am I even smart enough to know if species-5478 is the more intelligent being? Humans haven't interpreted the various forms of communication from lesser animals on Earth, so why assume that we can interpret the language or mode of communication, from something equal to, or greater than a human?

I honestly didn't think finding species-5478 was possible. In fact, looking for my brother's remains was the real reason I followed this route. It seemed like such a creature would take at least a few decades to locate… but discovering this tunnel has changed everything.

Our path narrows drastically once the overall slope dips downward. Centuries of rolling rocks and dust work as sandpaper smoothing out the path's rough spots. I consciously manage my center of gravity by adjusting MAJOR's weight to allow for sliding. It's easy to imagine the CP's engineers frowning on such behavior—over fears that I might break an ankle. Grey messages me once I reach the bottom.

"I did it."

"You found traces of organic life?"

"I wish! No, I'm talking about that hack you ordered."

I'd almost forgotten that I ordered Grey to do it. Finding the Nexus is paramount. I have to see the place where humanity integrated into the virtual world. It's the only way to know if we truly exist.

"Is our line secure?"

"Completely. Gravity boulders are interfering with the IVST's communications."

"What about the recorders?"

"I temporarily disabled them."

"Are they hiding anything from us?"

"I discovered a coded level in the VIA database that deals entirely with species-5478."

Remi cry outs through the crosscom, "What in da Hell are they hiding?"

"Hard to say. All I see are classified documents about its origins. E, are you sure we should be doing this?"

"Yes. We need to know what the VIA is hiding from us. Our lives might depend on it."

"Well… species-5478 doesn't appear to be from the Wasteland."

"What do you mean?"

"That footage we saw was not the first recording of species-5478."

I pause to consider the possibilities. "How long has the VIA known about 5478?"

"You're not going to believe this, but they have prewar footage of this thing!"

Remi is livid. "Those lying bastards! They violated da freedom of information act! What are they pulling?"

"I don't know, but there were sightings of species-5478 across the globe. It's unclear if these occurrences caused the war. The old government hoarded many secrets. They spied on their citizens, conducted covert operations in other nations, and even performed biological experiments on humans after openly declaring such acts unlawful. It was the ultimate form of controlled lawlessness, because for every law they created, counter injunctions allowed their negation. Nothing was truly sacred. People had rights until the government decided to take them away. This worked under the guise of freedom but only the government was truly free."

I furl a cybernetic brow. "Is there anything else?"

"Standard stuff. The VIA's former name was CIA, or Central Intelligence Agency. The group formed right after their assimilation into the virtual world. I have a member's list, special protocols, that sort of thing."

"Is there anyone on the list that we know?"

"No."

I continue strolling forward with a bit more attitude. "So they were working with the Institute of Virtual Science and Technology from the very beginning?"

"Yes."

Hannibal's anger begins radiating. "So a major government agency is hoarding prewar information from the public? This is a complete breach of our indivisic rights! This kind of crap ended the old world! What are we going to do, E?"

"Nothing, yet. If we break the story too early, we'll lose our chance to figure out what else the VIA is hiding. Labeling the Species Project as temporarily classified is just another lie. They have no intention on disclosing anything to the public. The VIA probably plans on erasing our memories once we return to the station. Make copies of those files and our experiences. Give both to Remi. Cover your tracks before moving to their next barrier."

"No problem, Major. Consider it done."

"E, is a nice enough nickname. Quit the lame argument."

I advance through the winding tunnel until the ground, walls, and ceiling expand into unnaturally smooth dimensions. The deliberate hand of craftsmanship reveals more of its presence with every step. My pace slows to emphasize the need for caution, but also to observe the construct of my surroundings. I redirect the power used to send my team their live feed and focus all of my sensory mechanisms into exploring this new region. Grey's instantaneous griping provokes me into transferring live feed duties to Hannibal.

These new walls are made of a concrete mixture that matches the standards used in the ancient world. They form a square corridor complete with holes in the ceiling meant to contain light fixtures. Strangely, the entire area seems free of major decay. After two thousand years, most things constructed from the ancient world should be nothing more than rubble.

The twenty first century has a reputation for creating provisional and shoddy products. My scanners also detect a minute increase in the electromagnetic energy saturating the air. It's plausible the blue film's power source is located somewhere ahead.

Remi asks, "Ehari, are ya fine? Why did ya cut yar feed? Grey keeps bitching about image quality."

"We're approaching something big, standby."

The corridor bends right before expanding to reveal something awesome. I stop just short of a jagged ledge overlooking a vast underground cavern. I fail to utter a word but Hannibal whispers my thoughts exactly.

"You are not going to believe this, but there is a lost city down here!"

Glass Box

CHAPTER 12

Remnants of an ancient metropolitan city lay sprawled before me like a lover awaiting my fondling curiosity. The paved highways circumventing the ruins interconnect with smaller roads at regular intervals. Some roads lead into the center of town while others connect to off ramps.

Unlike cities in the classic movies and shows, this city's perimeter contains larger buildings, whereas smaller ones fill its center. The coliseum of structures populates the entire cavern for miles in all directions. Each building contains honeycombed rooms with odd shapes and sizes. None of them appears suited for human habitation and favor storage over housing.

Architects in the virtual world are free of the physical world's restrictive natural laws. They design structures with fantastic shapes and sizes. Some even create buildings formed like flowers, abstract structures, or even moving animals. Here in the physical world, everything exhibits a distinct emphasis on structural stability. All skyscrapers within sight are rectangular and many have windows on all sides. Height seems to be the only variance for most. It's a depressing sight, especially when many of the smaller buildings follow a similar design. Supermarkets, factories, and malls favor each other while only the homes in residential areas provide some level of variance. Yet even there, many of the buildings exhibit similar layouts.

The electric film sheltering the ruins from Earth's climate is an enigma. Using advanced sensors produces no results, either. The luminescent curtain of bluish light appears to act as a barrier against the environment's exterior gases, rocks, and sediments. I use the dome-shaped film to gauge the ruin's radius and calculate two hundred square miles of area awaiting exploration. There seems no need to plan a destination as all focus revolves around a glowing spire of light in the ruin's center. I feel as though I'm inside a gigantic snow globe.

Hannibal lowers his shoulders when cooling fluid compresses within his arms. It appears as if he's sagging them with disbelief.

"This discovery is going to make us famous."

Remi marvels through the crosscom, "Are ya kidding me? That's da greatest find of our generation! Researches will need decades to investigate all of that crap! It's gonna be a geek-fest! Grey is probably going to be their guest of honor."

Grey asks, "What city do you think it could be?"

I shrug, "Your guess is as good as mine. This place is unlike any city that I've ever researched. I have nothing to compare it with."

How can a city like this exist? My recordings of the temperature indicate the air is compatible with prewar life. I boldly unlatch the seal on my environmental collar and allow the attached helmet to fold in-between my shoulder blades like the hood of a sweater.

Cold air hugs my face, and I gasp from the unexpected sensation. It's strange… considering the blazing global temperatures beyond the film. Not a single gust of wind or even a slight breeze moves about, though. I activate my nasal receptors and inhale a flavorful burst of scents. A few adjustments to my neural processor separate the mixture into individual aromas and odors. I smell concrete, granite, and asphalt for the first time. The experience gives me an instant head rush.

"So," Grey asks while monitoring the scene through Hannibal's feed, "what does it feel like to smell physical scents? Is it similar to the virtual world?"

I shake my head. "This is amazing! My head is spinning, like I'm high!" I release a burst of uncontrollable laughter as my body flutters from the momentary surge of euphoria. "I feel more aware when inhaling scented air. It's nothing like the virtual world! This level of sensory perception adds a completely new dimension to life!" Once my nerves steady, I point to the spiraling funnel of blue light sprouting from the city's center. "I want to know what that is."

Grey says, "It appears to be the dome's power source."

"Really? I thought it was a decorative light."

"You're the one who asked a stupid question."

"What does that blue, bioluminescent, spiraling film of light consist of? Where does it come from? What properties does it consist of? Should I be more specific? Maybe you want me to draw up a lesson plan detailing how to form simple conclusions using common sense?"

"Well then, you should be the first person tested, considering how common sense should have told you not to go cliff diving during a scheduled earthquake."

Grey is really getting on my nerves. Maybe he's pissed that I brought Hannibal instead of him.

I calmly say, "Listen genius, if that spire of light deactivates, the earth will probably crash down on top of us. Use all of that information we're sending you to find out what's powering the spire. That might lead us to species-5478. I'm sure someone with your limitless stockpiles of knowledge can figure that out."

Remi asks, "What are ya planning?"

"Can you establish a connection with Mother Nature?"

"Nah, there's still too much interference."

"Map the above land and document the exact location of these ruins. When you finish, return to base with Grey and report this discovery. Our presence might trigger some kind of collapse. We need to alert the VIA of this location. Come back with battery fluid and some charge packs. We'll be able to take our time when you return."

Grey sends another crosscom message. "What about cracking the VIA database? Is that assignment still on?"

"Absolutely. Let me know the moment you find something."

"Affirmative. Anything else?"

"Start looking for information about where the Nexus is located."

I hear a drawn out pause before receiving any feedback from Grey. "You mean, the virtual world's Nexus?"

"Is there another one?"

"No but… will the VIA even have information about the Nexus' location? That's the most highly classified intelligence out there. I'll probably have to reconnect to the virtual world to learn anything. Admin level intelligence will probably not be in the VIA database."

"We currently have access to the most advanced technology available. If we're going to crack their firewalls, then this is the time to do it."

"But, why do you want to find the Nexus?"

"I have a feeling these ruins have something to do with our virtual world. Besides, I want to see the place humanity calls home. Don't you?"

Grey clears static from his voice. "But if the

VIA discovers we hacked government barriers and found the Nexus, they'll delete us. Are you absolutely sure you want me to do this?"

"The faces we see in the media can't be the true administrators. I want to know who's running the Nexus. And don't forget, that they've been lying to us about species-5478. We have an indivisic right to the truth. All we need to do is alert the public of any important findings and they won't be able to delete us. If you're not up to this, quit the team, and find something safer. Maybe holographic knitting will suit you."

"Maybe I can stitch you a gag."

I feel like strangling Grey right now. "Do we have a problem?"

"No… I'm on it."

I wait for Remi and Grey to confirm their mission priorities before following Hannibal into the ruins. As usual, he's protective over my wellbeing and continually goes out of his way to stay ahead of me as we descend into the streets.

"So E, any guess as to what we'll find down here?"

"No, but this place must be species-5478's point of origin. Tracking a single entity in an environment like this is going to be challenging. The area is massive. There may even be multiple ways inside. But maybe we'll run into more of its kind."

Hannibal raises his metallic finger and points

towards the spire of light. "Where do you think it's coming from?"

"I have no idea. We need to get closer to find out. Keep your head on a swivel."

"I still can't believe we stumbled into this place."

"Stay focused. I feel the same way but don't let that pillar of light distract you. Look for threats in the environment."

We progress slower than expected. For some reason, time doesn't elapse steadily, as in the Nexus. My physical anxiety extends the passage of time and space, making the ruins appear larger than their actual measurements. Gathering preliminary information about the various artifacts along our path consumes a lot of time. Most objects are of human origin and seems to stem from the twenty-first century. Even though the city appears empty, its buildings are more than capable of hiding any number of things. Our scanners find no living organisms or even one power source other than the blue spire. What could sterilize all life with such efficiency?

Instead of restricting our journey to the streets, I lead Hannibal through various buildings in search of life. Fish tanks are empty. There are no rat, cat, or dog carcasses anywhere. In fact, we discover no roaches, mosquitoes, flies, or even a single germ within the entire span of our two-day hike. I'm also worried about Remi and Grey. They should have reported back by now.

Hannibal's voice is ripe with bafflement. "This is a little creepy, E."

"I agree."

After finding these ruins, I was sure that we'd discover a wealth of biological data. Instead, we have yet to locate a single microbial sample.

Hannibal takes the lead when I pause to study the bust of an Egyptian queen who seems to share a variation of our texture disease.

I fondle the bust and ask, "Do you think prewar movies lied about life in the physical world?"

"What do you mean?"

"You know, about the rat infested sewers and apartments. Is it possible those tales were just figments of a writer's imagination?"

Hannibal mulls the query. "What about the documentaries?"

"They could be faked, right?"

"I suppose," he shrugs. "I always found it a bit odd that people would willingly live in a house filled with roaches. It just never seemed feasible. Do you really think we've been lied to about ancient history?"

"I don't know. It's possible we entered a dead zone. Maybe there was some kind of biological weapon released here during the final days of the war."

"That would explain the absence of microbial life. But wouldn't there be traces of a toxin in the air or soil?"

"Maybe."

We stroll through a remarkably clean alley and emerge on a four-lane street parallel to the blue spire of light. Its mysterious power source remains hidden behind a collapsed skyscraper where a dull electric buzz echoes from beyond the building's debris.

Earth is such a volatile place! Who can fathom any physical city existing in such a world? Why don't earthquakes affect this place? Does the blue dome of light protect the ruins from vibrations? Nearly all forms of human technology fail to operate for any redeemable amount of time when outside. The Nexus functions only because engineers buried it deep within Earth's crust.

Hannibal pauses by a rusty fire hydrant and recons the area while I proceed to the spire. "Wait here. Just because our sensors haven't detected any life doesn't mean there isn't anything lurking about."

Hannibal doesn't argue with me and focuses on surveillance. "Are we keeping an open line?"

"Yes, but keep all communication restricted to emergency broadcasts. Our crosscoms might not be secure."

"Affirmative. Be careful, and good luck."

A stealthy insertion seems appropriate given the circumstances. Abandoned cars scattered throughout the main street become my primary cover. After darting around a variety of vehicles, I slip through a massive hole in the side of a pastry shop, and sneak to the opposite end of the building where something awaits.

Collapsing Inward: 1ˢᵗ Half

CHAPTER 13

A solitary onyx pyramid appears to be the blue spire's energy source. The structure is comparable in size to a large conical tent with a surface remarkably free of dust. It sits in the center of the skyscraper's rear parking lot and appears embedded into the ground. Oddly, I see no supporting equipment, signs, or any other indicator of the pyramid's purpose. It seems out of place compared to everything else.

"Hanni, are you seeing this?"

"Yes," he answers without hesitation. "Your video feed and sensor results are coming in clearly."

"What do you make of it?"

"Pyramids of that design were customary in ancient Egypt, but not really anywhere else. It looks out of place sitting there by itself."

"I was just thinking the same thing. How does it generate power?"

"Grey might know that answer. I have no idea."

I try sending another message to Grey and Remi but a magnetic storm aboveground is interfering with communications.

"I can't reach him. Can you?"

"Negative."

"Get over here and be careful. This pyramid makes me uneasy."

"Affirmative."

My sensors indicate the spire of light is actually a residual effect from an invisible energy stream ascending out of the pyramid. The stream refracts prewar particles lingering in the air, giving the spire its colorful blue hue. It's an enigmatic force without a classification. I find no thermal, chemical, electric, radiant, nuclear, magnetic, temporal, sound, mechanical, luminous, or mass based energy signatures.

The entire pyramid looks dark and featureless, like the portrait of a shadow. It's hard—if not impossible—to determine its composition exclusively through observations. Leaving the pyramid alone seems to be the only option, though. Tinkering with something like this is almost certainly a bad idea. Hannibal tries scanning the structure once he reaches me. I can tell from his agitated grunts that his efforts are producing no results.

"I can't find any relevant references for this thing in our database. Primary matches relate to ancient Egyptian burial and ceremonial structures."

I wonder, "Is there any connection between this pyramid and those made by ancient Egyptians?"

Hannibal flashes the area before answering. "I'm not sure. Give me a few minutes and I'll see if I can find a link."

I cautiously ease out of hiding to examine all sides of the pyramid. Hannibal watches me slowly circle the structure and while easing closer, my proximity inadvertently activates something within the pyramid.

"Ehari!"

Hannibal reaches for me as the pyramid emits an ominous humming sound. I try stepping back, but a triangular shadow envelopes my entire body, freezing me in place. Everything vanishes seconds later… and I'm alone.

Collapsing Inward: 2nd Half

CHAPTER 14

The terrorizing fear of death eclipses my other emotions but after a fleeting moment of disorientation, I focus on a vast expanse that I can neither see, nor perceive audibly. This vacuum is spatially palpable and extends in all directions. The enormity of space tugs lightly against me, suspending my body with some unseen force. What truly amazes is the effect this place has on my mind.

My consciousness actually precedes the present moment. I realize what my next action will be seconds before doing it. Is this a form of time travel? This… continual state of déjà vu is unnerving. I know that I won't see my hand before lifting it, and that I won't find anything when turning around to search the darkness. I even know beforehand, that I'll ponder whether I'm inside the pyramid, and that I'll be unable to reach a conclusion.

Then, a voice speaks to me…

"E… E, can you hear me?"

Light pours into my fluttering eyes. I squint at Hannibal's hulking body hovering over me.

"You're awake! Thank God!" When I try to sit up, Hannibal coaxes me in his most relaxing tone. "Relax. Don't try to move yet."

"What happened?"

"You activated the pyramid somehow. It blasted you with some sort of triangular wave. Do you remember anything?"

"My memories are fuzzy." I turn and examine the unfamiliar surroundings. Hannibal acknowledges my bewilderment.

"We're in the IVST facility. I had to carry you back to our chamber. You've been unconscious for a week."

I gasp, "A whole week?" Hannibal steps back as I reposition to the edge of his repair cylinder. Grey and Remi's cybernetic prostheticalanatomies are standing quietly in their hubs. "What happened to *them*?"

"They're in the virtual world."

"Why?"

"Something terrible happened."

"What?"

Hannibal activates a crystal monitor and displays news footage from one of Mandy Alyssum's recent broadcasts.

"There have been continuous bombings, riots, rivaling factions… society is falling apart." He then displays a diagram of the Nexus on another monitor. "Someone found a way to hack and merge different Realms with a new virus. The results have been catastrophic."

My lips parse. "Merging different Realms? How is that possible?"

"Your guess, is as good as mine."

"Hacking the Nexus or its Realms is theoretically impossible. If someone actually succeeded, the outcome will be… dear God… most Realms contain unique environmental variables that oppose one another. Combining conflicting atmospheric programs will eventually collapse the entire Nexus!"

Hannibal nods while highlighting the infected Realms on the Nexus diagram. "Luckily, most Realms haven't been merged, due to isolation. Give it some time though, and I'm sure they'll find a way to infect all of them."

"But who's capable of hacking Realms?" I realize the answer before finishing the question, and when I peer into Hannibal's mechanical eyes, he confirms my knowing glare with a slow nod.

"Scarlet was the first person I thought of, too."

"She'd need a lot of help to pull off a feat like this. Her new team must be involved."

"The Bloody Membranes? One of the reasons Remi and Grey returned to the virtual world, was to help the VIA stop them."

"And the other?"

"They wanted to find their families."

"Are they safe?"

"I don't know. The link went down seventy two hours ago."

"Why would Scarlet do it?"

Hannibal allows his shoulders to sag and stirs the vague sound of decompressing fluid. "She said things."

"What things?"

"Scarlet tried to get Remi and I to leave when you booted her from Mandible 9."

"Bull!"

"It's true."

"And you didn't tell me?"

"We thought it was pointless. There's so much bad blood between the two of you. Especially after that thing with Seti…"

I stand up and stomp around Hannibal. "I don't believe you didn't tell me she tried recruiting you! That bitch wanted to assume command of the team that I started! Now you're telling me she tried to strip members away after I kicked her out!"

"This is why we didn't say anything. You would have carried an eternal grudge. We know how much Mandible 9 means to you."

I can literally feel my face flush with rage. "Scarlet had reasons. What are they?"

Hannibal tries approaching but I back away from him. Only then does he grudgingly admit her motives.

"She mentioned Oliver Milke's underground movement and the coming apocalypse. Apparently, Oliver saw the coming of Christ in a vision. He believes the virtual world is obsolete and needs purging in order for those within to achieve salvation. I'm not sure if Scarlet wanted to join Oliver or stop him. She never made her intentions clear."

My mind reels with disbelief and I step away to contemplate the sheer insanity of it all. Is it possible a lunatic like Oliver Milkes can see Christ? I saw God… and my vision was no virtual glitch or well-crafted virus, either. *I saw God!* Did Milkes actually see Christ? Is this really happening? Am I truly alive or even awake right now? Could this be a nightmare?

Supposedly, the device containing our virtual world mimics the physical shape of Earth, but the tree-shaped Nexus within houses various Realms on its leafy branches. To me, it resembles the neural network of the human brain. Men like Oliver Milkes created their own planes of existence as a means of detaching from the main branch of humanity. I always believed this practice to be lunacy, especially when people view such actions as salvation. This is why past civilizations went to war. Besides… why does one religion feel they have to dominate the entire Nexus?

"I can't leave them in there."

Hannibal stammers, "You can't be thinking of going back! There should be at least two people manning this station! Besides, the virtual world might collapse on itself! I don't want to be left alone!"

"I need to speak with Mother Nature."

"How? We lost our link to the VBI and IVST."

"Is there any other way to open some kind of communication with them?"

Hannibal shakes his head. "I don't think so. I've tried everything but without a link there's nothing we can do from here."

"Well then… we only have one option left. I'm going back in to find out why the link is down."

"That's too risky!"

"Prepare the womb for my CP. We don't have any other choice."

"Are you sure?"

"Don't worry. I'll fix the link and bring Remi and Grey back. You guys are the only family I know. We don't have anything if we don't have each other."

Deus Ex

CHAPTER 15

Ablinding light envelops me as I await my transfer into the virtual world. Electrical power surges through my body like a raging fire. The unbearable pain eventually subsides as I awaken inside the same decompression chamber that I departed from; fixed onto the IVST's particle bed. My mind seems to have successfully transferred back into its original network of cranial and vascular threads and all within a matter of seconds.

Clusters of rotating nozzles lining the chamber's ceiling begin their descent while gradually releasing a photonic mist. These wispy particles of light synchronize with my skeletal frame before releasing skin textures from the chamber's underside. Dandelion-shaped flakes drift down like snow and accumulate into a thin sheen across my entire skeletal frame. The particles give my body a golden aura that dampens all light from the room's monitors. This particular stage of the process should reassemble my genetic meshing and complete the return trip.

My transition into the Nexus is not the same mire of listless bewilderment that framed my departure. I've maintained a clear mind and focused thoughts. Regressing to a photonic form of existence is easier than upgrading, apparently. Yet, although a smooth transfer, I arrive in the midst of a great upheaval.

"Di! You came back! We need your help," says Mother Nature.

I can barely hear Mother Nature's panicked voice above the distraught researchers. I push up, look around, and notice red warning lights gleaming throughout the room. My face almost certainly expresses how dazed I am.

"What's happening?"

Mother Nature runs to my side. "We are under attack!"

"By who?"

"The Calling is hacking into our facility!"

I exit the chamber after downloading a tank top with matching shorts and follow Mother Nature to the control room. Sensationally moving in my photonic body is like downgrading from a motorcycle to a scooter. All of my senses feel dull now that I've refused them with my neural link.

Cognition-wise the reverse is true. It's easier to focus on multiple instances while in a virtual state. Scientists, engineers, and programmers rush about in all directions. My three months of practical training affords me the ability to know what each person is doing, and why. I still have no idea what Mother Nature's real name happens to be, but the frenetic brunette wastes no time handing me something.

"This is an initiator for the emergency antiviral security system! Use it to stabilize the relay before the terrorists reach us!"

She pushes the tube-shaped cartridge into my hands—giving it to me with more force than I accept it. What makes Mother Nature think I'm the one to do whatever she needs? God didn't bless me with a quick and decisive mind even though my aura of leadership alludes otherwise. As such, I protest her demands.

"Hold on, I just returned! Why are you asking me to do this?"

"You are the only one here with any combat experience! The guards left to defend the Alpha section of the building. None of them returned! The terrorists probably deleted them!"

"Probably? What does this have to do with me?"

"Anyone who leaves to patch the relay will face hostiles along the way!"

"*The Suffering* was only a game! I don't have any real combat experience!"

"You are still the most qualified person here!" Mother argues, "This is not a game, Di!"

"But I don—"

"There is no time for delays," she insists. "We need you! The Calling is trying to destroy our decompression chambers! If their virus reaches this room the Species Project and our lives will be over! I need all of my people here working on decontamination protocols! Do you understand?

Am I getting through to you? Help us right now or die! All of us!"

Her anxiety is infectious. Imminent deletion is only half of the reason why Mother's commands are worth following. To me, physical Earth is my true home… and I'll do anything to return.

"Fine but… I need a weapon!"

When Mother nods to one of her colleagues, the scientist retrieves a rifle from a sealed storage locker. I can hardly believe this fool actually hands it to me! Seriously… it's a gun! Is he crazy? What era is this supposed to be, the ancient Wild West? Who in their right mind uses guns nowadays? Dear Lord… a gun? Really? Anyway… this *gun*, is nearly identical to the one that I used while playing *The Suffering*. I guess that accounts for something but I still complain.

"Are you serious? Do you really expect me to use this? A mechanical based rifle is old school tech! I could drop it! What am I supposed to do with this thing? Reminisce?"

Mother Nature taps her brow as she checks parameters on one of her holographic displays. "It is a prototype that uses 40 caliber density rounds."

"Prototype my ass! I need a photonic chain or compound bracelets! Anything but this!"

"The Calling disabled our energy cells! Older programs are the only things that will work! Just take the damn gun and leave before we die!"

Mother's seminal aggravation focuses my

attention and I grasp the weapon with both hands. The rifle fits into the cuff of my shoulder quite well, despite its archaic design.

"Is this an AR-98?"

Mother focuses on the holopad in her hand and inputs a flurry of commands. "No, that is an AR-S99. The weapon was upgraded with your post-game interview suggestions."

It's a major upgrade, considering the technology involved. Density rounds rip into virtual meshing like a buzz saw tearing through flesh.

"Where do I need to go?"

Mother Nature shrugs, "We have not figured that out, actually…"

I practically throw the rifle into the air out of frustration. "What does that mean? You give me an old-ass weapon with nowhere to use it! This is crazy!"

Mother hands me a tracking application. I scan the app with a custom antiviral mod before downloading the program to my neural link.

"Use that tracking app to find the relay," she instructs while directing traffic. "The Calling infected our building's mainframe with a unique virus that sealed everyone inside of this facility. This virus even alters architecture by randomly changing the layout of hallways. Drastic changes signify the relay is nearby. Our firewalls on this end of the facility will collapse if you fail to stabilize the relay in time. The entire building will compress if that happens."

"Like a collapsing building in the physical world?"

Mother confirms my simile with a jerky nod. "The virus will ultimately crush everyone into deletion if you fail to use that initiator in time. All you have to do, is plug it into the relay."

I moan at the prospect of photonic paralysis. "How much time do we have?"

"Maybe… twenty minutes."

Mother activates a hovering holoscreen and allows it to expand between us. She attends to a dizzying number of issues with it. The magnitude of her work is impressively grand.

"I found the guards! They appear to be holding the main incursion force at bay, but there seems to be a terrorist support team en route to their location! We will try to delay them, but time is running out!"

I charge the rifle's clip, tuck the initiator into one of my memory pockets, and then dash to the rear exit. "Don't worry! Consider the relay patched! Just hold out until then!"

A scientists unseals the room's portal and I slip out with my rifle poised to fire. Blood red warning lights fill both ends of the hallway. I see no errors yet, but the virus can be anywhere, so I move steadily while searching for environmental irregularities. Activating Mother Nature's tracking app forms a three-dimensional compass in the upper right corner of my neural lens. According to its triangular needle, the relay's location is approximately nine hundred cubes below me, on the southwest corner of the facility. I wonder about the Nexus while heading there.

My once unspoiled habitat is now a perversion of virtuality. I feel distressed by the photonic plane's lack of substance. My trip into physicality was brief but I already miss that uncanny sense of touch and the way aromas and odors—both pleasant and pleasantly foul—aroused my sensory receptors. Not to mention those tingly jolts of taste that cascaded through my tongue and even the claustrophobic grasp of gravity… dear God! I long for it all now! I feel so bare and handicapped without physical sensations! The virtual plane is now a lucid nightmare suffocating my consciousness. Experiencing life with superior senses was so wonderful, but returning to the anesthetic reality of the Nexus makes me feel drugged and trapped in a half-life that handicaps my senses with the same technology meant to save me from the ravages of physical peril.

Even if the Nexus remained virus-free in its original solid state, there's no comparing it to Earth. Life in the desolate, ravaged lands of physicality is more valuable than a half-life in pristine virtual gardens. I now understand more than ever what humankind lost through the ravages of war.

I use a nearby projection step to accelerate to the

stairport. The port's malfunctioning hub will only allow sequential transport to awaiting landings. I make four consecutive descents before black cracks begin forming in the walls. The Calling's malicious program is rooting itself into the architecture and changes to the stairport's design disrupt my ability to project any further.

Ehari: Damn… the virus found me!

Mother Nature: Stay calm. We will assist you.

I grab a guardrail as the walls melt like warm ice cream. The rectangular stairport slowly adopts a cylindrical shape while gaps appear at irregular intervals along the emergency stairs. I nearly panic when the virus creates a ceiling that it uses to seal me inside—what now appears to be—a bottomless well. Mother's programmers assist with an antiviral patch that manifests as dripping luminescent paint. Once their concoction seeps into the viral cracks, the stairs reform into a complete spiral. However, some sections of the wall continue circling about like rings and due to the hub's program corruption, the projection steps refuse to operate.

"You're a nasty virus, aren't you?" I shout into the abyss, "Running sucks!"

The hacker manipulating this aggressive virus chuckles so loudly that I hear his voice transiting through the walls. I hate cowardly taunts but at least I succeeded in goading this creep into revealing his proximity. He must be close in order to send messages through the architecture… but where could the coward be?

"Fine, I'll run!" I add with an erect middle finger, "By the way, your hacks are lame!"

I race down the steps after regaining my footing but the entire stairwell starts rumbling as though agitated by my taunts. The ceiling changes shape as the hacker uses his virus to mutate its surface into perilous impediments. Some sections transform into stalactites that fall each time the stairwell quakes. Chunks of stone dislodge from the wall and morph into dangerous objects. Blades, maces, and spikes are just a few of the weapons that reach out from the rotating rings along the wall. I barely avoid impalement, decapitation, and evisceration before dashing to the lower landing—nearly stumbling into the abyss after leaning on a broken guardrail.

I sling my AR-S99 and then scurry down the next flight of stairs. The hacker regains partial control of the steps and breaks the stairway segment directly ahead of me. I jump over the gap and barely grab an unbroken step on the far side.

Unlike the enemy hacker, I experienced real gravity in the physical world. Virtualized gravity acts like a child pulling on my legs for attention. The claustrophobic force that I endured on Earth is far worst. That suffocating monster might have pulled me into the stairwell's depths screaming for my life, but I shrug away this lesser version of gravity and effortlessly pull myself onto the stairs.

So many things about the virtual world feel

juvenile now. These walls disintegrate in a very blocky and mechanical manner, for instance. And the Nexus' failure to create a flowing stream of sensational photons for wind or gravity is more noticeable. Everything seems reduced to ones and zeros in this environment, resulting in an inferior rendition of the physical world, which gestates noticeable flaws.

I evade the next set of obstacles and stir a raging howl from the well's depths. Something inside the abyss is upset with my progress and climbs through the darkness towards me. I send a neural message to Mother Nature.

Ehari: Mother, what is that?

She fails to respond so I charge my rifle and fire blindly into the stairwell's bowls. There's no way of telling if my experimental weapon will function as intended but the rifle's red density rounds descend deep into the abyss and strike something enormous. My heartpulse nearly stops when the impacting projectiles barely illuminate a snakelike creature with demonic facial features.

The oblong rounds tear through its scaly body with such force that the beast alters course at the last second and retreats into the corridor directly beneath me. I follow its howls to the next landing only to find a trail of sparkling numerical data—evidence of a painful wound.

My tracking icon suddenly beeps when it triangulates the relay's new location, which is now somewhere along this particular level. I recharge my rifle before entering the corridor and dash towards the far end. Footsteps echo from beyond the upcoming corner. The approaching men could be from the terrorist support group that Mother spoke of, so I hide inside a nearby alcove right before they enter the hallway flinging streams of blue fire from their photonic chains.

These men are definitely from Oliver Milke's infamous hit squad! The assassins even use motion detectors to pinpoint my exact location and pin me inside of the alcove with suppressive fire. Hiding will do no good and the tenfold increase in danger gives me a dizzying head rush.

The first one yells, "Don't let her get any further!"

"Kill the infidel," another shouts with cultist delight.

Each of their streams strikes closer than the last. My hands jitter from the very real possibility of deletion. I can barely handle my own rifle but… the physical world imbued a savage understanding of true life within me—something these terrorists lack. Guttural fear of this magnitude isn't unattainable in the virtual world because the nerve it manifests only stems from physical fear.

I spray the hallway with blind fire before boldly leaning into the corridor with my rifle's stock pressed into my shoulder. The first terrorist in my line of sight screams when my density rounds tear through his neural brain and trigger a synaptic explosion. An anti-photonic vortex forms over the victim's shattered body. The funneling force attracts every neutrally charged photon within a twenty-cube radius towards its swirling core. I struggle against the tumultuous force and use the alcove to brace myself.

Everything inside the affected area warps inward as the vortex pulls the remaining men into its core. Their orbiting bodies become easy targets. I charge the rifle's launcher and eject a single density grenade at the floating terrorists. The radiant egg detonates within the group— splattering the corridor with meshing and synaptic data. I run through the carnage with a renewed sense of verve after the vortex finally collapses. Even my stomach cache holds when I stomp on their glittering remains. Am I now immune to virtual gore? Such a grisly sensation would have sickened my former self.

I follow Mother's tracking icon around the corner and halt when the corridor's dimensions undergo a drastic change.

The walls and ceiling expand dramatically—as though blown apart by an explosion—and form an Olympic sized stadium. An assortment of trees pops up from the grassy soil with their branches flapping like umbrella canopies.

The soil churns from the tunneling trees as if they were whack-a-moles. Before I make any progress, one of them tries impaling me when it spins out of the soil. I leap away from it but the tree continues spinning as its branches extend outward. The metallic leaves eventually detach from their stems when the centrifugal force maximizes, and they whiz through the air like throwing darts.

Mother Nature counters with anti-viral boulders that she drops from the ceiling. They smash some of the rising trees back into the ground and provide much needed cover.

Mother Nature: Our boulders pose no threat to you. We patched your neural signature!

I trust the VIA's patch, catch one of the boulders, and then shield myself with it when two palm trees spin out of the ground twenty-cubes away. Once the leafy blades detach from their stems and clang against the stone, I toss the boulder at another rising pair of trees and shatter them before their leaves detach. After crossing the stadium's halfway marker an entire blockade of pines ascends before me. Mother Nature counters by dropping a circle of boulders around my position.

Ehari: This is crazy! How am I supposed to make it through a forest of spinning, razor-leafed trees!

Mother Nature: The enemy hacker is using components of this facility to create those obstacles. There are finite amounts he can program from the data blocks used to construct that particular area.

Ehari: Drop some boulders directly on me!

The hacker tries expelling me from the circle of boulders by puncturing the ground directly beneath my feet with another tree, but Mother Nature smashes it with a boulder when I scurry temporarily out of hiding. Once my position is refortified, Mother drops a steady stream of boulders directly onto me.

I jump straight up and smack four of the falling boulders with an open palm—volleying them at the defensive line of pine trees blocking my path. Three of the boulders smash directly into their intended targets. The fourth bounces about and collides with three more. I make sure not to jump higher than the boulders surrounding me; least I lose my head to the maelstrom of pine needles swarming about like thronging files.

Mother Nature: Good job Di! Keep it up! A path is forming!

I continue volleying boulders until the trees stop rising and even toss a few like basketballs, over my barricade. When Mother Nature gives the signal, I roll the boulders used to fortify my position at the final set of trees blocking my path, and knock them down as if they were bowling pins. All remaining trees are harmless husks so I run across the stadium and through the exit.

Tremors cascading from the next corridor cause the walls to distort. I scream out, "Stop hiding, coward! Face me!"

Mother Nature: Di, stand still for a moment.

Ehari: Why?

Mother Nature: The virus is mutating faster than expected. We have no way of stopping it from modifying the architecture in your area, but protective measures are in place.

Ehari: What protective measures?

Mother Nature: We stabilized your center of gravity.

Ehari: Why?

Mother Nature: We are detecting changes in the floor's meshing.

The entire ceiling splits in half like an opening package. Both walls separate and collapse around the floor, which in turn, morphs into a cylindrical column. Darkness encroaches on the expanse of widening space the room once filled. A purple mist descends from the dark. It hovers above me like a toxic cloud swirling with phantasmal shapes. Below, lurks a sea of cubed bubbles. Churning algorithmic stews of this sort decompose virtual matter like flesh in acid. Mother Nature's antiviral countermeasures magnetize my body to the cylindrical floor's core. This prevents me from slipping into the broth of erasable data.

My tracking icon displays the relay's decreasing proximity. Only then do I realize the hacker possesses it.

Wormy code filaments drift about like algae caught in a rip tide. Their partially deflated shapes indicate a moderate level of viral corruption. The building will fully compress if the wavy filaments mature into erect rods.

Bladed pendulums rise from underneath the walkway when the hacker tweaks his virus. They swing about the floor's columnar axis from both directions. Each time I successfully dodge one of the pendulums another one swings into view. I rely heavily on my acrobatic skills because some of the pendulums move so fast that I have to flip, roll, and leap in order to evade their sharpened edges. These unimpressive traps are nothing compared to the pitfalls of God's physical world. Although a master hacker, my adversary lacks the murderous or sadistic talents required to incur my demise.

The hacker finally emerges from the mist in the form of a flying dragon when his pendulums fail to stop me. The enormous beast is sixty-cubes long and resembles a gigantic prehistoric reptile. It has blood red eyes, two spiralling horns, jagged teeth the length of my body, and a long snaking neck attached to a scaly torso.

This creature is the same red beast that climbed out of the well. I recognize the mythical monstrosity from emblems used by Scarlet's team of Bloody Membranes. The hacker is trying to form some level of symbolism by using this abomination as his avatar. I find such connotations contrived but I do admit... the creature is intimidating!

It emerges from the corner of my right eye—barely visible above the purple haze. The dragon circles about like a hawk eying its prey before swooping down when the pendulums detach and fall into the bubbling cubes.

I monitor the creature's approach and leap to the floor when the dragon's talons reach out. They brush against my back as I slide across the walkway on my belly. It disappears into the darkness and circles me as I rise with my rifle's grenade launcher primed.

The dragon needles the darkness and randomly weaves into and out of sight as it circles the walkway. My heartpulse drums when the monstrous creature begins howling. I can't hear the slow flap of its wings anymore and pivot in nervous circles as the dragon's deafening roars saturate the atmosphere. The game of hide and seek ends when I look up and spot the creature descending from above. When the dragon swoops down I fire a density grenade at its face and barely miss its gaping mouth when the beast veers out of the projectile's path. It flies below the walkway and glides above the bubbling sea of anti-algorithms before vanishing into the darkness.

Ehari: I need help capturing the hacker!

Mother Nature: Forget the hacker! You have to patch the relay the before time runs out!

Ehari: The hacker is carrying the relay!

Mother Nature: Then kill him!

Ehari: How?

Mother Nature: Destroy the hacker's wings and force him to crash into the bubbles!

Ehari: Will that work?

Mother Nature: Every program in this facility remains linked to default spacial properties. If you destroy the hacker's wings, he *will* fall.

Ehari: I need help tracking him! The hacker

keeps disappearing into the shadows!

Mother Nature: Use the tracking app!

Ehari: The darkness scrambles the app's signal! Can you illuminate my surroundings?

Mother Nature: Import currents are disabled in that area! We can only send program data to your neural link!

Ehari: Then give me some kind of light!

Mother Nature: Hold as we update your neural link…

Ehari: Hurry! The hacker is changing tactics!

My tracking app beeps each time the dragon slips into view but when I turn in its direction, the creature fades into obscurity. It seems to be moving twice as fast now and pinpointing the beast's location is just as hard. The dragon emerges from hiding and hovers above the bubbling sea as it inhales some of the anti-algorithms into its body. When I fire density rounds at one of its wings, the beast returns fire, and blows a massive ball of photonic fire at me. I dash away from the inferno and narrowly avoid the blistering blue sphere as my adversary disappears… yet again.

Mother Nature: We uploaded a flashlight mod to your rifle.

Ehari: Beastly! Activating now…

Mother Nature's mod is more than a simple flashlight. Triggering the underbarrel's new attachment releases a wide beam of light that penetrates the gloom's furthest depths. I have no trouble finding the dragon and fire the moment it aligns with my crosshairs. Some of the rounds rip through the creature's wings but rest are repelled by its scaly body. I lose my direct line of sight when the dragon flies underneath the walkway but continue targeting its wings as the creature glides underneath me. The beast gathers more ammunition from the bubbling anti-algorithms before rising into view and releasing another fireball. I counter with a density grenade and both projectiles dissipate when they collide. The roaring dragon circles once before coming straight at me. I empty my rifle's launcher out of desperation, and watch as one of three density grenades strikes the creature's left wing.

A cloud of blue light billows from the beast's wing as it shatters like glass. The creature howls miserably as it falls into a death spiral but as it descends, the dragon grabs the walkway with its tail and swings underneath it like a gymnast. I stumble as it lands next to me, right side up, where the beast perches like a bird! The dragon rears its roaring head and howls as my tracking icon identifies the creature's tail as the relay.

I steady my rifle as the towering monstrosity opens its mouth and fire at the dragon's face. The beast raises its remaining wing and absorbs my rounds, forcing me to retreat as the rifle's clip drains like a dying battery.

The dragon peeks over its wing and chuckles when I run away. Then, it closes the distance between us with a single forward step. I trust in Mother Nature's antiviral countermeasures and run underneath the walkway as the dragon tries crushing me with another massive stomp. My heart races as I deactivate my flashlight and circumvent the column. Instead of falling into the churning data below, my center of gravity remains fixated around the walkway. The dragon marches back and forth as it searches for me. It knows that I haven't fallen into the sea of cubical bubbles but has trouble pinpointing my exact location.

I notice the stringy filaments of corrupted code ballooning as they drift by. The virus appears to be maturing faster than projected but my options are limited. The dragon dominates the walkway and approaching it is suicide.

Suddenly…

The creature's thick tail whips around and smacks the walkway's underside a few cubes ahead of where I stand.

THWAP!

Then it strikes the area behind me before hitting another random spot.

THWAP!

THWAP!

The tail whistles like a snapping bullwhip as it lashes out two more times. One of these blind wallops will eventually crush me so I wait for my rifle to recharge before committing to a suicide run.

Before I make my move, the beast suddenly asks

in an human voice, "What is the physical world like? How does it feel to enter humanity's original dimension of time and space? Nobody thought returning to physicality was possible. The world went to hell when you proved them wrong. You are the mother of our destruction! Prophecy has declared you the Antichrist!"

There's something invigorating about a large creature speaking with a human voice. Fear of the dragon attunes my senses like never before. I hear flames blistering its every breath. The fiery bursts illuminate the walkway and mark the beast's location.

"Did you know the VIA tried to recruit Scarlet first? It's true. Ask your precious Mother if you think I'm lying. The agency wanted Scarlet to lead the Species Project with your team. I bet you didn't know it was all Mother Nature's idea, either."

Ehari: Is that true, Mother?

Mother Nature: Di…

There's no time for debating her betrayal. The dragon is swinging its snakelike head about as it searches for me. Every rumbling step he takes is so tumultuous that I fear dislodgement from the walkway's underside. I adjust my angle of attack after noticing fiery puffs brightening the eastern side of the bridge.

"You won't escape, Di! My virus is almost finished corrupting the building's code! It will delete you and your precious decompression chambers! You'll never see Earth again!"

The dragon harnesses his remaining anti-algorithms and then blows a searing stream of blue fire at the walkway. Flames circumvent the columnar structure and blister the underside behind me. I run into view as the stream nears, grab the initiator from my memory pocket, and plunge it into the dragon's snaking tail.

"No! You bit—" the dragon repeats in a computerized voice, "ERROR! ERROR! ERROR!"

I can see various complex algorithms spreading through its meshing as the initiator injects its anti-viral remedy. The dragon freezes from program lock and now resembles a stone statue with lifelike eyes—a sure sign that authorities have subdued the hacker within. He tries countering Mother's patch but lacks the time necessary to combat such a speedy upload. With his virus quarantined, control of the building returns to the VIA.

I notice a scaly pattern forming on the dragon's wings. Authorities will fail to notice the message I see, because the pattern stems from an imaginary game Scarlet and I invented as preteens.

The message reads, "Welcome home, E. Now the fun begins."

Conspiracy Theory

CHAPTER 16

Knowing the truth hurts in unimaginable ways. Beyond Scarlet's betrayal stands a house of lies constructed by my team. I'm a greater fool than imagined… a fool who lingered outside of Mandible 9's biggest secret.

Ugh, and Mother Nature… the nerve of that woman! What am I going to do about her? A person with moral countenance could never backstab with such efficiency! That bitch! I knew she was up to something! No one reaches her ranks without having slashed some throats. Figuratively, and literally speaking, of course. I know how to tread in a shark's tank without rippling water but how does one swim through a school of piranhas while bleeding? I'm so livid that forming a cohesive thought is… ugh!

Memories of projecting to the control room are fleeting. I'm suddenly at Mother Nature's station masked with rage.

"You betrayed me!"

I choke on my own words when the circle of scientists widens around Mother and I. She tries speaking but averts her glare instead.

"Well, guess I'm just a secondhand option, right Mother?"

"It is not like that Di—"

"No, it's exactly like that! You tried recruiting Scarlet and my team from right under me! She's a master hacker, idiot! Did you really think you could wipe her memory of the Species Project and then move on?"

"We had no idea Scarlet was so dangerous."

"How could the VIA not know that? She's a prodigy! Isn't that why you wanted her involvement?"

"The VIA is not infallible. We are correcting the error."

"Error? This is a monumental catastrophe! I saw footage of what happened! Scarlet uploaded viruses to all of the major Realms! She must have created it with information you gave to her! You better hope my friends are alive, Ma! And what is your damn name, anyway? Enough of this Mother crap! My involvement with you ends without your real name! Tell me who you are!"

Mother immediately responds by acknowledging her Master of Arms and the room's personnel clears out when she nods to him. This handsome and amazingly inconspicuous muscle-bound stallion supervises the evacuation with obvious disdain for my attitude. Mother calls him Izreh, while employees use the nickname Dropper, for his rumored ability at seducing women. I ignore Izreh's slighting glances by pretending only Mother and I are present. This is neither the time, nor the place, for flirtation. My attitude only stokes his fiery disposition, warming me. Does Izreh expect to drop all women with his looks and pompous attitude?

I impatiently ask, "Why the overly dramatic need for secrecy? We could have simply projected to another room!"

As with all lofty matters, Mother Nature assumes her usual place at the command console. "Please, calm down. You are asking for highly classified information, Di. We need this particular command station if we are going to discuss such intelligence."

Izreh seals the room after everyone evacuates. I take note of the portals on the eastern, northern, and western sides of the room. There may be a need to escape through one of them should this, "informative meeting" go south.

Mother's console faces the only empty wall. She grabs its stroke pad and uses the device to input a series of commands. The wall brightens as it holomorphs into a wallscreen. Mother Nature's VIA credentials are now on display. They mean nothing to me and I don't waste time reading them. The government can falsify anything so why should I believe in her profile's validity?

"Listen, Di. My name is irrelevant because I never was, I am not, and I will never be."

I pause to consider the familiarity of those words. They evoke a certain truth from a forgotten tome of knowledge. The algorithmic information in her profile catches my attention when I examine the wallscreen with greater intensity. Its significance eludes me and my anger swells.

"Stop with the riddles and just tell me who you are!"

"I am an artificial construct."

I step back and gasp, "A what?" Izreh scrutinizes my reaction as if measuring my total discontent based solely on facial expressions.

"I am a unique by-product of *The Suffering*. My programming was forged in the nuclear inferno that ended the game."

"Impossible! Constructs are imaginations. There's no way to… just… create intelligent virtual life! Do you think I'm stupid? Life grows within the logic stream and only from the genetics of real things that lived on Earth!"

Mother cycles her wallscreen footage to a secret unveiling involving herself as the first artificial construct. In it, the president speaks to senior cabinet members. I watch the conversation culminate to its disturbing revelation.

"The general populace has yet to realize," the president finalizes in a chiefly tone, *"that we can no longer reproduce inside the Nexus. A single child is all people of our current generation seem capable of outputting. These births will only stem the tide of extinction before regression takes place. This construct is a necessary measure for ensuring the propagation and evolution of our species. We call it, Mother Nature."*

I use one of my custom mods to scan the footage and discover official signatures on all of its data.

This means the government has legitimized artificial life construction. I find the idea repulsive.

"We have a birthing issue?"

"Yes."

"And our government thinks you're the solution?"

"Yes."

"Sorry Mother, but a construct is nothing more than a virtual Frankenstein. Our species will stop evolving if artificially born people become the solution to our dwindling population."

Mother gives me an expressionless stare. "You fail to understand what the president just said. The virtual world now serves to preserve human minds in an 'active-stasis' environment. A program error in the Nexus halts the expansion of human evolution and there is no way to patch it. Women have become partially barren as a result. Females can only bare one child now. However, that is only half of the problem. When two individuals give birth to a new child, their offspring now creates a merger of both parent's consciousness, instead of a new person. Such an act is not procreation but degeneration. The logic stream is failing to create new life, insomuch as preserving old ones."

"Wait… are you telling me, that our current generation marks the peak of human of evolution?"

"Your assumptions are correct. A flaw in the Nexus' design is causing a regression syntax error in your species' development. Human evolution now requires more than sexual reproduction in order to evolve. Nutritional input plays a major role in the growth process. The supplemental updates used in the virtual world are proving to be an insufficient substitute for naturally occurring genetic variants. Your logic stream has become nothing more than a continuum for preserving genetic codes. However, procreation may be possible with the introduction of a preservative carrier. This is why male scientists are countering the regression with surrogate females. Instead of letting both genders die out, the male chromosome will continue evolving."

"So this is the real reason why the government wants me to find species-5478. They think its DNA might be the cure for female barrenness."

"Yes."

"This wouldn't be necessary if they hadn't blown up the world!" I scowl at Izreh simply for being the only man in the room. He smirks like some magazine model posing for a shot. "So if we don't find species-5478, women will eventually die out and get replaced by artificial entities, leaving men as the only retainers of human consciousness. Scientists should be concentrating on making men and women more compatible. Virtual biology is nothing more than an elaborate means of recombining brainwaves. Isn't there a way of repairing the error?"

"No."

"What about CP breeding?"

"Cybernetic prostheticalanatomies are incapable

of large scale reproduction and manufacturing CPs in massive numbers will achieve the same effect as regression."

I clench my fists. "I'm not surprised to hear that you're some kind of artificial intelligence. It explains how you can multi-task so well. The agency probably thinks you're the perfect head for this division."

"You are correct. They do, because I am."

"Is that so? You never were, am not, and will never be, remember?" Mother Nature chooses not to respond. I grind my teeth at the frustrating realization that I've *literally* been taking orders from a tool! Mother's blank stare has officially lost its mesmeric reverence.

"So the VIA gave you the cryptonym Mother, because you'll be giving birth to these constructs?"

"Yes. I serve as the template. The government's surrogacy project aims to stabilize the birthrate by supplementing the population with artificial clones. Female offspring will retain my artificial intelligence gene. Male offspring will carry the human gene, and ensure the partial survival of the human race."

"It's appalling to know that men are willing to replace females with artificial clones just for the sake of breeding. How did women lose such ground within the scientific community? I always imagined humanity dying off as a male and female team and not with men existing as the last sentient humans. What can any man hope to derive from a soulless companion?"

Mother shrugs. "This is about the survival of the human race, not companionship. If that survival includes only one gender, so be it."

"You can't have a human race, with only one gender!"

"I am only a construct. I have no say in the matter."

"You said something about being forged in the nuclear inferno that ended *The Suffering*. What do you mean by that?"

Mother tips her head. "You all ready know what I mean."

"Do I?"

"Of course you do. The IVST discovered new algorithms from unique sequences that occurred in the game's final moments. Those algorithms helped finalize my creation."

"Where did they come from?"

"Unknown. The equations are presumed to be a random occurrence."

"I don't believe in random occurrences."

"No cause has been established. The sequences may simply be a glitch."

"So they just put you online?"

Mother nods like a robot. "I have been in operation for five months. A construct of my design is required to synchronize your cybernetic prostheticalanatomy during peak transfer loads in the birthing chamber. Other constructs will be modified to support child bearing."

"Surely you object, right?"

"No."

My lips curl. "After all you've learned, why not?"

"My knowledge base exists within a limited state cortex. There is no way for me to learn. I function to store and regurgitate information."

"That doesn't make any sense. I thought you were artificially intelligent. How are you able to make decisions if you process information like a basic computer?"

Mother Nature clears static from her voice before answering. "You know we are being monitored by personnel within the VIA headquarters, correct?"

"Of course. So?"

Mother points to her control console. "The VIA makes decisions based on the information I gather. They create new protocols in the form of updates, which the VIA uploads to my neural cortex. These updates become your new orders. I have restricted access over my conscious programming."

"So you're a remote controlled person. This is how the VIA plans on enslaving their new female surrogates. Otherwise, you might actually object to objectification. And the human operatives working here might not accept the idea of taking orders from an artificial construct—remote controlled, or otherwise. Now I understand why your status is classified. You're still in your infancy, after all. Now why is the Nexus in disarray?"

Mother uses a thoughtful pause to organize "her" thoughts. I find Mother Nature's artificial origins hard to swallow. Everything she does seems human. Yet underneath her soft smile lurks the suppressed consciousness of artificial life. I no longer want any part of these organizations and contemplate how to severe my ties with the Virtual Intelligence Agency and the Institute of Virtual Science and Technology.

Mother says, "Many Realms were bombed with a unique virus. Beyond that, information is scarce."

"What about my Realm?"

"I am sorry Di, but most of Newark was destroyed yesterday morning."

"How did that happen?"

Mother Nature glances towards me long enough to shake her head and then refocuses on the handheld cuffed in her palm.

"Compression."

"Compression? Isn't compression theoretical?"

"Not anymore."

Mother affirms my question by altering the wallscreen's imagery. A three-dimensional animation shows how Newark met its end. Viral goo erupted from a public portway and flooded the city from the inside out. The goo expanded like a lake before exploding. Images of death and destruction paralyze my thoughts. Newark is the Realm where I was born. It's the most diverse place within the Nexus, and where people of all backgrounds gather. I made my home there. Such a loss is shocking.

Mother adds, "Compression involves destroying all virtual life with a single virus."

"And Newark is ground zero?"

"Yes."

I pace about, dazed. None of this should surprise me. It was only a matter of time before our world's foundation destabilized. Still…

"So the entire Nexus is infected?"

"Not quite. The virus had trouble penetrating firewalls to certain Realms. Seventy percent of the Nexus remains unaffected. Unfortunately, opening ports between these Realms may cause the virus to spread, so unofficial travel is restricted between points."

I try devising some kind of inventive method for accomplishing such a feat but fail to think of any realistic way of tapping into the virtual world's logic stream, which exists outside of the Nexus and feeds data through a magnetic field.

"How was the virus planted into the logic stream?"

"It was not exactly planted…" Mother explains, "The virtual world's original programmers never foresaw intruders who could magnetically hack into the logic stream."

Her words leave me speechless. Magnetic hacks can only imply one thing. "So the virus didn't originate from within the Nexus?"

Mother shakes her head, "No. This problem is uniquely external."

"A terrestrial threat?" I ask with a raised brow, "Species-5478?"

"Yes, this threat is terrestrial but it stems from more than just a single source. We believe multiple hackers used laborbots to implant aggressive Trojans into the Nexus' magnetic field; which eventually combined inside the logic stream to form a single compression virus. The Bloody Membranes are prime suspects, but there may be more conspirators involved. Those responsible must be purged from the Nexus."

The thought is nerve-racking. Everyone I knew or could ever hope to know lives in the virtual world. Billions of people are susceptible to the compression virus.

"Have you determined where the virus came from?"

"The virus' exact origins remain a mystery but we have identified some of the perpetrators involved in its release."

I ponder all kinds of possibilities. "How can you be sure species-5478 isn't responsible for the hacks? It seems like a logical assumption."

"Evidence suggests species-5478 lacks the physical capabilities required for completing such a task. A handicap of this nature would almost certainly negate its involvement."

"So who are these perpetrators you're talking about?"

"Raul Fantis is the name of the hacker you helped stop. As you may know—"

"He's one of Scarlet's men."

"Correct." Mother alters her screen to display his profile. "Raul is the fourth member of The Bloody Membranes. We were unable to download any information from him, due to excessive corruption from our anti-viral patch that you uploaded into his mesh. It seems the rest of Scarlet's team is involved, along with a third party."

"So you think Scarlet's team is working with Oliver Milkes?"

"Either that, or…" Mother pauses to examine my face. She transcribes her mind's contents with a sour expression.

Mother wonders if someone from my team helped Scarlet mastermind the intrusion. I can only validate my own innocence. If my team held a secret about Scarlet from me, what else are they hiding? Is it possible one or more of my men helped Scarlet hack into the logic stream while I was unconscious? It's what the evidence suggests. We were the only ones outside of the Nexus during the incident. In fact, I ordered Grey to hack government files on my behalf. Hannibal remains on Earth. Is he the culprit? Who in the Hell knows what Remi's crazy ass is capable of. Anything is possible at this point.

"I can't learn anything from here. I have to find Remi and Grey. Where did they go?"

"Remi mentioned finding his mother and then departed right before the attack. He was last seen in the town of Pelorah." Mother pauses to check one of her neural messages. "According to my latest update, Remi was within three deca-cubes of his mother's house when the virus struck. Our trackers went off-line almost immediately afterwards. We lost contact with your entire team from that point."

"You lost all communications?"

"No."

Izreh leads us into Mother's office where she retrieves additional data from a secured cache. Mother then activates the holo function on her handheld with the new information. After a few seconds of scrolling, she projects holographic footage taken from my cybernetic prostheticalanatomy.

"Our link with your team was the only line of communication cut during the viral outbreak. The VIA was downloading footage from your hike when the interruption occurred. That is how we discovered the attacker's external origins. After reestablishing communication with Hannibal, we finished downloading all of the footage you took inside the pyramid."

"I don't remember how I got inside of it."

"We cannot figure out how you activated or entered the pyramid. You disappeared after stepping within forty feet of the structure and then reappeared as an image on the pyramid's surface. After thirty seconds, you re-materialized on the opposite side of the structure."

"What did my eyes record?"

"Your cybernetic prostheticalanatomy filters light in a variety of ways. You were using the physiology of prewar humans at the time, and probably would have saw nothing even if awake. When the footage is run through thermal imaging, environmental factors arise." Mother takes a few moments to tap her handheld. "This appears."

The holographic image reveals distinct anomalies floating around me. I have no idea what the various strings of light are or what they're doing slowly spiraling about.

"Grey discovered the anomaly and even has a theory about the pyramid that he will only share with you."

"He should be the first one that I speak to. How do I reach him?"

Mother consults her neural link. Her strained expression hints at some elaborate search problem. "Grey joined a team of VBI agents who were combating the virus. We lost their trail in East Newark. That entire area is one of the hardest hit by the bombing. It currently exists in a state of flux."

I shrug, "What does that mean?"

"The actual state of the city remains unknown.

I advise against going there. You may not be able to enter or return. Searching for Remi might be your best option."

"I need Grey and any discoveries he might have made. Is there anything specific you can tell me about how the city was destroyed?"

"Corrupted, is a better description. Information suggests that the bombing was initiated by Scarlet's second in command, Michael Brockman."

"Is he the one they call, The Enforcer?"

"Yes. Brockman unleashed the virus that Scarlet designed. She controls it from within Newark. Her virus infected people, animals, the city's climate, architecture, and electrical programs. Our investigation indicates the virus has roots in the underground purging canals. The Newark you knew is lost forever. Reformatting the entire city is the only way to reuse its data blocks. If you are going there, be careful. No one has emerged from Newark since the bombing and we may not be able to provide assistance if you make it inside."

The Ides of Scarlet

CHAPTER 17

From a distance, Newark resembles the brunt of an oncoming storm. Scarlet's malignant viral mist obscures the entire city inside its red smog and blots Newark's enclosure within a swirling core of toxicity. The night sky intermingles with the smog's fuming filaments and creates a weird distortion effect that warps the horizon with a magenta haze.

A program glitch causes my cloud simulator to malfunction in this area. Clouds randomly spawn and dissipate at different altitudes. The moon cycles through its phases within a matter of seconds. All of the stars have fallen into a persistent loop animation that creates an illusion where the firmament appears to drizzle meteoric showers.

I failed to encourage a single VIA or VBI agent to join me and they even reject the idea of forming just one search team. The bombing turned notions of rescue into a fool's errand. No one will help me find either of my teammates even though I have a victorious gaming legacy, voyaged into the physical world, and survived a virtual counter-strike. The sense of abandonment is overwhelming. This heightens my paranoia and doubts. Am I making a momentous error by looking for my friends?

I approach my destination from the northern lakes of Chi Isles and cross Allus Bridge to Newark. Aftereffects from the viral fog reveal themselves as I reach the city's southern border. Survivors give Newark a ninety rod—or ninety virtual mile—span for good reason.

The ground is dark and colorless. Static hovering in the windless environment generates corrupt textures that manifest as purple lesions commonly known as pixel herpes. These infectious errors contaminate everything they contact and even scar the atmosphere.

Scarlet's virus obliterated most non-organic programs from the suburbs. Not a single building, monument, or static structure remains. I see why the Defense Department's looping hazard warnings dominate the Virtualnet. The carnage littering Newark's outskirts is a testament to the defenselessness of the citizens caught in the anomalous static that formed after the bombing.

Entering Scarlet's dead zone is scarier than I imagined. Copious displays of death are everywhere. The virus stretched people and animals across the ground in a carpeted layer of mangled body parts, which literally covers every square cube of land meshing. I have no choice but to tread on their remains in order to advance.

Some of the bodies twitch when I step on them. My spinal codes tingle from the awkward gruesomeness. I even discover a small number of survivors fused into the tangled matting. Their bodies appear melted—like wax figures burned from the inside out. Never in my entire life have I witnessed such carnage. My teeth clatter from the sight of these people clinging to threads of life. The victims are not only deformed but also twisted together like mangled vines strewn across the ground.

I feel vulnerable even though Izreh's antiviral armor provides adequate protection against the volatile flakes of infected information drifting about, and send him a neural message after mustering my last remnants of courage.

Ehari: How can I help survivors?

Izreh: Helping victims is not an option.

Ehari: Are you crazy? There has to be something I can do for these people…

Izreh: Listen gorgeous, there is no way to aid victims of static fallout. Scarlet's virus contains paradoxical codes that detonated within a surge current. Victims have scrambled brainwaves. That flaky atmospheric static drifting around you is the shredded remains of over five million minds. The virus uses those filaments as infectious agents that pollute anything they encounter. Everything within its radius is contaminated. Nothing you do will save them.

The minds—the thoughts—the emotions of millions—gone. No, not gone… suspended rather, in a misty static. Some of the snow-like flakes land in my palm. I fondle the crackling filaments of shredded minds frozen in horror and sense the power of that shocking moment when Scarlet's virus tore everyone apart.

The media footage is the most gruesome thing I have ever seen. After the brutal evaporation of life following the explosion, Scarlet's virus magnetized hundreds upon thousands of onlookers in place and left them exposed to the spawning viral fallout. Contaminated particles attached to these helpless people and stretched their arms, legs, heads, necks, and torso's to photonic limits—all while conducting a seething current of positron fire—the flames of which, resuscitates the victims while simultaneously torturing them in-sync to the balance of life and death.

Many gamers sought this experience in *The Suffering*. We wanted to partake in a great human tragedy and now… I curse our indifference. How could we be so blindly disrespectful to those who died in such a disaster? The mere notion is nauseating. In fact, the idea of recreating this disaster for amusement is acutely disturbing.

Before the virus roots into my hand, Izreh's antiviral armor repels the sparkling flakes like ashes roused by the heat of fire. His armor appears as a thin blue sheen across my skin but it provides invaluable protection which guards against infection. I pray that it doesn't wither.

My surroundings confirm the perpetual cycle of war and terrorism. Humanity refuses to evolve beyond self-destructive ambitions. We fell to the faults of previous generations and the idea that a virtual environment would generate broadband peace always seemed erroneous to me. We now have proof that our fabricated world has done nothing more than transfer humanity's aggressions from one battlefield to another. How can our species serve the demigods of death and destruction so willingly?

Izreh: Scanners detect an energy surge three rods north of your position. Be careful.

Ehari: Scarlet has to die for this.

Izreh: We're doing everything to apprehend her.

Ehari: You're not doing enough.

I encounter more survivors while traveling across the devastated expanse. Stepping on their knotted remains always produces a miserable scream. Sometimes, when crossing an entanglement of body parts, I tread on multiple survivors at once. Listening to their wailing chorus is a grievous experience.

I try crossing the terrain with catlike movements even though it does little to ease the pain of those I walk across. Their ghostly moans form visible distortions that move through the air in amoeba form. These flotillas of sorrow deliver their whispering wails across the entire plateau. Nearing one of these distortions causes it to grow louder so avoidance becomes my policy.

Did those who envision the atom bomb, foresee the destruction it would wield? Did they consider the many lives that weapon was destined to destroy? Did those men cast their rock fully aware of the infernal ripple that would cascade throughout the waters of time?

Scarlet dreamed of this moment. She confided everything to me years ago, and exposed all of her darkest desires. Ending the world was her greatest ambition. The idea of it—the mention of it—the thought of it—the planning of it—Scarlet desired total destruction. I thought she was a crazy dreamer. Childish, even. It seems however, that I was the naive one.

I silence the muzzle on my AR-S99 after finding a toddler trapped in a tormenting mesh of mangled body parts. For the first time ever, I feel obligated to take an innocent life and it seems inappropriate to trumpet such an act with a bang. There's no immediate compulsion to pull the trigger, though. This miserable soul fascinates me in grotesque ways so I indulge my somewhat sick desire to study him.

The mere idea of taking an innocent life seemed taboo only a few hours ago. Yet, I now feel an unrelenting urge to act. It's strange how a moment in life changes a lifetime of living. Alleviating this child's suffering is not murder to me but an act of compassion. The viral fallout melted his body and now binds him in a state of great agony with the others who carpet the ground. Walking away is not an option. Nevertheless… although morally obligated to help, I'm hesitant.

The child's contorted face stares at me; I stare back, searching for signs of hope, but there's only agony. Not even a glimpse of peace remains. What kind of virus is this? Did Oliver Milkes help Scarlet design it? If so, how can someone who claims a religion create something so vile? I thought faith in God inspired divine creations.

Izreh messages me when I arm my AR-S99 but I mute his link in favor of contemplating life amongst the wailing dead. No one chose to accompany me into this dead zone, including Mr. Dropper. All opinions concerning my intentions are irrelevant. Raising the rifle is easy when I find the grounds to justify my motives. I take my time when aiming and place a single shot into the victim's head.

He dies instantly.

The *child* dies instantly.

Taking an innocent life is not as I imaged, though. There's no great revelation or moment of discovery. Nor is there any burden lifted or balanced leveled. In fact, I feel disheartened… and give a prayer for the departed before moving on; as I too, feel dead inside.

How can someone survive multiple days of this? What had that child saw in his abyss of agony that others will never know? What did that type of evil look like through his eyes—innocent eyes? What did it feel like to burn alive for days on end while writhing in such brutal pain? Did he even notice me? What kind of Heaven did that child see when he died, and departed this hell?

Time passes slowly. Deformed faces of the deceased spellbind my attention. Each expression uniquely exaggerates the viral potency of cyber terrorism. Ending the lives of survivors becomes easier after an hour. Muffled shots from my silenced rifle deliver quiet respite. Victims gasp and moan with relief as they die. I feel like a polite usher removing ill guests from a banquet hall or a doctor administering a fatal cure. When I restore audio with Izreh, he continues monitoring in silence. One can only assume the time for suggestions has long passed.

I feel stressed considering Grey's whereabouts. I'm beginning to wonder if he died during the outbreak. Most people would have considered this long before placing themselves in great peril. I don't even have a plan for finding him or Remi. Pessimism is quelling my spirit of determination but I continue to press on.

I finally reach the red haze defining Newark's urban boundaries and survey the environment. Scarlet's mist resembles a smooth marble countertop and not the formless contours of fog. The viral explosion shattered the city's loading zones into billions of circular pieces. These fragments form holes that drift about the mist's surface. Some are the size of a dime. Others are the size of a house. I think of ancient submarine portals when peering through the floating anomalies. Random areas within Newark are visible through each of these fragments. A few display nothing more than unpopulated streets or dormant buildings. Some reveal corpses, blood data, or some other disturbing image. What I find most troubling is that none of the fragments exhibit signs of life.

Izreh: When you enter Newark, pass carefully through whatever portal you decide to use. Their outer and inner edges are bipolar. Touching them will compromise the integrity of your antiviral armor. If you want to make an emergency link from within Newark try to find a body of water larger than nine hundred and forty-two u-liters. Submerging in the water might strengthen your signal.

Ehari: Thanks, but I'm not a mathematician, Izreh. What do forty-two u-liters equal?

Izreh: Are you all beauty and no brains? Try submerging yourself in bodies of water larger than a traditional bathtub. H_2O programs are unaffected by the virus and the photonic liquid might boost your neural strength.

Ehari: Affirmative. Wish me good luck. A handsome coward can at least do that much, right?

Izreh: Good luck, Ehari. I hope you take my advice, instead of ignoring it… like you did me.

Ehari: I hate it when people I don't know call me by my last name.

Izreh holds his breath when I jump through the largest fragment in range and emerge inside what's left of Newark's inner city.

The Blob

CHAPTER 18

Iland in an alley. The ground feels solid and although my surroundings appear stable, I need to leave my new enclosure of buildings to determine more. I try messaging Izreh but the signal is too weak. After easing down the alley, someone jams my neural link with a custom ringtone.

Scarlet: Finally… you have no idea how long I've been waiting for you, E…

I feel like a Neanderthal frozen in a block of ice. Is it really Scarlet? This is our first time communicating since I banned her from Mandible 9. I force myself to keep moving.

Scarlet: I knew you would come. You're the only person I know stupid enough to walk into the static fallout of a bombed city.

Ehari: You're the only degenerate I know evil enough to create such a place. What do you want?

Scarlet: I want you to suffer! You owe me your life!

Ehari: I owe you? How? You're the traitor!

Scarlet: Me, a traitor? Screw you! You betrayed me first!

Ehari: Whatever. How did you gain access to my neural link?

Scarlet: I dismantled the VIA's encryption codes. Child's play compared to my greatest feat…

Ehari: Hacking the logic stream? How did you do it? Why would you do it? The Nexus is our home! Life will become an illusion if we fail to preserve the fabric of our reality!

Scarlet: Our life is already an illusion! The Nexus is a fabrication of reality!

Ehari: The Nexus marks the evolution of reality! This world is a trophy of our achievements!

Scarlet: The virtual world is a concoction of doom!

I emerge on a cluttered street and pause to watch a nearby building crumbling apart. Something rises from the growing rubble pile but its billowing defragmentation cloud obscures whatever *it* is.

Scarlet: I refuse to exist in the imagination of others!

Ehari: That's impossible! Everyone immerses themselves within other people's creations… even in the physical world! Every building, toy, tool, or piece of art and crafted object, comes from the imagination of people! We live through the minds of others!

Scarlet: The actual physical world is NOT a fabrication of reality!

Ehari: How did you get an external signal? The VIA said the logic stream was magnetically hacked.

Scarlet: The VIA has no idea how the Nexus was hacked. If they did, you wouldn't be here.

Ehari: What does that mean?

Scarlet: Maybe you'll find out, before I capture you…

Scarlet's ambiguity makes me cringe.

Ehari: I know others helped you! How many of my people defected from Mandible 9?

Scarlet: That's a pointless question.

Ehari: Why?

Scarlet: Newark is under my control and there's no way to escape. You should be worried about yourself.

I turn about as all fragmentary holes leading out of the city dissolve into the red haze encapsulating Newark. My attention eventually returns to the crumbling building directly ahead. I ready my rifle before retreating into a nearby house and watch the blocky defragmentation rubble through an open window. The growing pile morphs into gray goo as though emulsified by an acidic agent.

Scarlet: Don't worry, it's painless.

Scarlet chuckles while her aqueous-based virus engulfs the entire rubble pile and its building. A frenzied gnawing sound rises from the bubbling mass—like a billion carnivorous ants feeding on a mountain of flesh. These rhythmic waves of gray dissolve every portion of the building with sentient hunger.

"Damn," I gasp, slinging my weapon, "buildings are deathtraps!"

Scarlet laughs as I dash into the next room. Scarlet:

Ousting me from Mandible 9 was humiliating! I was there in before the others! You did it right before *The Suffering's* release, too!

Ehari: Get over it! You were getting careless! You hacked government files without consulting me! You created dangerous viruses! You stole from accounts! You instigated information blackmail! Hell… you violated *all* of Mandible 9's rules of conduct and the Free Realm's laws!

Scarlet's viral goo surges like a rising flood as it pours through the windows and devours every object behind me. I dash through the room's portal, leap over a staircase banister, land in the living room, and then link with an active download terminal sitting on a counter. Gray goo drains into the room as my body's identification code loads into the internal conduit. I disappear inside the terminal and ride my SOS signal across town. Static interference disrupts the transfer and prematurely forces me out of the conduit. I exit through an abandoned office building's malfunctioning terminal, leave the building's reception desk, and receive a clear view of the house I just escaped through a glassy wall in the waiting area.

Scarlet: Our existence is dependent on cyber warfare. Why trust that existence to others?

Ehari: I trust no one!

Scarlet: You trust everyone! That's why you're here!

The bubbling mass of gelatinous code seeps over a download deli and pours into the neighboring streets as my anger blooms.

Ehari: Do you think you're some kind of god? You have to stop this! You have no right to kill innocent people!

Scarlet: And you do? I saw what you did on your way here. What gives you the moral ground to slay innocent children? Murder is a sin without rank!

I try appealing to Scarlet's reason but her sinister laughter reveals a new endowment to evil or at the very least, emergence of Scarlet's true self. I emphasize the word *evil*. Warning signs posted during our teenage years hinted at the woman she was destined to become. Scarlet's seeds of dementia originally sprouted in her paintings. The imagery canvassed from her twisted mind portrayed a disturbing venture into the darkest realms of self. Even more disturbing is how Scarlet's artistry once compelled me—perhaps, because I suspected her work to be an actual foretelling of future expositions.

Scarlet: You have three-minutes before my virus reaches you. What will you do this time? What if the next terminal fails or you run into a dead end? How long will it be before you face the inevitable?

I scroll through my neural link's various anti-viral apps but find nothing capable of eradicating Scarlet's neural Trojan.

Ehari: The VIA will reformat this entire city! You'll die if you stay here!

Scarlet: My life meant nothing to me after you ruined it. I'm willing to face deletion just to see you suffer!

I step out of the office and find a functioning skid sitting along the jumpwalk. It lacks a high charge but has enough energy to carry me a little further from Scarlet's virus. I hop on the skateboard-shaped device and activate its cruise function with the heel of my foot. The skid bobs across the ground like a rock skimming water.

Scarlet: Haven't you wondered what will happen if my virus reaches you?

Focusing on escape is hard with Scarlet buzzing in my head. I try using an anti-viral app to sever my link with her but the program requires a few minutes to complete its task.

Ehari: You're more than just aggro; you're sick!

Scarlet: You're the sick one! You're the one poisoned by the Nexus! This place is a prison… I'll escape in due time.

Ehari: You're demented! There's no escaping the Nexus.

Scarlet: Of course there is. You showed me the way.

I finally realize what Scarlet is after… the cybernetic prostheticalanatomy! My meshing contains the codes required to operate it, too.

Ehari: Even if you delete me, you'll never gain control of the womb!

Scarlet: I already control it.

Ehari: Hannibal is the only one left on Earth. He'd never betray me!

Scarlet: Once I have your genetic algorithms, sequencing a clone of your mesh will be easy. I'll have no trouble assuming control of the XX CP. Hannibal will never know the difference between you and me—at least, not until it's too late. Both worlds will belong to me after I delete him!

Her scheme has potential. Still… Scarlet was never this methodical when planning anything. That idiosyncrasy belongs to people like me. Oliver Milkes must be the real brains behind such measured tragedy.

Ehari: What did your virus do to these people?

Scarlet: You mean those degenerates scattered about? My EM-9 virus absorbed them.

My heart drops when I turn the corner and discover the way forward is blocked. Red haze fills the entire street. My neural map fails to discover any alternative paths but the antiviral app chimes when it finds Scarlet's intrusive neural Trojan. The application isolates her signal before purging it from my link. I demonstrate my ability to silence Scarlet by cutting her off in mid thought. This minor victory is irrelevant compared to my inability at finding an exit. I start panicking.

Scarlet: So you have an off switch now? Cute… but you'll never make it out of this city. Deletion is too kind a punishment for filth like you. I'll enslave your soul as punishment!

Ehari: You're crazy! Do you hear what you're saying? You've gone completely mad!

I head back to the main street and use the skid to surf into the next data block. It doesn't carry me far. I kick the skid away when its power diminishes and then dash into a program mill.

Scarlet: You look lost…

Ehari: Why does it have to come to this? Please, just stop!

Scarlet: No! I brought this entire city to its knees just so I could lure you out of hiding!

I scramble about searching for an exit.

Ehari: What happened to Grey? Did you delete him, too?

Scarlet: You're on a fool's errand. Everyone is dead!

Ehari: Liar!

Scarlet: You're next!

Ehari: You're the one on a fool's errand! Deleting me won't change anything!

Silence fills our neural links as Scarlet ponders my thoughts. Her deliberate pause conveys disbelief.

Scarlet: Did you ever ask yourself why someone delivered a bomb to your condo?

Ehari: Someone? You delivered it!

Scarlet: Wrong! My team changed the domain name on your address box. That's why the v-mail went to your neighbor's house instead of yours. I saved your life!

Ehari: Liar! Why save my life only to kill me now?

Scarlet: Like I said, your life means nothing to

me. I want your soul!

Ehari: What does that mean?

Scarlet: You exist inside the enthrallments of a man-made world. Your very perception of reality is a predisposed simulation.

Ehari: We're both in here! If my perception is skewed, then so is yours! But the state of reality doesn't matter when you have free will!

Scarlet: Our will only extends within the limits of the Nexus' parameters. We have the will to obey boundaries and laws. What is that, really?

Neural Link: Connection severed.

Ehari: Scarlet! Where are you! Answer me!

Neural Link: Connection restored.

Izreh: There! Ehari, I found you! I have you on the tracker but… there's a hazard alert! Get out of there! A virus is spreading in your direction!

My mapping sensor discovers no other way out of this zone. I pause as Scarlet's bubbling goo consumes everything before me with tsunami-like force. There's no way to escape it and as my hopes of survival dissipate, I fixate on the millions who lost their lives to Scarlet's madness. I have only a moment to contemplate my fate before the viral torrent crests into a wave, and engulfs me.

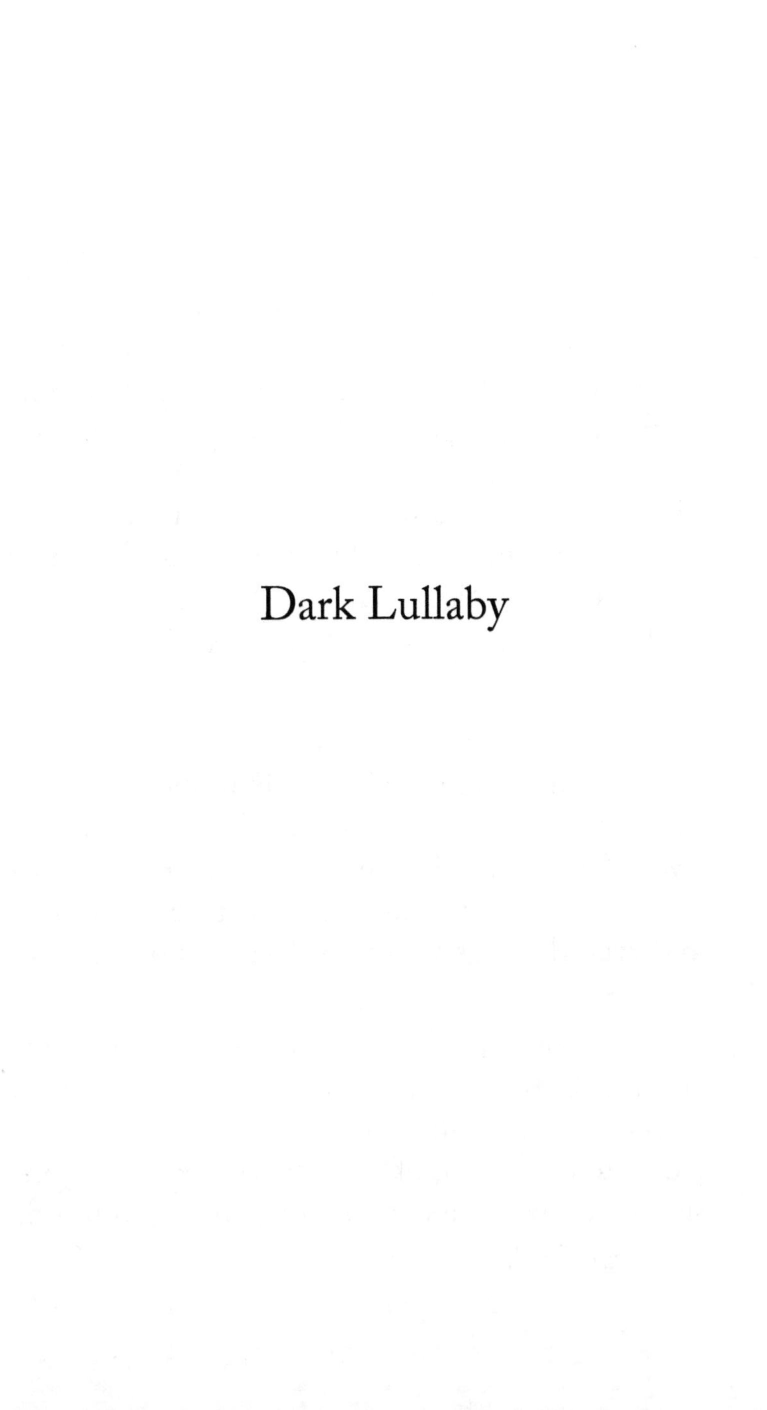

Dark Lullaby

CHAPTER 19

I'm neither asleep nor comatose and although fully aware, I fail to perceive anything beyond the confines of thought. Have I finally died? Am I a victim of some viral sedative? Did I become a virtual paraplegic? Darkness lingers about yet, something about it seems familiar. What is this place? I lose the ability to contemplate existence when my thoughts dissolve into a dreamlike state where all focus disbands.

I'm descending into a dark place…

It's cold…

Dear God, I see mom…

I'm in my childhood home. How did I get here? Am I dreaming? The environment appears authentic. Every facet of the house is intact. Familiar odors linger in the air. The ambiance, pictures, furniture, and even the rugs appear perfectly rendered.

But…

Everything appears larger. Volume is unnaturally abundant. Then I realize my childlike state, but it feels completely normal. Memories of adulthood fade into the chasms of my pubescence. I've become seven and half years old in both body, and mind.

Dear God… I see mom…

Mom lays pinned in one of the living room's corners. A pitted hole in mom's head exposes the dismantled remains of her synaptic threads. Post-processed data seeps from the vein-like strands hanging from mom's skull. I fall to my knees gasping with disbelief. Her blood data smears my kneecaps. This moment is all that matters now. Everything else ceases to exist.

Everything.

Everything I've ever known, learned, or pondered as an adult, dissipates like whispers in a wailing wind. I am a child again—raw and exposed to the world—my teary sparks fall into mom's glistening data and pop against the spillage until the faint sound stirs her killer.

"Ehari," he calls in an overly friendly tone, "is that you?"

I stand when a shadow fills the dining room's main portal. The murderer enters the room after I quietly sprint into the kitchen. He moves sluggishly, as if inebriated. The killer's lethargic steps embolden me into circling back to the main entrance where I peek through its cracked portal.

The burly man stands over mother's lifeless remains, fondles his groin, and then stares at her with sickly eyes. The circuit cutter gripped tightly in his left hand sparkles with mom's synaptic data. The tool appears fully charged. Some of the glistening residue slides down the rod's electric shaft and across the maniac's fingers where it forms blood rings.

My jaw drops when the lunatic withdraws

his penis and begins masturbating over mother's head. He affectionately strokes himself to erection before inserting his banana-shaped cock into mom's punctured cranial cavity. I'll never erase the image of her head smacking against his hips—eyes wide open—with that crooked banana-shaped cock ravaging the contents of mother's mangled brain. My juvenile understanding of the human anatomy can barely process such heinousness so I stand there transfixed by my first lesson in male anatomy. The data dripping down my shins leaves a glistening trail that the killer notices. He licks his lips and smiles while discharging electric semen into mom's skull.

"Ehari, I have a present for you!"

I back away from the portal as the killer chants one of mother's lullabies—as if to lull me into a false sense of security. There's a frightening amount of insanity, destitution, sickness, and cold murderous intent glazing the killer's stare. These are symptoms of the incurable Gordon's Virus; the virtual world's most feared contagion. This particular code originates from the most infamous serial killer of the same name. Some even believe the virus is an actual form of demonic possession, whereby Satan tears a man's soul from his meshing and assumes control of the corpse. This is exactly what I feel stalking me—a possessed man, beholden to the Devil.

So I run…

The murderer's bloodhound-like senses focus on the fleshy patter of my bare feet. He leaps into a feverish sprint and bursts through the portal after me. When I glance back and scream the notion of fright acts like a narcotic high that stimulates his murderous desires. The killer's eyes widen and for a moment, he appears not as a man but some deranged beast sent from the Underworld.

"Ehari! I'm going to atomize your little ass in the recycler! Do you hear me? Your life is mine!"

There's no compassion in his voice. My terror escalates with each panicked heartpulse. I run out of the side portal and towards the mock sewage disposal plant that my dad created as a Halloween funhouse. The killer is gaining on me and outrunning him seems doubtful as his footsteps near with each stride. I scream when his pace quickens and those murderous grunts grow louder as if to consume me with fright. He reaches for my hair, but Chi-Chi jumps out of nowhere and clamps the murder's wrist inside his jaws. I keep running and only look back after reaching the plant's archaic entrance.

My dog tussles with the assailant as I plead, "Stop it! Please stop!"

There isn't a single glimpse of humanity embroidering his stare. Nothing will convince the killer to spare me. He continues trudging forward as Chi-Chi tries pulling him back. Then, in a sudden explosion of rage, he lifts my black Labrador skyward after charging the circuit cutter's surge current, and stabs my dog in the stomach over and over and over again! I plead for the lunatic to stop as the sickening thump of rod and mesh collides. When Chi-Chi's intestinal threads finally spill out of his furry belly, he lets go of the killer's wrist and falls to the floor, wincing. Still unsatisfied with his most recent slaughter, the lunatic grabs my dog by the nap of his neck, and uses the rod's electric tip to decapitate him. I open the plant's old-fashioned door as the killer throws Chi-Chi's head at me. It strikes the outer handle as I slip inside and splatters the rust colored hinges with charged blood data. Chi-Chi's electrified sinew shocks my hands when I pull the door shut to secure its lock. The killer pounds against the frame with barbaric persistence as I pace about in search of an exit. I pause when he suddenly quiets. Did the maniac find another way inside?

Even the disposal plant's environment scares me. Most of the residing shadows are too dark for penetration with the naked eye and I rely heavily on the blades of light seeping through ceiling cracks to help me navigate. I'm perceptually handicapped when these grow sparse but keep pressing forward until the darkness encroaches on my last fragments of visibility. My fear of the dark grows until…

"Ehari!"

I jump when my name washes over me like frigid water. The killer's voice emerges from the adjacent room along with the sound of his circuit cutter sliding across a railing.

"Ehari! Get your scrawny ass out here you little bitch!"

Quivering, I sprint away just as the lunatic enters the room and begins stalking from the shadows.

Bloodlust stokes his every breath. The killer's echoing footsteps ripple through the darkness as I spot an aging air duck tucked behind a rickety compressor. I run for it as the murderer lunges from the shadows and grabs my sleeve when I slip in-between the duct's broken grate—but he loses the brief tug-of-war when I manage to pull my arm away. The lunatic strafes the duct with his rod raised.

"So you want to play hide and seek?" After a brief pause he yells, "Peek-a-boo," and jabs his circuit cutter through the flimsy metallic-like duct. The tip nearly pierces my shoulder as I barely avoid the next sparking thrust. "Peek-a-boo!"

I mistakenly tumble down a missing grate and fall into the awaiting sub-level. My left arm feels broken by the landing but I'm too scared to feel pain. The lunatic's footsteps thump down a nearby catwalk and the sound forces me to move.

"Where are you, Ehari? You're making me a little upset!"

Light pours through an opening directly ahead but who knows if the lunatic will see me emerge from it. I bolt out of the duct after eying no alternatives and run with all my might. The killer spots me and yells in frustration at the fence separating my half of the room from his. I sprint through a corridor leading to the main sewer junction as he searches for a way to follow.

Dear God... I see mom...

Her ravaged body flashes before my eyes and the blood data... those sparkling sheets of crimson decorated the living room's walls like shredded curtains. The memory causes a shiver to scuttle down my spinal mesh. I stumble through the darkness as a shattering noise echoes behind me. The killer laughs as I reach the junction and his nearing voice numbs my legs.

A single burning bulb illuminates the four way intersection. Only one of the dank corridors leads to an exit. The other two go nowhere.

Dear God I see mom...

I pause after glimpsing mom's corpse pointing towards one of the dead ends. I should be terrified of such an abominable hallucination but... it compels me in a loving way. The faint sensation is a minor reassurance when compared to the visceral yells of the lunatic that pursues yet... enough to give me pause. Instead of heading straight, I break the nightmare's tradition by choosing to follow mom's presence down the darkest corridor to my right.

Her bloodied hand and it's coiling index finger guide me through the shadows. I search for more of her—mom's whole body—eyes most importantly—but those parts stay out of sight. Her blood-splattered hand is the only visible part of her body. It glides through the columns of light hanging in-between ceiling grates. I can barely keep up but it isn't long before I reach a brick wall.

Dear God... I see mom...

Mom's crumpled body sits against the wall with its head down. A portrait of dad hangs atop her remains. Glinting light emerges from the small trinket cupped in his palm. He greets me when I step forward and reaches through the picture's frame with his offering.

The golden coin is familiar. Its portrayal of the first female ruler of Egypt reminds me of Grey. He gave me a similar token after I accepted his membership into Mandible 9. Taking the coin stimulates awareness of my true self; not just my child identity, mind you, but my complete adult self. As my mind seizes this realization, a throttling chuckle emerges from the building's walls. It revs up and down like one of those ancient American muscle cars before subsiding into an idling sigh.

The killer whines in a female voice, "You were always too smart for your own damn good…"

"Scarlet?" I twirl around as the corridor disintegrates into a sandy pile of photons. Memory input from the missing seventeen years of my life download into my neural cortex in a sudden flash of awakening. "So you planned on torturing me with a childhood memory?"

Scarlet emerges from the shadows. She continues using the killer's form as if it were her own.

"When my viral flood engulfs its victims, their most tragic memories become the catalyst for neural shock. The sequence repeats indefinitely. Torturing you should have been easier but that damn antiviral armor prevents me from taking full control of your mind!"

"Is there no depth you're unwilling to sink?"

I clutch Grey's token and back away. Although Izreh's antiviral armor provides *some* protection, Grey's coin is what actually simulates my awareness. He must be hiding nearby. Leaving such an item within Scarlet's viral plane requires his presence. Grey's hacking skills continue to impress me but Scarlet is not a fool. She'll find him eventually.

"All of humanity draws from the same cesspool of immorality." Scarlet backs into the shadows and melts out of view. "There is no such thing as right and wrong. I scoured the minds of others and saw the same filthy thoughts everywhere I looked! Decency is an adult fantasy perpetrated by heathens! The real people behind our social façades are nothing like the masks they wear in public! Everyone I killed viewed life with the exact same level of repulsiveness! They sinned in any way that circumstances allowed! They're degenerates! The consequences of their actions are the only things that stemmed their inner self-expression! All men and women use the exact same mind—with each person possessing a little piece of it! There wasn't a single innocent person within that entire city of hypocritical trash! They all shared in the darkness equally! Sexual perversions, murder, jealousy, deceit… there isn't a single malicious act or thought those people haven't acted upon! Even you, E… you killed a child! I killed a city of sinners! Who between us harbors true evil? Society's veil of wholesomeness is a lie! Your fabrication of reality pollutes the sterility of true consciousness! Humanity is a pustulant blister that erodes the face of Earth—and I have the cure!"

Oculus [neural recipient] Rift

CHAPTER 20

I awaken from a hibernated state but remain trapped inside Scarlet's gelatinous virus. Various objects and people appear frozen within the photonic goo. The other captives appear mentally locked inside their most tragic moments. All manner of things are scattered around me. I notice buildings, shop signs, damaged skids, and broken data blocks all bound like trinkets in ice. A blob of this sort hearkens back to our most primal fear as single celled organisms—engulfment by a larger cellular body—the original fight-or-flight response.

Grey: Ehari, can you hear me?

Ehari: Grey? Is that really you?

Grey: It is indeed! I knew you would recognize a copy of that Egyptian coin I gave you a while back, so I targeted an embedded pulse at your neural link, and used the coin as a conduit for externally increasing your synaptic power.

Ehari: Genius! You have no idea how good it feels to hear you! How did you find me?

Grey: Everything else in the city is either dead or dormant. I followed the commotion until it led me to you.

Ehari: Can you destroy the virus?

Grey: Not really. That virus is amoebic and the size of a small lake! Stopping it with the tools currently at my disposal is next to impossible.

Ehari: Well, I know you thought of something, am I right?

Grey: Indeed! I can help you escape Scarlet's virus with malware.

Ehari: You're going to infect her virus with another virus?

Grey: Correction, I've already infected her virus!

Ehari: How?

Grey: The coin data I relayed through your neural link contains the malware. All I have to do is activate it.

Ehari: You're amazing! Now hurry up and get me out of here!

The glimmer of blue light ascending from the coin in my hand is barely noticeable because Scarlet's goo has my entire body fixed into place. I manage to lower my head slightly, and examine the rising aura before it envelopes me. The light creates a kind of… vacuum, around my body that removes the virus' restrictions. I regain complete mobility as the glow dims to reveal my new confines.

Grey encases me inside a winged submersible that fits like a wetsuit. The craft is so tight that my head, torso, and limbs are barely movable. I lay sprawled in the submersible's t-shaped cockpit as Grey's holographic face emerges on the vehicle's concave windshield.

Grey: I call it, the E-ray!

Ehari: The what? That's a stupid name!

Grey: Are you kidding me? E-ray is a great name! I adopted the submersible's design from an extinct shark called a stingray.

Ehari: Well, the hack is amazing!

Grey: I know! Hard mental labor went into making that thing. It was going to be my escape vehicle if Scarlet's viral blob found me.

Ehari: Can you enlarge the cockpit? My body barely fits in here. I feel like I'm in a coffin!

Grey: Negative. Any bigger and the E-ray will lose its structural integrity.

Ehari: So how am I supposed to pilot this thing?

Grey: I designed the E-ray to function as an agile craft. You can control its movements via dual analog controls.

Ehari: How does it work?

Grey: The two pedals on the E-ray's footrests are for acceleration and deceleration. Press the right pedal to accelerate and the left pedal to brake or reverse. You'll also find four triggers on your analog sticks—use the bottom two for yawing. The left analog stick controls a spectral camera. Use it to view your surroundings. I haven't programmed functionality into the top triggers yet. The right analog stick controls rolling and banking horizontally or vertically. Tilt the stick forward to descend or backward to ascend. I designed the submersible to pierce Scarlet's blob like a shark swimming through water.

Ehari: Are you kidding me? How am I supposed to remember all of that? Can you remote pilot this for me?

Grey: Sorry E, but establishing remote guidance in my current state is impossible. You have to steer your own way to freedom.

Ehari: What's the quickest way out of here?

Grey: I have no real way of determining that. The blob is formless. Just keep moving until you find a penetrable outer edge. I can use light waves to map the immediate area. Standby while I program functioning radar.

Grey's image dissipates from the windshield when I grab the crescent shaped analog sticks he fixed into the frame. The E-ray responds as intended when I press the accelerator pedal and moves forward. It banks when I tilt the right joystick starboard and turns when I pull back. The submersible's temporal shields emit crackling sounds as I burrowing through Scarlet's viral concoction. I feel smothered inside Grey's E-ray… but I am impressed with how well it glides through Scarlet's photonic goo.

Ehari: Did you find Remi?

Grey: No, he found me.

Ehari: I heard he went looking for his mother.

Grey: She passed away in the attack so he came here to help with antiviral containment procedures. Our neural link collapsed sometime after.

Ehari: Were you able to reestablish contact?

Grey: No.

Ehari: Do you have any idea where Remi might be?

Grey: No. I've been searching around here, trying to find him but… nothing. I think he fled to another Realm.

Ehari: What did you want to tell me about the pyramid?

Grey: Disclosing that kind of information over an un-encrypted link is not advisable. We have to speak in person. Scarlet might be listening.

Ehari: Fine.

I feel like a tiny fish amidst a vast light-green sea. Determining up from down is next to impossible. Suspended objects give no clue as to what direction might lead out. To make matters worse, the viral goo shifts when I try moving towards less congested areas.

Ehari: Grey, are you monitoring this? Why is the virus moving?

Grey: I have no idea. The blob is not actually going anywhere, though. It seems to be gyrating instead.

Ehari: You mean, like a living organism?

Grey: Sort of, yeah.

I try gliding toward an empty area but the virus raises a mound of goo to my right and displaces a floating house. Grey panics when it moves towards me.

Grey: Get out of the way! Large blunt objects

will destroy the submersible's integrity!

Ehari: Crap!

I lean into the controls and change the E-ray's momentum from entering the building's sloping path. The roof bumps my submersible and I spin wildly about—losing all sense of direction.

Ehari: It hit me! The E-ray is unresponsive! What now?

Grey: Calm down. The house nicked your tail. I detect no damage. Regain your bearing and keep moving.

It's a suggestion easier said than done. I have to wait until the submersible slows to a near stop before I can establish a stable heading.

Grey: The radar is complete. Check your heads-up display.

An oval grid emerges on the lower portion of the windshield, between my control sticks. The enclosed three-dimensional map pinpoints every object within range. Grey's update allows me to avoid the next set of obstacles with great ease.

Grey: Be careful. I found an energy surge four rods above you.

Ehari: Where is it coming from?

Grey: Pinpointing the cause is difficult. It looks stationary though, and has an anthropomorphic form.

Ehari: I see it on the radar. Wait, that looks like a nucleus! I must be inside the replica of a cell!

Grey: What the... indeed! How did Scarlet

program something like this?

Ehari: She must be in the nucleus. That's my destination!

Grey: Why go there? You need to escape!

Ehari: I have to destroy the nucleus! It has to be the way!

Grey: The way to what?

Ehari: Destroying Scarlet's nucleus is the only way to break everyone out of this place!

Grey: How can you be sure?

Ehari: Everything forms around the nucleus. It's the nerve center of the cell.

Grey: And how will you destroy the nucleus without weapons?

Ehari: You're a genius, right? Use that ingenious mind of yours to program something!

The E-ray moves at five particles per second. These brisk speeds feel similar to the Jet Ski simulators I played in arcades. Even the engine hums and revs when I strum the throttle. I'm surprised at how fast the joysticks are beginning to feel like extensions of my limbs. Altering my angle of approach is easier than expected, too.

None of the goo's suspended objects poses an immediate threat now that I'm bettering the submersible's controls with functioning radar. Unfortunately, reaching the nucleus will take a while at my current rate. On the greater than or equal to side, Grey should be able to program a weapon or two by then. Of course, I have no idea whether or not Grey actually located the nucleus, or if his weaponry will even affect it.

Branching veins containing electric currents emerge around me as I approach my destination. All of the stringy conduits seem to extend from the nucleus. The goo shifts when I pass in-between some of them and displaces a large birch on my port side. Altering my speed avoids the tree so the virus tries blunting me with a broken section of road—whose broad surface hinders the object's ability to penetrate the goo in time. I easily dip beneath the impediment and continue forward at a swifter pace.

The trip calms until I notice something moving through Scarlet's vast lake of blurry and contorted objects. This… thing stands out against the gloom of static objects. Its rhythmic movement amongst the drifting debris is especially eerie.

Ehari: There's something heading towards me.

Grey: I noticed…

Ehari: What is it?

Grey: I don't know. Hide!

Ehari: Hide? Where?

I adjust my angle of ascent.

Ehari: Is it a machine?

Grey: No. It's some kind of amphibious creature.

Ehari: Can you be more specific?

Grey: DNA sequencing dates the creature to early prehistoric times. That's all I know.

Ehari: It's a counter-hack! Scarlet knows you're

hiding nearby! Get away before it's too late!

Grey: I can't leave you alone… besides, this is Michael Brockman's signature.

Ehari: Why can't you leave me?

Grey: Just focus on survival!

Ehari: Fine! Then tell me about Brockman! Isn't he The Enforcer from Scarlet's Bloody Membranes?

Grey: Yes. He's challenging us with a prehistoric mod. It's something of an inside joke. He thinks that ancient form can beat my E-ray…

Ehari: Where's my weapon?

Grey: Just keep moving. I'll have it ready in a few minutes.

I notice a temple floating nearby and head for the building's tower. Grey implements his first mod to the E-ray. According the new icon on my HUD, the submersible's tail should eject a propulsion coil that gives the vehicle a temporary boost. When I squeeze the left analog stick's uppermost trigger, a single thrust accelerates me to the building in a fraction of the time it would've taken using normal propulsion.

Ehari: Thanks for the enhancement but I still feel naked without weapons!

Grey: Don't worry, your main weapon will activate in two minutes. Stay out of harm's way until then.

I reach the temple's tower and slip inside an open window. The submersible's wings compress to allow entrance and then widen upon entry. Michael Brockman's creaturely form casts a dark shadow into the tower that skims the interior as I try hiding.

Ehari: Brockman is here!

Grey: I just finished your torpedo launcher. The mod will download to the submersible in about one minute. There's only enough energy to power five explosive discharges and avoid using the torpedoes inside enclosed areas.

Ehari: What good are torpedoes if I can't use them inside the building? What about pulse or string weaponry?

Grey: Pulses will have zero effect in the goo. Strings are ineffective, too.

Ehari: Torpedoes? That's it?

Grey: And remember your booster!

Ehari: Wait, he's swimming by my window…

Scanning Brockman's modified body reveals interesting results. His prehistoric form dwarfs my E-ray at over one hundred-cubes long. Brockman's four-fanged mandible functions as a set of fins when they expand and retract in the shape of an X. This grasping motion also initiates olfactory programs in his teeth. When he captures a living target, toothy secretions paralyze bitten prey. There are no eyes. The Enforcer's eel-like body billows through Scarlet's goo using a wormy tail fixed inside a spiral shell.

Grey finds no match for this abomination within the VIA's database, which eventually classifies Brockman's creature as a newly discovered dinosaur. I wonder… if all Nexus life stems from previous sources, where did Brockman find the genetic codes required to create something this ancient? Now that I think about it… where did Raul Fantis' dragon form come from?

The Enforcer unfurls multiple fins from his lower abdomen while circling the temple. The appendages help Brockman's bony tail thrash the tower. My submersible sways in the shifting current as pieces of the temple disintegrate around me. I flee when Brockman smashes through the building and enters the massive breach. He wades through tower debris as I flip the E-ray about and aim for his head. I finger the right analog's uppermost trigger and squeeze when the targeting reticule reddens.

Grey: I said be careful firing indoors!

I feel no kickback from the oblong missile ejecting from the submersible's launch cylinder. The torpedo penetrates Scarlet's goo like a soaring rocket—piercing with surprising speed and accuracy—barely missing Brockman's slithering head but striking his tail.

A crystalline bloom of energy bursts from the explosive detonation and shatters Brockman's spiral shell into a million splintering pieces. Photoproton reverb causes the temple to fracture into several sections. Blood data obscures some of the tail and building fragments floating about. Cascading waves of orange light knock my submersible back but I manage to keep the craft from slamming into the nearby wall. A bubbled moan escapes The Enforcer's mandibles. The damage isn't enough to stop Brockman from pursuing me and as I flee for cover, he closes the distance with a few wormy wriggles.

Grey: Use your boost!

When I squeeze the trigger, the E-ray's boost functions like an expanding spring that propels the submersible forward. To my surprise and delight, the uncoiling exhaust doubles as an antielectron bolt that deters The Enforcer when he tries following in my direct path. This gives me the time I need to maneuver out of the temple.

I circle the building while Brockman hammers the main doors with his damaged tail. He eventually breaks out of the temple and comes about like a predatory shark. Blood data seeping from his injury inks a cloudy plume into the goo. I ready another torpedo as The Enforcer weaves through some of the spreading debris and fire into his path, but Brockman dodges my attack by arching his snaking body over the torpedo. I rearm as the misfired missile strikes the temple's outer wall with a watery BOOM! Building debris blows about until the area now resembles an asteroid belt.

The Enforcer pauses within the debris field and uses his gaping mouth to funnel goo into his body. Shark-like fins expel the excess as an inverted whirlpool forms between us. Gravity shifts towards its twirling center. I try steering away from it, but the force is too strong.

Grey: Fire a torpedo into its mouth!

Ehari: There's too much debris! I can't get a clear shot!

Grey: Boost away!

Ehari: That won't work! I'll crash into something!

I swerve away from all kinds of clutter as Brockman tries swallowing me whole. When he swims forward, I flip the E-ray around and fire my third torpedo. The Enforcer waits until the missile is only a few cubes away from his widening mandible before blowing it back. I'm barely able to maintain control of the E-ray as the current pushes me away. The torpedo tumbles by and strikes a piece of building debris as I boost away from the explosion.

My ammo is limited and The Enforcer senses my hesitation. We circle each other for a few moments before I fire at Brockman's head. He tries once again, to arch his amphibious body over my torpedo but this time, I detonate the explosive remotely.

BOOM!

The Enforcer's torso hurtles into the gelatinous void while his head comets through one of the temple's fractured walls. It creates a bloody data cloud of obscurity that masks the defeated expression of my adversary. The glistening algorithms indicative of life fade into the dull shimmering redness of death.

Ehari: Did you see that? My timing was perfect!

Grey: You deleted Brockman but Scarlet lives.

Grey is right. I calm down, turn about, and trace the branching veins of electricity to their nucleonic source. I fear venturing any deeper. Few places provide viable protection against prehistoric creatures. Yet, after staring into the gloomy abyss for a few unsettling moments, I swallow my fears and venture onward.

Ehari: My radar isn't detecting anything between the nucleus and I. Do you see something?

Grey: No. I think that amphibious creature was Scarlet's only countermeasure. Be careful, though. There's no telling what the nucleus is capable of.

A life force emanates from the nucleus as I engage in orbit along its outermost ring of gravity. The sphere's dark inner core appears empty until I notice contours highlighting a female form. Scarlet's goo thickens around the nucleus as well, making it hard to get closer. I target the inner core with my final torpedo but can't seem to establish a reticule lock.

Ehari: I'm having trouble locking onto the nucleus.

Grey: Indeed. Some kind of transmagnetic field surrounds it.

Ehari: Will a torpedo penetrate to the core?

Grey: Possibly, but expect dampening.

Ehari: How much?

Grey: I can't say with any certainty.

I fire directly at the core after steadying my aim and clench when the torpedo enters its transmagnetic field. The oblong missile detonates prematurely and the field's dampening effect reduces the blast to imploding bubbles of orange light that inflict minimal damage to the nucleus.

Ehari: The field buckled! I need more torpedoes!

Grey: Indeed. There was a thirteen percent drop in the field's magnetic density.

Ehari: How many more torpedoes will I need to reach the nucleus?

Grey: Seven to eight should suffice. Maybe less, when you factor the field reduction percentage that occurs with each blast. Nevertheless, there's no way to harness the energy to make any more torpedoes.

Ehari: Maybe I can get close enough to damage the core with a boost…

Grey: That sounds dangerous. Combining a positron exhaust with that kind of transmagnetic field is like mixing hot oil and water.

Ehari: I was hoping you'd say something like that!

I cruise about in the E-ray and choose an attack angle that aligns with the inner core. Grey swears to himself through my neural link but his worries don't deter me. I advance into the magnetic field until it begins repelling the submersible. A sharp U-turn completes the maneuver. I fire the E-ray's booster with a sniper's precision and eject the coil directly into my target. The nucleus reddens when my antielectron coil dilutes its magnetic field. Yet, instead of destroying the nucleus, the inner core uses the E-ray's coil as a tether—binding my submersible.

Ehari: I can't break away!

Grey: Try cutting the power!

Ehari: It's not working! The nucleus is pulling me inside! Grey! What do I do? Grey!

Grey's thoughts fade into garbled static as the

nucleus pulls the entire E-ray and I, inside of it.

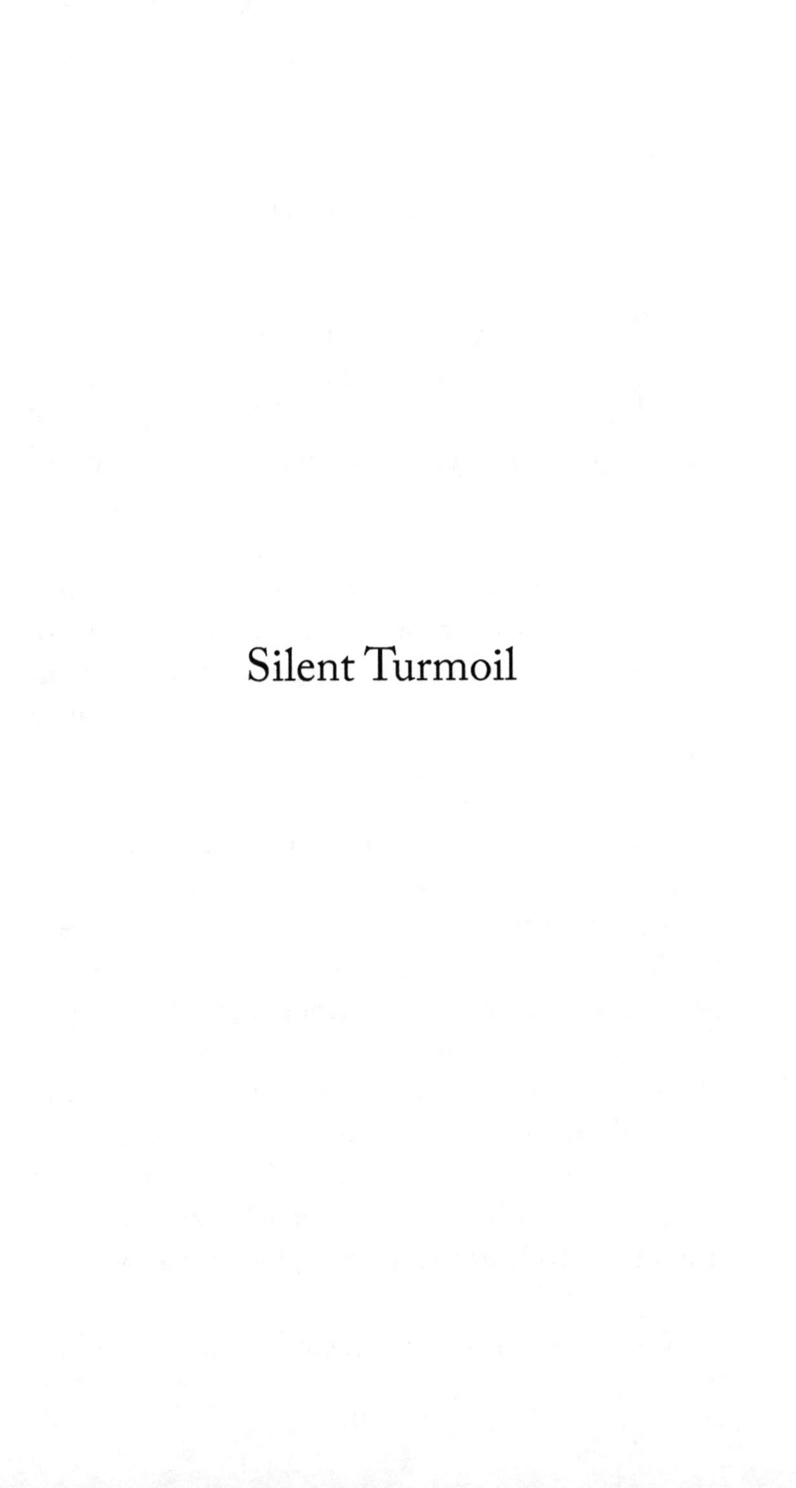

Silent Turmoil

CHAPTER 21

I discover a new form of energy inside the nucleus. Something… well, indescribable with current vocabulary. This extraterrestrial power is completely independent of virtuality and fills the entire nucleus with an otherworldly force.

The Nexus hosts various Realms that function like ancient Internet servers. Their protocols limit these dimensions to properties established by laws of science. This should prevent external modifications to the virtual world. So how did Scarlet cultivate a foreign force within the Nexus? Such fundamental laws should be unbreakable.

Grey's E-ray now drifts about like a powerless spacecraft. Yet, there's no void within the nucleus. An invisible force binds me to the core, where Scarlet floats in an embryonic state. Her heartpulse beats in the surrounding atmosphere. She begins communicating with an ancient code that uses phonetic harmonics. I understand everything Scarlet says without effort, and realize while listening, that these harmonics are a human being's natural form of communication. The frequencies attune to an untapped mode of the human psyche that was lost throughout the ages.

The first string of decipherable tones say, "I love

you, E. I love you dearly. You are the only person I love."

Veins permeating the viral goo redden from Scarlet's thoughts. When their charge oversaturates an electrical jolt strikes the nucleus. The shock paralyzes me with a distant memory from Scarlet's past. Its inducements are so strong that life expands through her viewpoint. I can see a park we often frequented as children. The memory is so vivid that it feels real.

"Why did you betray me, E?" Scarlet asks with another string of harmonics, "Why pretend to love me? I must have been nothing to you. Our friendship was a lie."

The entire sphere is set ablaze with the highly positive charge from a second jolt—kindling another memory. This one takes place at our favorite movie theatre. We're older now and leave the building after catching our boyfriends flirting with other girls in the dark. We make a blood data oath on the way home and promise never to betray one another.

"I don't want you to die, E. I want you to suffer. I want you to become soulless, like me."

Jolt number three cuts into my mind like a surgically implanted migraine. I writhe in pain as a seething memory roots itself firmly into my neural network. Scarlet's emotions now course through my vascular threads with adrenal potency. They pull me so deep into her thoughts that Scarlet's memories feel like my own.

I'm an expecting mother and a fetus kicks in my

belly. Love for this fetus overwhelms my senses. I rub my stomach and say, "I feel her sparking inside of me!" I feel other things as well. Unselfishness… sacrifice…

Another bolt of electricity simmers through the jellied veins and strikes the nucleus, shocking my every sense. The fourth memory consumes my mind with such turmoil, that I lapse into a mummified state as death circles about, stabbing the life out of me.

I awake on a familiar hospital bed awaiting my equally familiar gynecologist, Dr. Rochester. Patients in the neighboring room are unusually quiet and I notice low jumpway traffic on all four corners of the hallway. These Monday morning oddities are ominous. My aching stomach adds to the foreboding sense of anxiety. I feel certain Dr. Rochester bares bad news when he enters the hallway and stands on its projection step with his head down. His nature as an eternal optimist promotes itself whenever he looks up towards a patient's portal. Today, the doctor propels down the hallway while staring intently at his holopad. Only patients with terminal illnesses get a heads down approach.

Rochester enters my room and avoids direct eye contact. After a few unsettling moments he softly says, "I'm sorry Scarlet, but there's been a complication."

"What's happening?" I rub my belly and frown, "Why isn't my baby moving?"

"A fetus requires both parents to be alive and

well, in order for the mother to carry full term." Dr. Rochester states in his most respectful tone, "When Seti passed away, your fetus lost its ability to grow any further. An embryonic torrent can't survive without its father's active chromosomes remotely seeding the mother for at least eight and a half months…"

When I try sitting up, my aching stomach forces me back down. "Are you saying my husband is dead?"

Rochester gasps, "I thought Nurse Monroe informed you of the incident." He lowers the holopad while biting his bottom lip. "I'm truly sorry, but your husband was on his way to see a woman named, Di Ehari. There was an accident, and—"

"My husband is dead? What about my child?"

"I'm truly sorry," Dr. Rochester repeats, grimacing. "Your fetus also passed away after losing its father's support stream."

I faint when my entire body loses sensation. Ehari plagues my dreams until the worst possible nightmare manifests—awakening to a lifeless womb. The memory fades into Scarlet's nucleonic heartpulse.

I now understand the true meaning of turmoil. Interpretation is the real basis for this chaotic state of mind, not the act. What seems detrimental to one person is trivial to another. The depths of pain are not easily processed consumables. Grief, in its most tangible form, becomes a permanent part of the person who digests it. Scarlet's turmoil edifies every portion of her being. I never knew a soul could feast on such agony. Her malevolent feelings towards me alter my perspective of life with such force that I feel suicidal. Scarlet speaks during my revelation from somewhere nearby.

"I bombed Newark because my child, husband, marriage, and motherhood, died here, alongside our friendship."

The nucleus generates a tremendous magnetic pressure that builds against the E-ray's buckling hull. Extreme high and low densities fluctuate before Scarlet's heartpulse spasms out of control. She vanishes as a burst of spherical energy explodes from the nucleus and rattles my submersible. The E-ray's electrophotonic shielding reflects the blast before shattering like cracked ice on a car's window. Even the shield icon on my HUD distorts into wiry fragments.

Scarlet's viral goo decodes into a watery fluid after the nucleus blows apart. The enormous lake of contamination bursts within Newark's Upper Residential District—creating a spontaneous flash flood that fills the streets like an avalanche of snow descending from a mountaintop—decimating everything in its path with tsunami-like force. The submersible's heads-up display brightens when its radar highlights numerous hazards floating nearby. I grip the controls tightly, fully aware that crashing into anything without electrophotonic shielding means instant deletion.

Grey: Avoid hitting anything! The E-ray is susceptible to permanent damage without electrophotonic shielding!

Ehari: I know!

Grey: I mean it!

Ehari: I know!

Grey: Be careful!

Ehari: Are you trying to get me killed? Shut up! I need to concentrate!

There's no time for Grey to modify the E-ray for water navigation, which forces me to master the submersible's overly sensitive controls within a matter of seconds. The flood thrashes every imaginable object together like clothes in a washing machine. I can barely see anything through the grimy mixture and rely almost exclusively on the HUD's radar when steering.

HUD ALERT: Proximity Warning

I swerve away from a rouge object when it approaches on my radar. The warning activates at fifty-cubes, which—at these speeds—is practically right next to me. My heartpulse thumps harder when a red, crescent shaped bar pops onto the HUD.

HUD ALERT: Hydrodynamic Warning

I dodge another object after pushing the controls sideways but the item's immense size grabs my submersible with its undertow. The underwater current drags me down and my E-ray begins veering out of control after I try pulling up. I tap the submersible's booster, escape the impending collision, and set a steady course to the surface at dangerously high speeds. After nearly crashing into three more objects, I speed towards the jostling surface waves.

HUD ALERT: Velocity Warning

Visibility near the surface clears to at least one hundred cubes. Tumultuous waves crash into everything around me and an upcoming valley compresses the water into a raging current that increases the submersible's velocity. I manage to steer the E-ray above water and ride the waves like a speedboat. All manner of wreckage is colliding around me. I dodge floating bodies, a pylon, and even a download stand before an immense energy tanker emerges before me.

HUD ALERT: Proximity Warning

Grey: Turn back and boost away from it!

Ehari: No time!

Grey: Are you *trying* to crash into that ship?

Ehari: Shut up! I have to concentrate!

Grey is a fool. Reversing course is suicide. An entire city of wreckage is floating about and boosting headlong into such a mess is ignorant. Instead, I activate the submersible's targeting reticule.

Grey: Wait… you plan on… oh, crap!

Ehari: I need a torpedo!

Grey: I'm not sure if I…

Ehari: Damn-it Grey! Convert power from the booster and program one!

Most of the capsized tanker floats above water so I target the hull and fire the moment a torpedo comes online. It whistles ahead before striking the ship's aft and exploding. I ride straight into the breach and swerve into one of the tanker's corridors as fluid rushes inside. The ship lists as the torrent carries the vessel through the valley. It knocks me about pretty badly but the tanker provides adequate protection against external debris. When the ship comes to a halt ten minutes later, I breathe a sigh of relief as fluid begins draining from the corridor.

Grey: I don't believe that crazy stunt actually worked!

Ehari: Thanks for having faith in me.

Grey: I do but… you kind of, like… and then you… plus… forget it. The tanker set down in a field thirteen rods north of Yemi Province. All of the liquid is draining into a collateral glitch that formed into a canyon. Watch out for anomalies in that area.

The E-ray took more damage than expected. A single latch is all that holds the submersible to my body. I detach from the E-ray and examine the craft's battered surface with awe.

Ehari: How did this thing make it so far? I beat it to pieces!

Grey: I told you to be careful, remember?

Ehari: Yeah but… damn! I can shatter this thing with a single kick!

Grey: Well, you made it, didn't you?

Ehari: I did! Thanks again for another amazing hack.

Grey: You're welcome.

Most of the photonic fluid has already drained from the tanker but many rooms and corridors remain flooded. I wade to the ship's tilted deck for a better view of the city but my hope of finding survivors dwindles almost immediately.

Physical bombs have no power to unleash the chaos before me. Explosive ordinance—for instance—usually radiates a kaleidoscope of damage but Newark's wildlife preserve now resembles a marshy plateau of devastation. That collateral glitch Grey mentioned created a symmetrical gorge similar in size to the Grand Canyon. Most of the fluid has already drained into the dark reformatting pools exposed by the fracture. The amazing speed at which this occurred is mind-boggling. A swath of destruction leads from the fractured ground all the way back to Newark's Upper Residential District.

Bodies litter the entire scene. I see no survivors amongst the dead. Corpses appear moldy as though partially dissolved by some kind of bacteria. Lifeless virtual matter with relativistic origins normally reformats into photon bubbles but these bodies appear to have organically decomposed.

There's a staggering amount of destruction jumbled amongst the dead. The flood displaced many of Newark's buildings and smashed them into one another. Instead of crumbling apart, some kind of coding error has caused these structures to fuse together upon impact. The photonic liquid has strewed these clumped buildings about like scattered toys on a children's playground. Most of the garbage consists of consumable downloads and other recyclables. I descend the tanker's side and begin moving across the marsh once the initial shock subsides.

Ehari: Find any clues to Remi's whereabouts?

Grey: Sorry, but no. Maybe he… you know.

Ehari: I refuse to believe that.

Grey: You should at least consider the possibility.

Ehari: I will consider no such thing!

Grey: It might be easier locating him from outside of the Nexus.

Ehari: There's no evacuation plan without Remi.

Grey: Whatever you say. So how do we find him? Locating one person in a functioning city is hard enough, but Newark is in ruins now.

Ehari: Remi is resourceful. He found a way to survive just as you did. We have to figure out how. I want his last known location.

Grey: I have it but we face another problem. Newark broke into sections after Scarlet's outbreak destroyed the city's waypoints. Each section now floats atop reformatting pools. Remi disappeared on the largest surviving land mass. It includes most of the downtown area.

Ehari: How can I reach it?

Grey: There may be a way of getting there from the southern ports.

Ehari: How? Reformatting pools deconstruct

any data they touch. I'll be defaulted to my infant state if I fall inside one!

Grey: All you need to do is make it to the ports. I can mod a way across the pools.

All I need to do, huh? Grey makes it sound like the easiest thing in the world. *'All you need to do is make it to the ports…'* The southern ports are beyond the collapsed Zemi Bridge! How am I supposed to cross that?

A strong energy surge blows from the north, startling me with its presence and lifelike behavior. The approaching surge carries whispered words that spread across the entire marsh like gusts of wind. Each gust embodies an individual sentience independent of the overall energy flow.

Ehari: Where is this surge coming from?

Grey: It could be some kind of side effect from the virus.

Ehari: How are energy gusts in a dismantled and powerless city possible?

Grey: Technically, there's no way for a surge to exist under such conditions.

Ehari: I can hear whispers, too.

Grey: My scanners found no algorithmic matches for the surge or the whispers.

Ehari: What does that mean?

Grey: It must be a new form of viral mutation.

Ehari: Like what? Part three of the virus?

Grey: I have no idea, but you should probably seek shelter.

Ehari: Shelter? Are you crazy? The buildings are glitched!

Grey: Can you think of a better option?

No building in Newark provides adequate protection from anything anymore. All of their construction codes are destabilized. Any number of glitches might occur if I enter one so I decide to stay out of them while journeying onward.

Blast remnants from Scarlet's exploding nucleus smear the ashen bodies of those victimized by her initial viral outbreak. The residue shrivels the textures of its victims before permeating their meshing. This creates involuntary spasms and odd twitching commonly known as 'the corpse shuffle'. The new oddity involves breathing corpses. People within the Nexus have no functional use for such animations so why do some of these bodies appear to breathe? I move slowly and do my best to avoid touching anything.

Grey: Those corpses are exhibiting some strange signs.

Ehari: Are you talking about the breathing animation? I was just looking at that. What do you think it means?

Grey: It could be anything. My scanners detect no cause for the animation.

Ehari: Maybe it's a residual effect from the explosion.

One of the deceased husks startles me when it suddenly moves in a lifelike fashion. The corpse stares hauntingly into my eyes while contorting its body in weirdly inhuman positions. I back away and trip over a second body, which actually howls when I land next to it.

The animated corpse stares at me with hollow sockets and yells with absolute certainty, "We're all going to Hell! Every, single, one of us!"

I crawl away as the corpse levitates—one body part at a time—as though an invisible group of people decided to pick it up. The body fails to aggravate the mandates of gravity. Instead of stepping forward, it floats up and then hovers eerily like a ventriloquist doll with its crippled legs dangling about. Witnessing such a perversion of the human form paralyzes me with fear.

Grey: Run! Run! E, why are you standing there? Run!

The reality of living dead is far more frightening than the idea. The corpse moves forward as though manipulated by the invisible strings of a puppeteer. It lunges towards me while screaming, "We're all going to Hell!"

Grey: E!

Ehari: Dear God!

Grey: Run!

I roll away from the undead phantom when it reaches for my throat. A third corpse grabs my arm and auto activates the Fang Taser embedded in my wrist. The self-defense app releases two silvery threads that inject surplus electrons into the corpse's arm—breaking the electrostatic bond holding its limb together—shattering it. I nearly fall from the dizzying energy drain.

Grey: Behind you!

I stumble from lightheadedness and accidentally dodge the clawing swipe from a conjoined man and woman. A swift stroke of my hand releases another set of threads and when they wraps around the phantom's necks, one hard yank is enough to decapitate the howling abominations. Their shriveled heads and unified torso shatter at my feet as more undead rise from the mounds of scattered corpses.

Grey: Stay awake!

Ehari: But I feel so depleted—

Grey: Run! You have to run!

Ehari: I can barely move—

Grey: Run damn-it! Those things will rip you apart if you don't escape!

"We're all going to Hell," repeats the undead phantoms. "Every, single, one of us!"

I head for the southern ports but change direction when my vision blurs and wobble into a nearby house. Phantoms surround the suburban home while chanting fiendishly. I cross the living room and shuffle into the kitchen on weakened legs before collapsing next to a download dispenser.

The room flashes red as dawn penetrates its windows. Scarlet's virus has spread to the sun— which now rolls around the horizon instead of rising into the sky—encircling the city like a strobe light.

Grey: E, are you OK? Can you move?

Ehari: I… I… I think I dispersed too much energy. I have to recharge.

Grey: They're coming! Get out of there!

Grey gasps when some of the ghostly puppets push through the walls as if they were water.

The phantoms rhythmically chant like a tribe of cultists, "We're all going to Hell! We're all going to Hell! We're all going to Hell! We're all going to Hell!"

I consume an old power bar from a broken download dispenser and use the snack's energy boost to hobble into the hallway. Two phantoms glide across the living room as I head to the second floor but a stair glitch removed meshes from three of the steps. I fall through the unsupported textures and land somewhere between the basement and a data conduit. Light seeping through a split in the building's foundation catches my eye. I crawl towards it and notice the entrance to Princeton Hall half buried under rubble. With everything that's been happening, I'd forgotten about the subterranean portion of Newark.

Photonic smoke billows from the portal in curly puffs. Who knows what Scarlet's virus did to the underground portion of the city, but I have nowhere else to run and trigger the foremost projection step. I thank God when it activates and propel into the darkness as phantoms call out, "We're all going to Hell! Every, single, one of us!"

Crystal Paradise

CHAPTER 22

The Underground's architecture is renown for its beauty. Every square cube derives from geologically imprinted carats mined from the Earth's crust. Master jewelers designed every road, monument, and even the stadium-sized jumpwalks. A strategically placed lighthouse serves as the focal point. Its refracted light permeates every crystalline structure with an equal portion of radiance. Strolling through such a glittering world is the only way to appreciate its splendor. Unfortunately, this subterranean paradise is marred with viral deformities.

Rivers and lakes are now hollowed cavities that drift through the upper atmosphere like zeppelins. They form random shapes that further destabilize my simulator program. Clouds layer the ground in two-dimensional strips but continue their stormy routine—splaying showering fountains of water up from their inverted planes while casting random bolts of lightning into the sky—often popping the ballooning bodies of water with pinpricks of electricity—bursting them, and causing explosions of light similar to fireworks.

Many of the buildings lack textures due to a frame attachment error. Some of the detached textures form wrinkly piles of pastel colored sheets. Other textures lay sprawled across the ground as if they were discarded strips of wallpaper.

An energy restaurant has been "legged" in order to avoid the malfunctioning conduits running along the ground. The building strolls about like a prehistoric animal in the distance. Reaching it from my current location is unfeasible so I helplessly watch as it walks away—possibly with survivors.

Death idles about like a tax collector awaiting unclaimed revenue. Corpses of those who lost their lives in the initial outbreak lay splayed about like trash. None of these bodies exhibit breathing animations but I remain attentive to any signs of reanimation.

Trekking through this maze of corruption will take time. Viral hazards plague most projection steps, terminals, and data conduits. They trap anyone unlucky enough to enter Bonita Falls through a corrupt medium. Making it here without an error was a minor miracle.

I look about while fondling my Egyptian coin and observe the strong signal it casts. A kiwi-strawberry flavored cigarette finds its way to my lips. Igniting the tip wastes precious energy but the nicotine program soothes my nerves after a few drags. Exhaled kiwi and strawberry puff seedlings ripen into smoky fruit before dissipating. It's a worthy energy expenditure.

Ehari: Grey, are you there?

Grey: Yes.

Ehari: What happened?

Grey: You passed out on the projection step. You're lucky it malfunctioned after you used it. Those things might have followed you there, and… you know.

Ehari: How long was I unconscious?

Grey: About five hours. How do you feel?

Ehari: Only partially recharged. My linkage isn't completely blue, either.

Grey: You're running on backup power drawn from the step. You need to conserve your energy. Most of the conduits in that area are corrupt and saturating your vascular threads with a nicotine app isn't helping.

Ehari: Thanks for the advice, dad. What about Remi? Did you find him?

Grey: No. His signal remains dead and I found no other signs of life in that area.

Ehari: Really? What about that building I saw walking away? Aren't there people inside?

Grey: If so, they're not alive.

Ehari: Remi must be down here. There are too many abnormalities aboveground.

Grey: It's possible, but where?

Ehari: Where? I don't know where! Searching for Remi is like looking for a bit in a terabyte.

The Underground primarily functions as a citywide mall. Wares from all over the virtual world find exhibition in one of its four quadrants. I have a theory about Remi's whereabouts but traveling with the projectors off-line will make implementation extremely tedious. Walking under viral conditions is not just an annoyance; it's also a handicapping hazard. I begin scouring the immediate area for options once my cigarette depletes.

Few people are aware of my modding ability and self-proclaimed title as 'Jill of All Trades'. I create a portable projector in relatively little time by combining parts from broken projection steps and abandoned merchandise. There are even a few proton bulbs lying about that I use to power it. The finished mod resembles a small lawn mower motor. I connect my neural link to the app's control mechanism and use a custom HUD dynamic with new iconography that highlights green zones in the environment, filters viral traps, and hosts my reactionary functions. Once the parameters are set I merge the entire app into a pack mesh and strap it my back.

Grey: What are you doing?

Ehari: What I do best—modding.

Grey: I didn't know you could mod…

Ehari: Not many people know and I haven't had the time for modding lately. The cloud simulator was keeping me busy. I refuse to mountaineer the entire Underground just because the projectors are down.

Grey: Indeed… but, what did you just create?

Ehari: A portable projector.

Grey: That sounds dangerous. I know a few

engineers who ripped themselves apart trying to create similar devices. Maybe you should just walk.

Ehari: I *hate* walking long distances.

Grey: Where do you plan on going with that thing?

Ehari: The lighthouse.

Grey: How will you reach it? The portals are down.

Ehari: I'll find a way.

Grey: Do you think Remi is there?

Ehari: No, but I can use the lighthouse to find him.

Grey: How?

Ehari: I'll figure that out when I get there.

I connect my neural link's targeting reticule to the portable projector's activation switch and scan various green zones for a viable connection point. The neural link designates my chosen destination via pupil dilation and activates the projector. My environment blurs when I thrust to the targeted location but it reforms upon arrival. An extensive check for bodily glitches reveals no abnormalities so I plot another successful jump before feeling secure enough to save the portable projector's program to my largest memory pocket.

The lighthouse rests beyond thirty thousand cubes of hazardous terrain. My projector only jumps thirty-cubes at a time. Environmental factors seem unaffected by the PP's temporary warping of virtual space so the trip should go well if I can avoid anomalies.

I've frequented the Underground on numerous occasions but only explored a fraction of each massive quadrant. Buyer's Circle is where I end up. My current location—marked with a glittering diamond obelisk—is the convergence point for all districts. It's a popular tourist attraction but I've never visited any of the avenues that extend from here.

Grey: I detect intermittent signs of life in Bonita Falls!

Ehari: Survivors? How did you find survivors?

Grey: Someone is sending distorted neural messages from there. Most are distress calls from people trying to evacuate the area.

Ehari: My neural map is offline. Where's Bonita Falls?

Grey: The access port is about seven virtual miles north of your current position, inside of a gallery in the Fountain District.

Ehari: Are there any people in my immediate vicinity?

Grey: None that I can detect. Have you figured out what you're planning to do if you reach the lighthouse?

Ehari: Let me work that out. I have to reach the lighthouse just to see if my theory is possible.

I'm astounded by the scenery's mesmeric glints of light. I would've actually preferred walking to my destination under different circumstances. Yes, you heard me… I'd *walk* through here and actually enjoy it! I know I know… that's crazy, right? Of all people, imagine me, walking… but this place is so wondrous it'd be nice to stroll through it with someone you love.

It takes some time but I carefully project to the Fountain District after negotiating my way through various anomalies. The area caters specifically to aquatic art. An innumerable number of exhibits fill the gallery and sphere-boxing formats. Two imaging pillars set within a diamond-chiseled pavilion illustrate the options and history for each format. Both cater to diverse forms of art.

Sphere-boxing exhibits place the observer inside a global array containing three-dimensional pieces of static art. This method of observation allows people to reach out and acquire these "traditional" forms of art, which they fondle and observe.

Bonita Falls rests within the gallery format. Verbally activating this option opens a boulevard leading to pictorial representations of interactive exhibits. The exhibits hang along both sides of the avenue like paintings. I approach one of the walls after examining some of the art.

"Display Bonita Falls."

A portrait of an island paradise surfaces before me. I activate the overlay entrance subpanel beneath the picture. All other exhibits blur when Bonita Falls spatially magnifies to assume greater three-dimensional depth.

As the name suggests, Bonita Falls is a fountain based on the size and scope of a beautiful waterfall.

It's the type of art suited for owners of castles, temples, forts, or some other extravagant abode.

The actual exhibit consists of a tree-shaped waterspout that crowns a towering island in the middle of an elliptic valley. Its crystalline branches jettison pressurized streams of water into the sky, which rains down on the surrounding mountain range encircling the island. Water then flows into the valley through snaking streams sewn throughout the entire mountainside. As the streams travel about like racecar drivers they create a series of descending rivulets, which form thousands of waterfalls that fill the inner basin with a glistening lake.

Grey: That island is a relay point for distress calls but I can't figure out why the signal strength in this area intensified.

Ehari: H_2O programs were unaffected by Scarlet's virus.

Grey: That explains a lot… they're the paste holding all life together. H_2O programs make the perfect conduits for viral transmission!

Ehari: We need to find out if Remi is on that island.

Grey: I'm detecting floating mines in the lake and somebody fortified the beach with electron netting. Bypassing them is your first priority. I should get there to help you.

Ehari: How could you possibly reach me?

Grey: I'm already with you.

Ehari: The coin?

I retrieve the coin and notice Grey's face on the head's side. He winks at me.

Grey: Yeah. I hid inside the coin after linking with a power station. You have no idea how hard it is to compress a mind like mine, into a space like this!

Ehari: You sneaky bastard! You were afraid Scarlet was listening to our link, that's why you didn't tell me where you were! You thought I was going to die and wanted to make sure you'd stay hidden!

Grey: You have to admit, that you barely made it out of Newark.

Ehari: You're a coward! You could have helped me escape instead of hiding in my pocket!

Grey: I did help you escape!

Ehari: You helped yourself escape!

Grey: Coincidental trade-off… besides, we were dealing with a limited power situation. We barely had enough energy for one person.

Ehari: You could have had a little more confidence in me.

Grey: Sure. Now will you please find a way to stabilize my emergence program?

Ehari: I can submerge the coin—you, in water.

Grey: Good idea. I need a moment to prepare.

A glassy portal drops from a ceiling outlet when I select the Bonita Falls tour option on the guide subpanel. I peer through it, study my first available destination, and plot a route to the island.

The first path is unimpressive so I soft stroke the subpanel with my fingertips and scroll through more entry points. Something about the harbor entrance catches my eye so I pause for a closer look.

The harbor's diamond pier offers the closest protrusion to the island. Assorted boats line its wharf. Most appear haphazardly docked. Unsealing the portal causes the Bonita Falls cubicle to become a fully rendered three-dimensional space. The entire area unfolds around me. I follow a gravel path to the wharf. From there, it's a short walk across the diamond pier where arrays of colorful fish swim beneath my feet. I head for a yacht on the far end, board the ship's astern, lean over its guardrail, and flip Grey into the water.

Ehari: You're submerged.

Grey: I can tell. My neural link fully stabilized.

Ehari: Can you establish an outside line?

Grey: Negative. There's too much interference beyond Bonita Falls.

Ehari: Hurry up. I want to get to that island.

Luminescent bubbles trickle to the surface before a burst of light briefly illuminates the murk. I catch a glimpse of Grey's silhouette before he emerges seconds later. He swims to the yacht and uses one of his custom gravity mods to stand on the waves.

"For the record," he nods, "you're one hell of a survivor."

"I'm one hell of a survivor?" A sarcastic smirk

widens my face. "You're the one who compressed yourself into a tiny coin. I didn't even know a feat like that was possible!"

"My genius has no bounds, even in tight spaces."

I give Grey a quick hug. "Dork."

Grey checks his neural link for a signal. "Why not head to the lighthouse from here?"

"Have you been listening to those distress calls? A horde of undead surrounded the entire district! The lighthouse is blocked. We'll have to join the island forces if we want to survive."

Grey curls his lips. "We don't know who's on that island. It might be better if we find our own way."

"What other choice do we have? A few of those things are no problem but five million undead is a formidable force. Going to the lighthouse right now, is suicide. We need to establish a link with whoever is in command."

"I'm on it, Major. Doesn't this feel like old times?"

I wave Grey away when the island's emergency dispatcher responds to my first neural message.

Dispatcher: Di Ehari? It feels good to hear another friendly thought!

Ehari: You have no idea!

Dispatcher: Did you come from outside the city?

Ehari: Yes.

Dispatcher: Are you here to help us?

Ehari: Not exactly. We came here looking for a

man named Stephen Remi.

Dispatcher: Stephen Remi? I never heard of him.

Ehari: Can you link me to the person in charge?

Dispatcher: Sorry, but you have to meet them in person. Command links are down. I think they decided to redistribute the power elsewhere. Where are you?

Ehari: We're at the wharf, on a white yacht.

Dispatcher: We mined the lake and beach. There's no need for alarm, though. We can provide temporarily passage by deactivating that section of the minefield.

Ehari: Thanks. Who's in command?

Dispatcher: Depends. Chief of Security Dwar Parthis organizes our defensive protocols. Solus Miller controls the offensive details.

Ehari: So the island's residents divided into separate forces based on offense and defense?

Dispatcher: Basically. No one has ever dealt with army-sized forces before. Ancient combat has no real purpose in the Nexus. Anyway, when the residents couldn't agree on a leader or plan, they separated based on tactical disposition. Those who believed in a defensive strategy joined Parthis. Everyone else gathered with Miller.

Ehari: How big are these groups?

Dispatcher: About four thousand men and women evenly split.

Ehari: Separating in such a way seems like an odd form of compromise.

Dispatcher: At least both groups have the same goal of stopping those floating undead. We were attacked about three hours ago by a massive swarm of them. A lot of people died.

Ehari: I see… well, I readied the yacht.

Dispatcher: Please wait for approach and docking confirmation.

Ehari: Understood.

Grey helps prepare the yacht before steering the vessel along the dispatcher's coordinates. I join him at the controls and monitor the deactivating mines.

"What did you find during your analysis of my footage?"

Grey grunts, then his eyes widen like a child who'd forgotten his favorite toy at the park. "Sorry I didn't think of telling you any sooner, but there's another world inside the pyramid! I found it when adjusting the cortex filter on your footage."

"You forgot to tell me about a newly discovered world?" I gawk with bewilderment. "How is that possible with your ego?"

"Sorry, but with all that's been happening—"

"So what did you see?"

Grey shrugs, "I'm not sure. You were the only thing I actually saw floating inside the pyramid. It was foggy in there and numerical related data made up the bulk of what I discovered. Do you remember anything?"

"Yes," I nod, "there was a void. Like the void

of outer space."

"Really? That coincides with my theory."

"What theory?"

"I think the pyramid might be some kind of Nexus." Grey adds with a raised finger, "I'm not sure though, because the area within is not quantified."

"It's not?"

"No."

I think back to my brief time within the pyramid. It resembled a place of the mind—free of physical limitations and unlike the virtual world, there was no need to replicate physicality. Life moved within an ocean of transparency.

"So… you're telling me there's an entire world inside the pyramid?"

"It seems that way. I also think the world is filled with multiple planes similar to the Nexus' Realms."

"How do you learn all of this from numerical data?"

"I made adjustments to the cortex settings on your footage and recorded a few environmental readings."

"When was the pyramid created?"

"That, I don't know. And I don't know enough to guess."

"The Nexus was magnetically hacked from the outside. Do you have any idea how that could've happened?"

"No," he mumbles, "but I have a theory."

"Well, what is it?"

"Hannibal might be responsible."

"What? Hannibal? You're crazy!"

"Hold on," Grey pleads with open palms, "hear me out first! Hannibal is the only one who remained in the physical world when the rest of us returned."

"That doesn't mean he's responsible for the hack. Hannibal doesn't even know how to hack!"

"He could have been coached."

"By who? He's alone out there with no link to the virtual world. Besides… if that were true you would've found hard evidence by now!"

"How else could the virtual world be hacked from the outside?"

"What about Remi? We don't even know where he is. Why not accuse him?"

"I think Remi is too loyal. But who knows…"

"You're crazy." I back away from the controls and stare out of the cabin's windows. "Hannibal wouldn't betray us. He's an honorable man."

"I know you've been thinking it too, E. His brain injury could have done something to him that we don't know about. Hannibal might not be the same person you grew up knowing. Do you have any other ideas?"

"No, but Remi might. He has a knack for figuring this type of thing out. That's one of the reasons why we need to find him."

Grey brings the yacht to a halt inside the island's main harbor. I hear mines reactivating in the lake while the beach's electron nets power off. A pathway illuminates directly ahead.

"Ladies first." Grey says, stepping aside.

I have no fear when disembarking and take the lead. We follow the allotted trail all the way to a guard station. The awaiting escorts lead us to the island's colony where a curly haired guide named Estra—who wrestled professionally in another Realm—awaits near a flagpole. The guide takes us to private chambers where a complimentary energy allotment awaits. It's here that I receive a neural text from an untraceable source. It's an odd form of old-fashioned massaging when you consider that, a person can just as easily send a neural *message*, instead. The content appears limited by a lack of energy from the sender.

From Remi: I'm in the Pacific Vortex! Grey tried to kill me! Watch yourself, E. You're nex–

Law of Averages

CHAPTER 23

I didn't remember them by name and should have. Dwar Parthis and Solus Miller were teammates in *The Suffering* and one of my indirect contenders. Mandible 9 disqualified their group by outranking them in the Worldwide Contenders Board of Competition. It was a ruinous ordeal for both. Dwar lost major endorsements from sponsors and his longtime girlfriend. Solus' brother committed suicide after battling bouts of depression in the following weeks. My team was preoccupied with our training and paid little attention to the downfall of others. I vaguely remember seeing news coverage of Jonathan Miller's death, his mother rebuking virtual games, and fragments from the subsequent documentary about the "dangers" of virtual gaming.

Apparently, Dwar and Solus are now at odds and positioned themselves on opposite sides of the island. The mines and electron nets along the northeast shore are a part of Dwar's defensive strategy. His band of followers erected various battlements along the beachhead as well. The island's fortified amphitheater now serves as Dwar's base of operations. We meet our host inside the building's main office on the top floor, where Dwar and three of his top advisors gather around a holographic map of the island. Dwar separates from the group to address me personally.

"Di Ehari? Your face is all over the Virtualnet. I thought you died in the outbreak. What are you doing here?"

Dwar reminds me of Agent Grills. Both men have similarly stocky figures and rigid, well-defined facial features.

"I'm looking for a friend of mine, Stephen Remi."

"The loudmouth? Yeah, I remember him. We keep a detailed manifest of everyone under my command. He's not a part of my group and if Remi was in Newark when the bomb detonated he's probably a gonner."

"If we don't do something soon, everyone here will be gonners."

"Are you talking about those floating zombies? Don't worry. I've taken the necessary precautions." Dwar motions to his holographic map. "The entire northeast section of the island is fortified."

He leads us closer for a better look. I shake my head after glancing over the battlements.

"That won't work."

Annoyance reshapes Dwar's face with such distinction that he almost appears to be a different man. Bulging temples flexed from grinding teeth, exaggerate his expression.

"I hope you don't think I'm going to let you walk in here and start making commands, Di."

"I don't care about command structures, I just want to live. Those undead are more powerful than you think. Your barricade won't hold them back. There has to be another way."

"My strategy *is* the only way!"

I quietly project data from my neural link to Dwar's holographic map and overlay the battlement image with footage of my undead encounter. Everyone in the room becomes unsettled when they realize barricades won't stop the horde. I use their distress to reiterate my point.

"The horde passes through textures. They'll float right through your barricades and delete everyone inside your encampment. We need to come up with a new plan."

"We," Dwar announces, pointing to his inner circle, "are going to come up with a new plan. Now excuse yourself."

"I can help you think of something."

"Go! Now!"

Grey grabs my shoulder when I step forward. "Let's go. Maybe we'll have better luck with Solus."

"You know that's a stupid suggestion. Dwar is our best chance. Solus is crazy."

Grey nods, "That's why we have to make sure Remi isn't with him."

Because he's right, I follow Grey out of the building and back to the beach. We have to walk across the island now that Dwar and Solus decided to deactivate the jumpways and purge them for power.

I swear… walking sucks! How did primitive humans put up with it? They must have hated walking too. That's probably why they created automobiles and aircrafts. As we walk across the island at an agonizingly slow pace, Grey gestures to a variety of modified energy conduits.

"Do you see that? Dwar and Solus are draining power from the Market District."

"And?"

"They're hoarding all of the main energy! Even if we leave Bonita Falls, there won't be anything left for the rest of the district."

I pause by one of the conduits and examine it thoroughly. "Damn, you're right! Everything outside of Bonita Falls will go dark."

"It's worse than that. They're purging all of the nodes. The Market District will revert to a neutronic state. Nothing will work and every object in the district will freeze in place."

"Can we tap into any of these conduits or disrupt them?"

"I don't think so. Well, not without Dwar or Solus knowing. They linked the island's power directly to proton outlets on opposite ends of the island. Why would they do that?"

"It doesn't matter. There has to be a way of tapping into the conduits and creating some kind of energy spike. We could use the spike to puncture the Market District's architecture and escape."

"Yeah… that might actually work!" Grey savors the idea before pointing out the obvious. "The only problem is that we'd need a massive burst of power to breach the barrier. Maybe Solus is willing to see your logic."

"Doubtful… we need to come up with another plan just in case he's vision impaired."

Solus is an emotional man who probably won't agree to any proposals. It takes a little time but we devise a backup plan before reaching our destination.

Everything about Solus' suzerain setup troubles me. His arrangement resembles a medieval encampment. Instead of using energy to construct actual objects, Solus' members are utilizing their resources for body modifications and not a single einstein is wasted.

Solus' mob of followers flanks a collection of tents lining the southwestern beach. They part upon our arrival and open a direct path to a campfire, where Solus awaits.

Our host is a large man. Perhaps, one of the largest I'd ever seen. His curled hair, shaggy beard, and pitted face are reminiscent of barbarian explorers. Solus rises from a cross-legged position and steps right into his multicolored campfire, where he lingers within the coiling flames as some kind of dogmatic power display. I realize now, that the campfire is actually the proton outlet for his conduit. Solus and his followers seem to be taking turns overcharging their meshing with it.

He glares at me and says, "Yuz gotta lot of nerve

coming here, Di! My bro did suicide over yuz. Gimme one reason why I shouldn't kill yuz!"

Grey immediately steps ahead of me. "I won't let you do anything to—"

Solus uppercuts the air and releases a blistering ball of ionic fire at Grey, who barely blocks the attack using crossed arms shielded with neutrino studs that break on impact. The subcutaneously meshed joints in his left arm shatter as Grey stumbles into me and we nearly fall to the ground as Solus levitates above the campfire.

"Speak when spoken to or die where yuz stand!"

"Grey," I reach out sympathetically, "your arm!"

Grey pulls the injured limb against his chest as the crowd howls like a pack of bloodthirsty wolves.

"Solus is way too strong! I used half my power to block that attack! Another blow—"

Solus repeats louder, "Gimme one reason why I shouldn't kill yuz! If yuz don't, I'll tear apart every atom in yur body!"

I wasn't expecting this amount of hatred! Hiding my fear isn't easy. I cling to Grey while pleading, "I had nothing to do with your brother's suicide! I barely knew him!"

Solus grabs Grey with a magnetic chain, pulls him to his knees, and then yanks my friend away from me. Grey tumbles into the circling crowd where a trio of large men immediately restrains him.

"Yuz had everything ta do with ma bro's suicide! Yuz teased him! Yuz belittled him! Yuz degraded him! Yuz corrupted his mind!"

"It was trash-talk! Everybody did it! It was just a game!"

Solus smashes me into the ground with a crushing downward stroke of his fist. I don't even see the magnetic hammer he uses to strike me with, until it's too late. The blow scrambles my neural link so badly that static replaces the clear vision in my left eye. I realize there's no reasoning with him whatsoever. Even worse, I'm not sure if I can escape Solus or his crowd of wannabe supervillains and the uncertainty is paralyzing.

"A game? Yuz think ma bro's life, wuz a game?" Solus descends into the proton fire—his body glows as he absorbs energy from the outlet—and the flames grow when Solus levitates back into the air. "Let's play a game, with yur life!"

Solus abandons the fire and throws a blinding ionic ball with enough power to deatomize an entire group of people. I use my portable projector to avoid the sphere before it crashes into the ground and burrows out of view.

The crowd roars as Solus circles me. I dash into the campfire when he pauses to grandstand. Absorbing and using proton energy at the same time is impossible. As I recharge one of the onlookers flings electron arrows at me so I relocate. This only heightens Solus' rage.

"Leave her be! Yuz think I can't defeat this worm? Di's life is mine! Sine missione!"

"Sine missione!" The crowd chants, "Unto death! No mercy! Unto death! No mercy!"

Solus floats into the pillar of fire and harnesses enough energy to create a concentrated disc of protons. He stands atop the hovering platform before stomping down on it, and the entire disc drops like an elevator. I use nearly all of my power to ward off the disc as it presses my contorted body deep into the earth.

Everything blackens. Sounds muffle. My body is stifled. It takes a few seconds to realize that I'm not dead. There's no breathable air in the virtual world so I won't suffocate but my body will meld with the dirt if I'm under too long. It's the same result as asphyxiation—a painful death. I claw my way through the dirt and the cracked proton disc only to emerge inside a cylindrical pit about forty-cubes in diameter, and one hundred cubes deep. Solus seals this pit with another energy disc. His mob of followers gather atop the semitransparent lid and peer down as Solus descends the spiraling funnel of proton energy pouring from the conduit's compressed outlet rising from the pit's center.

Solus doesn't waste a moment and immediately hurls negatively charged electron bricks at me. I dodge them using my portable projector. Each brick smashes into the pit's inner wall and explodes into a fiery ball. My power supply drops to critical levels as I zip about—dashing through the column of proton fire whenever an opportunity arises. The small bursts of energy are barely enough to sustain my projector but Solus doesn't have the patience to wait for its full depletion. His anger surges with each missed brick—which grow progressively larger as if to symbolize Solus' increasing aggression. The pit shudders from the impacts, stirring photonic dust that clouds my movements. I dodge three more attacks and stoke Solus' rage as he searches the haze for me. The braided pillar of fire is the only thing that remains fully visible. I zip through the twirling flame four more times and absorb enough power to project about the pit's spiral walls until I reach the top, but the energy lid's surface isn't smooth. My hands stick to its anti-neutronic surface and bind me in place when I try breaking through.

The zerging group of followers glares down like wild Neanderthals and yells, "Kill her!"

Solus thrusts his arm up, grabs my waist with his magnetic chain, and then yanks me down. I project through the air before hitting the ground and attach to notches in the wall created by the exploding bricks. Solus tries bashing me with his hammer but this time, I escape the bludgeoning magnetic head and steal more energy from the flaming outlet before darting about like a fly to different areas of the pit.

"One hit is all I need to delete yuz! Juss one!"

Solus changes tactics once again and begins throwing simmering proton blades that boomerangs about. They screech through the air like living creatures—diving up and down—back and forth—and then fizzle out. Some of the curved blades hit

Solus but he barely flinches. Two of the blades nearly decapitate me but Solus quickly grows impatient as I continue proving my determination to live.

He pauses to create a massive atomic sword that quadruples my body's length, and then holds the blade upright like a knight of old. The energy Solus expends is immense and the effects are showing. His movements are becoming lethargic and the proton filaments surrounding his body dims with every weapon he creates. Solus moves about swinging his sword as I do everything within my power to avoid him. My neural link beeps as Grey tries messaging me but the column of fire and Solus' energy lid disrupts the signal.

Solus proceeds to gouge the pit's inner wall with his explosive blade and on three occasions, the lacerating force of his sword nearly severs me in half and almost collapses the pit. I continue evading his swings as chaos erupts aboveground. Solus' followers scatter from view as the ground shakes from a massive explosion.

Solus pauses to glare at me. "Yuz wuz a decoy!"

Solus leaps up and shatters the energy lid with a superman-like bound. I project out of the pit and emerge in the center of a frenzied battle that consumes the entire beachhead and the skies above.

A proton Frisbee flies pass me like a whining bird of white light as it severs three people in half. Another man dies when a woman crushes his head with a compression club. Two more explode after someone injects them with an electron syringe that fills their body with a steady increase of negatively charged particles.

What first appears as mutiny is actually a surprise offensive. Dwar is attempting to lay siege to Solus' encampment in an effort to claim complete control of both energy outlets. I catch a glimpse of Dwar and Solus converging in midair as Grey weaves his way through the onslaught to reach me.

"Dwar got the distress call," says Grey. "Your backup plan worked! This is our chance to escape!"

We head for the conduit's outlet as Dwar and Solus fall into the pit and begin tearing each other apart. I pull Grey in another direction when the spire of fire disappears.

"We're too late! They're clogging the outlet!"

"Get out of here before the outlet explodes!" Grey pushes me when I refuse to budge. "You have a portable projector!"

I shake my head and push back. "I'm not leaving you behind!"

"There's a surge in the conduit! If I don't hack into the outlet right now we'll never make it out of here! Don't worry! I have an escape plan! Meet me at the aquarium!"

Grey turns towards the pit and leaps inside before I can stop him. There's no way I can help. My portable projector is running on particles and I might not have enough energy to escape the battlefield. Unfortunately, fleeing seems to be the only real option left.

I project away from the beachhead as people continue dying in the most gruesome ways imaginable. The carnage is horrible. I pass armored warriors, mutated humanoids, vampire-like creatures, and even a conjoined group of people that merge into a giant. Both sides crush, rip, bite, and eviscerate each other like demonic creatures. By the time I reach the safety of a distant crag, light from the outlet's slender column of fire has expanded to encompass the full radius of the pit.

Ehari: Grey, where are you? The outlet—

A massive burst of fire rises from the pit as I await a response. The outlet explodes seconds later. A blinding light obscures the entire southwestern horizon before the entire beach crumbles into the lake and disappears.

Zero Code: If-Not, Then-Why?

CHAPTER 24

The conduit explosion that destroyed one fifth of the island deleted many—if not all—of the people fighting along its southwestern beach. Contamination fills the area so going back to search for Grey isn't an option. I head to the aquarium after he fails to signal me within a reasonable amount of time.

Most of Solus' half of the island lacks external power. Pier alarms and a few emergency conductors remain functional but everything else seems dead. Even the massive fountain in the island's center has stopped working.

The only way of reaching the aquarium involves a lengthy stroll through a prehistoric jungle path. Of course, my portable projector's energy reserves slump to near nonexistent levels, so that means I have to *walk* all the way to the rendezvous and every, single, step, annoys me.

The rough and uneven ground bends all over the place in weird directions and angles! If that wasn't enough, there are hilly areas that require climbing, or hiking, or whatever prewar humans called these arduous treks over rough terrain. What lunatic designed this path? Does he have some sadistic fetish for torturing people's feet? Every detestable moment makes me want to break my legs! Maybe he thinks we're in the physical world because he didn't even fix some of the rocks into place! Although it's an embarrassing admission, I actually trip and fall after sliding on loose gravel. The worst part is that I fell on my front memory pocket and corrupted my last cigarette. Now it won't ignite! If there's a Hell, it probably contains scores of people walking up paths like this. Maybe I died in Dwar's offensive and I'm already there…

I reach the island's aquarium and decide to calm my rattled nerves with a swim. There doesn't appear to be anyone in the area but caution remains a top priority. I keep my photonic dagger cuffed when dipping into a tank filled with several monk seals and a thriving coral reef.

Watching the aquatic life relaxes me more than the actual water. Real physical water has a way of… massaging the body on a molecular level. Maybe it has something to do with the hydrogen atoms.

At the very least, the program in this seal tank should strengthen my neural link, which I've set to transmit intermittent messages to Remi and Grey's signature. Maybe Remi will respond and even though Grey is the one who designated our rendezvous, he may need assistance getting here. I even set up a third link for Izreh.

I swim through the reef and find a functioning conductor nestled between rocks along the tank's floor. It's the only emergency backup source for the animals, in case of power failure. Zoo employees like me, know these things. There's no danger of drowning in virtualized water so I lay across the conductor's outlet and allow its radiating energy to recharge my depleted cells.

Even though I haven't stayed awake for five consecutive days, recent events have exasperated my usual thirty-five hour regeneration cycle, which I usually take during the weekend. I have a lot of respect for prewar humans. I'm not sure how they were able to accomplish anything sleeping eight hours a day every sixteen hours.

Some of the younger seals swim around me as I contemplate ways of escaping the undead horde. Watching their graceful underwater summersaults helps me idle. I drift into standby mode after thirty minutes and see vague events, things, and people, manifest before me.

I'm not supposed to see anything in standby except for the status menu that accompanies the dormancy of a deactivated consciousness. I've had this problem before and consulted with a physician about it. He told me that my synaptic pathways are probably misfiring and not completely shutting down. Apparently, seeing images or any form of playback while in standby mode is a mental error caused by uncompressed experiences.

I have other theories…

What if I'm dreaming? It's possible, isn't it? My neurology is relatively unchanged from that of prewar humans, so why not? The minds of all cognitive creatures living in the Nexus malfunction if we operate beyond our maximum time limits, because partitions in the solid-state portions of our neural networks degrade after our conscious access memories fill with overwritten data. Once our CAMs stop filtering properly, a perception error known as flashbacking occurs, and people begin seeing, hearing, or even feeling things that aren't real.

Wasn't this true of prewar humans?

After staying awake too long, they'd see things and would eventually go crazy. I believe the convoluted concentration of too much information was the problem. Sleeping was the ancient mind's way of offloading pertinent experiences to memory and clearing up the wet brain's RAM.

Essentially, being awake in the biological and virtual states holds identical meanings and purposes. The organic antennae that was the physical body, served as a tool for gathering and relaying information. Combining all aspects of the body like— eyes—nose—ears—skin—tongue—etc, rendered a live stream of the moment known as consciousness, which could even be achieved with fewer senses. The body expends its 'active energy' reserves during times of consciousness. Once depleted, the body enters sleep mode and uses 'passive energy' to repair and update its sensory devices.

Neural links and meshing replaced physical bodies. The advent of neural technology merges all senses previously associated with physicality, into a single medium. Physical bodies like the prostheticalanatomy that I used, have higher sensitivity per sense but lack the overall unification of a single sensory perception. Such a deficiency is like being born without a sense.

Prewar movie producers come to mind. They'd often use video and audio equipment to film excessive amounts of footage. However, producers only used a small fraction of that content to construct their movies. Only the parts deemed relevant formed the basis for their productions. Wet brains operated in a similar fashion. People needed to sleep in order to construct an episodic memory of the previous day's recording. All conscious creatures need periodic resetting before they can absorb more experiences. That's why I'm hesitant to accept that everything I'm seeing now, in standby mode, is nothing more than flashbacking.

What do I see?

I see an angel of light emerging from a triangular darkness. The angel places the entire world into my palms—I crush it—and in doing so, crush myself. Its meaning, if any, eludes me. There's more but after nearly twenty-eight hours of regenerating, I awaken…

COGNITIVE REACTIVATION INITIATED	
PATTERN BUFFER STRENGTH	0 - 25 - 50 - 75 - 100 - 125 - 150 - 175 - 200 - 225 ^ (224.90888090)

COGNITION POWER	SATURATION 95.9890 %	Synced wattage; memory fluctuation found in dream set [Seti-09]; anomalous sequence detected—INSURRECTION	
VIRTUAL ENERGY	PULSE RATE 36.56 BP	RECHARGE 89.67 %	PHOTONIC IO: DILUTED
MESH COHESION	LINKAGE 67,890 AR	LIMB ACTIVATION: ON	VASCULAR STREAM: ACTIVE
NEURAL STRENGTH	WAVELENGTH 72.89 API	FREQUENCY 95685.4 MHz	OUTPUT: WAKING

Grey: E, are you here?

Ehari: Grey? You're alive!

Grey: Indeed but, barely. Where are you?

Ehari: In the seal tank. Hold on, I'm coming out.

Two monk seals encircle me as I swim to the water's surface. They clap their fins as Grey helps me out of the aquarium. The water contains anti-adhesive codes that prevent droplets from attaching to my body so there's no need for drying off.

Grey looks like he's been through Hell. His forearm remains broken, so every movement he makes with it looks odd. Neither of us can fix fractures so his limb will have to stay malformed until we find medical help. The photonic explosion singed the lower half of Grey's body with a thin layer of golden ash. He even walks with a limp due to some unannounced injury.

I hug Grey before asking, "What happened back there? How did you survive the blast?"

"It was crazy… Dwar and Solus were at each other's throats when I dropped into that pit. They were beating each other up pretty badly."

"And?"

"And they didn't pay attention to me but there was no way to integrate with the outlet. It sustained too much damage. Attempting to reroute the power accelerated that explosion. I fastened a neutrino graph to my body and rode the energy stream out of there before everything went boom. It dropped me on the other side of Bonita Falls. That's why it took me so long getting here."

"Find any signs of Remi?"

Grey appears genuinely saddened by Remi's absence. He bites his lip before saying, "No. Nothing."

I use the Trinity optic lens gifted by Agent Grills to reprogram my outfit from a swimsuit, to something militaristic. The change occurs instantly.

"I tried linking with Remi underwater and got nothing."

"I don't want to sound glib, but maybe he's…"

We stare uncomfortably at each other for a few moments before leaving the seal tank. Is Grey's insistence on Remi's death pragmatic or deceitful? Remi's mysterious neural text comes to mind. Did it really come from Remi or is Scarlet the author? She could be trying to sow discord amongst my team. It wouldn't be the first time.

I assume residence in the aquarium's lobby and examine a mural depicting Newark before Scarlet's viral bombardment. Grey tasks himself with searching for an open link to the outside world.

"What really happened between you and Scarlet's husband?"

I lower my head a bit, in shame. How does one illustrate a relationship of the mind or truly explain untapped desire? Can you really articulate the density of emotional sustenance or the sprite of love?

"His name was Seti."

Grey taps his chest with the tip of his index finger. "You loved him, didn't you?"

"Loved, defines a cherished moment that can never be lost or regained. So yes, there was a time when I loved Seti. I loved him dearly, in fact. We shared our deepest intimacies, thoughts, and emotions. Life offered nothing greater and even to this day, no person has touched my soul with such intensity. The time we shared seemed endless but now... those same moments scar my psyche with fleeting impressions of happiness."

Grey looks up while gritting his teeth. "That sounds poetically... tragic." His eyes quickly dip below my gloomy stare.

"Sometimes, I wish my relationship with Seti was a fantasy and not this... curse inflicting emotional sterility. I still feel empty without him. He was so smart, and funny, and engaging… I couldn't get enough of him."

"You make loving someone seem like an addiction."

"It's more like, a binding." I check my neural link for incoming signals and notice something odd, which I keep to myself. "Have you gotten any outside signals?"

"No. So did you do… *it?*"

I grin, "We never actually consummated our feelings. Even though I cared for Seti, betraying Scarlet was not an option. She was my best friend."

"They say cheating with the heart is the worst form of betrayal."

"I can't control how I feel. I can only control how I act."

Grey seems amused. His voice lightens. "If that's the case, then Scarlet is indentured to her emotions!"

"Yeah… I think what hurts Scarlet more than anything, is how Seti never cared for her in the same way that he cared for me."

"So is it true that you met Scarlet at your parent's funeral?"

"Yes. We became friends at the wake and formed Mandible 9 during Junior High. Scarlet was the first member. We were best friends by the time Hannibal and Remi joined the team."

"So how did you end up falling in love with Scarlet's husband?"

My grievous sigh explains the gist of what I

have to say. "I don't know. We just… grew close over time. Seti would come to the condo and help with my cloud simulator program. We'd meet in the backyard and test updates together. He'd sit so close to me that I could almost hear his heart pulsing. I did everything to avoid touching him, because laying just one finger on Seti…" I pause to steady my thoughts. "We need to get an outside connection. Try linking with another station or rerouting the signal."

Grey picks up his equipment and tries following my orders but eventually turns towards me and asks, "Who was the man that killed your mother in the memory Scarlet tried using against you? He looked familiar."

I slap Grey without even thinking about it and he gasps with surprise. My teeth grind from the heartache of that terrible night and swallowing my raging emotions consumes large portions of mind-power.

"I'm sorry for hitting you."

"No, it's my fault. I had no right to ask such a personal question."

I stand up, approach one of the shark tanks, and study the hammerhead swimming within. Its graceful movements soothe my agitation. Words spill from me after watching the shark swim about.

"He was my dad."

"Oh crap," Grey ruefully nods through the tank's reflection. He tries thinking of something comforting to say but fails to conjure anything sincere enough to vocalize.

"My dad worked for the Institute of Virtual Science and Technology." I hold back tears adding, "He carried me into the backyard every day after work. We'd stare into the sky imagining what the clouds looked like."

"It sounds like he loved you a lot."

I nod, "He did. And I loved him."

"So is that why you like clouds?"

"I don't *really* like clouds. They just remind me of dad."

"How did he get infected with the Gordon's virus?"

I slump forward and let my forehead rest against the tank. "It happened when he was at work. Dad tried to help the VBI catch Gordon. He tracked that murderous bastard to an abandoned Realm where Gordon intercepted his neural link. Dad went crazy when he and Gordon shared thoughts."

"I'm sorry." Grey stands up and tries consoling me from behind. His loving embrace is welcoming, especially after so many cycles without a companion. I feel like melting in Grey's arms but pull away from his tightening grip.

"I don't feel like touching… right now."

"I'm sorry," he lies, before sitting down. I press my back against the tank and study him closely. After a meandering silence Grey asks, "So everything in your memory actually happened?"

"Yes. I knew something was wrong the moment dad came home. Instead of carrying me into the backyard, he went straight into the kitchen and grabbed a tool. Then he, he…"

I feel like retching a download. Even now, years later, I can barely wrap my mind around what happened.

Neural Link: Beep! Beep!

"Is that an outside signal?" I lean forward, grinning.

Grey's face brightens with surprise. "Yeah… it seems to be an emergency broadcast channel."

I join him in the middle of the room as we listen to our links. Negative info dominates the line. It's hard to remain calm, especially when all channels report similar news.

The first online reporter says, Reporter: It's the end of life as we know it! Our extinction has finally come! Undead are emerging from Newark! Are these the final days?

I scroll through various networks but the Doomsday theme remains the same. Thirteen additional Realms have been infected. Each had a prewar theme relating to the twenty first century. The footage secretes images of death and destruction into my mind. I can barely absorb it.

Their eerie messages hasten the erosion of civil society. Survivors are panicked and unsure of the future. Some people are rioting. Hostile Realms have begun warring with each other and someone prematurely leaked information about the Species Project to the public. Radicals demonize my excursion into the physical world and blame me for Scarlet's viral upload. The VBI, VIA, and the IVST are under investigation and like icing on the cake—officials have banned my cloud simulator program.

Grey tries looking in my direction but deflects his stare at the last moment. "I… what are you going to do?"

As I consider my options, one of the distant pier alarms activates.

"Phantoms," I stammer. "They're here."

The Calm Before

CHAPTER 25

The setting dusk highlights Scarlet's undead as their colossal numbers cut a dark swath into the horizon. The helix code she programmed into the horde allows them to penetrate any dexterity barriers separating blocks of Nexus data. With no need for portals, undead are entering Bonita Falls from every imaginable direction, thereby clouding the reddened horizon and sky with their ghostly forms.

Grey grimaces after spotting undead emerging from the lake and ground. "There are so many… what are we going to do?"

My face creases with determination as I brace for Grey's objection. "We're going to fight our way through them."

"What? You said that was impossible! We need help and power to do that. Dwar and Solus are probably recycled data and the conduit explosion decimated their forces. There can't be more than a few hundred people left!"

"I know."

Grey merges his hacking equipment into one of his outfit's largest memory pockets before standing. "And the power relays for both conduits are corrupt. If we try connecting to them directly, we'll be deatomized."

"I completely agree but right now, the only way out is through the horde."

"How do we make it through a swarm of floating undead? Those idiots drained most of the power so they can run around like superheroes."

I raise a brow. "What about the station you arrived from? Can we project there?"

"No. I depleted its power getting here. Maybe we should try the yacht."

"That's too risky. The mines will stay active now that the undead are coming."

"We can mod a sonar device," Grey explains with his hands, "and use it to navigate a safe course through the mines."

"What about the undead? They'll board the vessel and rip us to shreds."

"Maybe we can mod some artillery?"

"There are hundreds upon thousands of undead out there, Grey! Hundreds upon thousands! Maybe more! This island lacks the power we need to stop them! As a matter of fact, the undead's energy output surpasses the entire gallery on the voltage scale!"

"You brought us here and you're the idiot who wants to fight them!"

"And you're the fool who followed me!"

Grey turns away. "I still have the E-ray's specs. We can mod two more submersibles and then fight our way to shore."

"Where do we get the power for two E-rays?

Dwar and Solus already damaged the conduits. Even if we make two more E-rays and fight our way across the lake we'd never get pass the undead onshore."

"What about modifying the E-rays for flight?"

I consider the question's flaws. "The island's inhabitants already tried that. Airborne distortions are everywhere. Something will ice the aircraft into place if they don't fall out of the sky outright. Two people are stuck up there right now."

"Yeah, I saw them earlier today." Grey grinds his teeth with disappointment. "Those glitches are some of the worst and airborne distortions are hard to detect."

I start walking in circles now. Yes, I said *walking…* because there's something else gnawing at me. I back-hacked Grey's neural link after distracting him with my dad's story, and found an outside line. His secret channel has been active throughout our entire ordeal. Why was he hiding this from me?

Grey anxiously taps his neural link. "The last pier alarm has been manually activated. It sounds like something from a funeral procession."

Grey generally acts trustworthy and I need allies but what is he hiding from me? I follow him out of the aquarium and we stroll towards the island's observatory. The dome shaped building is one of the few places on this side of the island that Dwar chose not to fortify.

I point east. "Do you see the phantoms coming through the mountains?"

"Yeah. The undead are everywhere. It looks like an endless swarm of them. You were right. We have no hope of surviving out there. Our only advantage is that the phantoms move slowly. Hey, look over there, by the docks! Some of Dwar's people survived. They're actually trying to——"

Grey quiets when I place my hands on his chest and slide them down the curvatures of his torso. He recovers his composure quickly though, and takes me into his arms, and kisses my lips. I imagined this moment a million times with Seti but never once with Grey. Engrossed by my show of affection he fails to notice my charging portable projector.

I press against Grey's chest while transferring power from the projector into my Fang Taser, and then bind him in place by stinging Grey with the Taser's injectors. The fanged prongs download a paralytic program into his vascular threads as I pull away from the checkered film wrapping around Grey's body. The film instantly reforms into matted strings of pulsating energy. The strings should be powerful enough to confine him for about five minutes.

"What the..." Grey tries moving and growls when nothing happens. "What's going on?"

"I've suppressed you."

"Why? Is this about Hannibal? I'm sorry for accusing him of deceit!"

"This isn't about Hannibal." I grab the red expander from his front memory pocket and raise it into the air. Its balloon shaped antenna icon looks inflated, and indicative of someone who's been in constant contact with other Realms. "This is about you trying to delete Remi!"

Grey's eyes widen with surprise. His impulsive gesture is a form of non-verbal guilt. Such an incriminating mannerism is unexpected. Grey deepens my suspicions when he tries lying to me.

"What are you talking about? Let me go! I did nothing wrong! Why would I want Remi deleted?"

A lesser mind would believe his plea but I've played enough poker with Grey to know when he's lying. His high-pitched voice always gives him away.

"I know you're trying to hack your way free. Biding time by lying won't work."

I amplify the transfer rate from my portable projector. Grey moans when its suppressive power increases. I can only imagine how painful the crushing effect must feel, especially when I turn the power up even more.

"If you don't want me to compress your entire body into a ball of atomic paste, then tell me everything."

"I swear, E—"

"Listen carefully because my next words might be the last things you ever hear. If you lie *one more time*, then I'll turn the transfer rate to its full amperage and walk away. This is your *last* chance to tell the truth."

My bluff actually works! Grey wavers when staring me down before angrily relenting with grit teeth.

"Remi learned about my mission to kill you and tried to stop me."

I nearly flinch from his admission. Up until now, Scarlet reserved all notions of disloyalty.

"What happened to Remi? You have ten seconds to elaborate!"

"We argued and then fought. He tried to delete me, so I deleted him.

"How?"

"I knocked Remi into the Pacific Vortex…"

"How did he survive?"

"Survive? He's gone! Could an ancient human float in a lake of fire? Even if Remi *could* survive inside a vortex of anti-photons, finding him is like pinpointing a single man lost at sea."

"It's not impossible…"

"There's nothing you can do. He's gone."

"Why are you trying to kill me?"

Grey laughs while struggling to free himself. "I thought you figured that out already! You have no idea who am I, do you?"

I notice the exact moment Grey's sequencer key breaks the Fang Taser's bondage. He lunges forward thrusting a photonic blade as I step back. The blade's tip grazes my throat before I project thirty-cubes away. When I glance back, Grey is gone.

The Blood of Judas

CHAPTER 26

I discover Dwar and Solus' active neural channels while traveling to the observatory. They don't seem to know or care that I'm listening. Each man is giving orders to his own group. I'm surprised both men are alive but their luck seems to be running out.

It's not long before the first terrified thoughts emerge from Solus' group of superheroes. His neural banter diffuses into the screams of a young app designer; who meets his end at the razored hands of two phantoms. The victim's brief yet visceral thoughts douse the link with terror before stirring silence from everyone listening. Seconds later, nearby witnesses infuse the channel with their surging fear and chaos erupts before Solus delivers his first official order.

Dwar's group fairs no better. Two of their members—a young newly wed couple—die when a surging mob of phantoms cut them off from the main group. The husband is quickly decapitated but his wife's long and torturous death ends with her body parts in the hands of several phantoms.

"We're all going to Hell…"

I head towards a riparian zone as undead emerge from the island's range. Some of the ghostly puppets rise out of the ground like prejudged souls in The Book of the Dead. Each malformed body displays the "physical" mutation of its victim's torment. Those who suffered mental or introverted abuse appear as twisted variations of their former selves. Others have adopted limb extensions or some other grotesque body glitch. Desperately projecting down one of the zone's narrow paths is the only way to escape the undead, but there's no way to predict their emergence points. Hills, canals, and gullets, litter the uneven terrain. My projector works best on level ground. Negotiating rough angles with a portable projector is challenging. I hide inside of a nearby thicket and use the news channel's link to send a message to Izreh but connect with the bureaucracy instead.

Mother Nature: Ehari?

Ehari: Why did the VIA order my death?

Mother Nature: What are you thinking about? We would never—

Ehari: I just found an encrypted VIA frequency in Grey's neural link! He told me—

Mother Nature: What, that the VIA ordered your death? He is lying. Our agency needs you alive.

Ehari: Why?

Mother Nature: That piece of information is not transferable on an open link.

Ehari: Screw you! I need answers!

Mother Nature: Listen… Grey *did* work for us as an undercover agent but we terminated his employment.

Ehari: Why did you hire him?

Mother Nature: Grey was ordered to infiltrate your team and gather information on Scarlet or anyone in her inner circle. He became obsessed with you, instead.

Ehari: Why?

Mother Nature: Preliminary evidence suggests a plan to end your life but the reason remains unknown. We believe Oliver Milkes convinced Grey to join his spiritual revolution and ordered your assassination shortly thereafter.

Ehari: Oliver Milkes? Who is this guy? Why does he seem to be everywhere? And why didn't you tell me any of this before now?

Mother Nature: Oliver Milkes' identity remains a mystery and we only discovered Grey's intent a few hours ago.

Ehari: How did Remi get involved?

Mother Nature: We lost track of Grey after he returned from the Species Project's expedition. His breach of protocol raised red flags. Remi agreed to help us find him when asked.

Ehari: So you're more concerned with capturing Scarlet or Grey than with my safety.

Mother Nature: Of course! Look at what Scarlet has done. She poses a threat to the entire virtual world. We have to stop her. Grey broke numerous laws and betrayed the agency. More importantly, he might lead us to Oliver Milkes. Finding him is one of our top priorities.

Ehari: Is Grey, Oliver Milkes?

Mother Nature: We do not have the answer to that question.

Ehari: You bastards used me as bait…

Mother Nature: It was your idea to enter Newark, not ours. We just made the most of it. The agency's options were limited. We hoped Izreh's antiviral armor would protect you against the virus and tailed Scarlet to one of her hideouts after you successfully lured her from hiding. The information we gathered is leading to her capture.

Ehari: And Grey?

Mother Nature: We are having trouble tracking him. Grey was one of our best field operatives. He knows how to evade many of our search protocols. However, we have tools at our disposal that he knows nothing about. His capture is imminent.

Ehari: So now that you have Scarlet's general location has the agency decided to abandon me?

Mother Nature: No. We want to help you.

Ehari: If you want to help then get me out of here! This place is swarming with undead!

Mother Nature: Our options are limited on this end. Do you have any suggestions?

Ehari: I need an energy stream sent to my modulator.

Mother Nature: Do you plan to fight your way through the horde?

Ehari: Not exactly, there are too many of them.

I have another plan.

Mother Nature: Would you care to elaborate?

Ehari: That information is not transferable on an open link.

Mother Nature: Is that your attempt at humor?

Ehari: We're using an open channel! I can't risk alerting Grey of my intentions!

Mother Nature: What is your signature's new frequency?

Ehari: I'm sending it to your vmail. Focus the stream along a rotating carrier wave, between 0.9 and 2.4 terahertz.

Mother Nature: Anything else?

Ehari: Where's Scarlet's hideout?

Mother Nature: It is located within the subnet inside the tombstone plane. Tracking Scarlet's exact location will take time.

Ehari: Why? Running a harvester program should root her out within minutes.

Mother Nature: I wish that were true but Scarlet had to integrate with her virus when creating it. This gave her the unnatural ability to blend into the virtual world's diodactic frame. The agency will have to track her on foot, so to speak.

Ehari: She'll escape long before that happens.

Mother Nature: That is unlikely. The downside to Scarlet's diodactic integration ensures that she has no way of reentering higher Realms.

Ehari: So Scarlet contaminated herself with her

own virus?

Mother Nature: Yes.

Ehari: And, there's no way she can resurface in normal virtual space?

Mother Nature: Correct.

Ehari: How will you stop her if she finds a way to escape the diodactic frame?

Mother Nature: We developed an antiviral patch that protects other Realms from further contamination. The agency began deployment an hour ago. Our patch is the only thing preventing Scarlet from infecting the entire Nexus.

Ehari: I want to help find her.

Mother Nature: You will have to exit that area first.

Ehari: Hold on…

An undead boy suddenly rises from the adjacent garden and swipes at me with his weirdly elongated claws. I leap away and then project into the branches of an oak tree as he floats forward hissing with a detestable expression. More undead rise from the ground as I travel across the treetops and head towards the observatory.

Mother Nature: Ehari—

Ehari: Not now!

The observatory is less than a virtual mile from my current position. Dwar's remaining forces impedes the most direct path there. I have no idea if they'll be hostile towards me. Bypassing his troops will waste precious time and lead me into an open area with no trees or cover. Pushing through the maelstrom of violence is my only option.

Scarlet's undead continue their synchronous drawl. They're impossible to ignore… like drumsticks pounding against my tympanic meshbrane.

"We're all going to Hell! We're all going to Hell! We're all going to Hell!"

I stop projecting across tree branches when a head bounces off my shoulders and drops on the bed of roses directly below me. I remember the grizzled face. It belongs to one of the top advisors from Dwar's inner circle. His shocked expression—gaping eyes and mouth—appear to be screaming for help. The undead hovering above persistently rip apart the member's body. I feel like retching when falling limbs shower the surrounding leaves with photonic plasma. The glowing droplets fade into lifeless sparkles right before my eyes. I press on after regaining my bearing.

Male Follower: Jasper is gone! He's freakin gone! They got him!

Dwar: Stay together!

Female Follower: They're coming from everywhere! What are we going to do?

Dwar: Regroup!

Male Follower: We can't stop them! There are too many! There are too damn many!

Dwar: Regroup!

Female Follower: Oh my God! They're getting closer!

Dwar: Fall back!

Male Follower: Where? There's nowhere to go!

Dwar: Gather around me!

The screams of dying men and women saturate my neural link. It's too much for me to bear. I disconnect from Dwar's channel but can still hear them. Screams of the living and the howling undead encircles the area like a raging hurricane.

I skirt the remaining members of Dwar's group when they draw the attention of most phantoms in the immediate vicinity. His survivors have assimilated Solus' tactics and now use their energy reserves as weaponry. They're hovering above me in a jumbled mass when the undead draw near, and the sky brightens with colorful bursts of light as the group unleashes their best powers. Nothing seems to deter the undead from gathering around Dwar and his people. The growing swell of phantoms increases as the group falls—one after another—to the savagery of the horde.

I don't have the time or stomach to witness such a massacre and flee from the scattered phantoms drifting about the forest when suddenly… I hear whispering in my head… beckoning… urging me away from my destination. I try ignoring the whispers but they grow louder and by the time I reach the tree line, nothing else remains audible. An odd tone beeps through my neural link. When I activate it, my thoughts freeze.

Solus: When my first victim bowed before me, begging for his life, I lead him to his death in the name of Satan. –Gordon

I unknowingly fall from the branch.

Ehari: Viral Upload In Progress.

There's an unauthorized voice inside my head. It's mom! She's singing to me… it's not her… can't be… but the lullaby is so comforting that I don't want it to leave. The melody submerges my consciousness with a euphoric feeling. When the sensation breaks, I regain full clarity.

"What just happened?"

I unsteadily rise and look around, unsure of how I fell. Something is wrong with me, but what? I try downloading an antiviral patch but can't get a stable connection to the Virtualnet.

The observatory is sitting on a hill directly ahead. Undead are everywhere. Most don't notice me. I keep projecting towards the observatory but lose control of my mind and fall back to the ground.

Solus: They call me the father of all serial killers. I murdered my entire family, and relatives, at the age of ten. –Gordon

Ehari: Viral Upload Complete.

There's a voice inside my head. It's mom! She's singing to me… it's not her… can't be… but the lullaby is so comforting that I don't want it to leave. The melody submerges my consciousness with a euphoric feeling.

I see them now… the angels are descending from the heavens. There are thousands of them! I reach out for deliverance and pray they take me away.

When the sensation breaks, I regain partial clarity.

"Wait… am, I… infected with the Gordon's virus?"

I sit up and panic while trying to deactivate my neural link. Inputting the proper code is taking too long. Undead are nearing but running won't help. I have to purge the virus before it takes complete control of my mind! But… even though I input the code correctly, my neural link remains active and I collapse for a third time!

Solus: What kind of God creates Hell? –Gordon

Ehari: Warning: Viral Upload Detected In Neural Network. Anti-virus Software Initializing.

There's a voice inside my head. It's mom! She's singing to me… it's not her… can't be… but the lullaby is so comforting that I don't want it to leave. The melody submerges my consciousness with a euphoric feeling. I see them now… the angels are descending from the heavens. There are thousands of them! I reach out for deliverance and pray they take me away.

One of them descends before me. Mom? She reaches out offering an embrace. I move towards her, drunken with love. When the sensation breaks, I regain slight clarity and mom dissipates into an undead woman.

"Get away from me!" I scream, and roll across the ground when the phantom lunges for me.

A lone bystander catches my attention when I project away from the howling corpse.

It's Solus, but… he appears unusually distraught. His posture and body movements are unbecoming for someone brash. A sickly and depraved expression replace Solus' natural appearance. He's standing by a grove with a familiar gleam in his eyes. I recognize the abnormal stance, because my dad looked the exact same way… right before he killed mom.

Solus: I'm going to destroy your memories and violate your thoughts. I'm going to savor you. I'm going to rape your mind, over, and over, and over, and over… –Gordon

Ehari: Warning: Viral Mutation In Progress. Anti-virus Software Corrupted. Neural Contamination Imminent.

There isn't a second to spare—this may be my last moment of lucidity—so I project straight towards Solus with my photonic dagger withdrawn. He tries drawing his own weapon but it's too late… I've already passed him, and severed the arterial threads in Solus' neck.

Ehari: Viral Upload Quarantined.

A voice calls my name… beckoning… urging me away from my destination but it's fading into the undead's howls. A familiar tone beeps in my neural link and when I activate it, my thoughts remain clear.

Solus: He… hacked… my mind…

Ehari: Viral Upload Terminated.

Solus drops to his knees and stutters, "Gor… don… we… shared, thoughts. He… killed my, bro… Gre—"

Solus falls down as data spills from the gash in his neck. There was remorsefulness in Solus' eye—right before he fell—glimmering like sunlight—apologetic, even.

There's no time for contemplating what just happened. I turn from Solus' body, project to the observatory, and lock myself inside the building's domed aperture. Hacking the canopy is easy but I have to use a sophisticated program to calibrate the telescope; mainly because I'm pointing it towards the Pacific Vortex.

Aligning the telescope's tertiary mirror with the lighthouse sets the conditions required to create an old-school projection tunnel, which people used before the advent of projection steps.

"You won't leave here alive," Grey suddenly announces from somewhere behind me.

His reflection appears in the tertiary mirror. I study it while fanning Grey's temper. "What makes your life worth living?"

"My superior intellect is one of many reasons!"

"I can understand why you'd betray me. We were never truly friends, apparently… but why betray the VIA?"

Grey laughs. "The VIA? I was never loyal to them, either! They meant nothing to me, just like you and your family. You were all tools!"

"What does my family have to do with this?"

"Everything, fool!"

I finish inputting the coordinates before glancing over my shoulder. "You know nothing about by family!"

"That's where you're wrong, *Cloudy*. I know everything about you, your mom, and your pathetic dad."

"How do you know that nickname?"

"Isn't it obvious by now? Who else would know a nickname that only you and your daddy shared? I shouldn't have to spell it out for you, dumbass."

"You couldn't be…"

"I am." Grey's movements are shadowed in the tertiary mirror as he struts about like a king. "I became a master hacker at the age of eight and built my reputation on the creation of a single virus. The VBI sent their best agents to capture me after it went viral. I eluded all of them so the agency turned to the IVST for help—"

"You're a lying—"

"Your daddy was the only person who could track me but he didn't want to believe a child was capable of creating the Gordon's virus. In fact, the idiot thought I was infected and tried to save me! Underestimating his rival proved fatal. At least he was smart enough to leave a trail for the VBI to follow. But I got away and my virus continues circulating to this very day. I've become an urban legend!"

"Why are you confessing now?"

"Your daddy put fear into my heart that I never

felt before or since. I was scared of capture but terrified of someone outsmarting me. Evading your dad and the VBI was the only time I felt truly alive. I wanted to feel that fear again but *you* are not your father's daughter! Your intellect pales in comparison to that man. I have no fear of your ignorant ass! But… you're also the only person to escape my virus. Infecting a brute like Solus was a waste of time. I won't be able to live with myself knowing you got away from me, twice! I feel… imperfect. Corrupted. Eluded.

"Do you realize E, that I waited years for the opportunity to befriend you? I hoped you'd unravel my identity and come after me, but you're incapable of arriving to such conclusions on your own. Don't feel ashamed, though. Not even Scarlet could track me within her own virus! I have no equal!"

I turn around as my vascular threads brighten with rage. "You sick psychopathic bastard! My parents were good people!"

"Your parents were just another pair of losers! Their biggest claim to fame was being victimized by my virus! I'll credit you with one thing, Private E… you're the first person to escape the Gordon's virus, but you'll also be the last!"

"You're a pathetic excuse for a human being! I hope there's a Hell! You'll have a special place there right next to Scarlet!"

"Poor E…. are you mad, bitch? I owned you from the age of eight!"

I project straight towards Grey in a burst of rage

and unleash a gust of photizars with my modified Fang Taser. The shimmering wave reaches out and grabs an entire row of desks, but it misses Grey when he uses his own projection device to meld into the building's architecture. The objects merge as I pull them back and swing the entire sack over my head like a deranged barbarian. When Grey rises from the floor, I hurl the explosive bundle at him—screaming with rage when he scampers away from the observatory's walkway. The explosion throws equipment everywhere and phantoms push through the walls as we circle each other.

"When your daddy realized his mind was infected, he fell to his knees like a bitch, and begged me to save him!"

"Shut up! I'm going to rip your throat out!"

Grey smiles. "Sure you are, Cloudy. Now, as I was saying before you rudely interrupted me… that was the first time I brought a man to his knees. If you drop to your knees Private E, maybe I'll spare you further public indignity!"

A large group of phantoms lunge for me as Grey melts into the observatory's wall and travels to the ceiling. I tear a path through them with my Taser's threads and race blindly after Grey in a fit of rage.

"Letting the animal out, E? If you weren't such a retard, you'd know that telescope needs more power to set up a carrier beam. Nice try, but your half assed measures won't save you this time! You're stuck here!"

"Shut up! Shut up! Shut up! You're a degenerate

piece of malware! You hide behind programs and lies! You'll never be half the man my *mother* was!"

I can see phantoms pouring through the building's breach and Dwar dragging Solus' body towards the observatory. It seems that in the end, their friendship prevailed and by some crazy miracle, Solus is *still* alive… but barely. The damage I did to his neck is severe and he'll die without immediate treatment.

Grey unwillingly confronts a few phantoms passing through the roof while I engage more on the ground. The horde thickens as the last of Dwar's stragglers converge for their lives atop the observatory's canopy. Pieces of the rafters collapse onto the telescope as Grey and I hunt each other. The horde's numbers suddenly swell and our gladiatorial contest evolves into a fight for survival when the observatory fills with more phantoms.

"We're all going to Hell!"

"We're all going to Hell!"

"We're all going to Hell!"

Mother Nature: The horde is interfering with the energy beam. You have to clear that area before our feed will reach you.

Ehari: I'm not leaving until I kill Grey!

Grey: You should have killed me when you had the chance, mental case! It's too late now!

My fury peaks to new levels and I'm provoked into equipping my most dangerous body mod; a vortex template. It's a life-threatening tactic that often leads to instant deletion for those who conduct themselves improperly. Unlike addons, these types of body mods integrate into a person's skeletal meshing. I use mine to focus pure energy through my vascular threads, and into the mod's gloved straps.

Grey: So, you want to fight it out with body mods? All or nothing, huh? Let's go, dumbass!

Grey follows suit and arms his python template before leading me into the observatory's substructure. My hands transmogrify into vortex gloves as we descend into the building's bowls.

Grey glides like a film projection across the hallway's surface as I chase after him with my portable projector. We fight our way through each room hoping to find an area with enough space to face-off.

The undead chant, "We're all going to Hell! We're all going to Hell! We're all going to Hell!"

Grey uses his body mod to slash a phantom with his python fangs—it explodes seconds later. The shattered body parts decimate swarms of undead with collateral damage and the domino effect causes more phantoms to shatter. I project into a bordering room and narrowly avoid the maelstrom.

Grey: Nobody can stop me! I rule this world! I am a virtual God!

We travel deep into the basement where narrow corridors compress the undead into a mangled nest of interwoven bodies. My projector is useless here but Grey's python mod does its greatest damage within these confines.

Grey eviscerates a single undead on the far end of the main corridor before melting into its ceiling. The exploding phantom sends rippling shards into a tangled nest of phantoms and the growing tide of body shrapnel ricochets towards me. There's nowhere to run so I extend my hands as though wearing a Catcher's mitt and funnel the entire chattering stream into the vortexes undulating from my palms, but… the energy surge is too great and I scream when my vascular threads burn from excessive energy saturation. It's too much to bear and I release the dark stream milliseconds before my body explodes. The tremendous force propels me down the corridor where Grey lingers alongside an oncoming wall. I project through an office portal and escape his eviscerating swipe as the basement's meshing saturates with dark energy.

All of the rooms buckle inward when their construction programs fault. I catch two ceiling blocks and use the energy to jump up to the observatory where Grey awaits in the room's center.

I project straight towards him with my photonic dagger—barely missing the bastard's scrawny neck when he melts into the floor.

More phantoms lunge from the dome's darkest corners. I use my vortex mod to its fullest potential and rip them apart using a modified form of Wing Chung. I focus on movements that draw enemies into my funneling palms of death and even alternate the vortex' flow by switching which hand vacuums limbs, and which one expels.

I draw reaching phantoms into my grasp and dissolve entire arms, torsos, and heads but the undead are endless. They float about like tethered ventriloquist dolls as I slip between them using graceful martial arts moves mixed with projector leaps. When Grey ghosts into the observatory's ceiling, I draw the dome's atoms into my palms in pursuit, and tear the ceiling apart piece by piece.

Grey reemerges near the telescope and unleashes a projector clone, but I see through his façade and dismiss the phony holographic projection standing to my right. Grey thinks his custom cloaking mod conceals where he's actually standing but the genius hasn't considered his broken forearm—which disrupts the cloak's integrity—and the resulting distortion effect gives away his actual position to my left.

When Grey throws a particle sphere, his deadly golden ball completely misses me when I transport onto the telescope's tertiary mirror in half the expected time.

Then I notice Solus…

The tough bastard is *still* alive! Grey doesn't see him slumped on the ground and yells when Solus reaches out and grabs his ankle. He self-detonates before Grey can react and the entire room brightens from the explosion.

Solus' suicidal blast temporarily clears the room of phantoms and Mother Nature's energy stream activates as the telescope's mirror focuses on the lighthouse. Her stream—when combined with Solus' explosive power—creates a proxy spike that punctures the dexterity barriers dividing Bonita Falls from the lighthouse.

I project into the carrier beam and allow it to transport me—like a twig floating in a stream—to the lighthouse.

Grey survived the blast somehow, and emerges from the floor as phantoms tear at his legs. He leaps towards me with outstretched arms but I ensnare his fanged hands inside my vortex palms when he tries boarding the makeshift raft. Undead try pulling him back into the observatory while I struggle against them.

"You're a murderous monster! Die you sick bastard!"

More undead melt through the building's architecture and grab Grey, but I refuse to let go. We're locked in a death grip—neither gaining the advantage until finally, a large cluster of phantoms swarms over Grey and rips him from my palms.

"We're all going to Hell," they chant. "Every, single, one of us!"

The telescope's tertiary mirror shatters as I drift away and Grey—reaching out to me in fear—is the last I ever see of him.

All the King's Men

CHAPTER 27

It takes an hour for Mother Nature's energy steam to carry me safely to the lighthouse. I think of the night my parents died along the way. Words can't express what I'm feeling now that Grey is dead. I would have preferred watching the phantoms tear him apart just to ensure his demise, but life doesn't always wrap justice up so neatly. I escaped my dad's viral insanity that fateful night but he couldn't avoid the VBI agents who found and killed him shortly thereafter. Even though I witnessed mom's death at his hands, a piece of me still wanted dad's infected body to survive even though there's no cure for the Gordon's virus.

My mother on the other hand, gained a reputation for her cold and insidious ways. All of my memories of her revolve around spiteful and bitter moments. She was unaffectionate, callous, and did everything possible to make my life miserable. It shames me to admit it, but there was something pleasant about watching my dad knock the life out of her. I know that's a terrible thing to say…but truth can be a terrible thing.

I disembark in the lighthouse's pavilion and find Grills and Dennington waiting beside the lamp. Their presence isn't exactly a surprise but the agents' defensive posture causes immediate concern.

"You are standing on a restrainer net," Grills announces, tipping his head towards my feet. "Do not move or try anything impulsive if you value your life."

I shudder with alarm. There is indeed, a glowing lattice of anti-photonic energy beneath my feet. The net spreads across my half of the pavilion's floor, windows, and ceiling.

After looking around I ask, "What's going on?"

"We know you are looking for Remi," says Dennington. "This lighthouse is the best place to initiate a search."

"What do you want?"

Agent Grills examines me from head to toe before saying, "The agency wants you back in their custody."

Our eyes lock. "I don't like the word, *custody*. It implies criminality. I'm not going anywhere with you."

"Miss Ehari, I suggest compliance. We are here to help."

"I doubt that."

"A lofty investment was made on your behalf,"—Grills' tone becomes hostile—"it will be recuperated!"

"I'm sure any investments made on my behalf were not done for my benefit!"

Neither agent seems to realize that Izreh's anti-viral armor protects me from their restrainer net. Had one of them suspected as much, they'd probably order me to deactivate it. It's a secret best kept.

I scowl when Agent Grills assumes an aggressive posture. He raises the activator clasped in his right hand and threatens with flexing fingers to trigger the anti-photonic net.

"The VIA did not specify the conditions of your capture."

"Do you plan on deleting me?"

"No… but I certainly will, if you do not submit."

My scowl dissolves into something detestable. "You should know by now, that I'm not a submissive woman."

"I *will* delete you, Miss—"

Agent Dennington reaches out and grabs the activator in Grills' hand. His surprise speaks volumes.

"What are you doing?"

"This is wrong! If you delete her, we might lose our chance to find Remi!"

"Screw Remi! Let go of my hand or join Di in the net!"

When Dennington pulls the activator away, Grills tries stabbing her with a photonic blade cleverly hidden within the cuff of his suit, but he misses when Dennington backflips into an agile display of evasive gymnastics.

Agent Grills seizes the advantage with a withdrawn handcannon so I step off the net, approach him from behind, and kick Grills' arm up. The weapon discharges an electrostatic spear into the ceiling, frying a hole into its meshing as Dennington pushes Grills onto the anti-photonic net. She immediately triggers its trap before Agent Grills can escape the collapsing lattice of energy. The square threads of light ensnare the agent within a shrinking sack that compresses Grills into a ball of electrostatic paste. He curses me to the very end and dies screaming my name so loudly, that upon death, his voice cycles forward and reverse several times before fading.

Dennington immediately turns to me with open hands. "I am here to help you."

I step back and ready my portable projector. "Help me? You just deleted your partner!"

"My only objective is to help you reintegrate into the physical world."

"Why? Your faith precludes you, doesn't it?"

Dennington lowers her hands. "My faith aligns with the real Pope. I am not a follower of Oliver Milkes or any other false prophet. I worship the truth."

I glance at the sizzling pile of static on the floor next to us. "Truth is subjective."

"I am not an arbiter of evil, Miss Ehari. But I admit that I am not an angel, either. I am only trying to do what I think is right. I just committed a major crime in the eyes of the VIA and VBI—one that is punishable by deletion. That should justify a sliver of trust."

"Why delete your partner to save me?"

"My faith assumes the highest priority, not the agency."

Agent Dennington reaches out with intentions

on retrieving something from one of my internal memory pockets. I don't stop her, and watch as she removes the Trinity optic lens that Agent Grills gifted me during my visit to the Tia Muhammad Medical Facility.

"This is how we tracked you."

"Impossible. I removed the tracking program."

"The real tracking program was activated when you removed the surrogate."

Dennington holds up the optic lens and uses an advanced scanner to pinpoint the actual tracker. I confirm her reading with my own scanner and feel like kicking myself for falling into such an obvious trap.

She tosses the device through one of the pavilion's windows and into the awaiting vortex where chemical based programs shoot up like cardiograph spikes as the optic lens splashes into their v-shaped ripples orbiting the lighthouse. The photonic device sizzles with the ferocity of a fried circuit panel as the scripts holding it together disband. When the commotion settles, the entire Pacific Vortex continues its slow spin around the lighthouse, which centers within the dark system of ripples like a black hole.

"The Pope convened with every religious leader in the virtual world because he believes you are a saint who has been ordained by God."

"A saint? You're not serious, are you?"

"I am," Dennington confirms with a solid nod.

"I'm a normal, regular person. You're delusional

if you believe otherwise. It really burns me up when people try establishing divine kingships to others."

"I know what you saw at the end of *The Suffering.*"

"Really? Because I don't even know what I saw!"

"I think you do."

Dennington seems resolute but so am I. "I've cursed and killed people since that moment. There's nothing saintly about my actions."

"We are not saying you are a manifestation of God. We simply believe that you have a calling. Nothing will change our view."

"A calling? To what end?"

"Only God knows that answer."

Herein lies the problem. People like Dennington believe in something for no plausible reason. To me, that's the same as believing in nothing.

"You have me confused with someone else. I'm no saint. In fact, I'm as flawed and as corruptible as one can be. The furthest thing from perfection—"

"A saint is not the embodiment of physical or mental perfection. A true saint is a standard-bearer of righteousness—one who gravitates truth. Saints do what is right."

"History is filled with people who did what they believed was right. Most of them are the biggest monsters known to humankind. And what of my faith… or lack thereof? You're preaching to me without even asking about my beliefs!"

"Your beliefs are irrelevant to the truth."

"Really? Thanks for letting me know my 'saintly'

opinions are worthless. And truth… that word again… what makes you or your faith the possessors of it? How can you rally around something so abstract that its definition is based solely on individual interpretation?"

"Do you believe in God? Have you seen God? Why are you pretending to ignore what you already know?"

"Why are you pretending to know what I believe?"

We reach a stalemate of sorts, mainly because at this point, I'm unwilling to believe anything from anyone—*especially* government personnel.

"I am the only one who can help you reenter the physical world."

"Isn't that convenient? How do you know I want to go back or that I haven't found my own way?"

"I was helping Agent Grills monitor your every move, remember? He wanted to take you back to a VIA facility for permanent confinement. I am offering to guide you to the Institute of Virtual Science and Technology. They do not support the VIA's abduction plans."

"Why does the IVST want to help me?"

"Grey is deleted and the agency is tracking Scarlet. Your confinement is the next priority. The VIA tried and failed to duplicate your assimilation. Until they can figure out why, capturing you is among their greatest concerns."

"Tell them to speak with Dr. Panels if they want the secret behind my XX assimilation. Now why are you so insistent that I go back to the physical world?"

Dennington points to the Pacific Vortex. "Ask your friend."

"Remi? Do you know where he's hiding?"

"Not exactly. Even though Agent Grills discovered his distress signal, we had trouble pinpointing where it came from. The signal is scattered and there is no trace of Remi near any of the emergency buoys."

"That's because he's hiding inside the vortex."

Dennington muses of the possibility. "How is that possible? The recycling currents would have identified Remi as another contaminate and relocated him to one of the buoys."

"Exactly. And in doing so, he would have been deleted by now."

She shrugs, "So where is he?"

I debate whether it's wise to reveal my theory. Deleting Agent Grills earned Dennington no points. Just about every person that I know has lied or tried to harm me. Exposing the truth is a last resort.

"He's floating in the vortex, magnetically tethered to the buoys."

"I fail to see how that is possible. The curr—"

"Remi depolarized his meshing after falling into the vortex."

Dennington contemplates the idea before saying, "No one can disassemble their body and expect to live. Photonic depolarization is suicide."

"That's true outside of the vortex. Inside is a

different… matter, so to speak."

Dennington stares into the Pacific Vortex as she reacquires Remi's signal with her optic lens. It takes a few seconds before the wavelength is stable enough to transfer into my neural link.

"What do you make of it?"

I shake my head. "Well, honestly… I'm not sure. The signal in of itself appears useless. It relays nothing more than Remi's signature but there has to be something else we're missing."

"I agree, but what? I used my most advanced cracking program to decode any messages embedded in the signature. It found nothing."

I consider the signature's significance but more importantly, Remi's methodology. He doesn't have the complex mindset of Scarlet or Grey. Any message from Remi would be simple in nature but cleverly hidden. After racking my brain over hidden content the intermittent frequency at which the signature transponds grabs my attention.

"Remi is emitting his signature at a specific set of intervals."

Dennington's eyes suddenly widen. "You are right! What does that mean?"

"The emission rate is the code—Morse, in fact. Our team favored it during competitive gaming bouts against other groups because no one expected anything that archaic. We were able to relay secret messages this way."

Dennington begins deciphering the signal but

I've already decoded it. She looks around and says, "Remi dispersed himself across all four regions of the vortex. That is why his signal is *literally* all over the place!"

I nod, "We'll have to use the lighthouse's lamp to reassemble his meshing."

Dennington's eyes narrow. "You knew this all along, right? Is that why you came here?"

"Well, not exactly. I was considering another way of finding him. The lighthouse transmits energy to all quadrants of the Underground. Sending him a message with lamplight was my original idea. I had no idea he would actually be here…"

"And now?"

"Now I'm going to use Remi's distress signals as beacons and the lighthouse will help illuminate where he's hiding. I'll be able to focus the lamplight on Remi's individual body parts and use it to gather him from the vortex like a magnet collecting metal fragments from water."

Dennington approaches a window and stares into the Pacific Vortex. She glances back after a few seconds. "Will that actually work?"

I confirm her question with a thumbs-up. Now that we're on the same page, we immediately get to work adjusting the lamp's programming. It's my purgative to monitor her work. I even double check Dennington's modifications. She pretends not to care or notice. For someone who desires my belief in her saintly summations, clouding one's emotions over something this trivial doesn't incur any faith in her beliefs. I activate the lamp only when everything is complete and rechecked for a third time.

We modify the lighthouse lamp to shed five distinct energy beams. The four rainbow colored download beams should collect Remi's depolarized fragments while the white upload beam assembles them inside the pavilion.

With the beams modified as partial peer-to-peer file sharing protocols, the lamplight highlights Remi's scattered pieces and begins collecting them one bit at a time. The download beams, which we've focused on their prospective buoys, function as a BitTorrent. Each beam of colored light reaches across the swirling vortex and downloads Remi's body parts from the darkness. I can see portions of his mesh filling the cylindrical tubes of multi-colored light as if they were status bars on a classic computer screen. When all four downloads complete, they upload Remi's body to the final cylinder of white light. A problem occurs when the fifth beam fails to assemble his parts correctly. Something within Remi's mesh is distorting the process and I can't locate the cause until his upload completes. One minute per year of his life equals twenty-two minutes before the process ends. Unfortunately, another error occurs and Remi's body parts suddenly freeze inside the upload beam. The results are worse than expected.

"Oh my God," gasps Dennington, who appears overly distraught by his condition. "What went wrong? Why did the white beam upload Remi as a… mangled mass? It looks like an Axe murderer chopped him up!"

"It has something to do with his contaminated mesh."

"This is horrible! I never saw someone deleted in such a gruesome way!"

Agent Dennington appears ready to retch so I push her aside. "Damn Humpty Dumpty…"

"What?"

"It's a nursery rhythm. Basically…" I wave the explanation away. "Look, he's not deleted."

"What do you mean? Look at him! Remi's body is scattered throughout the final beam!"

"Calm down, he's still in stasis. Remi will be fine once we put him back together. This is just going to take a little more work than expected."

Agent Dennington looks baffled. "You mean… he is not finished downloading? Remi is still alive?"

"Yeah. In a kind of… three dimensional puzzle form.

Dennington cups a hand over her mouth. I can barely hear her say, "I do not believe this is happening." She examines the upload beam from multiple angles before leaning against a guardrail. "Can you really put him together?"

"Yeah, I think so. Heard of Holographic Tetris? I'm the current champion."

"Holo Tetris? Does it have something to do with Humpty Dumpty?"

"Not really. Anyway, I have to assemble him carefully. Connecting the wrong pieces can permanently damage Remi's meshing. Just stand back and let the Tetris master work her magic!"

Dennington checks her optic lens for Humpty Dumpty and Tetris references while I connect Remi's biggest pieces together. I find it no coincidence that the largest chunks involve his head. After uniting most of Remi's neck and torso, Agent Dennington is able to stomach the assembly of an entire leg and a piece of his shoulder. Her normal complexion returns by the time Remi's body nears completion. When I fix the last pieces into place, he falls out of the upload beam, lands on top of Agent Grills' remains, and then immediately jumps up.

"Whoa! That was beastly! I'm actually alive!"

Dennington runs into Remi's arms—"I missed you!"—and they kiss right in front of me.

"OK… so when did you two get together?"

Dennington speaks after freeing her lips from Remi's vacuous mouth. "Remi and I developed a… ah… relationship, at the Tia Muhammad Medical Facility."

"When did you have time to—" I pause, shake my head, and then step back. "Actually, I don't want to know. So, are you fine?"

Remi gives his backside an affectionate rub. "My ass doesn't feel quite right. Other than that, I'm great!"

"Well, I did have a little trouble putting your

butt together."

"Ha ha," Remi laughs while sneakily tucking a static charger into one of his memory pockets.

Dennington points to it and asks, "Is that what corrupted your mesh?"

"Uh huh," he says boyishly.

She smacks his shoulder. "Getting high in a solid state is bad enough but soaking in electricity while depolarized? Why would you be so careless with your life?"

"I was drifting in that vortex for days! I needed a way to pass the time…"

"You are an idiot!" Dennington hugs her buffoon affectionately.

"Besides," he adds nonchalantly, "I knew E would fix me up!"

Remi kisses Dennington's forehead. When she looks up, their lips lock for a second time. I can almost see their resource probers snaking together. It's a garish display of affection, especially for a VBI agent.

"Sorry about your mom," I interrupt.

Remi ends the kiss with a sad smile. "Thanks E. I'm fine now. I put her to rest at home. Scarlet has to pay for what she's done."

"Dennington said you have information for me."

Remi pulls away from his newest girlfriend and gives me a quick hug before asking, "Did you get my message about Grey?"

"Yeah. It was a timely bit of info. Thanks."

"There's more." Remi displays some of his optic lens data. "Scarlet is trying to hack into da physical world!"

"How? She'd need the IVST's birthing chamber program."

"She already has it! I was tracking one of da Bloody Membranes when I discovered Scarlet downloaded da program straight from your birthing chamber during da dragon hacker's attack. Raul Fantis was a decoy! Now that she has da program, Scarlet is trying to link with your cybernetic prostheticalanatomy. All of these virally bombed cities and Realms were meant to disrupt da VIA's ability to track Scarlet as she uses Hannibal's emergency connection to enter da physical world from their own servers!"

"So that is how she plans on getting out!" Dennington rushes to establish a link with Dr. Panels.

Dennington: We have a security breach! Scarlet compromised our channel with Hannibal!"

Dr. Panels: We lost control of the station channel an hour ago.

Dennington: What is the status of all cybernetic prostheticalanatomies?

Dr. Panels: The XX and XY CPs in the main birthing chambers are off-line. We cannot access them.

I clench my fists in frustration. "So we have no way to communicate with Hannibal, or integrate with the CPs? That means we're too late! Scarlet must already be there!"

"If she catches Hannibal off guard," Remi notes, "he's dead."

"If Scarlet finds the Nexus," I add, "we're all dead!"

"There might be another way to stop her." Dennington checks my expression before explaining. "The IVST has a fully functional backup CP in a hidden birthing chamber. It is an identical model to the cybernetic you integrated with."

"There's another CP? What are we waiting for?"

Dennington: Dr. Panels, prep the backup CP for emergency amalgamation. We are sending Ehari back out.

Dr. Panels: Sequencing in progress.

Ehari: I'm going to kill Scarlet if Hannibal hasn't done so already. She helped murder millions. I have to make sure she's dead.

Dr. Panels: You will not hear any complaints on this end. We will give whatever support you need. Scarlet is a worldwide threat. You have to stop her.

Remi gives me a nudge as Dennington establishes an exit out of the lighthouse. "E, there's something else I want you to know." He stammers a bit before tucking his optic lens away. "I'm not trying to get all mushy but… thanks for coming back for me. You saved my life. It took a lot of guts coming here."

"You know I had to come. What's Mandible 9 without its number one hothead?"

"Seriously, though… I know we're not blood

relatives, but you're still my sister. You're da only real friend that I've ever known. I don't want to lose you. Please be careful out there. Come back. I love you."

Remi hugs me once more and this time, I can feel his heartpulse quivering. I pull away from Remi and stare into his eyes. "I love you, too."

"I mean it, E. I just wanted to say that… I'm sorry. I'm sorry for everything that's happened to you. *Everything.*"

Metal Gear: Solid

Chapter 28

I've returned safely to the physical world, resurrected in the body of my new cybernetic prostheticalanatomy. I can barely see through the incubation tub's pink fluid, partly because the birthing chamber is darker than expected. The primary lamps are off and yellow hazard lights cycle in the room's corners. Hannibal and Scarlet are nowhere in sight. Danger buds in my guts, as if gravity is pulling cranial fear into my stomach. Such sensations are indicators of my physical whereabouts and stir my heart into beating faster.

Silence seems appropriate but it takes incredible concentration to emerge from the womb quietly. Resisting the temptation to lash out exhausts my body and mind in unimaginable ways. Regardless of the strain, I successfully control my nerves even though this cybernetic prostheticalanatomy delivers identical birthing pains to that of the first one.

After pulling quietly out of the incubation tub, I use an empty vase to muffle my vomiting. Preservation misters shower the room with a fine chemical spray. According to IVST protocols, these misters only activate when an organic anomaly enters the environment.

By the time I finish spewing amniotic fluid, my

hair spontaneously illuminates the surrounding gloom but detects no foreign elements.

I deactivate my hair's auto illuminate function and slip into a shadowy corner. A suit of armor hanging on the far wall draws my attention. I creep forward and retrieve it after scanning every inch of the room. The lacking auto-fit options of the physical world leaves me grudgingly dressing and adjusting the camouflaged combat gear—which is so thin, it feels like underwear. At least the armor comes with a Hemingway rod.

Grasping both ends of the rod completes the circuit necessary to morph the metal into a new shape. Advanced nanorobotics embedded within the alloy reorganize the Hemingway's atoms to allow on-the-fly molding of the metal. The rod reforms into nearly any envisioned shape that's equal to its mass. By linking with neural receptors in my brain, I'm able to mold the metal into a samurai sword that even has a matching scabbard. I magnetically fasten the weapon to my back before leaving the secret birthing chamber to investigate other areas.

Signs of battle litter my path. Dents in the corridor's titanium walls indicate pulse rifle fire. Frag charring along the floor is evidence of discharged grenades. I eventually enter the security room and find an assortment of broken weapons scattered about. All gun cabinets are missing their ordinance. There's nothing useful in the utility closets. Black lighting the area with my hair reveals Hannibal's cybernetic footprints, which seem to be everywhere. The purple light even highlights a second trail of footprints. They stretch from one end of this particular room, to the other. These elongated footprints don't belong to XX or XY cybernetic prostheticalanatomies.

A second anomaly is more disturbing. Although doorways are located on the northern and southern ends of the security room, the unidentified footprints are going from east to west. They lead directly into the walls where larger amounts of residue are visible. These splatters measure about eight feet and three inches in height.

I follow Hannibal's trail to the relay station. Voices emanate from inside. One belongs to Hannibal. The other seems to be coming from one of the station's microphones. Hannibal shouldn't have a connection to anyone. I feel like running into the room and hugging him but a sinking stomach sensation forces me to pause by the doorway. Trusting in primal instincts makes me uncomfortable but I relent just long enough to hear something disturbing.

An unfamiliar man says, "Scarlet just destroyed three more cities."

"And Ehari?"

"She escaped."

Hannibal grunts. "Where?"

"We don't know. I have my best people looking for her."

Hannibal pounds on something with his immense

Type XY fist. The vibrations are strong enough to reach me. "Look harder! She should've died ages ago! Do I have to go back into the virtual world and kill her myself?"

I feel ill now, and can barely believe what I'm hearing. Hannibal, of all people–

"She'll die. That's a promise," says the voice. "Now tell me, what happened there?"

"The creature found us."

"How? That facility is hidden within stone, metal, and amalgamated compounds!"

"The dark pyramid catalogs whatever enters it. When it dragged Ehari inside, the device scanned her prostheticalanatomy and recorded assessment data on its outer wall. I interpreted the inscriptions. It seems that species-5478 used her expedition footage to pinpoint our location. There was no keeping it out from that point. The creature actually walks through walls."

"How is that possible?"

Hannibal sighs. "Species-5478 is capable of moving through inorganic objects with systemic compositions of six elements or less. It cannot pass through highly complex compounds or mixtures."

"Did you kill that abomination?"

"No," Hannibal mumbles, "it escaped."

"Why did the creature go there? Was it trying to find the Nexus?"

"I don't think so. It appeared to be studying the Type XX Ehari used. I engaged the creature and forced it out of the facility with ion fire."

"Is the XX CP operational?"

"Yes. Why?"

"You have to disable it." The conspirator elaborates, "My sources suggest someone is trying to integrate with the female CP. I'm assuming it's the IVST but I've also heard a rumor that Scarlet found a way of hacking into the birthing chamber."

"Consider it destroyed!"

"Hurry! We can't allow anyone else to enter physicality. The Revelation to John must be fulfilled."

"Agreed. I've already prepared for the sacrifice. Good luck on your end, Oliver."

"You're doing the Lord's work, Hannibal. God bless you."

I hear an instrument panel deactivate, followed by approaching footsteps. Hannibal stops when his scanners detect me backing away from the entrance. My neural link activates within seconds.

Hannibal: Ehari?

He pauses to confirm his scan data.

Hannibal: Why am I asking? It doesn't really matter who you are, does it? You have to die.

Even though Hannibal's murderous intentions dominate my thoughts, I can barely contemplate how to respond.

Ehari: Why do you want me dead?

Hannibal: Why do I want you dead? Are you serious? I love you more than you can ever know!

I want you to live! The real question is why the IVST, VBI, and VIA, want you alive.

Ehari: No, Hannibal! The *real* question is why do you want me dead? I heard everything! You're working with Oliver Milkes! I don't believe it… Grey and Scarlet were actually right about you! Scarlet didn't deliver the bomb to my condo! You did! Why are you conspiring to kill me?

Hannibal moves forward slowly. Each mammoth step casts rippling vibrations across the floor. His body outweighs my own by at least forty tons. I'm not sure what I can do to stop him if he becomes aggressive.

Hannibal: I made a pact with Oliver years ago. He sent the bomb to your condominium. It was my job to detonate it. You and I were supposed to die together but Scarlet showed up at the last minute, realigned the bomb to Carol's, and tried to defuse it with her team. I came outside with just enough time to catch them and detonated the explosive before they could neutralize it—hoping the blast radius was large enough to reach you—it wasn't, so I waited for another opportunity. We eventually found the pyramid and your mysterious coma followed. Some of Oliver's people thought the device had already taken your life. Others believed the pyramid trapped you inside of it and that your CP was nothing more than an empty shell. There was no way of knowing for sure. Then, after you suddenly regained consciousness, I waited for the right moment to strike.

I remember the moment when Hannibal killed me, but didn't realize what was happening at the time. There was an instance of blinding light and paralyzing pain as I awaited transport back into the virtual world. I thought it was a nightmare.

Ehari: You electrocuted me while I incubated—

Hannibal: Yes…

Ehari: Why?

Ehari: You were vulnerable. It was the perfect opportunity to murder you.

Ehari: You're a coward!

Hannibal: I wanted to spare you pain but somehow… you survived.

Ehari: I didn't mention it at the time, but death is a requirement for cybernetic transference. You actually helped complete my transition.

Hannibal laughs. Hannibal: You should have stayed in the virtual world. When I kill you this time, I'll make sure you download into the afterlife!

[SCANNER]
|WARNING|

|RETICULE LOCK ESTABLISHED BY TYPE XY|
|CYBERNETIC- ARMAMENT MODIFICATIONS|
|DETECTED- ARTILLERY MODIFICATIONS DETECTED-|
|WEAPON CHARGING DETECTED- MINIMUM SAFE|
|DISTANCE EXCEEDED|

Hannibal upgraded his CP while I fought for survival in the virtual world. Only God knows what he's capable of doing. My scanner detects sion modifications to Hannibal's forearms. Instead of risking a head-on confrontation, I back away until he emerges in the relay station's doorway. I notice minor battle damage from Hannibal's encounter with species-5478, but his CP appears unharmed otherwise. Even the muscular marks that I made on Hannibal's chest remain and although I hide behind a nearby corner, his targeting reticule maintains its lock on me.

Ehari: Why are you doing this?

Hannibal: You and I grew up believing we had a disease that made our textures darker than everyone else in the Nexus, but I discovered the truth from Oliver and found proof in the ruins. My code originates from a place called Africa. This is the true cause for my darkened textures.

Ehari: No, we have Texitus disease—

Hannibal: That's a lie! We have no affliction! We're normal people!

Ehari: You're not making any sense! How can we be normal when everyone else has pale textures?

Hannibal: I found *real* recordings of the physical world inside of a library in the ruins. Videos… music… even literature and art! Those records revealed a world full of black, brown, and white people! They hid the truth from us by deleting our history from the Nexus! Race isn't about different hair or eye colors! It's so much more than that!

Ehari: That's the craziest thing I ever heard!

Hannibal: It's true!

Ehari: Then why are you targeting me?

Hannibal: We're prisoners in the virtual world! They've been using us as Guinea pigs! Death is the only way to break their chains of servitude!

[SCANNER]
|WARNING|

|SIONIC DISCHARGE PENDING|

[X-RAY PROJECTOR]
|MAPPING EXIT ROUTE|

Hannibal launches a sion from the arm attachment he'd been petting. The rocket whistles down the corridor as I duck into a utility closet and then explodes inside the corridor's intersection.

[SCANNER]
|WARNING|

|TOXIC COMPOUND DETECTED- PARTICULATE|
|POLLUTION VIA SIONIC DISCHARGE|

[X-RAY PROJECTOR]
|MAPPING EXIT ROUTE|

The blast releases miniature pellets that stick to the walls, floor, and ceiling. These pellets release an acidic gas that eats through the corridor's titanium alloy. I shut the utility door before the gas reaches me, cut into the ceiling's ventilation grate with my sword, leap inside when it swings open, and pull myself up the shaft. Even though acid eats through the door faster than expected, I avoid its corrosiveness by scaling up to the vent's cross section and crawling away.

Hannibal: Hiding is useless!

Ehari: The bombing at my condo must have damaged your brain! Think about what you're saying! Think about what you're doing–

Hannibal: You and I are the last of our kind! We are the suffering!

Hannibal's furious thoughts frighten me. He seethes with pure rage. The old Hannibal never possessed such a temperament. My X-ray projector maps the ventilation shafts and highlights three viable exits. Hannibal does the same. I can see him sprinting down the maintenance corridor and flanking my position. It's amazing how such a heavy and clunky looking prostheticalanatomy can move so fast.

Ehari: I still don't understand why you're trying to kill me!

Hannibal: A group of people went on a campaign of world domination thousands of years ago. Many nations fell to their invasions and the conquered lands were renamed Australia, Canada, America, and so forth. They slaughtered those who didn't submit. Billions perished. It was mass genocide. When nuclear war erupted centuries later, the oppressed found the pyramid and used it to escape annihilation. They fled to a new world. Your CP is the key to that world!

Ehari: Cybernetic prostheticalanatomies are for

reintegrating into the physical world!

Hannibal: Don't you get it? The government is using us! They think physicality is beneath them and want to finish the war by using you as a weapon! Your CP is a walking bomb!

Ehari: Impossible!

Hannibal: Listen to me E… the VIA kept our genetic codes active because only non-whites could enter the pyramid. They still haven't figured out why and used both of our families' lineages for experimentation! The Virtual Intelligence Agency even designed *The Suffering* so that only we'd pass it! It was part of our indoctrination! I learned while here, that they hoped the pyramid would accept you as a genuine human survivor. The VIA planned to destroy it with the bomb they planted in your CP's brain but the government underestimated the pyramid's technology. It remotely deactivated the bomb, subdued your CP, and planted a virus inside of you—that virus activated when I returned your body to the birthing chamber. Scarlet's obsessive hacks exposed her to infection and she became the instrument for transmission.

Ehari: This can't be happening…

Hannibal: I love you, E. I really do… but this isn't about us. The fate of an entire civilization rests on our shoulders.

Ehari: We can find a way that doesn't involve violence! I don't have to go back to the ruins! I'll stay away from the pyramid!

Hannibal: Too risky. Our CP's can be hacked too easily. Martyring ourselves is the only way to ensure the new world's safety.

Ehari: I thought you were my friend!

Hannibal: This is war! Friendships die on the battlefield!

Hannibal is unavoidable. I grab my sword when he pauses by the neighboring vent and transform my blade into a rectangular seal with four legs. He targets me as I fixate the table-shield into the shaft.

[SCANNER]
|WARNING|

|SIONIC DISCHARGE PENDING|

Hannibal launches a whistling rocket into my duct as I lean against the reformed metal. The makeshift plug holds the explosion at bay, but its concussive force dislodges the seal and pushes it forcefully against my back. The blast delivers my first physical sensations of extreme pain—a *horrible* feeling that multiplies my fear of death a thousandfold. I kick open a vent on the opposite end of the shaft after sliding for thirty feet on my backside. I calculate a perfect landing inside the adjacent disposal plant but part of my Hemingway rod sticks inside the shaft after refusing to reform into a sword. None of the acid pellets seems to have permanently damaged the metal but they've malformed it.

[SCANNER]
|WARNING|

|HEMINGWAY ROD CORRUPTION DETECTED-|
|MOLDING FUNCTION DISABLED|

I try moving but the deformed rod binds me in place when sionic compounds interfere with its morphing function. The metal even refuses to unlock from my armor so I try using a patch.

[SCANNER]
|PATCH DOWNLOADED|

|INTEGRATING 4:6 MALACHI CLASS REPAIR|
|PATCH- INITIALIZING|

Hannibal: Looks like you're stuck. No worries. I'll set you free!

I work frantically to execute the rod's patch while Hannibal barrels down corridors like a raging bull. He collapses his sion launcher for a missile variation.

Ehari: Hannibal, it's me! We've been friends for years! There has to be another solution!

Hannibal: Like what? Peace? Haven't you learned anything from *The Suffering*? We're a warrior species born on the most hostile planet in the solar system! There will never be peace amongst humans! We've slept our lives away in the virtuality of our enemy and this moment is all we have to awaken!

Ehari: This is murder! You're vile… just like those who destroyed Earth!

Hannibal pauses at the corridor's far end and

targets me with his missile launcher. I can hardly believe such weapons still exist. I try pulling the deformed Hemingway rod out of the duct but it refuses to budge.

[SCANNER]
|WARNING|

|RETICULE LOCK ESTABLISHED BY TYPE XY|
|CYBERNETIC|

Hannibal: We have to die! There's no other way!

[SCANNER]
|WARNING|

|MISSILE LAUNCH PENDING|

Ehari: Please! Stop!

[SCANNER]
|PATCH COMPLETE|

|4:6 MALACHI CLASS REPAIR PATCH INITIALIZED|

Hannibal fires his weapon as my rod pops free and snaps to my side like a rubber band. I have to backflip away from the roaring missile—which passes in between my legs and explodes after hitting a disposal bin on the far side of the room.

[SCANNER]
|WARNING|

|STRUCTURAL INTEGRITY COMPROMISED-|
|COLLAPSE IN PROGRESS|

[X-RAY PROJECTOR]
|MAPPING EXIT ROUTE|

The explosion is so tremendous the entire room disintegrates. I dash through the nearest doorway as the ceiling crumbles around me and barely make it into the facility's warehouse before the entire disposal plant implodes.

Hannibal: The survival of an entire world depends on our sacrifice!

Ehari: Let's go to the new world together! We can start over! Our lives don't have to end this way!

Hannibal: No good will come from polluting the new world with our knowledge and technology!

Ehari: But the virtual world is our home! How can you defend a place that you never saw? The new world that you're speaking of might not even exist! I've been inside the pyramid! There's nothing in there! The evidence you found might be a lie! Why are you helping Oliver Milkes?

Hannibal: Oliver showed me the truth years ago! Finding the library only confirmed his claims! They call him a false prophet but Oliver is a man of faith and righteousness! He's one of the few people who truly want to end this cycle of death!

Ehari: You can't end a cycle of death with more murder!

Hannibal: I told you before, this is war! The only way to end this war, is by making the ultimate sacrifice!

[SCRAMBLER]
|COMMAND PROTOCOL SIGMA:|

|DISPERSAL SIGNAL INITIATED-|
|CLOAKING FUNCTION ENABLED|

Even though I've distorted Hannibal's scanners and masked my movements from his radar, he has little trouble finding me. The warehouse has less open space than most other sections. Metal stacks and bins are everywhere but they're the only objects separating us. As I dash between them, Hannibal pursues with twin Gatling guns acquired from the adjoining armory.

[SCANNER]
|WARNING|

|RETICULE LOCK ESTABLISHED BY TYPE XY|
|CYBERNETIC|

Hannibal fires at me when I try sneaking into the armory and then blocks my path by guarding the doorway. I reform the Hemingway rod back into a sword before taking the offensive.

Ehari: I'm done running from you!

Hannibal: You have no choice! Your CP is no match for mine!

[CALCULATOR]

XX RELATION	XY RELATION
ARMAMENT DEFICIENCY = LOW NOMINAL	ARMAMENT SUFFICIENCY = HIGH OFFSET
SCANNER SUFFICIENCY = MEDIUM OFFSET	SCANNER DEFICIENCY = MEDIUM OFFSET
SPEED SUFFICIENCY = HIGH OFFSET	SPEED DEFICIENCY = LOW NOMINAL

[COMPUTATION]
|XX OPTIMAL PACE|
|= 38% >|
|XY OPTIMAL ROTATION SPEED|

I hide behind one of the stacks flanking Hannibal's position, sprint towards him when his back is turned, and slash Hannibal's shoulder blades with a powerful two-handed strike before he can face me with his enormous guns. I keep running as he swings about firing a wave of bullets and slide behind another stack. Rounds rattle against the metal as I consider my next move.

[CALCULATOR]

XX RELATION	XY RELATION
ARMAMENT DAMAGE = 0% EXTREMELY LOW NOMINAL	ARMAMENT DAMAGE = 0.068% EXTREMELY HIGH OFFSET

[COMPUTATION]
|XX KINETIC RATE|
|= 99.932% <|
|XY ARMAMENT POTENTIAL|

Hannibal: Was that supposed to be an attack?

Ehari: Big words… even for a giant with heavy artillery! I'm still alive aren't I?

Hannibal: Not for long!

My attack failed to penetrate with the depth I was expecting. Hannibal's armor is incredibly tough. Slashing will only inflict superficial damage but if I stab him, I'll probably lose my weapon…

I circle his position before charging straight for Hannibal. He turns towards me as I leap into the air with my sword pivoted towards his skull.

Hannibal raises the Gatling gun in his left hand when I try stabbing his face and shields himself with it. My sword sinks deep into the barrels as I land atop the gun, but not far enough to reach Hannibal's skull. When he turns his remaining weapon in my direction, I pull the sword through the gun's side—severing half the barrels as I leap away. Hannibal angrily hurls the damaged weapon as I run for cover.

[SCANNER]
|WARNING|

|INCOMING OBJECTS- INITIATE EVASIVE|
|MANEUVERS|

The Gatling gun breaks apart in midair with the larger half smashing into a nearby stack. I turn around while transforming the Hemingway rod into a club and bat the smaller half away.

Hannibal: You're going to die here!

Ehari: I keep hearing that, but it never happens!

Hannibal fires his remaining gun as I slide out of view. Rounds seem to spark against everything around me. I feel suffocated and search for an exit as the ground rumbles.

[SCANNER]
|WARNING|

|ADVANCING TYPE XY CYBERNETIC- INITIATE|
|EVASIVE MANEUVERS|

Hannibal abandons his position and rushes after me. I try doubling back to the armory but he's too close. A hail of gunfire follows every corner I turn. Then, when I begin to outrun him, Hannibal starts barreling straight through metal stacks as if they were made of Styrofoam.

[SCANNER]
|WARNING|

|ADVANCING TYPE XY CYBERNETIC- MINIMUM|
|SAFE DISTANCE EXCEEDED|

[X-RAY PROJECTOR]
|WARNING|

|NO EXIT ROUTE DETECTED|

Hannibal corners me when I avoid the crushing weight of three tipped stacks and bursts into view with his Gatling gun. He fires a second too late, though. I've already reformed the Hemingway rod into a shield that holds the bullets at bay. Hannibal forces me into the room's corner and charges as his gun depletes. My prostheticalanatomy's weight lightens as I leap above his body and Hannibal actually breaks *through* the titanium wall when he fails to ram me. I push away from the above corner, roll across the ground, and then sprint for the armory as he turns around.

Ehari: What's your body made of?

Hannibal: Blood and sweat!

I dash into the armory and grab the first thing I see. There's barely time to prepare the mine. Hannibal's thunderous footsteps are nearing at an alarming rate. I seek cover after exiting the rear hatch and slam it closed.

Ehari: I'm sorry it has to be this way.

Hannibal: So am I.

Hannibal enters the armory and inadvertently detonates the proximity mine that I placed in the doorway. Every single piece of ordinance inside the room explodes. The armory's exterior frame protects me from the blast as the entire room breaks away from the facility's main floor and drops into the basement. The explosion doesn't last long but the tremendous force emulsifies the armory and everything within it. When the tremors subside, a smoking pit seething with boiling liquid is all that remains.

I crouch by the edge and peer into the billowing smoke. My hair illuminates the darkness as Hannibal reaches out of the muck, grabs a broken beam, and pulls his severely damaged head and torso out of the mixture. The boiling metallic goo solidifies him in place as it cools in the air. Hannibal's eyes pierce the gloom—their red glow flutters with imminent pulse of death.

[CALCULATOR]

XX RELATION	XY RELATION
ARMAMENT DAMAGE = 0.0654% EXTREMELY HIGH OFFSET	ARMAMENT DAMAGE = 95.567% EXTREMELY LOW NOMINAL

[COMPUTATION #1]
|XX KINETIC RATE 94.913% > XY|
|ARMAMENT POTENTIAL|

[COMPUTATION #2]
|XY CYBERNETIC ESTIMATED|
|DEACTIVATION = 115.567 SECONDS|

Hannibal: You were always a hard target to hit.
Ehari: You were always a hard target to bring

down.

Hannibal: Listen to me, E… the virtual world is not our home. This place… this… Hell on Earth… this is where we belong. We have to die here. It's the only way to make things right. I tried to spare you from that moment when you'd have to make the decision on your own. No person should have to bear the weight of a world… alone.

Ehari: It didn't have to come to this.

Hannibal: Yes, it does.

Ehari: I can save you. Let me download your neural network into the virtual world. We can hide in the diodactic frame.

Hannibal: Like rats in a sewer? No thanks. This is where I choose to die.

Sparks from Hannibal's damaged neural processor briefly brightens the pit's darkness with orange light.

Ehari: Where's the Nexus?

Hannibal: Why?

Ehari: I want to see the virtual world.

Hannibal: Why?

Ehari: I have to see if our lives are a simulated illusion or real.

Hannibal: Impossible.

Ehari: Why?

Hannibal: There's no way of telling for sure. Seeing the Nexus won't validate anything.

Ehari: Why not?

Hannibal: Answer my question.

Ehari: What do you want to know?

Hannibal: What did you see at the very end of *The Suffering?*

Ehari: I saw… something magnificent.

Hannibal: You saw God, didn't you?

Ehari: Yes.

Hannibal: I knew it… you had a look in your eyes. It was transcendent. You really are a saint. Saint Di.

Ehari: No. I'm a sinner, like you.

Hannibal: No, you're not like me. You're different. You're blessed.

Ehari: Please, let me save you. I don't want you to die…

Hannibal: We're already dead, E–

The glow in Hannibal's eyes finally fades. I slowly back away from the pit, shaking with heartache. It's hard viewing Hannibal in such a state. My heart breaks as I turn away but after wandering about blindly my scanner detects an energy surge from a room on the far end of the facility.

"Hannibal, tell me you didn't…"

I confirm my suspicions after racing across the complex and sliding into the power room. The fight with Hannibal was only a distraction. All four reactors are overheating. The main console is smashed and its power lines—severed. When I try establishing a wireless connecting to one of the reactors my scanner detects a Diamond Class firewall. The advanced sequencing will need a minimum of one hour to crack. There's no other way of deactivating the reactors in less time. A simple calculation leaves me with a grim conclusion.

[SCANNER]
|CAUTION|

|REACTOR TEMPERATURE RATE INCREASING|
|BEYOND LIMIT|

|ANALYZING|

|…|

[SCANNER]
|WARNING|

|CRITICAL OVERLOAD = 25.743 MINUTES|

I don't waste a second and dash out of the room making additional calculations along the way.

"I need at least two minutes to reach the exit chamber—another three minutes to put on the environmental suit—the electric console requires command codes—then I'll have to open all three pressure sealed corridors before entering the final chamber, for a minimum of twelve minutes—just to get out!"

I don't foresee are the other traps Hannibal left behind. After taking a shortcut through the atrium, I trip a wire connected to a spring-loaded Axe and barely dodge the curved head swinging out from behind a counter. A grenade bouquet in the training room activates when I open the main door and detonates just as I close it. Then, I nearly run underneath two buckets of hydrochloric acid that Hannibal hid inside of ceiling panels only to confront another grim realization in the exit chamber.

"Wait, am I locked in?"

Hannibal smashed the consoles required for opening the chamber. There are no air ducts or external shafts leading outside. Hannibal even sealed the exits with a blowtorch just in case I found another way to open them. Incubating into the virtual world will take hours. There are no other escape options.

"You bastard! How could you do this to me?" I wail miserably and the mixture of frustration, grief, and uncertainty, fills the room. I sway from dizziness and then collapse to my knees when the prospect of death edges closer.

While brewing in the agony of defeat—at my most vulnerable—5478 arrives.

Neural Phenomenology

CHAPTER 29

I sense species-5478 lingering nearby. The creature's mind extends beyond its physical form. 5478 shares this portion of its consciousness by relaying mental content like a Wi-Fi hotspot emitting a signal. Unlike the invasive nature of sound waves, this "signal" does not automatically penetrate my thoughts. Instead, the helmet of invisible energy circumvents my mind and allows discretionary access to its information.

The facility's warning alarms blare in the background, signaling the reactor's fifteen-minute countdown. I barely notice them. There's little time for debating the possible consequences of interacting with species-5478. These final minutes may be all we have to communicate. I don't waste any time deliberating the issue and fearlessly seek a connection before I die.

[SCANNER]
|WARNING|

|OPEN NEURAL CHANNEL FROM UN-CERTIFIED|
|SOURCE- UPDATE REQUIRED TO INITIATE|
|DATA TRANSFER|

[UPDATE?]

|YES / NO|

I select, yes.

[SCANNER]
|NEURAL UPDATE IN-PROGRESS|

|...|

[SCANNER]
|NEW PROGRAM INSTALLED|

|SPHINX MEMORY ACCESS GRANTED|
|PHONETIC STREAMING IN-PROGRESS|

5478's upgrade allows me to experience the thoughts and feelings of those who lived in the past. The creature has managed to compress the consciousness of entire nations and lineages this way. Species-5478 shares its media content using human-based harmonics as the primary medium for communication. I realize in the act, that Scarlet was the first person within the virtual world 5478 contacted using such a method. Her intelligence was initially viewed as the most superior amongst human beings—so Scarlet became the primary target for first contact. When she utilized the upgrade to build her virus, Species-5478 severed ties with Scarlet after discerning her malicious intentions.

My newly acquired phonetic sense consumes the entire experience within a fraction of a second. My mind hungers for more information and I try absorbing the breadth of all knowledge pertaining to species-5478.

The creature's pyramid is the pinnacle of their technology. It molds light, energy, anti-matter, time, and even space—warping everything we perceive as reality into a medium of exploration. Manipulating super intense needle-like strings of gravity is the key feature used to link distant objects and even light to the pyramid. These specimens appear as two-dimensional film projections on the pyramid's surface. 5478 draws pieces of the universe into the pyramid for analysis before sending specimens back to their original destinations.

Species-5478 discovered new liquids, metals, gases, substances, and remarkably, life… in every corner of our galaxy. Like Earth, the variance of all species is dependent on the environments in which they evolve. A species' form predicates its intelligence. There are no exceptions to the rule. I analyze the profiles of many different entities. Some forms of life are wondrous while others are horrifying. All are spectacular to a human unaware of its celestial neighbors.

Species-5478 knows more about humanity than anyone expected. In fact, 5478 chronicled our entire evolution on its Sphinx memory, which is something akin to an organic hard drive. Through this perspective, I see humans almost as viruses demolishing our hosting worlds with uncontrollable urges to destroy and consume, as if unable to act otherwise. Glimpsing the human race through 5478's viewpoint makes me feel… embarrassingly parasitic.

An ancient Egyptian pharaoh by the name of Akhenaten, was the first human that 5478 ever contacted. According to the memory, Akhenaten saw God—a single Almighty God, who successfully foretold of future events. Since then, species-5478 has searched for the Almighty's presence within the fabric of our universe.

5478's interpretation of God does not involve a humanoid being with a curly beard who sits on a king's throne pointing fingers. Nor is God a reptilian entity that's beholden to 5478's likeness. That type of arrogance seems predominately human. 5478's God is similar to that of Akhenaten's—an all-encompassing entity that has no gender, bias, or even emotional barriers. Such things would limit the scope and magnitude of such a God.

5478 believes God exists outside of the known universe, much like an angler standing above a pool of fish—God has no urgent use for the elements of life that our immediate existence depends upon. To that end, 5478 wishes to share my experience of seeing God, but I'm hesitant; partly because I'm afraid 5478 might better interpret what I saw. Is it wrong to feel selfish after all that was just shared with me? 5478 may have more trouble deciphering the memory than I did—unlikely as that may be.

[SCANNER]
|WARNING|

|INTERNAL MEMORY REQUEST FROM|
|UNAUTHORIZED USER|

|ALLOW / DENY|

Time is running out. Should I share my inner thoughts with 5478? I've contemplated this scenario once before but now that I'm in the moment… I still don't know what to do. Species-5478 might kill me after getting what it wants but I'm dead, either way. Still… even though I'm clearly the inferior being, I can still demonstrate equal civility by sharing and allow the link to connect.

Granting access to my inner thoughts comes naturally. The doorway to my mind opens when our neural links bridge the communication divide and function as keys that unlocks the first partition of my consciousness. The impulse to know more about each other forms a binary connection whereby an equal exchange of numerical information occurs—in slight impulses at first—before growing stronger with each transfer—ultimately, evolving into a complex communion.

5478's thoughts are derived from emotions, memories, impulses, syntaxes, premonitions, mental pictures, signs, wavelengths, sensations, neural vernaculars, vibrations, forms of light, gravitational frequencies, pheromones, spoken languages, written words, hieroglyphics, numbers, patterns, secretions, emblems, gestures, scents, bioluminescent hues, temperature variations, something akin to melodic dialects, and a collection of technological mediums that converge their mind and body in remarkable ways. I realize through our connection, that species-5478 is not an alien creature from a distant world, but an ancient species that existed on Earth long before the proclaimed dominance of humankind.

5478 is more than a single creature; but rather, an entire species condensed within a singular state; its body is a world unto itself. Each cell-like entity within 5478 exists in a state of individuality—just like people—I'm essentially communicating with an entire race of beings through the body of their home world—a species within a species. The sum of communal thoughts creates a singular will and the opposing views forms parallels, doubts, presumptions, prejudices, likes, dislikes, and strange cognitive functions that are both foreign and common to human interpretation.

Their evolution began as a single celled organism but each cellular division gave rise to another microbial variation that recombined with the original cell. The advent of technology allowed 5478 to integrate inventions into themselves. Their body is now an organic machine hosting countless life-forms in a self-sustaining system. Within this realm is a biological nexus containing its own virtual world, and whose inner nexus provides the medium by which we're able to form a line of communication. Apparently, human neural links and 5478's biolink utilize many compatible binaries and features.

Life through 5478's perception ensnares entire generations within a mural of experiences. They witnessed the rise and fall of many intelligent species.

Some even surpassed the technological achievements of humans. Yet each species fell into extinction after refusing to prioritize space travel. The perpetual cycle of annihilation is an inevitable facet of life on Earth. Nature impatiently awaits acknowledgment and punishes disdain with extinction. Be it asteroids, plagues, or super-volcanic eruptions, each species that claimed superiority over the planet, fell to it— one by one—like children playing on a minefield.

In fact, the only species intelligent enough to devise a viable means of space travel that it endorsed and utilized as a primary objective for its survival, is 5478… known to themselves, as Kha.

Even though I feel obligated to use a plural distinction, Kha view their existence as neither a single entity nor a group—but more as an embodiment of consciousness. When I share my vision of God, Kha responds to me directly with a neural message.

Kha: Statement; God exists.

Ehari: I no longer believe in God.

Kha: Statement; We-I, believe in God.

Ehari: Why?

Kha: Statement; your vision is proof. It originates from beyond the borders of our universe.

Ehari: How can I believe in something I can't understand?

Kha: Statement; your mind requires extended saturation—mediation—evolution–then arrives understanding.

Ehari: What does God want?

Kha: Answer; you, me, us.

Ehari: For what?

Kha: Answer; unknown.

Ehari: Do you know why we exist?

Kha: Question; why is honey in a honeycomb?

Ehari: Because… a bee put it there.

Kha: Question; why are humans on Earth?

Ehari: I don't believe God put us here, if that's where you're going with this.

Kha: Question; is it possible to evolve from nothing?

Ehari: No. We evolved from materials that have always existed in one form or another.

Kha: Question; is it possible to evolve from no cause?

Ehari: No.

Kha: Question; what is the cause of evolution?

Ehari: Evolution caused itself through a sequence of natural events.

Kha: Question; can a sequence of natural events occur without a cause?

Ehari: If the events caused themselves.

Kha: Question; are programs derivative of evolution?

Ehari: Developer's create programs using the process of evolution.

Kha: Question; can you program characters in a virtual reality to perceive the programmer?

Ehari: Virtual characters can respond to the programmer's interventions but perception of the programmer requires consciousness.

Kha; Question; what is consciousness?

Ehari: Consciousness is awareness of oneself within a state of existence.

Kha: Question; is it possible to be aware of oneself within a nonexistent state?

Ehari: No. That's death. You can't be aware of yourself if you don't exist.

Kha: Question; is it possible for something to exist without being created?

Ehari: Only if it has always existed.

Kha: Question; what has always existed?

Ehari: The environment housing the universe.

Kha: Statement; We-I perceive God as the environment.

Ehari: How can God be the environment, if the environment has a beginning and an ending?

Kha: Answer; God is alpha and omega.

Ehari: How can God be alpha and omega, if God has always existed?

Kha: Answer; in the circle of infinity, there is always a beginning and an ending, which start and end at different points.

Ehari: If God is the environment, then what are we?

Kha: Answer; products of the environment.

Ehari: If we're not alive, then what are we? How

are we able to communicate with one another if we're not living entities?

Kha: Answer; your body renders the environment. Rendering does not equal consciousness.

Ehari: What about my awareness of self and the decisions I make? Surely these are indicator of consciousness.

Kha: Answer; "our" thoughts are the sum of environmental renderings, and "our" decisions are the derivatives of environmental forces. Every thought and action we make is a direct result of external stimuli—free will is a human illusion that masks the control mechanisms of environmental programming.

Ehari: Impossible…

Kha: Clarification; we are composites of the environment—the accumulation of base materials, no more alive than the atoms that bind us.

Ehari: I refuse to believe that. I view life as the sum of these parts.

Kha: Question; these parts, and their wholes, function similarly. Rhetorical. Question; ask yourself if we are the cause, or the effect of our environment.

I pause to consider the question. What are we, *really*? Does life truly run in such a scripted fashion? Every single human action *could* be seen as a reaction to external stimuli. The idea numbs my senses. If *everything* I do, say, and think is reactionary, do I actually control my own consciousness? Am I really choosing my own acts, or is the environment dictating everything I do like a cleverly written program in a virtual game? Is there anything I can think or do that isn't in response to the environment? *Anything at all?* If Kha's right and I'm just reacting to things around me, what am I? What is my life if nothing more than a sequence of reactions? How *isn't* that identical to a computer program awaiting external input from a controller? If the environment is our "HID", who controls it?

Ehari: We are the effect, but… if we're not alive, then what is death?

Kha: Answer; a reformatted state. True life.

Ehari: To what end?

Kha: Answer; to what end, is unknown. An impenetrable dark shell encapsulates our universe. Every deleted consciousness downloads into quadrants outside of the universe. Nothing else can penetrate the dark boundary.

Ehari: What does my vision of God mean?

Kha: Answer; unknown. The information is currently being analyzed.

Ehari: Why are you seeking a god of any kind?

Kha: Answer; to escape from our collapsing universe.

Ehari: I thought the universe was expanding…

Kha: Answer; the volume of space casts an illusion of expansion when distant light bends into the curvatures of the void. The universe appears dark because we exist in the event horizon of a reformatting vortex.

Ehari: Why are you using computer terminology to describe this event?

Kha: Answer; all matter within the universe stems from a central template of ones and zeros.

Ehari: So… the universe resets like an OS?

Kha: Answer; yes.

Ehari: Are formulas or mathematical equations the programs that restart events within the operating system?

Kha: Answer; yes.

Ehari: Do you think God is the programmer?

Kha: Answer; yes.

Ehari: Do you think we're living in a simulation?

Kha: Answer: Yes. The universe is formed with alpha-numeric symbols—the God code of Akhenaten. This code will unlock eternal life. Seeking the programmer brings purpose.

I consider the notion in silence.

Kha: Statement; escape death by following the light to freedom—prepare yourself.

There's so much to discuss that I don't want to leave Kha's mind. Exiting from the planes of a higher consciousness and returning to the seclusion of my unlinked mind unfairly lobotomizes my enhanced awareness of reality. After a brief, yet tumultuous struggle with my urge to learn, I disengage from Kha's link and hastily outfit one of the armored environmental suits hanging in a nearby storage locker. The facility's automated alarm blares on all speakers.

WARNING: Reactor overload in four minutes.

I gather a compression pack and headgear from the locker. After fastening my helmet into place I wonder, Ehari: How am I supposed to get out of here?

A slender, reptilian hand emerges from a splatter on the chamber's wall and motions in a human-like fashion to follow before withdrawing from view. I dash to the spot, reach out with my Hemingway rod, and poke the yellow residue. The rod easily penetrates the watery substance so I follow suit and step through.

Coruscation within the aqueous goo is so stunning that the chasm forming ahead is barely visible. This narrow pathway of yellow light shaped in Kha's form provides a brilliant pathway to the exterior. I can almost move with the same speed and dexterity afforded to me in an airy atmosphere. After negotiating the unrefined tunnel to its end, stepping into Pyramid Valley's pollution nullifies my ambitions for survival and when I look around, Kha is nowhere in sight.

I run as the ground rumbles from the seismic quakes of exploding reactors. Malfunctioning laborbots fall to the ground. Others stumble about when their connection to virtual operators fades. Debris of all types rolls down from the inner valley's mountainous walls. I negotiate the chaos and reach the safety of a loading dock. Here is where I realize that my link to the virtual world is forever lost.

A Trip to Nowhere

CHAPTER 30

Traversing Earth's hostile planes without any support is a frightening experience. I lived an entire lifetime neural linked to media and people. My former existence embodied a fusion of minds and technology interwoven within the Nexus' hive-like environment of free thought. Only two hours have passed since Hannibal destroyed the IVST facility but I've already generated suicidal thoughts. I'm sure the Nexus rests somewhere beneath tons of rubble at some unreachable depth. If not, there's no way of finding it, since all information pertaining to its existence now lies entombed within a smoldering inferno. I doubt even Kha's ability to penetrate such a mess. The ruins of a dead world are all I have left and my only company—ghosts. I never realized how distressing the mere prospect of isolation could be.

Daytime departed hours ago but a mountainous wall of fire left by a flaming tornado continues its slow burn. The blazing wall reaches thousands of feet into the air. It illuminates a particle mist hovering aboveground. I can actually see further at night because of this unusual lighting effect.

Antiparticles stirred by the onset of dusk have changed the ground's hue from sandy brown to bloodshot red. Odd earthly elements rise into the atmosphere and create strange multicolored clouds that cast radiant shadows across the soil. The ground softens into a toxic pudding when these abnormal shadows pass over them. All of the day's heavier rubble sank underground and probably formed into bedrock from the pressure and molten heat brewing below. Circular blobs of earth bounce about as if on trampolines and alternate from craters to rubbery mounds in the blink of an eye. My prostheticalanatomy alters its weight just enough to keep me from sinking into the bobbing earth but it's using more energy than I'd like to expend.

I spend hours searching for my brother's remains. Spending the rest of my life looking for him might be the only way to stay sane for any redeemable amount of time. How long could I last out here, though… by myself? How long would it take before the wind spoke to me in my brother's voice or shapeless clouds became living things formed in his image? Would I even know if I were going crazy? Is there a gradual slide into madness or does it rise up suddenly and snatch you away like a crocodile? What forms of delirium would solitude regurgitate after it eats my mind away?

My neural link suddenly beeps when someone opens a live channel and I jerk from the unexpected surprise. The source originates from somewhere nearby. Hannibal destroyed the IVST facility, so…

Ehari: Who is this?

Scarlet: Who else could it be?

I scan the horizon and see nothing. Scarlet is the last person on Earth that I'd choose to share my final days. Am I already going crazy? Suicide is becoming a rational inevitability.

Ehari: How did you escape?

Scarlet: I hacked my way into the original CP and awoke during your battle with Hannibal. It's a good thing you killed him. I'm not sure I could have done better. Species-5478 didn't seem willing to bond with me, like it did with you. I'm thankful it decided to save your life, though. I followed you out of the IVST facility using the path species-5478 created.

Ehari: Where's the Nexus?

Scarlet: Where do you think? Those idiots kept it underneath the IVST facility inside of a bunker! I thought they'd be smarter. There's no way of reaching the Nexus anymore… assuming it even exists.

Ehari: You're lying.

Scarlet: There's no point in lying! It's over! Everything is over! The virtual world is gone! We're alone!

[SCANNER]
|ANALYSIS|

|DISTORTION EFFECT IN PROGRESS- NEURAL|
|SIGNAL UNTRACEABLE|

My scanner is having trouble locating Scarlet within the atmosphere's antiparticle mixture. I hope she's having the same problem. Scarlet must be hiding inside one of the fissures scattered throughout the plateau's knolls. I keep a low profile and slide into a gully after failing to locate her.

Scarlet: Her name was Ehari.

Ehari: Who?

Scarlet: My baby. My child. The part of me that died. I named her after you.

I'm sickened by the disturbing level of calm in Scarlet's voice.

Ehari: Why are you refusing to see it was just an accident?

Scarlet: Conspiring to steal my husband was no accident.

Ehari: I did no such thing! We were just friends. How many times do I have to tell you that?

Large cracks form in the earth as gravity shifts. The wind changes direction seconds later. Air tentacles reach down from the stratosphere and disperse some of the sediments scattered across the ground. I feel things that my sensors aren't detecting. A premonition courses through my body. Is this what ancient humans called… foreboding?

Scarlet: You loved Seti more than you loved me!

I'm not sure if she's wrong. Balancing friendship and romance is an impossible task. Both require distinct versions and quantities of love.

Ehari: I… no, I…

Scarlet: Yes, you did. You still do. You never told me about the backyard. I had to find that out on my own. All those days of staring into the clouds with Seti as if he were your father, equals a love affair. Secrets are the proof of a guilty conscious.

My heart beats faster. The mere thought of Seti stirs a myriad of emotions.

Ehari: Why are you tormenting me like this?

Scarlet: Tormenting you? You?! What about me?

Ehari: What about you? You're a murderer! You seethe over the loss of a single child! Yes, it's tragic… but what about the millions you deleted? What about their suffering?

Scarlet: This isn't about some pathetic, unborn child. I unleashed *hell* throughout the virtual world because I love you!

Ehari: Seti and I are not slaves to your ambition! True love is not something you can bottle in a jar. It can't be contained!

Scarlet: You have no idea what true love is! Everything that happened is because of you!

Ehari: And what about Seti? I never invited him to my condo! I never provoked his feelings for me!

Scarlet: You never turned him away, either! That idiot… I never loved Seti. He meant nothing to me.

My heart… it's beating so hard the sensation is almost painful.

Ehari: What did you do? Please, don't tell me you—

Scarlet: Yes, I did. I murdered Seti.

Ehari: How? Why?

Scarlet: You know why. I used your cloud

simulator to spy on you and even planted bugs inside your home. I can hack anything, remember?

Ehari: Why would you marry a man you didn't love? Why spy on us?

Scarlet: I knew from that chance encounter in the arcade, that you and Seti were in love. I didn't want him to take you away from me. I couldn't let that happen… so I hacked into his mind and erased his feelings for you. Then Seti fell in love with you in a different way, and for a different reason. So I erased his feelings for you again, and then again, and again…

Ehari: You're a monster! Guilt paralyzed my heart years after Seti's deletion! You selfish bitch!

Scarlet: I needed a way to control Seti, so I planted a fake memory into his mind—and tricked him into thinking he'd proposed to me. But his emotions continued getting the better of him, even after we married. He kept falling in love with you… over and over and over again! It was infuriating! He never fell in love with me! Not once! I wanted to kill him on the altar… and when my pregnancy failed to suppress that devotion, the only option he left me with, was murder.

Ehari: But the child! The baby! Why delete your own baby? How could you do that?

Scarlet: The marriage and pregnancy were tools of dissuasion, nothing more. I spent years nurturing my relationship with you before Seti intruded into our lives. I hated him with every fiber of my being! His very existence repulsed me. Every moment that

I spent with him gnawed at my soul. Men disgust me! Seti was the very model of everything I loathe about that despicable gender. My pregnancy was the only thing he gave me of any value. I used the embryo to kill him by corrupting it with a malicious virus. The embryo infected Seti's vascular threads as he seeded my womb through the pregnancy torrent. When he left your condo and stepped onto the jumpwalk, my virus scrambled his signature just enough to cause the transfer glitch that fried him alive.

I scream out in horror after hearing Scarlet's confession. Her words stir eviscerating pain in my stomach and I double over as though stabbed.

Scarlet: Don't cry! I did it because I love you!

Ehari: You're crazy! I hate you!

Scarlet: I'm not naive enough to think you want a passionate relationship with me, but love isn't something you can bottle up in a jar, right? I grew bitter when you showed me no romantic interest—hateful, even. I was determined to make sure that if I couldn't have you, nobody would.

Ehari: All of you… you're all sick! You, Hannibal, and Grey! What in the Hell is wrong with you? Are you tied to Oliver Milkes, too?

Scarlet: My snooping uncovered Hannibal's secret relationship with Oliver. I followed up on his leads and discovered your true origins. I knew it was only a matter of time before you beat *The Suffering*. They designed the game so that only you or Hannibal could pass it. *The Suffering's* completion signified the end of your virtual training, and the beginning of cybernetic prostheticalanatomy integration. I decided to escape in your CP and destroy the virtual world after you exited, but Hannibal blew up the IVST docking station before I could find the Nexus. I would've preferred watching the virtual world crumble apart in my hands… but we're alone either way.

My body feels like it's on fire.

Ehari: How can… this is… I… you're insane!

Scarlet: This is true love! Accept it! The Nexus is gone! All we have is each other! You *have* to love me now! You don't have a choice!

Ehari: You… you tricked me into hating myself—into hating Seti!

Scarlet: That was no trick! Seti was weak! He couldn't stop me from killing him! Seti didn't deserve you!

Ehari: You're a monster! I'd rather die than live the rest of my life with you!

[SCANNER]
|ANALYSIS|

|MOVEMENT DETECTED 102 FEET SOUTH OF|
|CURRENT POSITION|

I spot Scarlet when she abandons her position. Monitoring the immediate area reveals no obvious reason for doing so and I can't figure out why she'd expose herself. Before I settle on a course of action the ground shifts beneath my feet.

[SCANNER]
|WARNING|

|TRANSIENT GRAVITATIONAL ANOMALY DETECTED|

Instead of buckling into the earth I'm lifted skyward on a large slab that elevates nearly fifty feet within a matter of seconds. I leap off as another chunk rises through the air next to me. The slabs elevate into the metalloid layer of iron and nickel drifting eight hundred and fifty-feet aboveground, where they shatter like glass. Instead of falling back to the ground, the broken pieces of rock scuttle across the metallic alloy's shiny underside. I have no idea how such a massive mass of metal can float through the atmosphere in such a fashion or why it attracts rocks. The metal island looks like an inverted mountain from my vantage point. I see gold, silver, and other metallic alloy layers following like a train of boxcars in the distance.

[SCANNER]
|WARNING|

|TRANSIENT GRAVITATIONAL ANOMALY DETECTED|

The ground spasms and I leap away from another slab before it can elevate me into the air. More chunks dislodge from the ground and rise skyward. Gravitational funnels forming inside the wriggling air tentacles act like straws sucking slabs of earth into the above alloy layers. The bluish hues from their cylindrical forms darken as the anomaly intensifies.

Scarlet: You didn't see that coming, did you? It's no surprise I can operate a prostheticalanatomy better than you can!

Ehari: Shut up!

Scarlet: Don't try to fight me, you'll never win! All you have is a Hemingway rod!

The alloy cloud's shadow continues causing gravitational aberrations on the ground. I rush in Scarlet's direction after spotting her outside the anomaly's effective range. The earth quakes beneath my feet as it tears apart. Larger pieces rise faster than smaller ones. Leaping off the biggest slabs becomes the only way to avoid smashing into the metalloid layers drifting through the air.

Scarlet: You were never a match for me!

[SCANNER]
|ANALYSIS|

|TYPE XX CYBERNETIC WEAPONRY- 1 PULSE RIFLE-|
|4 IV GRENADES- 1 SEISMIC DETONATOR|

I reach the outskirts of the gravitational anomaly then morph my Hemingway rod into a sword and shield. Scarlet is standing on an upcoming ridge and waits until I approach before leaping backwards and dropping out of view.

[SCANNER]
|WARNING|

|VOLCANIC LAVA DETECTED|

I pause atop the ridge and scan its valley. A river of lava flows along the base. Scarlet is running towards the orange flow so I slide down one of the slopes and chase after her. Our speeds synchronize and gaining ground is difficult, especially when she tosses an IV grenade into my path.

[SCANNER]
|WARNING|

|EXPLOSIVE DEVICE DETECTED|

The ignitron vanadium explosive releases a pulsing blast of white fire, which creates a crater of silvery filaments that contaminate the ground and surrounding air with decaying particles of light. Taking a wide girth to avoid its corrosive properties wastes valuable seconds. Another obstacle emerges by the time I reach the valley's base.

[SCANNER]
|WARNING|

|FREE FALLING OBJECTS DETECTED|

CO_2 gas rising from the lava, buffers the alloy cloud's shadow when it passes over the molten river. The anti-gravity field breaks and releases all of the hoisted sediments and boulders, which fall around us like rouge meteors. Scarlet leaps across a patchwork of rocks floating in the volcanic river and waves goodbye as they carry her away.

Scarlet: Seti didn't love you! He would have

never married me if he did!

Ehari: You deceived him!

Scarlet: Lie to yourself all you want, but it doesn't change reality! He was unworthy of love!

Ehari: Shut up!

Scarlet: He deserved to die!

Ehari: Shut up!

Scarlet: He married me, not you! He impregnated me, not you! How does it feel knowing I went to bed with the man you loved?

Ehari: You crazy bi—

Scarlet: We were destined to be together, E! Just accept it!

[SCANNER]
|WARNING|

|EXPLOSIVE DEVICE DETECTED|

I follow in Scarlet's path and leap across any islet of tectonic plating solid enough to float on lava. She tosses more ignitron grenades before I have a chance to close the distance.

The first explosive bounces off a rocky slab and harmlessly detonates within the molten sludge. I use my Hemingway rod to shield against the searing spray but her second grenade detonates atop solid scoria—destroying it—and cutting off my pursuit. Backtracking wastes precious time. Even worse—a mountainous slab of aluminum falls from the alloy cloud and plummets into the river.

[SCANNER]
|WARNING|

|VOLCANIC OVERFLOW IN TEN SECONDS|

There's no time to avoid the titanic wave of lava hurtling in my direction. My sensors indicate the Hemingway rod's density is lower than the lava's, so I reform the metal into a surfboard and ride the growing wave straight down the river. Avoiding the floating and falling chunks of rock becomes a game of death that culminates with the cresting lava. I surf along the base of the molten wave as it locks me into its rolling barrel and steer towards the river's eastern bank. Its funnel collapses behind me as I finally escape the scolding liquid and disembark safely on the embankment.

I reform my Hemingway rod back into a sword and shield when Scarlet fires at me from hundreds of feet away with her pulse rifle. Two of the shots damage my armor. I use my shield to deflect the remaining rounds before seeking suitable cover near a granite outcropping.

Ehari: Why are you trying to kill me?

Scarlet: You take too many chances with your life! I can't have you doing something that will destroy your prostheticalanatomy! I'll go insane if I'm alone out here...

Ehari: You're already insane! If you want a companion then why fire at me with a pulse rifle?

Scarlet: I won't let you run up and kill me! All

I have to do is disable your CP, and then reactivate your neural core!

Ehari: How? Hannibal destroyed the IVST facility!

Scarlet: I don't need or want you to have full functionality! Your brain is all that matters.

Ehari: I won't be your slave!

Scarlet: You don't have a choice! I'm the one with the gun!

A flurry of oblong rounds strikes the granite when I try advancing. There's no way of attacking Scarlet from within the valley, especially with my weaponry. As she closes the distance between us, another alloy cloud passes beyond the molten river and re-agitates the gravitational anomaly within its shadow.

[SCANNER]
|WARNING|

|TRANSIENT GRAVITATIONAL ANOMALY DETECTED|

I hold my position and allow a large section of rising granite to elevate me into the air. This time, I wait until it lifts me a hundred feet before leaping onto a slower ascending slab. Scarlet continues to chase from below after losing her line of sight.

Scarlet: You're not half as clever as you think!

[SCANNER]
|WARNING|

|DISRUPTER CHARGE DETECTED|

Scarlet skewers my vicinity with a swarm of pulse fire before discharging her weapon's grenade launcher. The spherical orb strikes a rising slab directly ahead of me and explodes; there's barely time to shield against the fiery debris.

[SCANNER]
|WARNING|

|ELECTRUM IMPACT IMMINENT|

I try my best to avoid colliding with the gold and silver layer hovering above me but as I rise higher, my prostheticalanatomy has trouble counteracting the illuming effects of the anomaly. After being lifted eight hundred and forty-feet my CP barely reaches a state of near weightlessness as I smack into the alloy layer's underside. Scarlet continues firing at me as I scramble to my feet and run upside down across the alloy's surface. She unleashes her final pulse grenades—both strike ascending rocks and detonate prematurely.

Ehari: This isn't the virtual world! There's no way to cheat the laws of physics! Hacking won't help you here!

I duck inside a shifting alloy plate's hollow interior. It's a risky maneuver. The cavernous space has the potential of crushing me with a single collapse—and all without a moment's warning. Luckily, the risk pays off. The advantage shifts into my corner when Scarlet loses sight of me and rides a slab of stone up to the alloy layer.

Many of the hollowed layers contain winding burrows with barely enough room for maneuvering. Other channels have spacious ceilings housing pillars of homogenous metals that keep the lower and top halves quartered. I dash through one of the smaller burrows as Scarlet trails in my footsteps. She fires at me repeatedly so I wait until Scarlet nears before blocking a narrow burrow with my shield. When she bends its foremost corner, I morph a single spike through my shield's center and try impaling her with it. Scarlet avoids the attack and retreats.

[SCANNER]
|WARNING|

|EXPLOSIVE DEVICE DETECTED|

I leave the shield fixed into place as Scarlet drops her final ignitron grenade, and we both run before it explodes. My shield holds the explosion at bay but the burrow collapses. I escape through a wall fracture, enter a new channel, and morph the remaining half my rod into a small halberd, which I use to chop several columns of electrum. Scarlet finds me seconds later.

[SCANNER]
|WARNING|

|RETICULE LOCK ESTABLISHED BY APPROACHING|
|TYPE XX CYBERNETIC|

A final swing of the sword is all it takes to cause

a catastrophic collapse. Scarlet tries to escape the crushing alloys, but the angle of my cuts ensures the brunt of the collapse falls on her half of the channel.

[SCANNER]
|WARNING|

|COLLAPSE IMMINENT- MAPPING EXIT ROUTES|

I have only seconds to enjoy Scarlet's screams before the collapse pushes me onward. The nearest of three burrows leading out of the channel becomes my avenue for escape. I race through the glistening pathway and eventually emerge in Earth's toxic atmosphere before the electrum collapses inward.

Slabs of earth are continually sucked up by the straw-like funnels of gravity and pummel the metallic underside. Dodging them isn't easy and juggling the various pitfalls takes all of my concentration. The balance between urgency and safety shifts as the gravitational anomaly persistently rips the ground apart. Using my Hemingway rod as an inverted umbrella sail is the only way of riding one of the descending currents below the gravitational event horizon. Then, as before, I use the rising slabs as steps that lead back to the ground.

A shallow cave grants a secure hiding spot that shields me from further air trips. I peer out of it, gasping with a strange mixture of relief and grief.

The scarred landscape, bleeding with molten seepage, substantiates the anomaly's abusive hand. Hours pass before all alloy layers leave the area. I use the time to contemplate how I'll commit suicide.

475

A World without God

CHAPTER 31

Returning to the alien ruins completes one of the most difficult tasks that I've ever undertaken. Hiking to the ancient city requires submitting to solitude. Loneliness is my antithesis for living. It requires abandoning my humanity and regressing to a lesser form of self. I refuse to embark on such excursions into madness. Even though the prospect of communicating with Kha intrigues me, it's no match for mental evolution with my species. Discovery is more than knowing; discovery reaps its greatest rewards through the allocation of knowledge. What's the point in learning the universe's secrets if there are no humans left to share in the spoils?

I indulge my curiosity and search for Hannibal's evidence. Proof of a government conspiracy will pave the way for my suicide. It's easier to end a life that you loathe so I follow the revised route Hannibal used during his return trip to the IVST facility and find the library he mentioned.

There are no signs of human activity aside from Hannibal's trespassing. Antique media fills the entire building. Kha appears to have gathered these relics during the final moments of the war, where they've remained untouched for thousands of years.

I find everything from holos, pads, tablets, books, parchments, records, films, billboards, magazines, CDs, DVDs, tapes and magnetic recordings, cassettes, paintings, microfilms, all manner of drives and even stone carvings. Every item is of human origin.

I find Hannibal's evidence pile nestled between two bookshelves. Sifting through the material sickens my soul because everything he said proves true.

There *was* a place called Africa! It was in fact, a continent filled with Africans! An entire race of dark-skinned people lived there! The continent even had multiple countries! I had no idea such truth existed...

I even learn about a library in Egypt that stored the summation of African knowledge. This library was eventually raided by a man named Alexander the Great and later abolished after its contents were plundered. A renaissance was born in Europe soon after, but the location to Kha's pyramid remained a mystery. Sadly, Hannibal's revelation was only partially correct.

He forgot to mention America.

Or rather... Sinwa.

This was the name of my home before the conquerors arrived. They ravaged, raped, and decimated the land and its people. Millions of men, women, and children perished—ruthlessly, slaughtered like vermin. Descendants of those who now control the virtual world annihilated them. It's a nauseating realization. I wouldn't be surprised if every person that I ever met was a prearranged meeting by the Virtual Intelligence Agency. Is my entire life really a lie? Am I nothing more than a tool? The classic movies, shows, and music that I love all come from the exact era of my descendant's genocide. That isn't a coincidence.

The suffering...

The Suffering...

Hannibal's descendants were enslaved and later freed. Africa remained in the possession of Africans but my people faced the ultimate suffering. Tribes like the Navajo and Hopi had no power or voice in their own land, even centuries after the genocide and the election of an African American president. They obliterated my people's culture by "reeducating" the women and within a few generations, wiped out thousands of years of being.

Cultural extinction...

Dogs thrived in America, whereas my mother and father's bloodline passed into obscurity when their lives warranted no recognition within the war dance of life.

I only have scraps of knowledge that barely cast light on my culture. Fragments of my ancestors' history survived through a few ceremonial chants but the totality of my existence has been stripped away and replaced with a chasm of spiritual amnesia.

My ancestors were secluded to reservations that held less technological advances than some "third world" countries. There wasn't even a national memorial constructed for the millions who lost their lives to the invaders.

No holidays of remembrance unconverted to shopping events.

No apologies.

No remorse.

No recompense.

We are the forgotten; the reviled vagabonds of humanity. What gave others the right to sack and pillage our home? My ancestral generation and people are but a vague memory now and I am nothing more than a whispering ghost.

The invaders never faced accountability for their crimes, either. Instead, numerous nations disregarded the genocide in favor of the American way of life. They dressed in American clothing and feasted on American food. Some spoke English and adopted just about every tradition conceived by the invaders. They were in effect, co-conspirators to the crime—dancing to the drum beat of a war already lost. Will humans readily allow genocide against other races if the offenders share the plunder with those who witnessed the atrocity? Perhaps they feared sharing my people's fate. Fear is the ultimate justifier of violence, after all. Or perhaps, they just didn't care.

"I love America," says some blonde girl in the magazine I'm flipping through. She smiles broadly in a makeup ad while displaying two exaggerated thumbs-up. "It's the greatest nation in the world!"

Great to who, exactly? Technology doesn't create civilized behavior and having it, doesn't make one sophisticated. Scarlet and Grey proved that. There's little enlightenment within our civilization. We are dominated by barbarism.

I feel like retching but instead, I cry so hard that tears fall from my eyes. I wonder… if this girl could see the Earth now, would she retain such affection for those who ravaged our entire world? Probably… because after seeing humans through the eyes of Kha, I know we're all selfish creatures who live in the moment. The madness of self spares nobody.

I leave the library after spending days researching ancient cultures and hike to the pyramid in a dreamlike trance. Time stagnates into a pool of memories where only the most significant moments rise to the surface.

There's darkness churning inside of me now—as if I'd eaten a seething, fuming vat of vitriol. I never felt such gravity before. A weight of unfathomable density burdens my every step.

Seti's smile—its meaning—highlights everything that made life worth living. He forced me to look beyond myself and peer into the depths of what I believe to be, my soul. I'm not even sure how my one true love slipped through my fingers so easily. Just thinking about him stirs eviscerating pain and limitless joy. I contemplate all the time we spent together and wonder how two people, who were incredibly close, fell so far from one another's grasp.

What went wrong? How did Seti end up with Scarlet? We loved each other dearly. I still have countless holographic letters from him that I replayed after his death. Seti went out of his way to visit me on those rare occasions when the projection steps were down. He'd actually *walk* all the way to my home just to spend a few minutes with me. Our love was unrivaled. We seemed destined to be together and in that moment of certainty, Scarlet took him away.

I've learned since then to be wary of sure things. Losing Seti was a crushing blow. I spent years harboring my feelings from others and never wanted to experience such a shocking loss ever again. Yet, to know that Seti felt the same way and that he planned to reveal his love to me strips him away for a second time.

I hate myself for not following my instincts! I hate Seti for falling into Scarlet's grasp! I hate that neither of us had the mental acuity to see beyond Scarlet's selfishness and our juvenile interpretations of love! I hate Scarlet for killing Seti and his child! I hate that Scarlet's child, wasn't my own! I hate the memory of Scarlet's pregnancy! I hate feeling Seti's child growing inside of her and wishing it were my own! I hate feeling Seti's child dying inside of Scarlet! I hate that I wasn't mature enough to handle a relationship with the only person that I ever loved! I hate knowing my happiness revolved around a single moment in time that's forever lost! I hate thinking back on all the moments I shared with Seti! I hate thinking about all the moments I could have shared with Seti! I hate feeling such immeasurable pain that I can't think straight! I hate the way life bristles with heartache! I hate the way I feel! I hate losing my brother to the Wasteland! I hate the VIA! I hate the VBI! I hate the IVST! I hate my mother's killer! I hate my father's killer! I hate this uncontrollable urge to find and destroy the virtual world! I hate the virtual world! I hate everything about the virtual world! I hate what my life has come to, because of the virtual world! I hate how all of my family died in the virtual world! I hate! I hate I HATE!

Suicide is all I can think of. Everything is a reminder of what I must do. The billboards depicting smiling models who appear to mock my existence with their snobbish expressions. The expensive dresses inside the wedding shop designed for smug brides wanting to flaunt their happiness at those of us with no grooms. The celebratory displays in the Museum of American History bragging of victory over a conquered land and its people—by ignoring the land's original inhabitants. The toy store filled with various reminders of the childhood and children that I never had. The family restaurant spitting on my parent's grave. The college mocking my fraudulent friendships with its posters of student unity. Everything around me feels like an affront to my life.

I reach the inner city and find Scarlet sitting cross-legged before the pyramid. I'm not surprised to find her alive. She sustained moderate damage in the alloy layer's collapse but her body appears mostly functional. There's an easel propped in front of her. It supports a canvas that drips with black paint. Her back is to me but Scarlet's head turns just enough to indicate awareness of my presence.

"There aren't any empty canvases left... so I painted over one of Rembrandt's portraits."

Scarlet seems to have lost her rifle in the alloy cloud but I spot something shiny resting against the easel's legs. I reach for my Hemingway rod as Scarlet faces me.

"If art is a reflection of a person's soul, what does my painting say about me?"

"You're soulless."

"Why? Is it because I despise God's reality? Screw this place! I hate *everything* about it! All of the perversions, sickness, and pain, come from God's creations! How can any of us be faulted for the sins of our so called, 'father'? Everything we did in order to survive this sick reality... all of the suffering... we're the products of absolute madness! I spit in God's face! I shit on everything God stands for! God is a joke! A sick joke! Saying the name stirs vomit in the foot of my throat! We live in a world without God!"

"Shut up..."

"Listen E, our lives are our own. God is not our savior. God doesn't even exist. If anything, God is the architect of our destruction. The very idea of God is more powerful and destructive than a trillion nuclear bombs. We should abolish God from our lives, and love each other."

I fondle the hilt extending from my sheathed sword before pulling the weapon free. "I'm going to kill you."

Scarlet slowly stands after grabbing her salvaged half of the Hemingway rod that I abandoned in the alloy cloud. Her right arm trembles. She hobbles about as though injured and uses the rod as a crutch.

"I discovered Kha's secret as I waited for you. This pyramid is more than a fancy telescope. It can also send objects back through time. I didn't think time travel was possible but the pathways are all around us. They're directly relative to the present. Light from distance stars can take billions of years to reach Earth. Those ancient photons are touching the planet every day. They're the DNA strands of time. Kha mirrors the past using ancient photons to reflect previous events. The past isn't something we go into, it's something that comes to us. Kha can change our fate and save everyone from a desolate planet. So why is Kha letting us destroy the world? Earth was Kha's home before it was ours."

Tears water my eyes. I try not to cry—especially in front of Scarlet—but I feel too much pain and it can't be suppressed. Years of hopelessness—misery— memories of what was—dreams of what could have been—pummel me in a tsunami of emotions that wash my inhibitions away.

Scarlet casually steps into the gravitational aura surrounding the pyramid as I circle her in the opposite direction. She found a way to alter her follicles and appears submerged in water as her fiery red hair drifts through the shimmering field. Scarlet strokes the pyramid's surface before stepping away and returning to normal space-time. Her reflection stares at me through the pyramid's dark surface.

"This device is the ultimate weapon of war. No species should control such power."

[SCANNER]
|WARNING|

|CRANIAL WARHEAD ACTIVATED BY TYPE XX|
|CYBERNETIC- 2 MINUTE MINIMUM TIMER|
|INITIATED|

Scarlet turns towards me and charges. She morphs her lance-shaped rod into a sickle when our weapons clash. I tilt my head just enough to evade the curved blade when it reaches out to reap my life. We separate after I morph my sword into a spear and jab at Scarlet's neck. Her sickle transforms into a two-headed battle axe when I morph my spear into a Waldo. We gage each other briefly before colliding once more—furiously—violently—moving like two cobras searching for a single venomous strike.

Scarlet leads me into the pyramid's gravitational field—we move into and out of it as the battle demands—attacking in bursts that push our CPs to their limits by accelerating beyond the speed of sound. Our clashing weapons reverberate through the air and the clangs of battle follow us like clapping bystanders in an out-of-sync video.

Showering sparks from our weapons move slowly as they drift inside the bands of gravity bending the folds of space surrounding the pyramid. We move through the embers of light as if they're auburn snowflakes.

[SCANNER]
|WARNING|

|CRANIAL DETONATION BY TYPE XX CYBERNETIC|
|IN 1 MINUTE|

The plasmatic fluid in our veins bubbles from exertion. I refuse to back down and Scarlet—intent on my deactivation—follows me to the limits of our cybernetics.

We clash swords while skirting the pyramid's gravitational boundary and when Scarlet's right arm drops from overexertion, I deliver my deathblow yelling, *"Die,"* in a muted voice dampened by spatial lag, and sever Scarlet's throat as she thrusts her weapon forward.

We come to a sudden stop outside of the pyramid's aura. My word catches up just as plasma gushes from the open veins in Scarlet's neck.

"Die!"

Plasma pours from Scarlet's mouth as she forces a smile. Her weapon's hilt sticks out of my chest. Its blade, pierces my back. I drop my weapon and try to pull Scarlet's sword out, but it's too late. I've already lost too much strength and my arms can't pull the blade free. We drop to our knees almost in unison. Scarlet falls a bit faster than I do but we end up at the same place.

"I love you," she whispers, before giggling evilly.

No words can express what I'm feelings. I stare blankly as the end approaches. My heart's every thump grows weaker. I feel no pain. Is this Déjà vu?

Death swallows Scarlet first. She screams horribly when her time arrives and within that moment, dies.

[SCANNER]
|ANALYSIS|

|TYPE XX CRANIAL DETONATION DEACTIVATED|

Scarlet's sudden fluctuation terrifies me. What did she see in her final moments? How could someone who lingered so lethargically on the precipice of death pulse with such vigor during her final breath? I don't want to die but it doesn't matter. My life is slipping away faster than I can hold onto it.

Kha returns like an angel harvesting souls, and emerges from the pyramid in a new form. Kha's evolved state is inexplicably beautiful—Heavenly, even. I don't have the senses required to view Kha's complete natural state anymore but I weep with wondrous delight at the being of light that stands before me.

The virtual world rests in Kha's cradled hands. Kha gives it to me as if it's a trophy. The blocky orb glistens in my palm. I hold it closer and see my reflection in its surface.

A mental signal wraps around me. I feel its sentiment. Kha has always known about the virtual world's whereabouts. When the reactors exploded, Kha retrieved the Nexus from the IVST facility right before the vault collapsed. They've been waiting a very long time for humanity to destroy itself. Our sphere is the final addition to their human exhibition. Kha now has 4,689 exhibitions on similar planets throughout the galaxy. Earth, however… is *our* home, and Kha's ruins cradle the history of both our civilizations.

There's an impulse to destroy it—to crush the entire virtual world with my hands. The impulse is more than a slight feeling. I really want to destroy the virtual world! Such irony is fitting—the Trojan Horse that killed its creators. I have every right to end the lives of those who derided my existence. The Nexus embodies everything that I've come to despise in humanity but more importantly, it entombs everything I love. My hands shake with fury as my final moments near.

How should I view the end of the virtual world?

My father raised me to believe that only God can destroy all life and that humankind doesn't have the power to obliterate "divine" creations. Yet here I sit, descending into death like an angel or even worse, the Devil. The Nexus is slowly dying and my hand helped trigger its demise. All of human history has culminated to this moment and I feel like the very hand of death that I reviled my entire life. Does this make me a god, or does the credit go to those pale souls who centuries ago, created the instruments of destruction that I now wield so valiantly? Perhaps my theology is all wrong. Maybe I'm an instrument of Christ or even better, God…

Should I try reconstructing the old world? Is it possible past men were destined to build whereas my generation was fated to destroy? It's not likely. I'm no slave-master culling the misfortunes of men. Nor will I clean up future mistakes, seeking darkness in the light of Heaven. I prefer to save the world that past injustices created. Why? I reek of man's attitude, that's why. In fact, to despise God, is to love the true nature of humanity. Surely, you've despised something that created you. Ah… but you choose not to believe in man? Well then, enjoy your paradise in Hell. The vacation will last an eternity.

Our world is a relic now—one that we doomed with the fires of human angst. The Nexus has enough internal power to operate for a few thousand years. But humanity has no way of interacting with the physical world now that the IVST facility is rubble. They'll see a dark and endless universe peppered with stars. No more bright universe. As the Nexus' batteries continue draining, the sky will appear to grow dim as the stars die sequentially. Then, various species will go extinct. Power failure will occur when battery reserves drop to critical levels, and everything will freeze in place, permanently. The limits of the Nexus and the reality of those within it are now limited to the boundaries of their imagination.

I cannot destroy the virtual world or its people—regardless of what it contains. It's my home and of course, Remi is still in there. He means the world to me.

There's enough time for Remi and Dennington to know the joys of parenting. If they get started soon, both can have a child and grandchild before the Nexus' internal power starts fading in noticeable ways. I hope the rest of the world learns how to enjoy what little time they have left. Every moment of life is precious.

I hand the Nexus back to Kha and close my eyes. The drudgery of existence narrows as death seeds my life in the soils of rebirth. I glimpse the era before my first conscious thoughts—that flicker of conception when reality compresses the entirety of consciousness into a single synaptic spark. I stare into this eye of eternity—the eye stares back—only now, in this instance, do I understand my vision of God.

Kha hovers above me as I fall to the ground. I can feel Kha's mental signal wrapping around my mind. All partitions open. Kha offers salvation, but at the ultimate price; I must be willing to restart life completely anew.

[SCANNER]
|UPDATE|

|GENESIS OS AVAILABLE- USER ACCESS GRANTED|

|SCANNER|
|SUICIDE WARNING|

|CURRENT OS DELETION PENDING:|
|COMPLETE NEUROLOGICAL WIPE REQUIRED TO|
|INITIALIZE UPGRADE|

|ALLOW / DENY|

The offer to preserve life at the cost of one's soul—the opposite of God's promise. I shouldn't accept… but I remember life as a child, before the horrors of adulthood when every moment became eternal and each day was new. I want to feel that innocence again—just for a moment, so that I can recapture the grace of God.

My body, heart, and mind ache so much but even now in the midsts of such pain, I soak up every moment before accepting a new life.

(Aten)
(Buddha)
(Jehovah)
(YHWH)
(Krishna)
(Allah)
(…)

[SCANNER]
|WARNING|

|NEUROLOGICAL REFORMATTING IN-PROCESS|

Everything I knew, felt, and became, slips away.
I am a soul without form, lost within a void. Darkness rests upon the deep.

And the spirit...

God?

God slips away, too.

Life is terrible... at times, wonderful. The memories... the many memories... I indulge in the precious ones before they're deleted. My dad and our time watching clouds. That occasion when mom baked my lop-sided birthday cake. My older brother's obsession with teaching me modding. Mandible 9 in its prime, and Seti... my dear Seti...

I reach out to embrace him, and feel his touch. I view Seti through Scarlet's memory and try holding onto him—wrapped in a wedding embrace—Seti becomes the last person I see before my mind goes blank.

[SCANNER]
|UPDATE|

|NEUROLOGICAL REFORMATTING COMPLETE|

|GENESIS OS INSTALLED|

A new world unfolds as my neural network downloads into Kha's biological Nexus—and I am reborn.

[THE END]

Kha:

CHAPTER 32

Our thoughts reach out to you from across time—your mind connects to our future, and you become a part of us. This is the memory of who you were. Knowing it, changes who you are. Never forget it.

The past…

What is the past? Who lingers there? Who are you? What gives you the right to destroy and plunder our Earth? Does the world belong only to you? What vanities are greater than the sum of all life?

The future…

What was the future? Who lingered here? Who were we? What gave us the right to interfere with history? Did time belong to only us?

There is no answer.

Despise the selfish and uncaring. Be sickened to the pits of your souls by those who waste the fruits of a plentiful world with mindless disregard for those around them and those destined to come. The weapons of war they brandish so haughtily are not a means to an end; they simply define the end of all meaning. Men attain immortality through death and not with desperate attempts to postpone the inevitable end. Their fanatical mission for survival is what created the first weapons of war but ironically, those arms exasperate humanity's demise.

They don't have to live on the hellish Earth in which we exist. Where's the divine justice in that? We see justice as an imagining of children. Reality barters no such goods. Our life is proof of that purchase.

Bitterness doesn't describe the terrible ache we feel whenever we come home. We can never truly convey such pain. We only hope those who know of our misery will understand why your war must never happen. Our Earth is a daily reminder of past mistakes. The ashen soil and red sky are signposts affirming insatiable appetites that consumed everything and everyone like a ravenous plague.

So know this…

We hold the fate of billions in our hands but we are not monsters and seek peace even in our time of suffering. You are a part of us now and we understand what it means to exist in the moment. Our future remains a mural of possibilities. This message is a plea for help. We're asking that you unbind us from this Hell on Earth. Avoid the suffering, and the need for a virtual world. Look around you. This is our home. We're all humane, if not human. Earth lives. Don't let her die. Do something. Anything. The time, is now.

-Kha

NEURAL UPDATE IN PROGRESS
[MESSAGE TO CURRENT RECIPIENT:]
[THIS DATA PREDATES PRESENT TIME-LINE]
[FUTURE EVENT ENDING]
[THE SUFFERING]

ABOUT THE AUTHOR

Juan Luis Sims worked as an Aviation Support Technician in Jacksonville, Florida and Pensacola, Florida while enlisted in the U.S.M.C. He was born in Chattanooga, TN and raised in Rochester, NY writing various unpublished works. He currently resides in Phoenix, AZ and works as a private contractor.

jlsimspublishing@gmail.com

fictionalwriters.com